The Reluctant Hero

Also by Michael Dobbs

The Edge of Madness

The Reluctant Hero

MICHAEL DOBBS

POCKET
BOOKS

LONDON • SYDNEY • NEW YORK • TORONTO

First published in Great Britain by Simon & Schuster UK Ltd, 2010
This edition published by Pocket Books, 2009
An imprint of Simon & Schuster UK Ltd
A CBS COMPANY

3 5 7 9 10 8 6 4 2

Simon & Schuster UK Ltd
1st Floor
222 Gray's Inn Road
London
WC1X 8HB

www.simonandschuster.co.uk

Simon & Schuster Australia
Sydney

A CIP catalogue record for this book
is available from the British Library

B Format ISBN 978-1-84739-323-4

Typeset in Palatino by M Rules
Printed in the UK by CPI Cox & Wyman, Reading, Berkshire RG1 8EX

To Alice.
A beautiful god-daughter.

PART ONE

The Friend

PROLOGUE

Guilt. A relentless hunter. And no matter how hard Harry Jones ran, he couldn't escape. He'd turn a corner and there it would be, peering out from the shadows, or sometimes he'd catch a fleeting glimpse of a woman in a crowded street from the corner of his eye, and the whole thing would rush back at him.

Julia. His wife.

And his fault.

It had been a lifetime ago, yet it still felt as though it was yesterday when Zac Kravitz had breezed through town – except that wasn't entirely true, for Zac never breezed. He was Delta, US Special Forces, a man who moved around with about as much subtlety as a November gale full of snow heading off Lake Huron, where he was born.

Oh, but the man had his uses, and no one could doubt his commitment. They'd first met in the early nineties when Harry had been acting as an adviser to a Colombian government anti-drugs detachment, and Zac had tagged along as an observer. The mission had taken them into the mountains for a little search-and-

3

destroy against the cartels. Sounded like fun, but someone had forgotten to remind the Colombian troops that sometimes it rains in the tropics. The weather had closed in, fouled up their extraction, and that had put all their lives on the line. For three days they'd been forced to play a game of blind man's buff with heavily armed drug-runners and a jungle full of fire ants. One of Zac's gadgets had saved the day – typical of Delta types, they loved their toys, and he'd brought along a prototype sat-nav system that had dragged them out of the rainforest mire. While in Harry's view the former college football player was the sort of guy who had spent his younger days throwing one too many tackles with his head, after Colombia he was welcome, any time.

Loyalty to his own. It's what kept a soldier motivated. So when Zac sent a message to tell Harry he was passing through England with his wife in tow and had a couple of days to spare, Harry suggested they all spend one of those days down on his boat in Dartmouth. Zac, his wife P.J., Harry. And Julia.

It was a twelve-metre yacht named *Guinevere* constructed almost entirely of wood, an old racing yacht with teak decks, its original petrol-fired engine, awesome maintenance bills and a pedigree stretching back nearly fifty years. Too much of a handful for most, but that had never bothered Harry. Zac was already pulling the tab off a beer as Julia cast off and *Guinevere* slipped out into the estuary, her sweet lines catching the eye as she headed into a gentle sou'westerly, the bow barely breaking the swell. There was no way Harry could know he'd already been 'pinged' by an Irish Republican active service unit. Provisionals, out for revenge.

Northern Ireland. It had been a peculiarly dirty war and in his SAS days Harry had got his hands grubby, clambering down into the gutter to play the game by the Provos' own rules at those times when Queen's Regulations ran out of ideas. Now it was payback time. Harry's past was catching up with him.

They sailed to Salcombe for their lunch, pie and pickle, carried by light winds, nothing above ten knots, returning as dusk was beginning to gather. By the time they reached the red marker of the Homestone buoy, the purple-green hues of the stones of Kingswear Castle at the mouth of the Dart had come into view. *Guinevere* was almost home. Harry was at the wheel, Zac up front winding in the Genoa sheets with P.J. standing at the bow, arched and pert like a Victorian figurehead silhouetted against the fading light. Julia was below, using the heads, while in front of them they could see the bustle of the harbour traffic as on all sides boats scurried to their berths. *Guinevere* was drawing close to the castle when a speedboat, a Sunseeker, cut across their bow, a little too close for comfort, but it was one of several craft in the vicinity and caused no more than momentary irritation to Harry; there was no shortage of dickheads on the river nowadays. These particular dickheads came back for another pass. As they did so, from out of the growing darkness, a rocket-propelled grenade hit *Guinevere* just above the waterline. It blew both sides out of the stern.

Harry knew nothing of what happened next. He was knocked unconscious and thrown clear of the cockpit, dislocating his shoulder. He was left helpless, oblivious, saved only by his life jacket. Zac, with all the fortune that had enabled him to survive the threats of Islamic revolution and irate husbands, found himself in the water. P.J. was close by, conscious and screaming, and soon other boats were circling, fellow sailors desperate to help those in peril. They plucked P.J. from the sea, while Zac helped others lever Harry onto the deck of a yacht, where he quickly began to stir. But of Julia there was no sign.

When, eventually, Harry opened his eyes and began to make sense of what was around him, he saw *Guinevere*'s bow section pointing uncertainly towards the sky, swaying on a dark, oily swell. A dozen craft of varying sorts were circling, not daring to draw too close. When the grenade struck it had ignited the gas cylinders in the rear galley. The explosion had not only thrown Harry from the boat but also burst *Guinevere*'s fuel tanks, which were now spewing thirty gallons of highly inflammable petrol. A lake of fire was forming around the boat, sending spirals of sooty smoke into the night sky. *Guinevere*'s funeral pyre.

A hush fell across the scene as the onlookers watched her die. The wind had slackened and the lapping of the swell subsided, and from the centre of the burning lake they could hear a knocking sound. The kind of sound someone might make who was desperately trying to smash a way out.

Harry was still concussed, his thoughts scrambled, his shoulder screaming in pain, yet he fought off protective hands as he struggled to his feet.

'Julia!'

He screamed again, then again. The pounding from within the dying yacht seemed to increase.

She had been in the heads, protected from the blast by a main bulkhead and surrounded by stout wooden timbers. These had been her shelter, and would now provide her coffin.

As Harry cried out, Zac dragged his attention away from P.J., who was still coughing up water on the deck of their rescue boat. No one else moved; what could be done? *Guinevere* was surrounded by blazing fuel. Only the fact that she was slowly sinking kept her from burning, and she would be gone long before the flickering tongues of fire subsided.

To try the flames risked anyone's life and promised almost certain and serious harm, yet Zac accepted the gamble. He stood on the gunwale, filling his lungs with air, then he hit the water, diving as deep as he could beneath the fire. He needed to cross thirty, forty feet of burning sea before he came to *Guinevere*, and the next they saw of him he was clawing his way up the steeply angled deck and disappearing through the forward hatch. He took the fire with him, on his back, his shirt ablaze and so, it seemed, was his hair.

Inside, all was unremitted darkness, but guided by the sounds of the desperate knocking, he found the head. It was already three-quarters under water. The door was stuck tight, wedged by the solid iron stove that had been wrenched from its mooring in the main cabin. Normally it would have taken only a moment to shift it, but on a sinking boat, beneath the waterline, with the stench of his own burning flesh in his nostrils, it was a different matter. Yet Zac did it. He was Delta, never been beaten. *De Oppresso Liber* – Free the Oppressed. And Zac did just that, got them both out. Saved Julia.

So that Harry could be responsible for her death just six months later.

Ta'argistan, Central Asia. Population 9,763,402, if you believed the official statistics, which no one did. It was an inflated figure, dreamed up solely to extract maximum benefit from various credulous international aid agencies. This had once been the land of Joseph Stalin, an outpost of the Soviet empire before the Wall came down, and his spirit continued to haunt the streets. It still retained not only a fair scattering of ethnic Russians and their language but also much of their brutalist architecture and more than a few statues of Lenin.

Yet it was by no means a colourless place. It was a land of mountains, ravines and sweeping plateaus, of infinite skies and tumbling melt-water rivers that marked the route of the fabled Silk Road which had once linked the Orient with Europe and Africa. Before the Soviets, long before, this had been a land of nomadic horsemen, without frontiers, through which Scythians and Turks and marauding Huns had passed like weather fronts, and where Genghis Khan and his sons held sway. Now it boasted a President elected by a huge majority – if you believed those official statistics – and there were many in the international community who struggled to maintain the fiction of 'Ia'argistan's democratic underpinnings, because what it lacked in terms of natural resources it more than made up for in location. It was a most compelling piece of real estate, bordering on both Russia and China, Afghanistan, too, and nudging up against a host of other '-stans'. In truth it was a state that should never have existed, the by-product of the nineteenth-century mania for drawing lines on maps, a country brushed by Islam yet where the myths and fierce traditions of the mountain tribes still held sway, a place of intrigues and competing ambitions, of clans and khans and, as one early Chinese general had suggested, a place of bones.

Ta'argistan also possessed one of the largest nuclear-waste dumps in the world, a series of huge shafts in the Celestial Mountains into which the Soviets had tipped everything from spent fuel rods to clapped-out X-ray machines. It was a country that had never properly digested its history. It stirred uneasily, waiting, like a lamb before the encroaching storm.

CHAPTER ONE

'Buck up there, darling!'

In response, Harry manufactured a smile in apology to his guest, then went back to staring out of the taxi window.

It was freezing in London, a night when the air grew sullen and felt almost solid. New Year's Eve, that time for reminiscing. How he'd grown to hate it. A tune kept running through his head, one he'd picked up shortly before his Finals at Cambridge more than twenty years earlier. It was like a sea shanty, one he'd heard sung in mournful Irish tones as he was wandering along the Backs one stifling night in June, and it had stuck.

'So I called to the barman to pour me another,
Me soul was fair bleeding for want of a wet,
And the good resolutions I made to my mother,
Are the good resolutions I drink to forget . . .'

He knew it was a nonsense, of course, he could never forget. Yet some memories didn't even have the decency to fade, so there were nights when he took himself back to that riverbank in Cambridge and drank to a simpler life, trying to soak away the confusion that had crept in between the cracks. He hadn't planned that this should be one of those nights, but things weren't going much to plan any more.

The Right Honourable Henry Marmaduke Maltravers-Jones, M.P., P.C., G.C. and Guest, the formal invitation had said. The Guest, in the decorative form of Bernice, a sports marketing consultant, now sat beside him as the taxi drew close to their destination. Winfield House was the official residence of the US Ambassador to London, set in a dozen acres of parkland in the heart of the capital. It had been built by Barbara Hutton, that elegant yet troubled heiress to the Woolworths empire who had been in search of a retreat far away from the pressures of home; a dozen acres of land on the other side of the Atlantic that were patrolled by the Royal Parks Constabulary seemed to offer an ideal solution. The house hadn't had an easy birth; the officials of the Crown Estate wanted Ms Hutton to use grey brick, she had insisted on red. Solid British bureaucracy versus the mobile might of American money. The dollar won, of course, and in 1937 Winfield House had risen, in defiant blushing tones, from the rich earth of Regent's Park and was greeted by everyone as a splendid addition. The dream was not to last. Eight years, two failed marriages and a whole world war later, Ms Hutton had grown distracted, her mind and heart elsewhere, so she had offered the house to the US government. The lease changed hands for the sum of one dollar. The way the London housing market was headed, it might not fetch much more even now.

The taxi drew to a halt at the entrance gates. A US Marine resplendent in his high-collared dress blues bent to inspect the invitation card that was handed through the window. The interior light glittered off the eagle and anchor insignia of his cap badge. 'Welcome, Mr Maltravers-Jones,' the young marine said, as a colleague in the sentry box confirmed Harry's name on a guest list. 'Happy New Year, sir!'

Harry winced. 'Yeah, you too,' he replied as the taxi passed into the tree-lined driveway that led to the main entrance.

'Why, Harry, darling, I knew you were quite a mouthful, but not a Maltravers-Jones,' Bernice said, giggling.

'Henry Marmaduke Maltravers-Jones,' he sighed in explanation. 'Hardly the last thing you want voters to see before they place their mark on a ballot paper, is it? Not when I'm supposed to be a man of the people.'

'It seems I scarcely know you,' she said coquettishly, trying to brush aside his dark mood. She stood six foot tall in her heels and was delightful company, both in and out of his bed, where she had visited frequently and increasingly regularly in the past four months, but even as she laughed in his ear and squeezed his thigh, Harry knew their relationship was over. He was still having difficulty explaining that one to himself, and only God knew how he'd manage to explain it to her. He couldn't find fault; Bernice had freckles, and fingers that could squeeze the most breathless sounds from a violin. She did much the same with Harry, too, yet inevitably she wanted more. Most women in their mid-thirties did. She wanted more than his bed, she wanted the man himself, and Harry was wealthy, exceptionally well connected, a soldier turned politician, with so many letters after his name she still hadn't worked out what they all meant, a man with grey eyes and a body that was remarkably well toned for someone in his forties. And, if it also carried a considerable number of searingly outspoken scars, it only added to his allure in her eyes. Oh, and he was unattached. The perfect package. She snuggled closer.

As they climbed from the taxi, waiting on the steps that led to the large double doors of the ambassador's residence was a short, stocky man dressed in livery with not a hair to be found on his polished black head. 'Evening, Mr Jones,' he declared, his words condensing in the cold air. His hand reached out. Most guests simply handed across their coats, Harry shook it warmly.

'How are things, Jimmy?'

'Can't complain,' the other man responded in a husky voice that carried an easy Southern lilt. 'Still got a job. Times like these, that's sure a blessing. And one that gets me to see all the fine ladies first. Evening, miss.'

'Take care, Bernice,' Harry warned as they were ushered inside, 'former Master Sergeant Jimmy Jackson was US Airborne.'

'Which means?'

'Not a man to mess with. Or take for granted.'

'And there was me thinking you liked me only 'cos I know how to mix a drink, Mr Jones.'

'I guess there is that, too,' Harry smiled, before turning back to Bernice. 'Jimmy and I first met – what, twenty years ago? In the desert. I'd just dragged an Iraqi intelligence colonel from his bed, but it turned out he had lots of friends who took an instant dislike to me. Jimmy here took care of them. Came all the way to the outskirts of Baghdad to do it.'

'Hell, when we first got that shout I thought it was just a pizza delivery,' Jimmy responded.

'That particularly deep voice he has, the one so many women find irresistible, is in fact the consequence of a bullet in the neck that Jimmy took that night. It was meant for me. Got himself a Purple Heart and a Silver Star for his troubles.'

'Seem to remember you got yourself a few scratches, too.'

'Did I?'

They were jousting, swapping shared memories, while Bernice was slowly beginning to understand the significance of some of the scars she had discovered on his body. 'But . . .' she began to stammer in surprise. 'It sounds dreadful.'

'You try delivering pizza in downtown Miami. It ain't so very different,' Jimmy said, taking her coat.

The two men laughed, in the manner of old friends, but Bernice's mind was still back in the desert, under fire. 'It never leaves you, does it, the times you soldier-men have together?'

'No, miss. And I'm sure glad of it. Why, what'd we have to think back on in our old age if we'd been – I don't know. Bankers?'

She moved closer to Harry, squeezed his arm. 'Harry Jones, there's so much I don't seem to know about you,' she said softly. She made it sound like a challenge, one she was more than willing to take up. She didn't see the flicker in his eye.

Jimmy Jackson was more than merely a doorman, he was the ambassador's personal valet and knew how to deal with many kinds of situations, those that stretched from amusing an ageing duchess to diverting aggressive drunks, and that ability also enabled him to know when the time had come to extract himself. This was one of those moments. 'You folks have a fine evening. I'll see y'all later. Fix you that drink,' he said, turning for the cloakroom.

'You better,' Harry replied. 'Feeling I'm going to need it.'

The bolt slid back uneasily in its track. As the door swung open, Prisoner 7217, Extreme Punishment Wing, stirred, rubbing his eyes, struggling to focus. He rolled from his straw mattress, the only furniture in his stinking cell. It had been gnawed yet again by rats, but he took no notice. He had been here too long to care. He clambered to his knees.

It was many moments before he realized what was happening. It took time for everything nowadays, but that didn't matter. Time was the only thing he had, yet it meant nothing. How long had he been here on the Punishment Wing? He had tried, in the early days, to keep track with scratchings on the mould-infested walls, but he'd been overcome by confusion after a couple of months as the mould grew back, so he had stopped. After that, he lost his grip on most things.

A voice penetrated the fog of confusion. 'Mr Mayor,' it greeted, almost jovially.

That was right, he remembered now. He was the mayor, from one of the towns twenty miles south of the capital. How considerate of the visitor to remember. This voice, this new man, stood beneath the single bare bulb that lit the cell, and the yellow light seemed to strip him of all humanity, making his appearance pale and ethereal, like – an angel. Or a ghost, perhaps. He'd called him Mr Mayor, not 7217. The prisoner remembered his number more clearly than his name. So much had been lost along the way.

The angel seemed to have read his thoughts. 'Mr Mayor,' it repeated, 'I wanted you to know that I am a man of my word.'

Had he met this pale-faced apparition before? the

prisoner wondered. He couldn't decide, every thought led to confusion. From the corner of his eye the prisoner saw something move, something dark, elusive, a rat, fleeing the disturbance. In the early days he had tried to block the holes in the damp stone walls with straw from the mattress and handfuls of hardened filth, but it had been pointless. There were too many holes, and just too many rats.

'You remember? The promise I gave you, Mr Mayor?' the angel continued.

Prisoner 7217 nodded fitfully, not meaning it. It had become his default response to anything they said.

'I said you had no need to worry, that we would never execute a mayor.'

He looked up from all fours and nodded again, this time more purposefully. A memory came back, confirming what the angel had said. It was what had kept him going all this time.

The angel slowly pulled back the sleeve of his grey serge uniform and consulted his wristwatch. He smiled. 'But in a few minutes, your term of office will be over. You will no longer be mayor.'

Yet again Prisoner 7217 nodded, his head drooping as he struggled with the weight of this new thought.

'Happy New Year,' the angel whispered. Then he turned and left.

In the great hallway of Winfield House, beneath crystal chandeliers that were reflected in huge gilt mirrors hanging on three sides, the ambassador waited with his wife to greet their guests.

'Why, Harry Jones. Welcome back to our little home,' he exclaimed, his face lighting up. No one but a truly wealthy man could have called Winfield House a little home and got away with it, but David Bracken was one of those few. He was a tall, ascetic man who had made several fortunes in the information-technology sector and spent much of it wisely, some of it on the recent presidential re-election campaign. The post to the Court of St James's had been his reward. Yet Harry quickly noticed that despite the splendour of the surroundings there was a muted atmosphere to the occasion. In previous years Harry could recall encountering many kinds of entertainments – a soprano from the New York Metropolitan Opera, rooms filled with life-sized Disney characters, an entire wall filled with tropical flowers. But now these flourishes were missing. And it was Californian chardonnay rather than champagne. The ambassador apologized. This was to be a modest affair, he explained, no extravagance, a subdued celebration to match the mood of such tight-fisted times. He always carried a little frown of concern around with him and had always been regarded as the serious type, which was considerably more than could be said of his wife. In many people's view she hadn't proved to be one of his better investments.

'Why, Harry,' Sonia Bracken exclaimed, stretching up to peck his cheek and revealing more than a modest mound of freckled flesh as her husband concentrated on greeting Bernice. 'I haven't seen you for such a long time.'

They both knew Harry had been avoiding her. The last time their paths had crossed, in an overheated seaside hotel during a political conference, she had made it abundantly clear how keen she was to do her bit for the Anglo-American alliance, and how willing she was to be both inventive and discreet about it. She'd muttered something about increasing the size of his majority. When Harry had declined her offer, she had taken umbrage, like any rejected woman, and now her eyes, once filled with lust, were as cold as uncut diamonds. 'I've missed you,' she lied, 'but what's this? Why, Harry,' she said, carrying out a close inspection, 'you have put on weight.'

Well, a couple of pounds, maybe, but that was none of her damned business. Anyway, he'd been busy – or, more accurately, distracted these past couple of months by . . . by what he wasn't entirely sure. There seemed to be an emptiness that had crept into his life and neither his job, nor Bernice and certainly not the overflowing Sonia Bracken could fill it. Harry's eyes dropped, first to the remarkable creation at her neck that he suspected had come straight from a showcase at Tiffany's, then beyond, until they were loitering in the pink chasm between her over-sculpted breasts.

'At least it's all my own,' he whispered, moving on.

*

Two guards dragged him from the cell. He stumbled, wasn't able to walk properly, couldn't lift his feet, he hadn't used his legs in so long. He was confused, and afraid.

As he passed the other cells, Prisoner 7217 forced his head up. Through the narrow bars of the doors he saw the faces of other prisoners, grey, like dirty chalk, their eyes flooded with pity, and with fear, fixed upon him as they watched their own futures being dragged past. Their cracked lips fell open but they uttered not a sound.

He'd heard that men often fouled themselves when they died violently. It was one of many whispers that scuttled around with the rats. He prayed it was not true. He had a deep, almost animalistic desire to stand tall, to make a good death of it, for his family, and particularly for his son, Daniyar. Yet as he stumbled once more he ridiculed his own stupidity. A good death? What total shit! What in God's name was he thinking of? It wouldn't make any difference how he died, once he was dead.

As for his family, they would never know. His son was only five, wouldn't even be able to recall his father's life, let alone its end, a life that was nothing but a grain of wheat, blown by the passing wind.

Would there be pain? He'd often asked himself. Come to that, would there be anything at all? He wasn't much of a believer, couldn't pretend he expected to wake up in Paradise tended by several dozen virgins, but he could hope, always hope, force back the liquid that was laying siege to his bowels and find something solid to cling to. He stamped his feet on the stone floor in anger until he could feel pain, shouting at them to work. He wasn't going to be dragged any further. And as he levered himself upwards he gave a half-choked cry of triumph. Yes, it did matter how he died, not to anyone else but for himself. He was going to die as he hoped he had lived, cursing them all, defiant to the last.

He was scrabbling around inside his head, snatching at thoughts, images, grabbing at those things he knew for certain and which might give him something to lean on. He was aware of a long passage that lay ahead. The stones of the old walls were damp, uneven, the ancient light fittings casting lurid shadows that flickered darkly before him as he passed, then were gone, like life itself.

He made out a flight of stone steps at the end of the passage that led down to a wooden door built of ancient planks. The hinges swung open quietly as the door was drawn back, flooding the passage in front of him with unexpected brilliance. He blinked in the sudden rush of light; it was as though the gates of paradise were beckoning. He tried to laugh, find some comfort in the thought. Then, once again, he saw the pale features of the angel.

They both drank more than was good for them. While Jimmy Jackson served Napa chardonnay to most of the guests, he always seemed to have a crystal glass filled with some fine single-barrel bourbon on his tray when he passed Harry, which was often. And as Bernice grew relaxed, she let her own defences down, while failing to notice his.

'To the new year,' she said softly, raising her glass, her other hand snaking around his waist and pulling him closer. 'I hope it's going to be a very special one, Harry.'

'What way?'

'You and me.'

The words seemed to roll into one.

'You make it sound like . . .' He struggled to find the right description, but she wasn't to be denied.

'Like Bonny and Clyde? Yes, and bubble and squeak, and—' She was about to say love and commitment, and wasn't it about time they got their stuff together, but something held her back. 'That's how I feel about us,' she whispered. Her eyes had filled with emotion, but as she looked up into his, she realized she had made a most terrible mistake. It was as though she had taken a telescope expecting to see the stars and had discovered only the deepest, most intense black hole that sucked everything out of her night.

For a moment neither of them spoke. There was no point. She knew that words wouldn't change a thing. And even before he could squeeze out an apology she had broken away and disappeared in the direction of the powder room. It wasn't her fault. She wasn't to know that tomorrow would be the tenth anniversary of Julia's death.

Then Jimmy was at his side once more, his tray bearing yet another bourbon of quite exceptional proportions and his eyes full of understanding.

'How many tumblers of this stuff make you a social drinker, Jimmy?'

'Two, I guess.'

'And an alcoholic?'

'Three. And that's your third.'

'In which case, I'm already there and it makes damn-all difference. Geronimo, Jimmy,' Harry muttered as he emptied the glass in one. 'And room for another before you throw me out of here, I guess.'

It was over. Not just the evening but Bernice, their affair, another little chunk of his life. It was approaching midnight, no point in waiting, time to leave, there was nothing more for him here. And he was beginning to feel the effect of all the bourbon. He made his way to the washroom, which he was glad to see was empty. He took his time, relieved that he could be on his own at last, and was washing his hands when the door swung open. Harry didn't look up, not wanting to engage in small talk, concentrating on scrubbing his hands.

'Hello, Harry,' a voice said. 'So this is where you're hiding. I've been looking for you everywhere.'

Harry looked up to find the pale eyes of Hervé d'Arbois staring at him. He was a man close to seventy years of age, not tall but most elegantly presented. The hair was gently silver, the nose aquiline, the fingers long and elegant, giving the impression that they had never strayed far from a keyboard. The voice had a gentle Parisian veneer, like so much of the rest of him. The cufflinks were in the form of gold Crosses of Lorraine. Hervé d'Arbois was one of those ubiquitous Frenchmen who had been quietly running the country for the past hundred and fifty years, no matter what the colour of the government. His life represented a waltz through the corridors of privilege: the Sorbonne, two years at ENA – the École Nationale d'Administration in Strasbourg – balanced by national service in Algeria during the bitterest days of the war for independence. Later he'd served a term as a European Commissioner. D'Arbois had spent a lifetime seducing power. Harry had got to know him in Brussels where he discovered that a single phone call from d'Arbois could achieve in a matter of minutes what months of laying siege to the European Parliament could not. A most useful man, was Hervé, one to whom people listened. But not Harry, not tonight. The bourbon had kicked in, as though it had a point to prove, and his temples were throbbing. He wasn't in much of a listening mood. Harry splashed water on his face from a running tap.

'It's simply that I believe you know him. At least, you *knew* him,' d'Arbois was saying as Harry at last emerged from the waterfall.

'Sorry, didn't catch that. Who?' Harry muttered as he headed in the direction of the hand-dryer. The noisy rush of hot air forced d'Arbois to wait until he was done.

'Zac. Zac Kravitz.'

Harry's heart began to race in alarm. It wasn't simply the alcohol.

'Harry, I am all but retired, a man of leisure, but I still hear many things. Old habits, you understand. And the word is that your friend has got himself into – as you say – a spot of bother. Rather a bleak spot, too.'

'But . . . how? *Where?*' Harry demanded in confusion, the words echoing back accusingly from the tiled walls.

'Ta'argistan.'

Harry, his brain cells already battered, bruised a few more trying to recall where the place was.

'I'm not familiar with the detail,' the Frenchman continued, 'but it seems Mr Kravitz has been moving in the murky commercial underworld these past few years. Mercenary work, commercial intelligence, something of the kind. The sort of stuff that leaves dirt under the fingernails.' D'Arbois sighed, producing a brilliant white handkerchief and polishing his rimless spectacles with meticulous care.

'Zac, he . . . sort of went AWOL. Hid himself away. I lost track,' Harry mumbled, partly in explanation but also in apology. He should have kept tabs on him, but it had all been so long ago, in another life. Even P.J. had upped and left him. 'He always was a bit of an awkward bugger.'

'Which is why it seems no one wants to help him.

Not his government, certainly not his business associates.'

'But what the hell's he done?'

'I only pick up –' the Frenchman waved his glasses in a vague circular motion – 'whispers. Rumours. But he seems to have upset someone. Someone very important. His associates don't expect to see him again. It happens, you know, in a primitive place like Ta'argistan. Get yourself in trouble with the government there and – *poof!* – you disappear. I only mention it because I seem to remember that you were a friend of his, once.' He delayed delivering the final word, as though it made the matter of no importance.

Harry stared into the mirror. The antiseptic lighting seemed to have bleached all the colour from his face, yet at the same time highlighted the creases. How could it do both? he wondered in confusion. From beyond the door, at the outer limits of his storm-tossed senses, he could hear the crowd had grown suddenly still, and a clock was beginning to chime.

'We should go and join them, Harry,' d'Arbois said, and before Harry knew it he was gone. Through the part-open door there swept a tide of cheering as the clock struck midnight. He pushed a few stray strands of his hair into place and followed the Frenchman, but the other man had already disappeared, lost in the throng of celebration. As Harry scanned the room, he spotted Bernice. She was in the arms of a commercial counsellor from the Spanish Embassy. The energy of their enthusiasms suggested something more intense than an exchange of diplomatic courtesies. So, she was a survivor, nothing wrong with that. His fault, anyway. And she wouldn't be needing a lift home. Harry stumbled for the door.

In his mind he was walking through a meadow. He was panting, filling his chest with barrels of cool mountain air that seared his lungs; he'd been racing with his elder brother, Chingiz. He'd won, his first time. He was growing, getting quicker, had taken Chingiz by surprise, a shortcut through a thicket of lucerne. The sharp blades had cut his bare feet, which now stung furiously, but it had been worth it to beat his brother. They had run from their home to the river that was gorged with spring melt water and which thundered down the valley, dragging brilliant pebbles and even large boulders with it. A profusion of flowers clogged the banks, forming a blanket beneath the blossoming rose-willows, whose branches bent towards the cascade of tumbling water. At last, winter had surrendered.

As he turned, in the distance he saw his grandmother, bearing a pitcher of sour milk and a headscarf bulging with bread. She had been the one who raised him, while his mother spent her days in the fields. Now she was drawing closer, beckoning to him.

He held it all together, kept his thoughts and fears from running amuck, even when they bound his hands behind him and kicked him up the rough wooden steps of the scaffold, right up to the moment they began mocking him. He heard them wagering money on whether he would be a 'stiff-dick' – one of those poor wretches who, at the bottom of the rope, somehow got an erection. As he heard their laughter he stumbled, fell, overwhelmed by disgust. How could they? They wouldn't put a dog down like this!

He picked himself up and looked towards his destination at the top of the stairs. His eyes came to rest on the noose. It held him like a cobra's eye. It seemed remarkably heavy to him. Rough twisted hemp. Almost an inch thick. With a double-tied knot. *Allah O Akbar! God is great! May He be merciful . . .*

He began repeating the prayer as he made his way up the last few steps, trying with his words to shame the guards, and to drown out their mockery. God is great! But where was He?

They offered him a hood, but he declined, his eyes brimming with hatred. Why should he hide from them, help them sleep? And while he was shaking his head in contempt, they shackled his feet in irons, so that now he could do no more than shuffle inches at a time. Then one of the guards approached. He had the noose in his hand and was reaching out for him.

'May God shit on your soul and on the memory of your mother!' the prisoner spat, no longer able to contain his fear. What difference did it make if they beat him again, broke his bones? But they didn't, not this time.

'Yeah. You just tell him when you see him,' the guard smirked through crooked teeth. 'In about forty seconds,' he added.

Was it so close?

The noose tightened around his neck, rough, scratching, its ferocious knot nestling behind his left ear. That's where it would happen. About the second vertebra. Snap clean through his spinal cord, if they had got it right. Instant unconsciousness, he had been told. But how did anyone know? Then he would hang there, slowly strangling, even as the heart raced to respond. That's when the priapism would happen. Unless, of course, these barbarians couldn't even arrange an execution and his body fell too far, when the head would be wrenched completely off his body. *Allah O Akbar! Allah O Akbar! Allah O Akbar! Be merciful . . .*

A patch of white stood out in the middle of the scaffold. The trapdoor.

He tried to imagine a field of fresh white tulips spreading in the early sun, but the illusion wouldn't last. He couldn't concentrate. Too many scuffed heel marks.

He could do no better than hobble now, swaying as he moved forward, inch by inch, his mind stuttering along with his feet.

Allah O Akbar! For pity's sake . . .

His voice rose as he prayed. He could feel his bladder screaming. And there, directly in front of him, was the angel once more, his smile like quicksand for the soul, beckoning him forward. He couldn't think of a single reason why he should any longer do as he was told, but he did so anyway, afraid that if he stood still his bladder would betray him, yet even as he stepped forward, the noose seemed to slip around his neck, and was tightened, savagely. He could feel the knot pressing into his neck.

He began to struggle, but only inside. It was as though a wall was closing around him, blocking his view. Stand tall. See beyond it. To the meadow once more. *God is great! Stand tall!*

He stretched to the very tips of his toes, stretching to see if his beloved grandmother was still there, waiting. God rest her soul.

And there she was, so very close he felt as though he would be able to reach out and touch her, her weathered skin the colour of freshly turned earth, her smile like a new moon, wrinkling her face like a flood plain in spring. And tears in her eyes. Why tears?

He felt his footing slip, and for a moment he lost sight of her, the wall once more. *Stand tall! Stand tall!!!*

And there she was again.

It took Harry three attempts to get his key in the lock. Once inside, however, he proved more adroit at filling a glass. He was already so drunk that very little was making sense, nothing lined up properly; his thoughts were half-formed, his emotions wholly exaggerated.

Today was the day Julia had died, just six months

after Zac Kravitz had dragged her from the sinking boat, Harry had led her off-piste and into the path of an avalanche. There had been no warning. One moment she was there, skiing almost within touching distance, then the mountain had moved.

Snatched away, just when they needed each other most. No, not so much needed – *wanted*. Since her escape from *Guinevere*'s clutches, life seemed to have taken on an added richness, as if every day must be lived to the full, in case it was her last. And Harry was at the centre of it all, with a look, a word, a scribbled message, a smile, and they had tumbled closer together. At least, that's the way he remembered it. Never had they made love so generously, or so frequently, and Julia had taken the lead. It was as if she was in her own race against time.

He hadn't realized how desperate she was to become pregnant, and hadn't even realized she had succeeded, not until the doctors in his Swiss hospital had told him. She may not have known herself. Harry had lost not only Julia, but their child.

There had been plenty to fill his life these past ten years – enough, in truth, to fill quite a number of lives. Plenty of women, too, even another brief marriage, but no one like Julia. And in the lonely reaches of this night, it seemed to hurt as much as it had done that first day when he had returned home from the Alps, entirely alone. Now he sat in the dark, with his drink and his coruscating guilt, as streetlights pointed sharp fingers of accusation at him through the half-drawn curtains. He began to mutter feebly, his tears washing the dribbles of whisky from around his lips, his voice like ripping sandpaper.

'*So I called to the barman to pour me another,*
Me soul was fair bleeding—'

He choked on the words. Harry drank to forget. Yet no matter how hard he tried, it had all been stirred back into his life by two words.

Zac Kravitz.

Kravitz had never been a true friend, a soul mate, he had been too much of a head-banger for that. Impetuous. Sometimes arrogant. Harry sat and began ticking off all the reasons why Zac didn't matter to him any more. He owed him, of course, for Julia, but hidden somewhere deep inside was a voice that kept insinuating it would have been better if Julia had gone down with the boat. Harry would surely have found that easier to deal with than Switzerland. Then he wouldn't have felt it was all his fault.

Julia, in those last six months, had brought more light into his life than he had ever known. He owed Zac for that.

The American had been callous with his own wife, P.J. She'd eventually left him, but that wasn't so strange. Delta types often demanded too much, or too little, from those who loved them: Harry knew the same might be said of him – would be by Bernice. So P.J. had left the scene, taking their three kids and the dog with her, and soon afterwards Zac had gone missing, deliberately hidden himself away, turned his back on everyone, his badly burned back. That's why he'd been forced to quit, honourably discharged, his career gone down in flames with *Guinevere*. Yet the same could have happened to anyone in Special Forces, at any time, and often did, because when you live on the edge there's always the danger you will fall. Harry would have done anything for Zac, and had tried, but he couldn't do a damned thing after Zac had taken himself off and hidden in the shadows. He was a man who knew how to cover his tracks.

Besides, it was all so very long ago. What the hell was the point? Harry cried, first in despair, then in anger at Zac for coming back to screw up his life. He fumbled for his glass, grabbed at it with both hands, only for it to fall, spilling the last of the whisky on the rug.

The bedside clock showed it was shortly after 4 a.m. Harry sat bolt upright in his bed, naked, and sweating profusely. He stared round in alarm. The bed beside him was cold, empty. Distant memories of his evening began creeping back. Yes, he'd screwed up again.

Fragments of the dream that had woken him began to return. He scrabbled for the elusive pieces, but the only thing he was able to see was Julia's face. Under the water – or was it melting ice? Fading. Sinking. Her lips forming one word.

Goodbye.

In fear and impotence Harry began pounding the empty pillows beside him. He'd have given his life to have again those last six months, and his soul to have had six months more. But as he hit the pillows, blindly, in rage, the anger was pushed aside by despair and remorse, which hurt even more. Harry grabbed the pillow and buried his head in it to hide his tears.

He lay still for many minutes, trying to find a route to safety through the war that had broken out within his mind. Somewhere outside, above the streets of Mayfair and in a night made endless day by wasted lights, seagulls who had swapped cliff face for roof tops bickered and pranced. It seemed as though they were mocking him, but it came nowhere close to how much Harry mocked himself. A man can spend a lifetime arguing about the balance between honour, duty, position, reputation, those things by which others measure him, but in the end it's what's inside that matters.

Harry sat up in bed once more. 'Fuck you, Zac,' he said quietly, before heading for the shower.

CHAPTER TWO

New Year's Day had set in misty and frozen, as bleak as the year it had left behind. The sky was low, like beaten tin, and the air filled with tiny needles of ice. As Harry stepped out around the Serpentine, the lake at the heart of Hyde Park, he left a trail of dragon's breath in his wake. He kicked out at a pebble, which scuttled for many feet across the persistent ice before disappearing into dark, reluctant water.

He had sat on his patience for as long as he could before calling d'Arbois. That had been shortly before eight, an hour that on such a day would normally have caused outrage, but they were both members of the 24/7 club, both Europeans who had grown used to the fact that events which shaped their world nowadays occurred in distant parts and different time zones. It was God's revenge on the imperialists. Anyway, as the French Foreign Minister had recently been overheard muttering, no one slept soundly while the new US Secretary of State was awake and functioning.

'We need to talk. About Zac,' Harry had said, without preliminaries.

'We already have,' a reluctant d'Arbois had replied. 'I know very little else.'

'Even so.'

They had agreed to meet at one of the coffee shops overlooking the Serpentine. In midsummer the place would be overrun with excitable children demanding ice cream and another ride on the boats, but today it was almost deserted. They sat at one of the tables outside, wrapped to the ears in their overcoats, out of earshot of the members of the skeleton staff, unwilling to risk the remote possibility that any of them spoke much English.

'Hervé, thank you,' Harry began, acknowledging the kindness the other man was showing by disrupting his day.

'It is always a pleasure to help a friend, Harry. And you sounded . . .' He hesitated while he searched for the appropriate word. 'Restless. That's not like you.'

With the words wrapped in d'Arbois's gentle but occasionally stiff accent, Harry couldn't tell whether the other man was expressing concern or administering a scolding – no, not a scolding, he decided. The Frenchman was a man of many sides; his judgements were usually political, rarely personal.

'I wasn't in much of a frame of mind to take on board everything you were saying last night,' Harry said, scooping some froth from his cappuccino. 'Run it past me again. Please.'

The Frenchman looked out over the grey surface of

the lake, his eyes settling on the naked trees at the edge of the park. With his dark cashmere overcoat and silver hair he seemed to be as one with this monochrome day. 'There is precious little to my tale, Harry. I brought it to you only because I knew of your past liaisons with him. And I have heard nothing but snippets – fragments – in the margins of other conversations.'

Harry didn't need to guess too hard at what was meant. Spy talk. In Algeria, d'Arbois had come into contact with the DGSE – the Direction Générale de la Securité Extérieure, the French equivalent of MI6 or the CIA – and those who were brought under its wing were rarely allowed to escape. Contacts would be maintained, oiled over drinks, meals and many years, particularly with someone as influential as d'Arbois. It would be beneficial to both sides. D'Arbois was renowned for the depth of his connections along the corridors of power and those at the DGSE would want to share them, scratch each other's backs. Anyway, chances were they'd all gone to school together and slept with each other's sisters. It was the French way. Since d'Arbois's retirement from most of his public roles, he had been courted by many private concerns – international companies, defence contractors, financial institutions. Knowledge is profit, and Hervé knew a lot of people. It kept him in cashmere.

'These Central Asian republics are cowboy country,' he continued. 'Since the collapse of the Soviet Union, Kazakhstan, Tajikistan, Turkmenistan and the rest have become cheap copies of their old masters in Moscow. They've lost their Soviet shackles but not the mindset and dark habits. Mix all that with the oil and gas and other natural resources that have been found in some of these places, and you have the makings of some of the most unappealing regimes in the world. And yet,' – he paused to sip his coffee – 'much of this seems to have passed Ta'argistan by. For most people it was little more than miles and miles of barren rock. Then the rumours started to grow. Some new mineral source has been discovered there, so it was said, some fountain of riches that will turn it into the Switzerland of Asia, but . . .' D'Arbois shrugged. 'Nothing has come of it. That hasn't stopped the adventurers and buccaneers circling, of course. Apparently that's when your friend Zac came into the picture. There was talk he made a personal enemy of the President. I'm not sure, I can only guess, but perhaps he even tried to organize a coup.'

'That doesn't make sense. A coup? For what possible reason?'

'Who can tell? Ambition, greed, revenge? None of it's new. Leaders in every country live under threat, sometimes from unlikely sources. As for Ta'argistan, it may be an inhospitable jumble of rocks but they've been fighting over it for a thousand years, tribe against tribe, khan against khan. Throw in the possibility of oil or gas or gold . . .' He spread his gloved hands. 'Anything could happen. And does.'

Harry frowned, trying to follow this through. 'Will they put him on trial?'

'Why should they?'

'To make an example of him. Discourage others.'

'Believe me, if they dragged everyone suspected of malevolence to the dock, it would become their leading industry. No, they manage these things in the shadows. They prefer the dark ways. They don't have to fry testicles in Victory Square to prove their point.'

'But won't the US government help?'

D'Arbois shook his head. 'Did the British government help when the son of Margaret Thatcher got himself involved in some ridiculous coup in Africa? No, not even then. Such matters are too embarrassing. It's better to look the other way. Move on.'

'To the next fuck-up.'

'Leave the bodies behind.' The Frenchman uttered the words quietly.

That had never been Harry's way. He'd once carried a dying colleague for two days on his back through the Iraqi desert. You didn't leave your mates behind, particularly mates like Zac. 'I want to help him,' he replied.

'Too late. He's beyond help. It's possible he is no longer alive.'

'But I owe him.'

'Your loyalty is admirable, my friend, but in this case I fear it is misplaced. Zac Kravitz is one of those unfortunates who has dropped through the drain of history. You owe him nothing. Enjoy yourself. Celebrate the

New Year. Put all this behind you. I should never have mentioned it.'

Celebrate. Forget. *So I called to the barman to pour me another* . . .

'There is nothing for you in Ta'argistan,' d'Arbois insisted softly.

Nothing but Zac Kravitz. The man who saved Julia.

Suddenly they were interrupted. A dog, a hideous over-engineered creation barely larger than a cat with stumpy legs and bulbous eyes, had fled from the clutches of its female owner and come to forage. It was scratching at the Frenchman's trouser leg, its damp paw placed firmly on his polished shoe. Harry thought d'Arbois was bending to stroke it, but instead he picked it up until it was dangling by its kitsch jewel-encrusted collar. Almost carelessly, he tossed it back in the direction of its owner, not hard enough to cause damage but more than enough to make his point. Both dog and owner yelped in surprise, then began to stare at him, moist eyes bulging with accusation and pain. The Frenchman stared straight back, so forcefully that they wilted and withdrew. He wiped his shoe with one of the paper napkins that had arrived with the coffee.

'You must forgive me, Harry. I have a plane to catch. Zurich by five.'

'On New Year's Day? The gnomes must be hard task-masters.'

'No, just very busy.' He stared at Harry, as if struggling to make up his mind whether to reveal some

close-held secret. 'Look, there's one of your British parliamentary groups going to Ta'argistan in the next
couple of days. Roderick Bowles – you know him, of
course? – he's leading it. Perhaps he could help.'

Roddy Bowles help? There had to be a first time.
'Thank you, Hervé.'

'I must rush.' D'Arbois hesitated. 'I'm so very sorry
to be the bearer of such disturbing gossip. But that's all
it is Harry. Gossip.'

As he departed, striding away into the grey morning,
the Frenchman wrapped his arms around his chest
for comfort. He'd heard that Harry had been off form
recently, turning down ministerial posts offered by
the Prime Minister, wandering around town with disgracefully unsuitable women – unsuitable, at least, for
an Englishman. Then there had been last night. Harry
Jones, of all people, beginning to show the fracture
lines, as if he had supped too greedily of life's riches
and was being dragged down by excess. D'Arbois
had seen it happen so many times before.

Nearby, a duck came in to land on the lake, its wings
thrashing the air in increasing concern before it was
dumped arse-first on the ice. It suddenly found itself
sliding along, out of control, before eventually stumbling to its feet and trying to restore what remained of
its ruffled dignity. A bit like Harry, the Frenchman
thought. Definitely slipping. Losing it. Wouldn't have
happened in the old days, not at all. There was a time
when he'd never have been able to fool Harry so easily,

pulled the wool over his eyes all the way down to his underwear.

His triumph amused him, made him feel invincible, even at his age. D'Arbois stepped out around the lake with an added spring to his step, humming a tune by Berlioz.

Harry sat beside the Serpentine, watching a world that was wrapped in a blanket of frost, overwhelmed by a sense of foreboding that was far more than a hangover. Dark thoughts made him anxious, impatient. He reached for his phone.

His career at the sharp ends of the military and political establishments had left him one of the best-connected men in the country. His name opened doors, ensured his phone calls were returned, but even Harry Jones couldn't change the fact that it was New Year's Day. He knew the Foreign Secretary well, had even been offered his job, but also knew the man was away skiing in Whistler. In any event, he would be likely to know little about Ta'argistan and sweet nothing about Zac. Any question would be handed over to his senior officials, who in turn would bump it down the chain of command to a relatively junior desk officer sitting at a crowded work station somewhere in the bowels of the Foreign and Commonwealth Office. These junior officials were normally friendly and efficient, but – it was New Year's Day. When Harry phoned, instead of finding the desk officer for Central Asia, he was put through to an amenable, bouncy duty clerk buoyed up by an overdose of caffeine who seemed to be running the entire world, yet who was unable to reveal any more about Ta'argistan than Harry had been able to discover by logging on to Wikipedia from his mobile phone while sitting in Hyde Park. Much the same when he tried his contacts at MI6. Absent on leave.

It became quickly apparent that Ta'argistan didn't register on the British radar. It hadn't been part of the Empire, didn't have a vote in any assembly in Brussels and wasn't likely to come to Britain's assistance if she was invaded by Iceland. There was no Ta'argi embassy in London, no British embassy in Ta'argistan. And when, stretching his wings, he called the US embassy in Grosvenor Square, he was promised by the receptionist that someone would call back, but they never did. Ta'argistan wasn't part of the American empire, either.

Harry glanced at his watch. 11.17 a.m. Not even daylight in Washington, DC. No help there, then. His frustration grew. It was easier being lost in the Columbian jungle than chopping his way through the distractions of the holiday season.

It was at this point that the dog returned, accompanied by its owner, who was dragging behind her a community support officer, a doleful man wrapped in a fluorescent jacket and brandishing a notebook.

'That's him,' she cried, pointing a finger of accusation with the merciless passion of a Grand Inquisitor.

The sparrow that had been foraging on Harry's table flew away in distress.

The PCSO approached. He was in his late fifties and had the air of a man who in a previous life might have been a quality inspector at a ball-bearing factory. He also bore an excessively cropped moustache that bristled with attitude. 'Good morning, sir. This lady says you've been manhandling her dog.' His moist, pink nostrils flared in disapproval.

'I'm afraid you are mistaken. I never touched it.'

'No – but his friend!' she interjected.

'Never met the man before. A Frenchman, I think.'

'Do you know where he's gone, sir?'

'Said he had a plane to catch.'

'Do you mind if I take a few personal details, then?' the officer replied, bringing forth his notebook.

'I do rather. In a bit of a hurry. But so should you be. Isn't that him, on the far side of the lake?' Harry waved towards a figure that could just be made out across the frozen waters, an entirely innocent stranger who happened to have silver hair and be wearing a black overcoat.

'Yes, that's him. Come on!' the dog owner cried, dragging the bemused beast behind her as she set off in pursuit, its eyes bulging once more as the collar tightened around its neck. With a mean glint in his eye and a bristle of disappointment, the PCSO detached himself from Harry and went after her.

Harry stirred. He had already come to the conclusion

that she was one of those implacable women who would be back, demanding her rights to vengeance. He could sense some ridiculous headline being squeezed out of it all; the tabloids would always oblige, and he would find himself pilloried for an act only a little less despicable than child molestation. He was achieving nothing here, chasing shadows. It was time to move on.

As he looked out across the grey, ice-pinched park, he wondered what it was like up in the mountains of Ta'argistan. Not pleasant, he assumed, but he didn't know, and his ignorance made him feel impotent. He sighed. He knew he would have to swallow a bitter pill. He needed Roddy Bowles.

Harry had got it right. It wasn't much fun in Ta'argistan right now, even in its capital city, Ashkek. It was a town built with too much concrete, in too much of a hurry and with too little imagination, a place where the winds whistled down from the gaunt, grey mountains to scour every corner. And the cells of the ancient central prison in what was simply called the Castle had no heating.

There was one empty cell. It had been vacated a few hours before by Prisoner 7217, and he wouldn't be coming back. Ever. A cell that stank of shit and rats and damp and mould, and despair.

It was into this cell that they threw what was left of Zac Kravitz.

*

Roddy Bowles didn't want to see Harry. Understandable, perhaps, on New Year's Day, but there was form between them, no outright confrontation but an implicit and unambiguous awareness developed over the years that the chemistry between them would never be right. Bowles not only didn't want to see him but would have preferred never to have anything to do with him, yet Harry had insisted. With reluctance that wasn't entirely covered by a veneer of politeness, Bowles had submitted.

He was a politician in his early fifties, small, lean, with greying hair cropped unfashionably short which revealed that he was thinning behind. Bowles hadn't made it centre stage in Westminster; a stint as a junior minister had come to an untidy end when the *Evening Standard* had uncovered some compromising business arrangements allegedly undertaken by his wife, after which he'd devoted his career to cheering from the wings, where he had worked hard to keep one step ahead of the script. He'd spent his time spotting whose star was rising and who was standing on the unsteady trapdoor of life, applauding all the time, even as the bolt on the trapdoor was being withdrawn. His efforts had got him a knighthood long before it was due – he claimed it was for personal services to the Prime Minister, but if you asked him what those services were, he would smile and tap his nose as if you had no right to know. In truth, he'd got his K because he'd nagged in the right places, and they'd hoped that granting it would keep him quiet.

'Hello, Roddy. Apologies for bothering you,' Harry said as the door to the Bowles' apartment opened.

'Never mind, never mind. You're always welcome, you know that,' Bowles responded, making light of the fact that never once had the two of them shared so much as a cup of tea together. 'Come in.'

He led the way into his top-floor apartment, situated in a mansion block in the heart of Belgravia. Harry had expected to find a low-ceilinged, almost mean attic as was typical in these old Victorian buildings, but walls had been taken out and ceilings raised to construct a remarkably large, well-lit reception room. It was furnished in simple but elegant style, with comfortable modern sofas, fresh flowers and a wonderful Georgian desk with a view over Eaton Square. The walls carried not the usual clutter of political cartoons and self-serving publicity photographs but some fine Impressionist paintings, and Harry also spotted an ancient Roman green glass pitcher on the desk and something on a side table that might have been out of Damien Hirst's stable. The place had been kitted out with remarkable taste and an open mind. So unlike the rest of Roddy. There was also a woman's coat thrown over the back of one of the chairs.

'The curator of my pictures,' Bowles explained, sensing the imperceptible rise in Harry's eyebrow. 'We're thinking of bringing up some new canvases I've acquired from the country. She's, er . . . in the bathroom.' It sounded like a confession. Time to move on.

'You said you had something urgent you wanted to discuss. I'm intrigued.'

Bowles indicated a seat for Harry, and sat down opposite him, as though conducting an interview. He was wearing a double-breasted blazer and it was buttoned. Harry remembered that Julia had always harboured doubts about men who wore such jackets and kept them buttoned, even when sitting at home on a sofa. She said they hid more than a man's bulging gut.

'Roddy, you're leading a parliamentary group to Ta'argistan.'

'Yes, in three days' time.'

'I'd like to come with you.'

Bowles appeared bemused. 'But . . . why?'

'Lots of reasons. I'm curious. All this talk about Asia forging a brave new world – I want to see a bit of it myself.'

Bowles chuckled, like a tutor with a confused child. 'Yes, but Ta'argistan at this time of year is a pretty remorseless place. Even in the capital they can't guarantee power supplies. A bloody icebox, I can tell you. God knows why they suggested we go at this time of year, but that's why it's only four days. You'd be better off in the Caribbean or Courchevel – anywhere, in fact.'

'I'm not looking for a holiday. And I suppose . . . well, let me be frank. It's the anniversary of Julia's death. Could do with getting away somewhere completely different, take my mind off things. So I'd like to be part of your group.'

'And I'd love to have you, Harry, be glad of your support, and if I could help I most certainly *would*,' Bowles replied, banging his fist on his knee for emphasis, 'but the Ta'argis are an inflexible lot, no imagination. Still polishing Joe Stalin's boots. And they've been very clear that they can only accommodate five of us. And since they're footing the bill—'

'My bills aren't a problem.'

'Maybe so, but the arrangements and accommodation are. Five, they have said, and five it will have to be.'

'Surely you can squeeze another one in.'

'Out of my hands, I'm afraid. We're already fully subscribed. I've got that twerp Bobby Malik, Sid Proffit – what an old buffer he is. There's Ian McKenzie to make up the Scottish quota and Martha Riley for decoration. A rum lot, I'll agree, but also a full house. I'd love to have you on board, Harry, a man with your qualifications, but . . .' He spread his hands wide in surrender to the facts. 'I'm so very sorry.' The words were syrup, but there was no disguising the stone that lay beneath.

The noise of someone moving about crept from a room nearby. Bowles rose to his feet, the interview at its end. 'Wish I could ask you to stay for coffee but, as you can see, I'm tied up at the moment.'

Or likely to be later, if the rumours were true. He might bring his paintings up from the country, but never his wife.

He led Harry to his door and shook his hand, a rather awkward gesture between colleagues, before propelling him out. 'I'm sorry to disappoint,' he lied, briskly closing the door.

'Oh, but you haven't,' Harry whispered, as he headed for the stairs.

When, at last, Zac became aware, he found himself in a place that had been stripped of every shred of colour. Some pain was like that, so intense, so personal, that it tore away all subtlety from the world and left nothing but obliterating darkness and flashes of blinding, impenetrable light. He lay immobile in the filth, curled up, like a child, his hands tucked between his thighs, instinctively trying to protect those most vulnerable parts of a man's body from any further injury. The pain they had inflicted had been, literally, unimaginable. The sort of pain that makes a man do anything, say anything, to make it stop.

And Zac had. Given them everything. Every name, every contact, everything he knew, not that there had been much.

Zac had been part of the Circuit, the name insiders gave to that expanding world of private armies that stretched from Algeria to Afghanistan, from Nigeria to Venezuela, anywhere there was a mixture of money and danger. They filled gaps where local security forces were ill-trained or under-staffed; even the US and British governments used such men to guard the outer perimeters of some of their more exposed embassies. It was a world of mercenaries, of guns for hire. Mao Zedong had once declared that power grows out of the barrel of a gun, and so did big fat profit.

Zac had been hired to help with the training of Ta'argistan's paramilitary forces. Nothing unusual in that, it was happening all around the globe, but Zac was still that irrepressible football player, didn't know when to stop, not until he'd been knocked clean off his feet. That had happened the day they dragged him off and accused him of sharing the sweated sheets of the wife of the most powerful man in the republic. That sort of liaison put a man way out of bounds. The President could scarcely admit to being a cuckold, so instead Zac was accused of treason, of being in contact with opposition groups and plotting the overthrow of the government. In a land of mists and suspicions, it was an accusation that took hold all too greedily. Now Zac lay shivering on a cold stone floor. He'd told them everything he knew, even things he had simply imagined, but it wasn't enough. They thought he knew more.

They hadn't beaten him, not at first. They'd tried to squeeze information out of him through isolation in the Castle, and humiliation, depriving him of food and clothing and of any concept of time. They had degraded him and begun to treat him ever more brutally, like an animal, and for one period of exquisite foulness even as a catamite. Torment both body and

mind, leave a man to swim in his own fear, not knowing where they might drag him next, and he will crack.
Rip out the soul and the words will follow. But when he
failed to give them what they wanted, what they
thought he knew, the treatment had become ever more
savage.

No amount of training could have prepared Zac for
what came next. Name, rank and serial number didn't
get him past the first deliberately busted finger, bent
back until it snapped. Every man has his breaking
point, and Zac had reached his at a relatively early
stage in his torture. No shame in that. Yet although he
was unable to resist the physical pain, Zac still fought
them, in his mind. When they'd grabbed him he'd been
playing chess with an old Ta'argi at one of the concrete
tables in Victory Park where grizzled chess players
gathered; he loved the passion of these whiskery men,
even though he didn't understand a word of their language. Not that his interrogators saw these encounters
as being innocent. As he had sat, bent in concentration
over his endgame, they had clubbed him from behind,
but before they dragged him away he had snatched at
one of the chess pieces, the black horse. It was nothing
more than a cheap wooden carving, but to Zac it
became priceless. He had managed to keep it throughout all that was to come, in his clenched fist, in a pocket
or a fold in his clothes, between his toes, in his mouth,
anywhere. Yes, there too. The struggle to retain that
chess piece became his own private battle with his

tormentors, one they didn't even know about. It gave him a sense of control, so that when they lacerated his body and filled every pore with pain he was able to survive it, claim victory over them, so long as he could feel the small wooden horse biting into the flesh of his palm.

When he was thrown back in his cell and left in the squalor on his floor, his horse would come to life, and in his imagination he would ride it away into the mountains, to freedom, to places where it didn't hurt any more.

How many weeks Zac had survived like this he couldn't tell. Time no longer had any meaning, only the moment mattered. But he was aware that something had changed, he was in a new place, a different cell. This cell was deeper, danker, than any that had gone before. It was as though they had brought him to the deepest hole on earth, lit by a single bare bulb. As his eyes began to regain their focus, he looked up and saw a guard towering over him.

'Where . . . where am I?' he muttered feebly as his tongue snagged on a loose tooth.

The guard looked at him, and for a moment Zac thought he saw pity in his eyes.

'What does it matter?' the guard said sadly. 'You won't be here long.'

The names spilled by Bowles as members of his group included one Harry knew well. Ian McKenzie, a Scot with a parliamentary seat in Kent, was one of nature's enthusiasts, a rare creature who saw good in most people. It was a grievous weakness for a politician. 'That man'll never climb the ladder,' one Chief Whip had remarked. 'Spends too much bloody time on his knees being nice to the weeds.' It wasn't that McKenzie had no ambition. Several years earlier, during a ministerial reshuffle, he had been at home affecting a total lack of interest in the matter yet straying no further than the pond at the end of his garden, when his wife had stuck her head out of the kitchen window and yelled at him that Downing Street was on the phone. It had transformed him from monkish indifference to a man with the energy of a rutting greyhound and he had leapt to respond. Yet, tragically for those who like happy endings, in his bounding haste he had tripped over the step and given himself a head wound that would later require half a dozen stitches at A&E. What caused far greater indignity was that the call turned out to be from a correspondence secretary enquiring about nothing more life-enhancing than a constituent's letter. Afterwards, true to his good nature, McKenzie had shared the joke with his many friends. It was one of the few ways that year he'd managed to get coverage in the newspapers.

'Mac? It's Harry Jones.'

'Harry! Happy Hogmanay, my friend.' He was somewhere outside, his voice raised, almost shouting down the phone.

'You, too, Mac. Look, I need a small favour.'

'Anything for you.'

'You're going with Roddy Bowles to Ta'argistan in a couple of days.'

'Getting stuck into a bit of training for it even as we speak, as it happens.'

'Where?'

'Val-d'Isère.'

'I admire your dedication.'

'I'm in the line for the ski lift right now, just about to thump some little French teenage shit who thinks he's got the right to jump the queue.'

'Sounds like you're having a wonderful time. You should stay.'

'Oh, fat chance.'

In the background Harry heard a youthful cry and a Gallic curse before McKenzie came back on the line.

'Sorry, Harry, all yours now.'

'Stay, Mac. Call in sick. Would you do that? Just tell Roddy you can't go. I'd like to take your place.'

'You can't be serious, old mucker.'

'Never more so.'

'But it's the middle of bloody winter there. And Roddy's such a prick.'

'What are you saying?'

'He practically broke my arm to get me to agree in the first place. You know what he's like. I've been kicking myself ever since – must have been pished. No, come to think of it, must have been completely bloody paralytic. I've spent the whole of Christmas trying to figure out some way of wriggling out of it.'

'Why not simply say no?'

'You know what a hideous bully he can be. And –' he sighed – 'I owe him a couple of favours. He never stops reminding me. Payback time.'

'So you'll help?'

'Harry, if I was a true friend, I'd save you from yourself. But if you're wanting to spend a few days cuddled up to Roddy Bowles in the frozen armpit of Central Asia, it's all yours. Call in sick? What sort of malady do you want me to contract? Something lurid, I hope.'

'Anything that stops you rushing back. But let me be the one to tell him first.'

'Whatever. Look, I've reached the head of the bloody line, got to dash. Totally raving mad, you are, Harry. God, I hope you'll not be living to regret this. Tally ho . . .!'

The connection went dead.

It was the following afternoon before Harry called on Roddy Bowles once more.

'Why, Harry. This is becoming a habit.' Bowles opened the door with such reluctance its hinges might have seized.

'I was passing,' Harry lied. 'Thought it better than the phone.' That was truthful, at least, beard the bully in his own den, face him down. And gather intelligence. The woman's coat was still slung over the chair.

Harry glanced round the room. 'So how's the curating going, Roddy?'

'You mentioned some coincidence,' Bowles said, making a point of ignoring the question.

'Yes, poor Mac. He's the one who first mentioned your Ta'argistan trip to me. Got me interested.'

'And?'

'Well, tripped over his bloody skis, the idiot, hasn't he? Got himself a case of mild concussion. Can't fly, and so can't be on parade.'

Bowles took a deep breath and with ill-concealed impatience brushed away imaginary fluff from the front of his double breast. He could see where this one was going.

'He called me from the hospital. Worried about disappointing you,' Harry continued.

'I'm not sure the man's capable of disappointing me,' Bowles replied tartly.

'That's why he asked me to take his place on the trip.'

The eyes flared icily. 'Impossible.'

'I know it's a coincidence, but it solves all your problems.'

'That's where I'm afraid you're wrong, Harry. You know I have to offer any spare place to others. There's a waiting list, you know.'

'What? You leave the day after tomorrow.'

'Which is yet another reason why it won't work. Visas. You'd never get one in time.'

'But I've already applied online. It'll be waiting for me at the airport.'

Suddenly Bowles snapped, tugging furiously at the sleeves of his blazer as though to keep them from reaching out for Harry's neck. 'I will not be bounced like this!'

'Bounced, Roddy? But I thought I was helping. After all, you said you'd love to have me on board.'

'I'll not allow you to go behind my back.'

'Roddy, how can you say that? I've done no such thing. As soon as I heard from Mac I called you at home.'

'What?' Bowles snapped, his voice rising in alarm.

'Yesterday evening. Spoke to your wife. Asked her to give you a message.'

And suddenly Bowles was in retreat. 'Ah, I see,' he sighed in the manner of a deflating balloon, and colouring as though his collar had suddenly tightened several sizes. He glanced away, unable to meet Harry's eye. His attention became fixed upon the woman's coat. He knew Harry had seen it, too. 'My wife and I, we, er . . . haven't been in contact the last couple of days.'

Harry allowed a moment of suffocating silence to settle on his quarry, but he couldn't let it last. He had to allow the man a means of retreat. He might yet need the bastard.

'I'm sorry if I've put you out, Roddy. That wasn't my intention, I assure you. But you said the Ta'argis were expecting five and – well, five it will still be. I thought I was doing the right thing.'

'Yes. Of course.'

Harry waited for Bowles to say more, but although the man's lips were working furiously, no sound came forth. 'I'll see you at the airport, then, Roddy. Have a good evening.'

As he left, the door seemed to close so much more easily behind him.

Zac pushed his fingers into his ears to blunt the incessant sound of screaming.

The noise continued for a long time before he realized the screams were his own.

CHAPTER THREE

They hadn't yet arrived, but already the character of the group was beginning to take shape. Bowles stood at the helm, still fully buttoned, the officious and, it had to be said, efficient captain. He'd done this trip before, knew the form, and wanted everyone to know it. Sid Proffit, dcar fellow, was a member of the House of Lords, in his late seventies and happy to claim the status of 2I/C on account of his seniority and enthusiastic naval whiskers. He still retained a roguish twinkle, which became evident as he summoned the cabin attendant to refill his glass. Bobby Malik was the serious type, quiet, diligently wading through the briefing papers he had brought with him, the youngest in the group, a new arrival to Westminster after a much-heralded victory at a by-election. He seemed uncertain why he had come or what he was doing here. Harry barely knew him but concluded that, like Mac, he had been a victim of the Bowles press gang.

And then there was Martha Riley. Martha was late thirties, petite, provocative and, in Harry's view, over-flowing with attitude. Their brief encounters around

Westminster had always left him with a headache; she seemed somehow to resent him and his success, as though it was undeserved. She was American-born, a New England liberal with a New York edge, which made her exceptional if not quite unique in the history of the House of Commons. The first woman ever to sit in the chamber had been the American-born Nancy Astor, a woman with an attitude built on her husband's uncompromising wealth and with a tongue as generous as a pocketful of razor blades. The British electorate had waited ninety years before they'd dare repeat the experiment; in Harry's view, they'd jumped the gun.

She was a difficult woman to pin down and almost impossible to categorize. Martha was witty, frequently saucy, and occasionally in private she had a mouth like a garbage can, yet she confused many men by also being surprisingly puritanical. Several of her colleagues at Westminster had attempted to drag her off to a secluded corner, but so far as was known she had resisted all such encounters, sending the befuddled lecher away with the sound of buckshot in his ears. Her views on the male of the species were unequivocal. She had, she said, married well, to a man who was exceptionally wealthy and took frequent liberties. In her turn, seven years later, she had taken his house and a great chunk of his fortune, and never looked back. 'I was born screaming, and I haven't stopped since,' she would declare. Now she was complaining about the meal.

Harry sighed and closed his eyes, trying to catch a

little sleep. It was a flight that would last almost ten hours and he'd need all his wits around him when they arrived. He had no clear plan, only doubts. He'd spent the past two days immersing himself in everything Ta'argi, and it had proved to be a pretty cold bath. He had taken what he could from the Foreign and Commonwealth Office, followed that up with Amnesty International and Human Rights Watch, and tried to fill the gaps with Google.

He had also pursued the US Embassy, not for what they knew about Ta'argistan but for what they might tell him about Zac. There he'd run headlong into a wall of silence, or it might have been simple ignorance, so he had appealed to his friend the ambassador, who had promised to get someone to call back. A military attaché eventually did.

'Captain Zachariah P. Kravitz.' Harry hadn't known he was a P. That, at least, was something new. Nothing else was. 'Yes, sir,' the attaché continued, 'he once served in the US armed forces, but that was some time ago. Hasn't lived in the United States itself for almost ten years. He is no longer reporting on any of our radars, sir.'

'And what does that mean?' Harry had asked.

There was a short, baffled silence. 'It means precisely what it says, sir.'

'Not on our radar? What's he supposed to be, some kind of jumbo jet?'

'That's all I've been given, sir,' the young attaché

replied awkwardly. He was clearly reading from a statement; these opaque words came from somewhere higher up the food chain. He coughed, as though something were sticking in his throat, then began reciting once more. 'But I can tell you that we regard Ta'argistan to be an aspirational democracy, and consequently a government which the United States considers friendly.'

Friendly? Not if half of what he'd been told by an elderly Russian from Human Rights Watch was true. Harry recognized the American's impenetrable jargon for what it was. A warning. Deep water. Keep out.

Roddy got them upgraded to business class. Had to give that much to him, the man had clout. They took off shortly before midnight, leaving the clamouring lights of London behind them for a flight that lasted many hours, flying against the sun. Roddy's upgrade proved a blessing, for it enabled them to catch a little sleep, although as they woke they found the world outside already fading as they headed for the dark side of the planet. Beneath them unfolded endless miles of emptiness, snow like suffocating gauze on landscape lit by a cold steel moon. It seemed devoid of any trace of life. No roads, no traffic, no villages, not even an occasional campfire. Harry glanced across the cabin at Martha. She was no longer complaining or even talking, but had her eyes closed and was concentrating on her breathing as she gripped the arms of her seat. Strange woman, Harry thought, full of contradictions.

Attractive in her own way – in fact, more than that when she allowed herself a smile, but years of working out as a professional ball-breaker had tugged away at the corners of her mouth. She was ambitious, never hid it, and the accepted wisdom in the corridors of Westminster was that she was destined to get her over-due leg-up to ministerial rank as soon as the Prime Minister decided the time had come to wring a few more necks in the dovecote. Perhaps then she would learn to smile. Martha had been in Parliament six years, her career still ahead of her, whereas Harry . . . Harry was a maverick, did things his own way, was temperamentally unsuited to dancing to another man's tune, a grievous sin in Westminster. There were some who thought his time was past, and perhaps they were right, while it seemed likely that Martha would soon be pulling a ministerial salary and disappearing from view in a chauffeur-driven car, off to some official engagement which she would use as an excuse to lec-ture the rest of the world. Harry resolved to buy himself a pair of stout earplugs.

But that was tomorrow's business. Right now, the flaps of the 757 were dropping beneath the wings as the plane began its final descent. Ahead, Harry could see the first flickers of civilization. The glowing lines of a runway pointed towards a distant medley of lights that was the airport terminal, but suddenly, and seemingly at the last moment, they disappeared. In the blink of an eye there was no terminal, no runway, nothing but renewed darkness. The engines roared ferociously in protest.

The aircraft was lifting and turning when a voice came on the intercom, a woman, the First Officer. 'I'm sorry, ladies and gentlemen, nothing to worry about, but they appear to be having a bit of trouble at Ashkek. A power outage, by the looks of it. Hey ho, not great timing. It happens in this part of the world. They're supposed to have an emergency back-up system, but I suspect their gennie's frozen, so we're just going to cruise round and hold for a bit to let them sort themselves out. Meanwhile, sit back and relax. We'll be on the ground in no time.'

She was as good as her word. It may have seemed a lifetime for the faint of heart, but it was no more than a few minutes before the wheels touched down with barely the hint of a thump upon a snow-skimmed runway and the aircraft whined slowly to a halt. Not until then did Martha open her eyes. Hazel, with a hint of marmalade, to go with bobbed hair the colour of chestnuts. Did it come out of a bottle, like the Prime Minister's? Harry wondered.

He was soon distracted from drawing any further conclusions about Martha by his first sight of Ashkek. The single terminal was drab and ill-lit, even with the power restored.

'What are we doing here?' the youthful Malik muttered, his brow creased in disappointment as he shivered in a blast of chill wind.

It was a question Harry hadn't entirely resolved for himself. 'Your first parliamentary trip?'

Malik nodded.

'There are alternatives. You might prefer to discover a passionate interest in the film industry, or maybe space travel.'

'What do you mean?'

'Hollywood and Florida. And you'd be surprised how many of our parliamentary colleagues have developed a previously unknown but unrelenting desire to study the impact of rising sea levels on places like the Maldives. That's what this game is about. Just be careful not to get trampled in the rush.'

'I'm not like that,' Malik protested, a little piously, 'I don't see my job as a matter of privilege.'

'Then welcome to Ta'argistan.'

There was a welcome, of sorts. While most of the passengers joined the shuffling queue to have their passports checked, Bowles and his group were taken to a VIP lounge, a solemn affair with severe furniture and dusty artificial flowers, and two armed guards on duty outside the door. There the group was greeted by an official with agitated eyes and stiff English who introduced himself as Sydykov. He collected their passports, offering them tea while he dealt with the formalities and their luggage. That got Martha going.

'I've got three bags,' she declared, slowly, her voice rising as though speaking to a village bumpkin. 'Three,' she repeated, holding up the appropriate number of fingers. 'One is small, so please make sure it isn't over-looked.'

Harry winced at the performance. He could tell a military man even in his civvies. Sydykov seemed to reciprocate, coming across to introduce himself to Harry more formally.

'Your rank?' Harry enquired, shaking his hand, noticing its firm grip.

'I hold the rank of major,' Sydykov replied.

'In which service?'

But the man simply smiled and moved on, as though he hadn't understood.

Sydykov was there once again as they gathered in the foyer of their hotel two hours later, his smile still stretched in that fixed, dutiful manner, as stiff as the covers of the passports he handed back. The visitors had been given time to unpack and rest and were now waiting to be driven to the Presidential Palace for dinner, their first formal engagement of the tour. Martha Riley was still behaving like grit in a shoe. She looped her arm through the major's, as though they were now old friends.

'Now, I don't wish to complain,' she began, 'but I couldn't find any sign of a hairdryer in my room.'

With her free hand she ruffled her hair and returned his smile, while he appeared temporarily speechless, almost stunned.

'And may I ask what that elderly lady is doing, sitting outside our rooms at the end of the corridor?'

Sydykov stiffened. 'She, Mrs Riley, is there to ensure your comfort,' he replied, his lips now taut in exasperation.

'I asked her about the hairdryer, of course I did, but she didn't seem to understand. How can she help us if she doesn't speak English?'

Once again Sydykov seemed anxious to move on. 'Forgive me, Mrs Riley, while I make arrangements for your hairdryer.'

'That's so kind of you,' she said to his retreating back. 'A girl's got to look nice for the President.'

Harry found himself torn between rising irritation and the gentle tickle of amusement. How could she be so crass? Hadn't she realized who the hell Sydykov was? Yet the sight of a major in the internal security service being used as a dog to fetch a stick held its own small pleasures. This was touted as a goodwill visit, yet they weren't even trusted to wander around the hotel on their own. He'd already spotted the additional plain-clothes security, two of them sitting stiffly in the foyer. The hotel was constructed in the monumental, almost brutal style of the Soviet era and its public parts had all the sense of fun of a funeral parlour. The foyer could comfortably hold two hundred, yet there weren't twenty. There was no crowd to get lost in, everyone stood out, particularly two goons.

Harry's mind went back to the researcher from Human Rights Watch whom he'd met in a coffee house in Bloomsbury, near the British Museum. He was an old, wizened Russian named Pyotr whose crooked back and pronounced limp told of a life of troubles behind what had once been the Iron Curtain. He had a cracked voice and a thick Slavic accent, and as he spoke tears formed in his eyes. Harry couldn't decide whether they were caused simply by his age, or by the sad tales he had to tell of a land filled by perpetual snows and suspicion. Now Harry was here, and the old Russian's stories seemed to be coming to life.

Sydykov had returned, bringing with him a hairdryer, a preposterously large contraption that Martha immediately claimed and held aloft as though she had just won an Oscar.

'Thank you so much, Mr Sickof.' She made a point of mispronouncing the name. 'Back with you in five minutes, gentlemen,' she declared, disappearing in the direction of her room.

They waited for Martha, then they waited some more. Bowles tapped his foot in exasperation, Proffit meandered off in search of a drink, Malik sat in a corner studying his briefing notes while Harry asked himself yet again what the hell he was doing here. He had no plan, or at least nothing he regarded as shower-proof let alone watertight. The closest he'd got was a plan so simple it bordered on the preposterous. Its sole merit lay in the fact it was so outrageous, it might just take everyone else by surprise, too, catch them napping. He would simply ask them to release Zac.

Outrageous, certainly, but perhaps not as stupid as it

sounded. There were ties between Britain and Ta'argistan. The Central Asian state was desperate for aid, for experts, for sound advice, anything that might help it drag itself out of their yurts and into the twenty-first century. Many homes were still heated with dried camel turd, their walls built of mud, and the industrial infrastructure consisted of little more than haystacks and holes in the ground. The Ta'argis also needed help in clearing up the irradiated rubble left behind by the Soviets. In return for help in these matters, Britain's rewards were likely to be less tangible. She'd gain a friend in a sensitive part of the world, and Britain had grown rather short of friends in recent years. If they were lucky, the Brits might discover that the Ta'argis, like some of their Central Asian neighbours, were sitting on an endless supply of oil or natural gas or uranium, buried somewhere deep inside the Celestial Mountains. That was a long shot, of course, but modern diplomacy was little more than a crap shoot, and you had to be in the game to stand any chance of winning.

A new world was waiting only to be discovered, yet for the moment it would have to wait on Martha. Sydykov paced up and down the foyer, examining his watch, his smile growing more forced with every glance. When, finally, she reappeared, blown and brushed, Bowles exploded in a theatrical gesture of impatience. 'Really, Martha!' he snapped.

'Why, Roddy,' she said as she breezed past in the

direction of their waiting bus, 'you'd spend more time with your hair, if you had any.'

His hand came up defensively to the sparse patch on the back of his head, as though to brush it away. He gave a snort of rebuke. Then he followed.

Soon they found themselves heading for the White House, the Presidential Palace. It proved to be an uncomfortable, angular building of six floors set in the centre of the city behind ornate railings, its name coming not in imitation of the US President's home but from the pale stone cladding used in its construction. Harry recognized the style; Soviet, nineteen-sixties, built off a plan drawn up in some office in Moscow, presumably the same office that had supplied the plans for Lenin's mausoleum. The entrance was guarded by young soldiers in exaggerated flat felt hats the size of dinner plates who snapped to attention as the visitors approached. Inside, the reception hall was vast, largely empty, like an aircraft hangar, every step echoing on the pink-marble floor. By contrast, the lift up to the top floor was claustrophobic and slow. They found themselves disgorged into a reception room, where they were greeted not by the President but by a man of slightly less than average height with a lean, pinched face and hair plastered thinly across his skull. He was wearing circular rimless glasses, and the eyes behind them were bright and almond-shaped, betraying the presence of something Mongol in his genes, yet his skin was pale by the standards of most mountain men, as though he rarely saw the light. With his sloping shoulders and modestly cut suit he gave the impression of an academic, a professor who loved nothing more than spending his days with books. Sydykov made the introductions.

'May I introduce to you Mr Amir Beg,' he said, 'the President's chief of staff.'

'Welcome to the Presidential Palace,' Beg said, offering a polite bow but without shaking hands. His English was halting but, as his guests were to discover, usually technically precise. 'The President will be with us shortly. I'm afraid I can offer you no more than fruit juice, since the President himself doesn't touch alcohol.' He waved to trays carried by young girls in colourful native costumes.

'That wasn't in the bloody briefing,' Proffit muttered in a theatrical whisper from the back of the group.

'You never read the briefing,' Bowles responded, leading the charge for the trays.

Apart from Beg and Sydykov there were only three other Ta'argis present, officials from various economic ministries; it was destined to be a small gathering. The room, like so much else in Ashkek, was stiff with formality and too large for their number, and fruit juice wasn't going to help. Two oversized portraits of the President hung at either end, and the only splashes of colour came from cultural artefacts and murals on the walls. Many of the designs featured horses.

'Used to do a little hunting myself when I was

younger,' Proffit ventured, tugging wistfully at his whiskers.

'We Ta'argis are – or *were* – nomads,' Beg said. 'We claim descent directly from Genghis Khan. Our horses represent our freedom.'

'Then Martha here should feel at home,' Proffit exclaimed jovially. 'I've always suspected she was in direct line from Cochise and the Sioux.'

'Cochise was an Apache.' She arched an eyebrow. 'And I'm half-Irish.'

'The other half?' Proffit enquired.

'Pure skunk.'

Proffit was about to offer several further observations about her probable genealogical roots when the large carved wooden doors at the end of the reception room swung open. Everyone turned, and fell to silence as Mourat Karabayev, the President of the Republic of Ta'argistan, strode through the doors, accompanied by two large hunting dogs close at his heels. He was tall for a Ta'argi, in his early fifties and only a little overweight, with a full head of dark waving hair swept straight back from the temples. He had the high, prominent cheekbones so characteristic of his people, and a small but deeply incised scar just below his right eye. He also had a nose that at some point in his life had been badly broken.

'Mr Bowles, it is so good to see you again,' he said, extending his hand and sniffing – his broken nose seemed to give him the need to snuffle repeatedly. 'And

all of you: Mrs Riley, gentlemen, you are most welcome. I am sorry if I have kept you waiting. You must
be hungry. Let's eat!'

His suggestion was more than hospitality; it implied
a man short of time and, perhaps, with limited
patience. At a brisk pace he led them through to a
neighbouring room that was much smaller, with windows on two sides facing out across the city, where the
lights were beginning to change as shops were shut-
tered and in their place the nightspots came to life. Yet
the view inside the room proved far more tempting. In
discretely lit display cabinets hugging every wall was
housed a collection of gold artefacts, exceedingly old
and in remarkably fine condition. Items of jewellery,
ornamental horse harnesses, burial goods, Buddhist
figurines both seated and standing, ancient coins,
amulets, with every piece crafted from gold. The display was overshadowed by yet another portrait of the
President, watching protectively over a dining table set
for ten. Karabayev took his place in the middle, looking
out over his city, Bowles sat opposite. The two groups
didn't mingle but found their seats on either side of
the table – like North and South Korea, Harry thought.
Beg was at the President's right hand, and Martha next
to Bowles. It made Harry wonder if Bowles had been
responsible for the British seating plan; he was left in
no doubt when he found himself ushered to the floating seat at the very end of the table.

The meal was simple – meat that might have been

mutton, with cabbage and potatoes. And cheese. Mountain food. Alongside the fruit juice, they were also offered a drink of sour-smelling liquid that was described as fermented mare's milk, but even Proffit took only a cursory sip. The glasses were kept topped up, and they talked: of aspirations, of industries, of economic ties and political ambitions, all the many things that might turn the myth of the Silk Road into a modern reality. Then Karabayev raised his glass of mare's milk and offered a toast: 'To friendship.'

'To trade,' Bowles responded.

'To aid,' the President added.

Bowles smiled and sipped his fruit juice.

'And in return for that aid?' It was Martha. As usual, there was a note of challenge in her voice.

The President stared across the table. 'In return? Why, our friendship. We are a proud and independent people, Mrs Riley, a natural ally of the West. Friendship in a turbulent world has its own value, I think.' But he could see he had failed to impress Martha. 'Is there more you would want?'

'I'm a democrat, Mr President. You want my friendship, I want more openness. Human rights. Free elections. I hope you'll forgive me speaking candidly' – her lips were working as though chewing a large wad of tobacco – 'but I keep hearing claims that the last election was rigged.'

An uncomfortable silence settled upon them all. While he considered his answer, Karabayev threw morsels of meat to the two dogs, whose jaws snapped hungrily. Then he sniffed, pretended a smile, showing a set of perfect white teeth that Harry suspected might even be his own.

'Yes, democracy. A delicate flower, Mrs Riley, too easily trampled by . . . careless criticism.' He threw more meat to the dogs before wiping his hands and turning his full attention to her. 'You shouldn't listen to lies peddled by the disappointed. And might I suggest you take care when you offer lectures about democracy? After all, your own government was elected by barely a quarter of the voters while your head of state isn't elected at all. And as for your House of Lords . . .' He turned to Sid Proffit, a.k.a. Lord Proffit of Chipping Sodbury. 'I hope you will not take this personally, but the entire world sits back in bewilderment at a house of Parliament filled with nothing but placemen and hereditary aristocrats. It is . . .' – he searched for the appropriate term – 'quaint. But scarcely democratic.' He held up his hand to stall the imminent outpouring of rebuttal from Martha. 'Yes, yes, I know, you have your own way of doing things, but so do we. In Ta'argistan we like to work in harmony with the people. The government and governed are as one. All in step.'

Harry could almost hear the tramp of marching boots echoing through the streets.

'It is an ideal more easily aspired to than achieved, I know,' the President continued, 'but that's why the foremost task of my loyal lieutenant here –' he placed his hand on Amir Beg's shoulder – 'is to ensure that it becomes a reality.' He made it sound as if Beg was a spin doctor. Beg smiled, nodded his head to acknowledge the recognition, although his knuckles showed white. They usually did, Harry had noticed. They were remarkably uneven, like a mountain range, as if at some point they had been badly broken. Perhaps that was why he didn't shake hands.

'If you want more aid, we need to see progress on human rights,' Martha persisted.

'We have nothing to hide.'

'Really? That's not what I hear.'

'And what is it, precisely, that you hear, Mrs Riley?' Karabayev sniffed.

'All nature of things. Domestic violence on women being the norm. Bride kidnapping. Harassment of the gay community. And I can give you a list of opponents who seem to have disappeared inside your prisons.' As she was speaking she reached out to stroke one of the dogs that was prowling around the table in search of more treats. In return what she got was a deep, glottal growl and a curled lip that revealed large yellow teeth.

'I'd advise against that, Mrs Riley,' the President warned. 'They're not pets.' His voice had grown quiet, almost soft, but he was no longer even pretending to smile. 'As for lists, I can offer you lists, too, if that's what you want. About your own country. Unless I am very much mistaken, Britain has the highest prison population in Europe. Isn't that so? And the highest levels of crime, the highest levels of homelessness. And what did your Leader of the Opposition say just last week? I seem to remember he talked about cities littered with drug addicts where the streets are patrolled by pimps and prostitutes.' He brushed a piece of imaginary lint from the front of his jacket. 'We can all play games with statistics, Mrs Riley, but I find it a fruitless exercise. In Ta'argistan, we do our best, in difficult circumstances.'

Beg joined the battle. His accent was less fluent than his President's, yet his voice conveyed remarkable passion. 'Twenty years ago, there was no freedom in our country. The half that wasn't used as a training ground by Soviet special forces was used as a dumping ground for its nuclear industry. And we need no lectures about prisons, Mrs Riley. Both the President and I had the pleasure of spending several years as guests of our Soviet masters. If our hands aren't yet as clean as you might like, it's only because we haven't finished washing them of foreign dirt.'

Karabayev took up the reins once more. 'Please don't mistake us for barbarians, Mrs Riley. Look around you. These beautiful artefacts were being fashioned at a time when in your own country I believe the natives wore animal skins and daubed their bodies in coloured mud.'

She was about to protest that she had been born an

American, but held her tongue. Somehow, she doubted that waving the Stars and Stripes would help.

'This place was the crossroads of many ancient civilizations. We are a proud people, an ancient race. We ask for nothing other than respect.'

'And a little aid,' she reminded him.

Karabayev was on his feet, his face stiff. 'I'm sure we could swap stories all night, but you will have to continue without me, I fear. Affairs of state, you understand. I shall leave you in Amir Beg's capable hands. Goodnight.'

With a final snuffle, he was gone, pursued by the dogs. Bowles glared at Martha, she fixed her gaze on her mare's milk, and Sid Proffit took another, and longer, exploratory sip. Meanwhile, Harry's heart sank. The President had disappeared, and with him had vanished any chance Harry might have had of simply asking for Zac's release, as an act of friendship. Martha had really mucked that one up. Blown it to pieces. It had always been a long shot, he knew, but so much less painful for him than any of the alternatives. His eyes were drawn once more to Beg's obliterated knuckles. Something about this man told Harry that nothing would ever be achieved here without very considerable pain.

Bowles' eyes continued to glow red with anger, as if with a little more focus they might encourage Martha into an act of spontaneous combustion. There would be words later, yet the hole in the evening was quickly filled as Beg nodded towards Sydykov and the President's chair was removed. One of the servant girls – Harry wanted to use the term waitress, but there had been a feudal touch about the entire proceeding – took Beg's chair and put it in the President's empty place. Harry couldn't help but feel there was something symbolic in the act; it was as though Beg was staking a claim. And as though in proof of his independence, another nod of his head brought alcohol. Beer and vodka. From Kazakhstan and Finland.

'Bit of a miracle,' Proffit declared jovially, wobbling his whiskers. 'Fruit juice into wine. Whatever next?'

'I thought it was forbidden,' Bobby Malik said.

'Not at all,' Beg replied, draining his glass of vodka and holding it out in his crooked hand to be refilled. 'It's simply that the President has a gastric complaint which is inflamed by alcohol.' He looked around the table and smiled. 'I don't.' He seemed entirely at ease standing in for the President, and for another hour the dinner continued as those present broke up into groups around the table and Beg talked with animation and considerable informality one by one to his guests.

It was near the end of the evening before Beg joined Harry, who was standing admiring one of the displays, a figurine of beaten gold, a mountain goat whose right leg had gone missing somewhere along the centuries. Yet the damage couldn't detract from the elegance of the craftsmanship. Karabayev had been right. Nothing like this could have been produced in Britain at that time, not for another thousand years.

'Beautiful, is it not?' Beg enquired.

'I find it stunning. The rest of the artefacts, too.'

'They were uncovered almost ten years ago in burial grounds in the south of our country. Yale University gave a grant to help us preserve the collection.'

'More aid.'

'A necessity of life in a country such as ours.'

As Harry turned to face Beg, he realized the Ta'argi was smaller than he had realized, a good seven inches shorter than himself, forcing him to lean down to make sure he caught everything that was said. It made their conversation almost conspiratorial. It was the chance he had been looking for.

'Mr Jones, you are most welcome in my country. I know very little about you – you haven't visited us before. You have kept very quiet this evening – and you are not drinking.'

'Don't worry, nothing religious. Just pacing myself.'

'I hope we haven't bored you. I would like us to become good friends.'

Harry was trying to judge the moment, and this was too soon, but it wasn't a situation he controlled and his time was short. The other man had given him an opening, so he felt obliged to gamble. 'We have a lot in common, Mr Beg.'

'Really?' Beg smiled, as if the thought gave him pleasure.

'Yes. Like you I spent much of my professional life at war with the Soviets. Although not perhaps at such close quarters as yourself.'

'Then you have been fortunate.'

'I tried to help some of the resistance groups.' He made it sound like charitable work, which was deliberately misleading. What Harry had done, during his time as a member of the SAS, was to help train the mujahedin in Afghanistan.

'I hope you and your colleagues will be as keen to assist us now the Soviets have gone.'

Harry offered no immediate reply. He'd been sent into Afghanistan not to deliver aid but to show the rebels how to use their Stinger missiles and blast Soviet helicopters out of the sky, in mountains not three hundred miles from where they were standing.

'It's that work which brought you here?' Beg pressed.

'Let me say that my work has given me a wide range of interests,' Harry responded.

'Indeed?' Beg raised his glass to his lips and sipped; he had to use both hands, gripping the glass with difficulty, he couldn't fully unbend his fingers. 'And may I ask what your interests are in Ta'argistan?'

Harry admired the way in which Beg seemed to pick up on every nuance. He wasn't a man to be underrated, and that made him entirely the right man for Harry's purpose.

'I have heard a story that an old acquaintance of mine is here. You know how stories fly around.'

'Indeed.'

'An American. By the name of Zac Kravitz. The suggestion is that he's found himself in difficulty and is having trouble getting home. That causes great pain to his many friends and family.'

'Indeed,' Beg said for the third time, in the manner of a professor listening to a student's dissertation and unwilling to commit himself.

'May I be blunt?'

'It seems you already are, Mr Jones.'

'I don't want to follow the path Mrs Riley seems intent on treading, making wild public protests about injustices. In truth, Mr Beg, I don't know whether any injustice has been done. I neither know the facts nor care much about them. But I and his friends would be exceedingly grateful to get him home. Exceedingly grateful.' The words were repeated slowly, as though dragging a great weight.

Beg's eyes bored into Harry from above his spectacles, unblinking, assessing, until finally he used his knuckle to move his glasses back up his nose. 'Then I think what you are suggesting mirrors Mrs Riley's path precisely. Financial aid in return for – certain considerations.'

'But entirely privately.'

One of the servants came to replenish Beg's glass but he waved her away impatiently. She scuttled to a safe distance.

'I would ensure that a substantial sum of aid was

made available without strings,' Harry continued, 'and directed through whatever channels were deemed appropriate to prevent it becoming a matter of public controversy.'

He was offering a bribe. Beg took no offence. Such things were accepted practice along most stretches of the Silk Road. Harry knew what the next question would be. He would be asked to state how much, then they would haggle – which raised the question, how much was Zac worth to him? How do you place a value on a friend's life? Harry was a man of considerable means, his father had been a swashbuckling pirate and had died in the arms of a disgracefully young mistress, leaving behind a fair fortune, and even though the stock-market chaos and Harry's short-lived marriage to his predatory second wife had kicked painful chunks out of it, still there was enough. Life in this part of the world was valued pretty cheaply, although Harry suspected Beg's appetites might be larger than most. Somewhere in the middle there would be a compromise, a figure that would satisfy them both. Yet what Beg said next took Harry by surprise.

'It is a very interesting proposition you make, Mr Jones. But it suffers from one small flaw.'

They were like two men facing each other on a tightrope, each waiting for the other to make his move.

'We have no American prisoners,' Beg said quietly. 'Goodnight, Mr Jones. Take great care.' He moved away and the evening was at its end.

Harry had gambled. He had failed. He had no fall-back plan. And in the process, he had made himself a marked man.

Tiny spaceships of snow hovered inquisitively around them as they climbed back into their minibus for the journey back to the hotel. The roads were still crowded with night traffic – a surprisingly large number of German and Japanese cars, Harry noticed, all old, mostly imported second-hand from Western Europe, and some almost certainly stolen. For a while they followed a Mercedes van that still bore the fading logo of a German haulage company. Nothing here was quite what it seemed. Through the darkness and the snow, the people of Ashkek scurried about their business.

The bus swayed and bounced along the darkened road and over substantial ruts, although whether these were caused by poor maintenance or uncleared ice it was difficult to tell. As they had seated themselves, Roddy Bowles and Martha had what in diplomatic circles would have been termed a frank exchange. He had challenged what he called her unpardonable rudeness to the President. She had countered that it would have been difficult for him to hear let alone understand what was being said with his head stuck halfway up the President's arse. He had accused her of flagrant discourtesy. She had replied, in earshot of all, that she would have taken his advice about manners more seriously if he hadn't spent so much of the dinner with his hand creeping up her thigh. After that they decided to suspend hostilities until another day, and found seats at opposite ends of the bus.

Sydykov, who was still in harness, had spent much of the journey back to their hotel on his mobile phone. Eventually he stood up and faced the guests, clinging on with both hands as the bus swayed and bucked.

'I have to offer you all an apology,' he said. 'But the weather has got worse. A lot of snow is coming. As you know, we had intended to take you into the Celestial Mountains tomorrow morning to visit our latest hydro-electric project, but the roads will be unreliable. So I'm afraid we shall be forced to change the schedule. I'm sorry to have to ask, but is there anything you would care to do tomorrow morning instead?'

In the half-light of the poorly illuminated bus, a discussion began that teetered between accepting an invitation to morning coffee with the Deputy Prime Minister and a discussion about tourism and transport, when Martha's voice cut through the babble.

'I'd like to visit the central prison.'

'The prison? But – why?' Sydykov replied uneasily.

'Human rights. The President said we shouldn't be worried about it, and a visit to the prison would help convince us.'

From the rear of the bus Bowles could be heard muttering about their trip being turned into some sort of publicity stunt. Sydykov, too, had his objections. 'But we have had no notice.'

'That's the point,' Martha replied. 'An unannounced visit. Couldn't be better.'

'I am really not sure it will be possible without preparation—'

'No, no, Mr Sickof, that won't do at all. President Karabayev assured us you have nothing to hide – his words, not mine – and I respect him as a man of his word. Do I need to take the matter up with him?'

It was a threat that left Sydykov swaying with uncertainty. He wasn't one to second-guess the presidential whim. Then Bowles joined in.

'This is ridiculous. We can't let you hijack the whole proceedings,' he protested from the back of the bus. 'You can't demand that our hosts make special arrangements just for one.'

Sydykov shrugged his shoulders, as if to indicate reluctant agreement, until another voice interrupted them.

'That's not a problem. I'd like to go, too.'

It was Harry.

'Excellent! We have a quorum,' Martha exclaimed.

At that moment, with the hotel in sight, the bus hit another pothole and Sydykov was thrown back into his seat. He didn't get up again, but instead began agitatedly banging the buttons on his mobile phone.

The guard had been reluctant to leave the other man alone with the prisoner.

'Why should you worry? Look at that,' the visitor

had said, nodding towards Zac's pathetic form, huddled in the shadows of the corner. 'A butterfly with broken wings. I need no protection from that.'

The guard knew better than to contradict him. He saluted, and left them alone.

For a while, after the door had been slammed shut, the visitor said nothing, standing quietly, thoughtful, his hand against his nose to fight the stench until eventually Zac stirred and looked up.

'You are an interesting man, Mr Kravitz,' the visitor said quietly. 'You come to my country to cause trouble and deep offence, so we lock you up and throw away the key. Yet still you seem bent on causing trouble – you, and your friend, Harry Jones.'

Zac shook his head in confusion, aroused by some distant memory.

'Oh, did you not know? Mr Jones is here, in Ashkek. He is asking about you.'

Slowly, heavily, with a body that refused to cooperate, Zac levered himself up into a sitting position, his back propped against the wall. 'Harry?' he mumbled through cracked lips.

'Yes. He wants to buy you back. A most interesting man, your Mr Jones.'

Zac stretched his legs, clumsily, and began to wriggle, like a fish on a line, as he tried to rub the pain from his shoulder.

'In fact, I think he may have saved your life,' the visitor continued. 'You were due to die tomorrow.'

Zac raised his head, perplexed. His lips moved, but no words came out.

'Did they not tell you? The President in his wisdom had decreed it. But now . . .'

Life, hope, began to stir once more in Zac. He leaned forward, expectant.

'We shall keep you alive,' the visitor continued, 'and play the game. We can't let you go, you understand that, don't you? Not at any price. You really shouldn't have been caught fucking the President's wife. Not that you were the first, of course, and I think our beloved President suspects that. But you were the first to get caught, and that makes a difference. Now he demands retribution, and even though he is only half a man, he is still the President.'

The visitor began to laugh, but gagged on the first mouthful of fetid air. He spat on the floor in disgust.

'So we will wait for your friend Mr Jones to leave us.' He paused. 'And then, I'm afraid, you will die.'

His smile was thin, surgical, like a wound. He was done here, for the moment. Amir Beg kicked the door to attract the guard.

CHAPTER FOUR

The hotel room was what passed for five-star in Ashkek – clean, comfortable, and fiercely overheated. Whether the tropical temperatures were a constant condition, Harry doubted; he'd already seen enough hesitation of the lights to suggest that the power supply couldn't be taken for granted. The hotel was topping up while it could.

He'd been in bed half an hour but couldn't sleep, his mind tumbling through what he had seen and heard. Could it be that, after all, Zac wasn't here, as Beg had claimed? But Beg's denials carried no weight. Harry had offered him a bribe; a corrupt man would have reacted to the temptation, and an honest one to the insult. Yet Beg had offered nothing but professed indifference. That couldn't be the end of the story.

As Harry lay on his bed, staring up at the whorls of plaster that decorated the ceiling, he heard a knocking at the door. A tentative sound. Not the secret police, then. When he opened it, he was astonished to discover Martha, wrapped in one of the hotel's meagre dressing gowns and, from what he could see, little else. From her perch at the end of the corridor, the old hag watched everything.

He couldn't resist staring at Martha in surprise and more than passing approval before engaging once more with her eyes. 'Am I supposed to invite you in?'

'You'd better. Unless you want to disappoint Stalin's Granny over there,' she replied, nodding in the direction of the crone.

'This isn't what I expected,' he said, closing the door behind her.

'Don't expect anything at all. You're not my type.'

He was mildly surprised to feel a flicker of disappointment pass over him.

She stood in the middle of the room, her arms folded defensively across her chest. 'I want to know what you're up to,' she demanded primly.

'What *I'm* up to?'

'There's something odd going on – and you're in the middle of it. Don't pretend you've come here just to take a look at a few factories and—'

Suddenly he held up a finger to his lips to demand her silence. He hadn't made a close inspection of his room but he assumed it was bugged – nothing too sophisticated, not in a city that couldn't even afford enough coins for the electricity meter, but there were basic precautions that needed attending to. He went over to the bedside radio and switched on the BBC World Service, then he sat on the bed and patted the place beside him. She gave him a sharp look, then set-tled down suspiciously on the duvet.

'Look, I'm not an idiot,' she began in a low voice, leaning closer to him, 'the whole thing stinks. Sydykov's suits are far too well cut for him to masquerade as a tour guide. This place is crawling with security. I hadn't exactly expected Ashkek to be a holiday camp but this is like something out of the old Soviet Union. If this is an aspiring democracy, as the Foreign Office would have us believe, then I'm Mother Teresa.'

Humility had never been her strong point. In Westminster, many people simply referred to her as the Power and the Gloria, but not within her hearing.

'I agree,' he said.

'So what the hell were you doing sucking up to Amir Beg? Can't you tell what he is, for God's sake? I just don't understand what you're up to – appearing out of the blue, with no notice, no previous interest in the place. All evening you say nothing, even more odd you drink nothing—'

He winced, she'd hit too close for comfort. He'd only wanted to keep a clear head. 'Since when has what I drink been any concern of yours?'

'I don't know what causes more trouble – when you're drinking or when you're not.'

He was growing angry with her. Ridiculous woman. 'Do you always burst into men's bedrooms just to insult them?'

'It's not my habits that are the issue here. Anyway, I

assure you, I'm not your type. But Amir Beg seems to be. That cosy chat of yours – you've got something going with him, haven't you? You're like Roddy Bowles, I'm sure he's up to something, too – except you don't have his line in bullshit.'

He shook his head. 'No, never like Roddy Bowles.'

'Then what's going on, Harry? Why did you suddenly volunteer to come with me to the prison? I don't need you holding my bloody hand, or contradicting everything I say and denying what I see.'

Ah, so that was it. She thought he was a stooge, intent on keeping her in her place.

'I won't have it,' she spat, even as she whispered.

Somewhere in the background the BBC was offering a weather forecast. Bleak, and getting worse. Harry stared at Martha from close at hand. Her hazel eyes were indisputably animated and, it seemed, observant. Perhaps he had underestimated her.

'Don't take me for a fool, Harry.'

'I don't. Many things, perhaps. But not a fool.'

That was the moment he decided he would trust her. He wasn't sure why – perhaps it was simply that aching feeling of being on his own for far too long. Anyway, it was only sense to let someone know what he was up to, in case the whole thing went disastrously wrong and he got his balls caught in a wringer. So he turned the radio up and told her: about Zac, about Julia, about loyalty and ties and his attempt to bribe Beg. As he talked, she sat and listened quietly.

'I'd hoped they might simply be persuaded to let him go,' he concluded. 'That's why I came here, to ask them, quietly. But . . . well, you got there and sank your teeth in first.' He couldn't resist a wisp of criticism.

'Ridiculous. If Beg won't release your friend for a substantial bribe, he was never likely to let him go for nothing.'

'Fair point.'

'You're risking your whole career, you know that. If you get caught offering a bribe . . .'

He didn't bother to reply.

'You haven't seen this Zac for years. And it doesn't even sound as if you like him too much.'

'Not the point.'

'Julia meant that much to you?' Suddenly, her stridency had softened. It was a stupid question, and she knew it as soon as it was asked. 'Harry, I'd like to help.'

'You can't,' he replied, brushing her aside.

'Why not?'

'Because.'

'Of what?'

Harry sighed. 'Because it seems I can't get him released using the usual flattery or even excessive bribery. So the only option I think I've got left is to break the bastard out.'

Neither of them spoke for several minutes as they considered what he had said. Then some thought seem to strike her and she stiffened. 'You're a total dickhead. You know that, don't you?'

'You're not the first to reach that conclusion.' Harry shifted his position on the bed to find himself a better defensive position.

'So you're just going to – break him out on your own. Single-handed. Is that it?'

He shook his head, not bothering to reply. How could he? He hadn't any firm idea of what he was going to do.

'You don't even know for sure Zac is here,' she persisted.

'That's right. But this is just the sort of hole at the end of the earth he'd end up in.' He knew it sounded pathetic.

She studied him intently, gauging the next thrust. 'You know, Harry, you're not at all like your reputation.'

'How's that?'

'Turning down a woman's offer. Although I guess I'm a little older than your regular diet.'

He shook his head once again, as though trying to ward off troublesome flies. First drink, now women. God, she wasn't doing much for his self-esteem this evening.

'Must be your time of life, I suppose. Roddy's such a clear case, but you . . . I've seen it so often. Men reach a certain age, start getting terrified that they're losing their masculinity and might be shown up by some woman.'

'Martha, what's bitten you? I can do without the

feminist outrage right now. It's simply . . . Look, it could turn nasty.' He scowled, but she wasn't to be so easily denied.

'What? Not nice work for a woman?' She laughed, but the eyes were hard, there was no humour in her face.

'For anyone.'

'I can't believe it. You sound just like an echo of my wretched father. He tried to stop me going to college, you know, even though I was a straight-A student.'

'No, I didn't know—' but the words were wasted, she cut straight across him.

'He thought such things – education, ambition – were wasted on a woman. A Neanderthal who believed women were meant for other duties.' The words came spitting out, like bullets from behind a barricade. 'Then there was that pathetic excuse for a husband, who tried to insist my life's mission was to stay at home to look after his poodles. So don't patronize me, Harry, don't you dare. I've had it all my fucking life!'

'That was never my intention.'

'But that's what you're doing!' The skin on her neck flushed with emotion.

'You don't even know Zac.'

'You haven't known him either, for Chrissake, not for years.' She had to struggle to step back from the edge of anger on which she was standing, suppress the anger that had bubbled up, and to lower her voice. 'Anyway, you've got no bloody choice in the matter.'

'Meaning?'

'You can't do anything without me.'

'What, you're going to help me smash down the prison door?' he said, incredulous.

'No, you idiot. But if you're determined to make yourself a complete pain in the butt on this trip, you're going to need some help.'

'With what?'

'Let's start right here, shall we? You can't even get out of this room without being spotted, not without help. You need to distract the Wicked Witch of the East out there.'

'And why would I need to get out of the room unnoticed?'

She brought her face very close to his. 'You need help. Local help. You don't even know for sure Zac's here, or where he is! You need to make contact with those who might know. The opposition, right? And while you're doing that I can give you cover from the bad guys. Scramble their thoughts. Distract them just a little.'

He had to give it to her, she was excellent at doing that. Even the trivial act of borrowing a hairdryer had thrown Sydykov's plans into confusion.

'I suppose with your *Boys' Own* background you know how to break a man's neck,' she continued. 'Well, I'm a woman. I do things differently. I break their attention span.'

When he looked up, he noticed she was pouting, almost mocking, claiming victory.

'Martha, don't underestimate what we're up against.'

'A hormonal New England feminist and an unreconstructed male chauvinist. Why, sounds like one hell of a team to me.'

While Martha distracted the old woman with questions about the hot-water supply, and the woman tried yet again to explain that she didn't understand a word of English, Harry slipped unnoticed from his room. He couldn't risk being spotted leaving through the foyer, so he used a side door and stepped out into the night. It was still snowing, and Harry gave thanks; it would give him cover, and hide his tracks, but he shivered, he wasn't dressed for this. The snow also made it more difficult for him to find his way, and in any case he only had a small tourist map he'd bought from Stanfords in Covent Garden, but Ashkek was a small city built on a typical Soviet grid and he quickly found his bearings. He headed for the Marriott Hotel about half a mile away; it felt further as he slipped along on the ice. By the time he saw the lights of the hotel in the near distance, the damp had wormed its way through the welts of his shoes and he was feeling distinctly uncomfortable. He hated being unprepared, but this whole saga stank of the makeshift and for what must have been the hundredth time Harry scolded himself for ever having started. To set out without a plan was folly; to set out without the right boots was straightforward madness.

It was heading for midnight and the hotel wasn't busy. A solitary taxi waited in the rank. Its driver had his head arched back, as though sleeping. Harry pulled open the back door and climbed in, trailing snow. The driver started at the interruption and turned to examine his prospective passenger with irritation and a glow of suspicion; it was clear from the cut of Harry's coat that he wasn't a local.

'*Dobryi vecher! Ya britanckyi politic*,' Harry announced in his rehearsed but clumsy Russian. From his pocket he produced his parliamentary pass, complete with portcullis and washed-out photograph.

The driver stared sullenly.

'*Ya khochu pogovorit s Vsadniki.*' *I want to talk to the Horsemen.* He pushed the parliamentary pass into the driver's hand so that he could examine it.

It was Pyotr, the old Russian, who had told him, over their second coffee. Ta'argistan was a concept that was not yet fulfilled, a mixture of Ta'argis, Kazakhs, Uzbeks and Russians, with even a few Ukrainians, Tatars, Tajiks, Dungans and Uighurs thrown in for good measure. Over the centuries many different peoples had come, and they had passed on, leaving some of their number behind to engage in a timeless struggle for supremacy. Karabayev, a Kazakh, had taken control of the country one hot, sultry summer's night when his predecessor, an ethnic Ta'argi, had died in his sleep. The former President's passing was as sudden as it was unexpected, and few believed it was unassisted, but no one was going to argue with the huge number of armed police and militia that had suddenly appeared on the streets. Ta'argistan woke to discover their world had turned and Karabayev, the Vice-President, was in control. To some outsiders this might have given an impression of harmony and peaceful transition, but in truth Ta'argistan was no tribal melting pot but a cauldron, perched over a slow and blistering heat.

There were religious differences, too. During Soviet times the authorities had trodden hard upon organized religion, but as soon as the Soviet tanks had withdrawn behind the mountains the priests, mullahs and monks had emerged once more to fill the spiritual space. Their efforts had helped to rekindle a sense of separate identity amongst many, and to erect frontiers inside the state. So the Ta'argis were farmers, the Uzbeks and Kazakhs traders, and the Russians were, amongst other things, taxi drivers. 'You want to get hold of the Opposition,' Pyotr had said, wiping foam from his thick moustache, 'you ask a taxi driver to meet the Horsemen, that's what they call themselves. Whether the driver will take you, of course, is another matter. If he thinks you're setting him up, you'll find yourself out with the rest of the rubbish in a frozen ditch on the other side of the airport . . .'

'Horsemen,' Harry repeated.

The light inside the taxi had gone out, leaving Harry in darkness that was interrupted by the occasional glow of the driver's cigarette. Outside the Marriott the snow continued to fall, trickling down the windscreen in slow, meandering rivulets.

'British politician. Friend,' Harry insisted.

The driver muttered something – a curse, judging by its rough edges, an invitation for him to fuck off – and took another slow, uninterested drag of his cigarette. Yet suddenly he was alert, his eyes gleaming. Harry, with the skill of a magician, had produced a hundred-dollar bill and was thrusting it at the other man. In a country where most people's annual income was less than three thousand, it was bound to get some response, and the driver's face flooded with a mixture of both greed and suspicion. This wasn't any innocent enquiry, not with that amount of money on offer, there was danger here, for them both. Yet Harry was undoubtedly a foreigner, and the note was new, crisp, freshly printed, not the sort that normally circulated in the black markets of Ashkek. Where this one came from, there might be many more. In one move, the driver snatched the bill and slammed the car into gear. They took off into the night, the tyres scrabbling for purchase on the ice.

Much to Harry's relief, they weren't headed for the far side of the airport. Instead, they arrived outside the railway station, a relatively elderly and relaxed building that someone had decided to spruce up by painting it in garish shades of green, pink and white, like an Italian ice cream. Beside it stood an even older building, a hotel, one that had been in the process of reconstruction when the recession struck and the money dried up. Now it stood abandoned, its empty windows staring out lifeless into the night. There was little sign of activity at the station, either. The driver drew to a halt, managing to clip the kerb as he did so, stopping beside a ramshackle shelter made of pieces of wood and corrugated iron. He disappeared inside and Harry followed. The shelter was cramped and stuffy, with only a tiny twenty-watt bulb for light and heated by a foul-smelling stove that stood in the centre. Huddled around the stove Harry found not only his driver but two other men, one of whom was glaring angrily at the driver, his face full of suspicion. The driver was jabbering and pointing towards Harry.

'Do you speak English?' Harry demanded, anxious to take control of the situation.

'*Ingliz?*' the angry man repeated from beneath an enormous nicotine-stained moustache. Then he nodded.

'I want to meet the Horsemen.'

'Why?' The voice was deep, the accent thick.

'I want to help. I am a British politician,' Harry explained yet again. Once more he produced his pass, allowing the man to examine it closely. 'And I want your help, too.'

'What help?'

'That is for me to discuss with your leader.'

From his wallet Harry brought out a printed business card with a portcullis and his personal details on it. He also brought out another crisp hundred-dollar bill. The man took both, examined them, then threw the card into the fire. 'We know who you are,' he growled. 'This is small place.'

'Then you will do as I ask?'

The bill was first stretched between his thick fingers then folded carefully before disappearing inside an inner pocket. 'Maybe.'

'I must know. I have very little time. And there could be more money in it for you.'

The man tugged at his moustache while he examined Harry, as though he would find the truth written on his forehead. 'We see. You must go.'

'But when will I hear from you?'

'Tomorrow. Tomorrow evening, perhaps. Or never. Now go.'

'I must see him,' Harry insisted, stepping forward.

Suddenly, the other man had a knife in his hand. The speed with which he had produced it was more than enough evidence for Harry that he knew how to use it. 'Go!' the man repeated, his voice cracking with menace.

There was no point in haggling, it might even be counterproductive. Harry knew he had overstepped some invisible mark and the matter was now in their hands. He backed off. Outside it was snowing more heavily than ever, and it had grown colder, the snow more fierce, bullets of ice that were beginning to rattle off the roof of the shelter.

'Any chance of a lift back to the hotel?' Harry asked.

'We busy,' the man with the moustache muttered,

the light of the fire still dancing off the knife in his hand. Then he turned his back and began talking animatedly with the others.

With a sigh, Harry stepped out into the snow.

Harry had less than three hours' sleep that night, and had to fight his way through a wall of numbness before he made it down to breakfast.

'You always look that bad when you spend the night with a girl?' Martha greeted, offering a smile that was half-welcome, half-amusement as he sat at her table. 'I hope I was worth it.'

'Remind me never to let you share my bed again.'

'Must be tough being a man of your age. Running out of staying power already.'

She was about to persecute him a little more when they were interrupted by the sight of the advancing Roddy Bowles. He had clearly adopted a new tactic and was sidling over to their table, wrapped in a conciliatory smile.

'Good morning, you two.'

'Roddy,' Harry acknowledged, unwilling to commit himself.

'Er, Martha . . .' Bowles' lips puckered as though chewing lemon rind. 'We got off on the wrong foot yesterday. I hope you'll forgive me. Suffering from a little jet lag, I suspect – you know, arranging these trips can be hell, so many balls in the air. Barely got any sleep these last few nights.'

Perhaps it wasn't all bullshit. Harry's mind wandered back to the woman's coat that had been cast so casually over the back of the chair.

'That's why I was put out by all those last-minute changes,' Bowles continued. 'Damned snow. You'd have thought in a place like this they'd know how to cope, but . . .' He shrugged and made a stab at gentle humour. 'Where do they think this is? Bloody London?'

Martha made a point of concentrating on her bowl of fruit, digging out the pips.

'Anyway,' he struggled on, 'everything's sorted. Just as you asked. I understand the arrangements have been made for your visit to the central prison . . .'

It seemed he'd been talking to Sydykov.

'I like to run a tight ship – and keep one happy family,' Bowles continued, strangling his metaphors. 'Wouldn't want any silly stories floating around when we get back home about – what's the best way of putting it? – how we fell in or out of bed with each other, would we?'

So, he'd definitely been with Sydykov, who'd had the nightly report from Madame Guillotine. Martha hadn't stayed in Harry's room above an hour, but that had been more than enough.

'Thank you, Roddy. You're something special, really you are,' Martha replied, not looking up from her bowl.

'Good. Enough said. I'll leave you in peace, then. Enjoy the morning.' With a triumphant wobble of his lips, Bowles departed in search of his breakfast.

'*Ilex aquifolium*,' she said in the direction of his retreating back.

'What?' Harry enquired.

'I have a large bush in my back garden,' she said. 'Roddy reminds me of it. *Ilex aquifolium*.' Her eyes caught his for a moment, and she smiled. 'It's a form of holly,' she explained. 'The prickless kind.'

There was little that was romantic about Ashkek. Decades of being run by bureaucrats in Moscow had pressed a heavy hand upon its culture, squeezing out most things that offered a reminder of the old days. Meandering tracks had been replaced by mindless boulevards, its native style smothered in concrete and stone cladding. Then the Soviets had left, taking their money with them, and for the last twenty years almost nothing new had happened, and most of what was left behind had begun to crumble away. The towering figure of Lenin still stood on his plinth, reaching for the sky, but the marble slabs at his feet were cracking, falling off. Old women sat huddled in the underpasses, squatting on plastic bins, offering pirated DVDs and cheap cigarettes for sale, while rusting cranes hung over abandoned construction sites, marking the spot where dreams had died.

Yet the Castle was an exception. It was too massive to have been swept aside simply by a little snow or neglect. It had begun life as nothing more than a stopover on the Silk Road, but as the centuries had passed it had grown to be used as an armoury, a barracks, a palace and now a prison that squatted, brooding, beside the road leading west out of the city and into the mountains. It was constructed of massive stonework beneath lowering gables and heavy slate roofs, with high walls many feet thick that over the centuries had withstood both cannon and siege. Yet, as Martha and Harry drew up outside, with Sydykov and a driver for company, it was clear that the Castle's walls weren't intended to keep the unwanted out. They were there to keep them in.

'We will use the tradesmen's entrance,' Sydykov suggested with gentle humour as their Mercedes drove past the massive main entrance and entered through a much less symbolic gate that opened off one of the many side streets. They parked in a cobbled courtyard. Armed guards saluted; Harry noted that their vehicles were mostly ageing Ladas. Nearby a battered, oil-smeared truck was being loaded with bags of rubbish by prisoners whose every move was watched by still more armed guards. As Harry climbed from the back of the car he counted three floors to the roofline, with an indication of a basement or cellar area, too. On the lower two of those three floors the windows were covered in bars. Everything seemed to have been built of rough, old stone, the walls, the floors, even the staircase they climbed. Sydykov led the way. Harry hadn't expected refinement and he found none. With every step, the stale smell of institutional squalor seemed to set more firmly in his nostrils.

They were escorted into a large, overheated office on the top floor, in the middle of which, waiting to greet them, stood a serious-faced man of around sixty with a square head and a face that was almost flat.

'Good morning. I am Governor Akmatov,' he said, in Russian, extending a hand. He indicated they should take seats in front of his ornately carved partner's desk. For all its size it was surprisingly empty of decoration – a telephone, a desk light, a pen tray, a wooden photo frame. There were no papers of any sort; it didn't seem to be an office that relied on such things. A bust of the President stood on a wooden column against one wall, and nearby was a noticeboard with what seemed to be some form of illustration of the prison. Harry couldn't be certain; he stared, cursed silently. He tried squinting. Damn, it didn't help. He'd been wondering about his eyesight for a few months but had done nothing about it. There came a time for every man to acknowledge his weaknesses, but it was always something for tomorrow. Now, once again, he promised himself he'd arrange an eye test. Soon.

A tray of tea arrived, Akmatov played host, and ten minutes went by as he ensured they had everything they wanted. The next thirty were spent with him, through the translation of Sydykov, giving a detailed description of the penal code under which he operated and the many human-rights treaties he was required to observe. As he droned on, Martha began to grow restless. She sipped her tea, fiddled with a bracelet, rummaged in her handbag, and began to glance point-edly at her watch until a new noise cut through the litany. It was Harry's mobile phone, warbling out the music of the *Dambusters March*. He loved it as a ring-tone. The tune began to reach its crescendo, and he apologized, taking himself off to a far corner of the room while Martha continued to pepper the governor with questions. Harry quickly brought his conversa-tion to an end, mouthing that he would call back later, then fumbled with the buttons. 'Sorry,' he offered awk-wardly, 'I'll switch the thing off. We can do without any more interruptions.'

When she was offered a third cup of tea, Martha held up her hand. 'Thank you, Governor, very helpful, I'm sure, but we haven't come here for tea. We came to see the prison. Can I suggest, Mr Sickof, that we get on with it?'

Sydykov's lips tightened into the thinnest of smiles as he turned to the governor and began a rapid exchange. The governor picked up the telephone and soon two new officials joined them, who began describ-ing everything from budget allocations to food allowances. After another five minutes, Martha stood up.

'The prison,' she demanded.

'But of course,' Sydykov countered. 'We are ready for you. It is simply that we wanted you to understand what you are about to see.'

'Mr Sickof, I understand all too well what I am

112

seeing. In New England, where I was born, we call it a snow job.'

'I'm afraid I don't . . .'

'When the snow comes down on you so hard you can't see a damned thing.'

He nodded, as though accepting the insult, and rose from his chair. 'But you will understand, I hope, Mrs Riley, that we are a poor country, and this is not a hotel. We have few resources. Those we have we prefer to direct towards more deserving causes – our schools, hospitals. I know of your interest in human rights, but pregnant women and children have their human rights, too. Please remember that as you find your way through the snow.'

'I'll do my best,' she replied, heading determinedly for the door.

Soon they were being led on a tour of administrative offices, laundry, the exercise yard and the kitchens, which seemed rudimentary beyond belief. And just before Martha's exasperation was about to burst forth once more, they found themselves sitting in a cell, small and spartan, considerably colder than the governor's office but no worse than would have been found in many prisons around the world, talking to two shaven-scalped prisoners – although it soon became clear that the conversation was to be as much with Sydykov as with the men. The prisoners could have been saying anything, but all Harry and Martha heard was what Sydykov told them. Of adequate food, of fair treatment, of generous exercise – although Harry had noted that the kitchen fires were cold and the exercise yard covered in unbroken snow. As they spoke, the prisoners' eyes kept darting in agitation towards the door, where the governor stood, monitoring their every word.

Sydykov was extolling the benefits of the parole system when Martha got to her feet once more. 'I would like to see other prisoners. And more of the prison.' She was like a mongoose at a snake. Gave no quarter.

'Anything you wish,' he said slowly, his tone calm, almost mechanical; neither of them was any longer bothering to hide their mutual animosity.

Harry turned to the governor and made his voice heard, almost for the first time. 'Do you have different classes of prisoners?'

'No,' Sydykov replied without bothering to translate the question.

'And you treat foreign prisoners in the same way as the locals?'

Sydykov shrugged. 'There are so few foreigners here. Uzbek smugglers, the occasional Kazakh car thief – all Kazakhs are a little crazy, they inevitably end up getting caught. That sort of thing. They receive the same treatment.'

'I was thinking more of Western prisoners.'

Sydykov stared at Harry, long enough to let him know he understood where this was headed. He spoke briefly to the governor before turning once more to

Harry. 'As you know, tourism is not yet well developed in our country. We hope to expand all such links – with your government's help. We need a better airport, new roads, investment in improved hotels, and much more. These are our plans, the things we want you to take back to your government. Tourism could be a key growth area for us – we Ta'argis are renowned for our hospitality. It is a tradition from our nomadic past.' He was delivering a lecture in response to what had been a simple question, wanting to establish with Harry who was in charge of this exercise. But the point had been made. 'For the moment, Mr Jones, we get no more than a couple of thousand Western tourists, mostly trekkers who head for the mountains. They cause very little trouble. We did have two German guests who had accepted too much of our hospitality and were discovered drunk in Victory Park. We gave them a small fine and put them on a plane back home. Two years ago.'

'No Western prisoners right now?'

'No Western prisoners right now,' Sydykov repeated softly.

They held each other's eye, testing their resolve, before Martha spoke up again. 'Right. The rest of the prison?'

Sydykov tore his eyes away from Harry and glanced at his watch. 'There is little time, I'm afraid. You are due to have lunch with the Prime Minister and we cannot be late. But,' he added quickly, forestalling her imminent outburst, 'we will do our best. Please – come.'

And for twenty minutes they were hauled around facilities at an almost reckless pace. Everywhere they found conditions were simple, primitive by some standards, squalid in parts, but no one made complaints. Whenever they paused to interrogate inmates, Sydykov declared that they were entirely content. The way he talked, they might have been there at their own request.

All too soon their headlong charge had led them back to the courtyard and their car. The driver was already holding the door open.

'I must apologize for the rush,' Sydykov said, 'but such visits are difficult to arrange at short notice. I hope you will accept that we have done our best.'

And that's what the record would show. They'd met the governor and senior officials, been shown any number of facilities, talked with several prisoners, and even if those discussions hadn't been at length or in private, what could a reasonable man or woman expect squeezed between dinner with the President and lunch with the Prime Minister? Sydykov would make his report back to Beg; it was a game, and the morning had been a victory for the home side.

It was only when he stepped into the fresh air once more that Harry became fully aware of the reek of decay that had clung to them throughout their visit, the sort of stench that couldn't be scrubbed from the air, no matter how hard the prisoners toiled. That's when Harry knew Zac was in there, somewhere, at the heart of it, in a place they hadn't been shown. Rotting. His nose told him what he hadn't seen.

In every corner of the Castle they had found armed guards and closed doors, and ancient, stout locks whose keys dangled from the gaolers' belts. CCTV, too. As they passed out through the gates once more, with Martha squirming in frustration beside him, Harry took a fresh look at the walls. Damn, but they were thick. Take an entire squadron of Dambusters to blast a way through that lot. He couldn't take this place by storm, and there was nothing he could do on his own. He found himself catching his breath, his heart racing in anxiety. Yet as they turned into the main avenue, he was reminded he wasn't entirely on his own.

'That,' Martha spat, 'was a complete waste of time!' She didn't care that Sydykov heard her – indeed, she insisted on it. From his seat in the front, the Ta'argi official allowed himself a faint smile of satisfaction and stared straight ahead. What he didn't see was that Harry had caught Martha's eye, and squeezed her hand. They had at least one advantage. They now knew more about the enemy, about his strengths, but also his arrogance, and arrogance was a weakness.

There was also the not inconsiderable matter of the photographs that Harry had taken of the governor's office on his mobile phone. It hadn't been a waste of time, after all.

CHAPTER FIVE

The afternoon was taken up with a sumptuous but swiftly taken lunch in the Prime Minister's residence and a couple of desiccated briefings from ministers and officials about the country's economic needs. Bobby Malik had tried to play his part, reeling off figures he had found in the briefing papers he had brought with him about the amount of British aid that had been provided to the country.

'Yes,' the Prime Minister responded through a mouthful of sausage stuffed with meat and preserved mutton fat, 'your aid programme. You have sent many consultants and advisers who have visited, told us of our shortcomings, then returned home. We would have preferred a power station.'

After that, Malik retreated and kept his counsel, and neither did Harry take much of an active part, sipping distractedly at the watery beer. His mind was elsewhere, wondering about those he had met the night before. By this evening, they had said, or not at all. As the pale light outside the window began to fade, Harry found it increasingly difficult to maintain his spirits.

Were they serious? Would they come? It would soon be dark, how long could the definition of an evening be stretched? Or were they already raising their glasses and drinking to yet another foreign fool?

By half-past six it had been dark for more than an hour, and Harry knew it was over. The evening was well upon them and they had been transported to an ice-hockey game – their 'culture time', as Bowles had referred to it. They wouldn't get to watch the whole thing, because they were expected to attend yet another official dinner at the Ministry of Transport and Communications. They would be transported directly there from the game. No downtime, no opportunity for anyone to make contact. Somewhere deep inside, his heart raced even faster and Harry felt sick.

The ice hockey was taking place inside a ramshackle indoor arena that Harry suspected might once have been an aircraft hangar. It was noisy, cold, barely above freezing, even in the stands, with row upon row of seats around the rink supported on scaffolding. The conditions were primitive, yet the game was pursued with an intensity that was infectious. The players were young men who, when the summer came and the sun had chased the snows from the steppes, would swap their ice skates for short, shaggy-maned horses and do battle in a fierce sport that required them to fight for the carcass of a headless, black-fleeced goat, just like their forefathers had done, except in the old times the victims had been human. It wasn't that the ancient

Ta'argis had been heartless, simply practical; goats had often been more valuable. The equation was simple. Survival had required victory – over the elements, of course, and the enemy, but also sometimes over each other. Now clouds of condensation were beginning to form up amongst the metal rafters as the sons of the survivors fought, while on all sides spectators bellowed their encouragement. Even Sydykov, that most emotionally constipated of men, was performing little jumps of excitement in his seat and waving his glove in enthusiasm. Beside him Martha, unimpressed, shivered.

They were offered mugs of thin soup to keep them warm, far too salty for Harry's taste, but piping hot. Martha wouldn't drink but clung to it as a hand warmer. Vendors roamed between the seats, selling paper twists filled with candy and nuts, doing their business in those moments when the crowd wasn't on its feet and screaming. One of the vendors, an old, wizened man, offered Harry a bag, but his fingers were frozen and he fumbled, dropping it to the floor. As they bent to retrieve the bag, their heads came close together. The old man whispered something in Harry's ear, so quietly that no one else could possibly have heard, and Harry himself had difficulty.

'Take a piss,' the old man said. 'Five minutes.'

When Harry looked up to catch his eye, the man had already gone.

Five minutes later, Harry made his excuses. He walked the twenty yards to a miserable wood and brick shack with no door and 'M' painted hurriedly on the wall. *Muzhskoi* – Male. The paint had dribbled and long since faded. It was as primitive as could be, nothing but a bare enclosure with cracked tiles underfoot and a sheet of corrugated iron covering one long wall, beneath which ran an open gutter. The place reeked of ammonia, so sharp it made Harry flinch. A solitary man in a long serge overcoat stood facing the primitive urinal; Harry crossed to join him, standing so close that the other man splashed Harry's shoes as well as his own. When he was finished, the man bent to fumble with his flies, and spoke softly.

'Same taxi. Eleven tonight. Do not be late.'

The man buttoned his coat carefully, then left. From outside came another eruption of excitement, so loud that it made the air shake. As he started to fasten his flies, Harry couldn't resist offering a silent cry of satisfaction. The game, after all, was still in play. Yet when he drew breath, he choked, the fetid air sticking in his craw. Nothing was simple in this country, not even taking a piss.

They were shuttled from the hockey match to their dinner at the ministry in a fleet of cars. To Harry's surprise, he found himself alone in the back of one of them as they drove in procession through the dimly lit streets. To his still greater surprise, he discovered that the man in the front passenger seat was Amir Beg.

'I hope you found your visit to the Castle this morning useful, Mr Jones,' Beg said over his shoulder.

'It was helpful. Thank you.'

'I sense your caution. It is understandable.' He turned to face Harry, his face all but obscured in the darkness, apart from his almond eyes staring from behind the spectacles. 'Mr Jones, I hope you will allow me to speak freely. It is very easy for small countries like mine to be misunderstood. We have no great wealth, but that does not make us savages. Some like to pretend we are still in the Dark Ages, but we try our best and look forward. We want to improve. That's why I was glad to arrange your visit this morning. I want your help in dispelling these wild rumours that we abuse human rights. I would like to think I can rely on you in that, after your visit. And if there is anything else you would like to see . . .'

Harry was taken aback by this approach, not certain where it was headed. He didn't want to commit himself. 'I'll let you know,' he said.

Beg twisted his body still further and hooked his arm over the back of the seat to enable him to look at Harry full in the face. 'You also raised the issue of your friend. You thought he might be here.'

'Not my friend. A former colleague, from many years ago,' Harry replied cautiously.

'Whoever he is, or might be, whatever you've heard, I'd like to help. Put any misunderstandings to rest. Perhaps you can give me a little more information.'

Harry examined the eyes, touched the inner soul, and knew this was not a man to trust. He shook his head. 'It was nothing, apparently. A wild tale somebody had picked up. They obviously panicked and asked me to look into it while I was here. You yourself said last night you don't have any American prisoners.'

'That's correct, but . . .'

There was a moment's silence between them as the car bumped along a rough stretch of road.

'May I be frank with you, Mr Jones?'

'Please do.'

'I am not always told the truth. Not the whole truth, at least. Those like Sydykov and his kind, they love their little secrets, cling to them as if they were their mother's breast. I suspect you find much the same in your own country.'

Harry nodded; he had a point.

'It's possible at some point your American might have passed through the hands of the security forces,' the Ta'argi said. 'Much the same once happened to me. I know the pain.'

In the light of the passing street lamps, Harry saw Beg's broken knuckles glow deathly pale, and some instinct inside made him shiver. This man had been attentive, solicitous, had said all the right things, a perfect host. But nobody came out of the Soviet camps perfect. Harry knew this was nothing but an act.

'If you could tell me any more about your colleague,

I'd be happy to use my powers to investigate a little further,' Beg continued. 'With your help, of course.'

Play the dumb fool, Harry told himself, tell him no more than he must already know. 'His name is Zac Kravitz. From Michigan, I think. I last saw him more than ten years ago, so there's not a whole lot more I can tell you, apart from the fact that he's gone missing. And that he has friends who are very concerned for him.'

'And why would he have been here in Ta'argistan?'

'I'm not sure. I know he's well travelled. A tourism consultant, perhaps?'

They were pulling up in front of the steps of the Transport Ministry, their time drawing to an end. Harry and Beg were staring at each other, not in hostility but rather to size each other up. They both seemed to understand that the hostility would come. No need to rush it.

The driver was at the passenger door, holding it open. Beg wrinkled a brow, like a chess player calculating his next move, and the one after that. His eyes suggested he knew he would win.

'Well, if there's anything else that comes to mind, please let me know. Enjoy your evening, Mr Jones.'

Enjoy his evening? In three hours' time he'd be standing on a freezing taxi rank in shoes that were still damp from the previous night's outing. He was exhilarated by the prospect of what he might be about to discover, yet it was already overshadowed by an instinct that was screaming of danger. Does Beg know? Harry wondered.

Could he have found out already? This was undoubtedly a desperately serious man. Harry climbed the steps, wondering what he was walking into.

'Having second thoughts?' Harry asked.

'Plenty,' Martha replied.

The day's formalities done, she was lying next to him on his bed, wrapped once more in the thin, tight dressing gown for the benefit of the old woman in the corridor. Harry, whispering into her ear to the accompaniment of the BBC, had been bringing her up to date on his encounter with the man with the paper twist of nuts, and with Amir Beg.

'Somehow I'd always suspected,' she said, continuing, 'that sharing a bed with you would have its ridiculous complications.'

'Thought a lot about that, then, have we?'

She dug an elbow into his ribs and called him a sorry bastard, but there was no malice in it.

'Harry, you've got to take care,' she said, her tone suddenly more serious.

'About sharing a bed with you? I promise eternal vigilance.'

She rolled over to face him. 'But you don't even know if your friend is here.'

'He's here all right.'

'How do you know?'

'Instinct. Experience. And Amir Beg. The bastard's lying.'

'You can't be certain of that.'

'I am. The man was smiling.'

'Yeah. I know the type.'

As they continued talking, suddenly the radio crackled and the BBC faded into silence. The lights flickered, fought back, then succumbed completely. A power cut. It was several seconds before it came back on.

'My alarm call. Time to go,' Harry whispered. He stood up and squeezed his feet once more into his damp, protesting shoes. 'How do I look?'

'Like you need a serious session with a colour consultant. I'm just not sure – a scarf, maybe? Save you getting yourself arrested by the fashion police.'

In retaliation, his eye ran teasingly up her body, but by the time he had reached her face, he found it stiff with concern.

'This isn't just a playground, is it?' she said. 'Your friend, he must be in very serious trouble. Which means we could be.'

'That's possible,' he said slowly. 'Roddy Bowles finds you in my bed, he's going to be furious.'

But she wouldn't be distracted. 'What's your plan, Harry?'

He looked away, buttoned up his coat, anxious she might find something disagreeable hidden in his expression. 'A plan?' he said. 'Bugger it, I knew there was something missing.'

*

No snow tonight, just intense, penetrating cold. He felt conspicuous on the street, doing his best to hurry along on the slippery ground. Once or twice he stopped, bent to fix a shoelace, glancing behind him, trying to see if anyone was following. When he turned a corner he hid in the doorway of a baker's shop behind a pile of empty plastic boxes, and waited for several minutes, but no one passed. He pulled up his collar against the freezing air and carried on.

The taxi was there, parked a little further away from the entrance of the Marriott than the previous night. He climbed in the back. The driver set off, saying nothing. He, too, seemed anxious about being followed. He drove slowly at first, excessively so, glancing in his mirror, tugging nervously at a cigarette, then he put his foot down and doubled back on himself, turning several corners. He parked in the shadows, waited several minutes, then repeated the entire exercise. Only when they had passed the angular outline of the Monument to National Independence for the third time did the driver seem to relax.

They didn't head to the railway station, but drew up outside a dimly lit doorway in a side street that ran off Victory Square. A sign declared this to be the entrance to the Fat Chance Saloon. It seemed closed. The driver nodded, and Harry tried the handle. The door opened onto a short flight of narrow wooden steps, badly worn, that led down to the basement. Harry descended cautiously; it was a great place for an ambush. As he reached the last step and opened another door, a fug of tobacco smoke hit him and began to attack his eyes. The Fat Chance had been created inside an old cellar with a low barrel ceiling, inadequate ventilation and several side alcoves, where young people sat crowded around computer terminals. A piano was tucked away in a corner; the pianist was taking a cigarette break. The Fat Chance appeared to be some combination of Internet and jazz club, the sound of an old Blood, Sweat and Tears track trickling out from the speakers, to the accompaniment of clicking keyboards from the alcoves. The jazz enthusiasts seemed to be taking a holiday, only two tables in the main section were occupied, but it seemed to Harry to be the type of establishment that might never be busy, a place that had the atmosphere of merely going through the motions. The atmosphere was close, claustrophobic, only kids could survive here and Harry knew it would give him a thumping headache if he stayed too long. A waitress appeared at his elbow; she was middle-aged with tired, deep-set eyes that didn't offer even a flicker of welcome. She nodded that he should follow her. They threaded their way between the tables to the far end of the cellar where she drew back a rough patterned curtain that screeched on its metal rings to reveal a larger alcove that had once probably been an old store room, the brick walls and ceiling freshly painted to cover the damp that was already beginning to find its way back through. At the table sat four men. One of them was the man with the nicotine moustache from the previous night, the second a young man, late twenties, with a chest like a gorilla and massive shoulders in the shape of a horseshoe, whom Harry assumed was some sort of minder. The third was young, barely in his twenties with straight dark hair down below his shoulders and who stared enquiringly at Harry through heavily tinted glasses. A little like John Lennon, Harry thought. The last of the men was older, rheumy eyes, prolific eyebrows. It was he who appeared to be in charge and instructed Harry to sit down. As Harry did so, the waitress placed a glass of beer on the red-and-white checked table cloth in front of him. It was frothy and looked desperately thin; he didn't touch it.

'So,' the older man said, 'you have been asking to meet some people, or something, called the Horsemen.'

'That's right.'

'Tell me, Mr Jones, who or what do you think these Horsemen are?' He wasn't looking at Harry, as if he wasn't worth the trouble, but instead inspected the end of his mean, self-rolled cigarette, the sort that required almost constant relighting.

'Someone who doesn't care for your President or his friends. Someone I hope might be willing to help me, and in return receive my help.'

'For what purpose?'

'I believe a friend of mine is in the prison here, in the Castle. I want to get him out.'

What happened next went so quickly that Harry was

only vaguely aware of all the pieces. The gorilla got up – to get another beer, Harry assumed – but no sooner had he passed by than Harry's arms were snatched and pinned behind the chair, which was tipped, then dragged back from the table. Any noise was drowned out by the piano player, who chose that moment, presumably under instruction, to pick up his playing – a Beatles melody, the acid years, Harry later recalled, without being able to be more specific. His memories of the moment were fragmented because, while he was tilted back and with his arms still pinned, he was hit, very hard, just below the ribcage in the solar plexus, with a blow that seemed to go straight to his backbone. The pain screamed through his body and for a moment he was paralysed. His diaphragm went into spasm, he couldn't breathe, couldn't protest, couldn't even be sick. The gorilla let him fall forward, his face striking the table, where it lay in the spillage of the beer while he gasped for breath.

'You ask too much, Mr Jones,' the third man sighed. 'You say you want help, but I think you already have too many friends. Like Major Sydykov. And you already know about our prison, you were there this morning. I think you are a friend of the President, too, not the sort to be a friend of ours. So what are you really doing here?' His tone was dry, unemotional, not soaked in accusation, yet there was no doubting the menace in his words.

Harry forced his face up from the table, his eyes bleary. 'I'm looking for someone,' he gasped.

'Yes, yes, these Horsemen. So you have said.'

Harry shook his head, the spilled beer dribbling down his forehead. 'No. An American. His name is Zac Kravitz.'

As his stomach muscles went into spasm once more, in the background the pianist changed the tune, beginning to thump out his version of 'Here Comes the Sun'. Up to that point it had been a particular favourite of Harry's.

'I think Zac's in there somewhere, in the Castle,' Harry continued, still choking. 'He's the only thing I'm interested in.'

The man examined the end of his cigarette once more, frowning as he discovered it had died. He relit it, sucking in a slow lungful of nicotine. 'So, you are a friend of the unfortunate American?'

The words revived Harry like a shower of ice water. He pushed himself back in his chair, disregarding the threat of further violence, his voice urgent. 'You know him? He's there?'

'Oh, yes. He's there. And in very deep trouble.' The man stared through the purple tobacco smoke, suddenly perplexed. 'Yet you are smiling, as though this is good news.'

'This is the first time I've known – for sure, you see. That helps.'

'How can that be?' the man asked, picking a fleck of tobacco from his tongue.

'No bloody point in trying to break a man out of prison if he's not there.'

The other man began to laugh, drily. 'You want to break into the Castle?' He wrinkled his brow in curiosity. 'Then your defence is complete. You are clearly mad.'

'It's why I wanted to find you,' Harry gasped, sucking in deep lungfuls of air. He began spluttering again; too much smoke. God, it hurt, his stomach muscles weren't what they once had been. But the pain had been worthwhile. As he stared across the table, through bleary eyes, Harry felt sure he had found the leader of the Horsemen. 'I want your help to get him out.'

The humour died on the other man's face. 'What foolishness is this?' The tone was harsh, his lip curled. He suspected a trap.

'My friend's in trouble. I want him out. And I'm willing to pay, a very large amount of money. It's the same deal I offered Amir Beg last night, except you will have the added reward of causing huge embarrassment to the government.'

'You expect us to do your dirty work for you?' the man spat.

'No, not at all. I want you to help me. Whatever happens, whatever we do, I'm part of it.'

'But you are a politician,' the man sneered.

'I've had my moments.' Harry picked up a paper napkin and wiped the beer and sweat from his face. He was feeling better. They were talking rather than breaking his neck.

'You would risk your life for him?'

'Yes.'

'And why would you do that, Mr Jones?' It was a fresh voice, that of the waitress. For the first time Harry realized that she hadn't left, had witnessed everything from the background. Now the men were looking towards her, waiting for her lead. It left Harry confused.

Why would he risk his life? It was an excellent question, one all soldiers are asked, but normally respond to with little more than a quiet smile. 'I owe him. He saved the life of my wife many years ago. But it's even more than that. Difficult to explain.' Not the thing most soldiers talked about. Unless you'd been there, been part of it, how could you understand?

'I'm a patient woman. No need to rush.' She took a seat in the middle of the table, like a judge. Her dark eyes had an air of authority, of experience. It wasn't just the grey at her temples but a sense that she knew about life and was accustomed to its many lies. An air of profound sadness clung to her.

'Zac and I, we fought together. Put our lives on the line for each other.'

'Friends.'

'More than that, much more. A soldier's code.'

'Tell me about it – please.'

Her voice was soft, but insistent. The rest were silent, waiting on him, and on her. Even the cigarette had been allowed to die. They were putting Harry to the test.

'OK,' he began, struggling to ignore the pain that was still burning through his gut, 'it's like this. In my country you join up, become a soldier, for many reasons – the excitement, the challenge, those strange things men call their ideals, or maybe it's because you're just trying to escape from what or where you are.'

'You have a choice? Interesting.'

'Then, one day, you find yourself out there facing the enemy. And they're trying to kill you. Rip the life from your body. You're never the same after that. How do you put it into words? The bullets are tearing at the air around your head, your heart is flooding with fear, every instinct screams at you to run, to get out of there, to save yourself, but . . . you stay. Why? Sure, for Queen and country, and for the people back home, all those things you've sworn to protect, but it's difficult to find much of a focus when you watch men torn to pieces and know you're supposed to be next on the list. You stay put, not for your ideals, or because anyone orders you to, and no way for the money you're being paid. You stay for the other guys.

'You're in it together, you see. This is what you've chosen, and there's an instinct even more powerful than self-preservation, a fear even greater than that of your own death. A soldier would rather face a firing squad a thousand times over than just once have to look his own colleagues in the eye knowing he had failed them. You share the risk with them because they share it with you, and together you're part of something that is so much more powerful and important than a collection of individuals.'

'I think all of us here share that, Mr Jones,' she said gently.

'It's how you measure yourself, as a man. The loneliest place on earth is looking in a mirror and being ashamed of who you see.'

'Some people never bother to look in that mirror.'

'I guess I must be the vain type.'

She steepled her fingers in front of her mouth, preparing a verdict. 'Mr Jones, you must know that they intend to execute your friend. He has only a short time to live.'

It jolted him, more pain, yet somehow it was no surprise. 'Why? What has he done?'

'This is Ta'argistan. Reason is not required.'

Harry turned, confronted them all, eye to eye, before coming back at the woman. 'Then you must help me! You are the last chance I have of getting him out alive.'

'I think you are right,' she said. 'But we cannot.'

'I was told you were the opposition.'

'Yes, an opposition, of sorts, but not a resistance movement. We have no army. We are teachers, lawyers, bakers, postmen, engineers, taxi drivers. Even bar owners. Simple people, not soldiers. We try to fight with ideas, not AK-47s.'

'You must help!'

'He may be your friend, Mr Jones, and I pity him, but he is your friend, not ours.' Her voice grew firmer as he pressed, while desperation began creeping into his.

'I'll pay you. Richly.'

'We are not gangsters, either! We cannot help you.'

And the gorilla's hand was on Harry's shoulder.

'I won't accept this,' he said, clenching his fists in frustration. 'I want to talk to the leader of your Horsemen.'

Her hooded eyes flinched. 'But you cannot. He is dead.'

He stared at her in bewilderment.

'My husband . . .' The words and their memories were clearly a struggle. 'They took him. Last spring, when the snows began to melt.'

'And since then?' But he could see the answer in her face. Despair. Confusion. And defeat. The widow sat in his chair, but she would not take his place.

'I am so sorry,' he whispered.

Cold, dead eyes stared back at him.

'But that is why you must understand,' he pressed. 'Zac, he saved my wife's life.' He thought he saw a flicker of some emotion in her features, but whether it was of sympathy or resentment, he could not tell. 'What price would you pay, to get your husband back?'

'Goodnight, Mr Jones.'

Harry was hauled to his feet. He tried to fight back, but it was pointless. The curtain was drawn back once more, its metal rings clattering along the rail like the bolts of the rifles in a firing squad. Only at the last moment did he turn upon her, with violence in his tone.

'You say you fight with ideas. You want ideas?' he

spat. 'I'll give you one. From a man named Edmund Burke.'

'An Englishman?'

'A stubborn bloody Irishman, as it happens, and all the better for it. Nearly three hundred years ago. "The only thing that's necessary for evil to triumph," he said, "is for good men to do nothing".' Harry didn't even try to hide his contempt. 'I think he meant women, too,' he shouted as he was bustled out.

A chair went flying, Russian curses were tossed about. Then a new voice joined in.

'Mr Jones.'

Harry was almost out of earshot when he heard his name being called. It was the young man with the shoulder-length hair. Everyone stopped. Harry turned.

'How would you have done it? The escape?'

'No, Bektour!' the woman said sharply. 'Such knowledge is dangerous. We don't want to know.'

'It's not the information that's dangerous, Mother.'

'Even so.'

He shook his head, his neatly brushed hair rustling around his shoulders. 'Information is power, Mother,' he said softly. 'You know we cannot leave it to them. Father would have understood.'

Harry remembered the kids huddled together in the other alcoves around computers, sharing monitors, often squeezed together two on a chair. 'So that's what you're doing here,' he exclaimed, 'you're running an Internet group.'

'We are what the comics call cyber-activists, Mr Jones,' the young man said. His English was excellent, with a slight American tinge. 'We set up websites, form chat groups, offer news, all the sort of stuff the authorities try to cover up.'

His mother snorted in exasperation.

'Yes, it's not like the old ways, and it has its risks,' he continued. 'They keep trying to close us down, but they have difficulty in finding us in cyberspace, and when they get close, we move on. We use foreign servers, keep changing our encryption programs, we constantly do battle with their blocking software. It's like a game of tennis, first they serve, then we return. They try hard but they're not very good at it. We are better, even though we only wear T-shirts and jeans.'

'They won't bury you in cyberspace if they catch you, Bektour. They'll bury you right here, alongside your father,' his mother snapped.

'In which case there's nothing much more to lose by listening to what Mr Jones has to say,' Bektour replied, with all the politeness of a loving son but with a sense of weariness that implied this was another round in a very old argument. 'Please, Mr Jones,' he said, indicating he should take his seat once more. 'Humour me, and forgive my mother.'

Harry was angry, hurting, in two minds. Why indulge these people with their family squabbles? Yet it meant, for the moment, at least, he wouldn't be thrown out into the snow and left entirely on his own.

'How would I get Zac out?' he muttered, taking care as he sat down once more that the gorilla wasn't behind him. 'I'm not entirely sure. It depends a little on you.'

'I keep telling you,' the mother spat, 'we are not the Taliban!' But already her tone had changed. She was no longer leading the discussion but was staring at Bektour in the manner of an old lioness who had lost her position in the pride. She was hurt, and more than a little afraid.

'That's the point,' Harry said, 'we don't need the Taliban or any army. If there's any commotion, let alone any shooting, it's over.'

The gorilla returned, but this time only to place a fresh glass of beer in front of him. Harry accepted it as an offer of conciliation and took a sip. It tasted as if it had passed through a goat.

'It's not just a matter of getting him out of the prison, you see, we've also got to get him out of the country,' Harry continued. 'He doesn't stand a chance if the security forces are put on alert. Everything has to be done quietly. No explosions. No guns. No violence. We're not trying to do a remake of *The Dirty Dozen*.' A fresh spasm of pain surged through his stomach. It didn't seem to appreciate the beer, either.

'So where would we come in?' Bektour asked, pulling his hair back from his face, his eyes alert, expectant.

'You have people on the inside.'

'How do you know that?' the mother hissed in suspicion.

'You knew I was there this morning, with Sydykov. You must have friends working there.'

Bektour took a sip from his own glass and replaced it very carefully on his beer mat, lining up other beer mats in a row beside it, everything very neat. It seemed to be his way. 'And what if we did?'

'We need local knowledge. Intelligence – *information*, as you put it. Look, I know I was shown only a small part of the prison this morning. Useful, but not enough. I need to know precisely where Zac is, and how to get to him, what sort of security system they have, details of the inspections, that sort of thing. The Castle isn't Guantánamo Bay, it's old, decrepit, not up to date. From what I saw they have very old-fashioned locks, only a very small CCTV system, and the guards all seemed to be the kind who are a bit dozy by the middle of the night. Timing will be everything.'

'You could have all the time in the world and it wouldn't serve any purpose,' the mother said. 'Your friend is in the Extreme Punishment Wing – in the basement. You talk about locks, but you don't even know where the door is.'

'We may be in luck.' Harry reached into a pocket and pushed his mobile phone across the table to Bektour. 'Can you read the photos on this?'

'But of course,' the young man said. Within moments he had produced a laptop, into which he plugged the phone with its camera, and soon they were viewing the images Harry had surreptitiously captured that morning in the governor's office.

'Zoom in – right there!' Harry instructed, jabbing a finger at the screen.

The wall chart from the governor's office came into ever-closer focus. Staring out at them was a detailed plan of every floor of the prison.

'You expect just to walk in and out?' the mother said, incredulous, cutting through the shimmer of excitement.

'Easier than tunnelling, I suppose.'

'Nobody has escaped from the Castle in four years,' she protested. 'The last man to try was caught less than five hours later, wetting himself in the back of his mother's wardrobe. He was never seen again. This is a small country, Mr Jones. It's not easy to find a place to hide.'

'I can get him out of the country if you'll help me get him out of the prison. How did the last man do it?'

'Through the sewers. In that part of the town they are old, large, almost the height of a man,' the man with the moustache said. The others were listening, too.

'But now they are blocked with bars,' the mother interrupted. 'No one can get out that way again!'

'We won't be breaking out, not at first. We'll be breaking in. They won't be expecting that,' Harry replied.

The mother – one of the men called her Benazir – sat chewing the inside of her cheek with exasperation, yet for the moment she seemed to have run out of further objections.

'If we can get him out,' Harry continued, 'we'll have shown that Karabayev and his gang are vulnerable. And also that they are liars. Through Zac we'll be able to show the world what they're up to. The biggest propaganda victory you've ever had. Think about that!' His finger was pounding the table in emphasis. 'They'll lose every friend in the West, put all the aid they rely on at risk. They'll come under enormous pressure. I'm in a position to arrange that. It might just change the whole deal here in Ta'argistan.'

'It could end with a massive clampdown and our heads nailed to Karabayev's door,' Benazir retaliated.

It was Bektour who spoke next, his words slow, delivered with remarkable restraint for a man so young. 'The Berlin Wall, the Soviet empire itself, was pulled down not by bombs and missiles but by people. Ordinary men and women who decided they'd had enough. Many of them were no younger than me. Isn't that what Father told me, just before they took him? He always said there had to be a better way, one worth taking risks for.'

'I lost your father, Bektour, I will not lose you!' It was a cry of anguish, and she looked round at them all, her eyes beseeching support, but no one spoke.

'Give me one man on the inside, and we could handle it,' Harry said softly.

'We can give you two,' Bektour whispered. 'Isn't that right, Mother?'

But her eyes were closed, her head hanging in defeat.

'You'll need more than simply a couple of doors opening on the inside, Mr Jones. If he's spent any time in the Punishment Wing, your friend will be dead weight. You won't be able to manage him on your own,' Bektour said.

Benazir moaned softly.

'I shall be with you,' her son continued.

'No!' she gasped.

'Me, too,' the gorilla said.

'Thank you,' Harry replied, then he paused. 'There's one other thing . . .'

'Yes?' Bektour asked.

'I said that timing was crucial. I'm sorry, but it has to be done tomorrow night.'

'Tomorrow?' Even Bektour spluttered in surprise. 'God help us.'

'My delegation leaves in two days. I can't stay longer.'

'You clearly don't want us dying of boredom, do you?' the young man replied, tugging at his hair.

His mother looked up. There were tears on her cheeks. Her eyes were filled with pain for her son, yet as they settled upon Harry, he saw nothing but pure, liquid hate.

CHAPTER SIX

They spent the night crowded round the table, the limp beer replaced by dark coffee, trying to construct a plan. They were joined by others, summoned by telephone, while the man with the moustache disappeared for more than an hour and returned with two men who, judging from their raw eyes, had been dragged from their beds. Prison officers, their friends within the Castle who had spotted Harry on his earlier visit.

For Harry to have any chance of success he needed equipment, information and a whole load of luck, yet the most vital ingredient of all was time, and of that he had almost none. They pored over the governor's floor plans, ordered more coffee, scratched out diagrams across paper napkins and on spare envelopes, while Harry tried to devise a way in, and a way out. All the while Benazir, the mother, hovered miserably in the background.

The officers from the prison had the toughest time. Harry took one to another alcove and grilled him. When he had finished complaining about his interrupted sleep Harry interrogated him about alarm systems, about locks and inspections, and in particular about the timings of the guards' patrols, along with all their comings, goings, shortcuts and idle habits. Then he did it all over again with the other guard, looking for inconsistencies. He had to gain a picture of the Castle, one that he was able to fit alongside what he had seen that morning.

As the hours raced by, Harry built a plan, revised it, reconsidered it, then came back to where he had started. It couldn't be much of a plan, not in the circumstances, but it was based on one crucial piece of information: the sewer. It was the only access point that might not be guarded. When he put it to the prison officers, they merely sucked on their cigarettes and shrugged. Perhaps.

Harry also needed a team, men with muscle, but when Bektour tried to persuade the officers to be their guides through the labyrinth, neither was willing to take the risk. Perhaps his mother's reluctance was proving infectious. It wasn't just their jobs at stake, they explained, but their necks, and those of their families, too, and their attitudes made it clear they thought the plan belonged where it started, in the sewer. Yet despite this setback, hour by hour, man by man, a team was built. Equipment was identified, men sent out into the night to forage, to beg and borrow, to steal if necessary, but the one thing they couldn't find was more time. Harry had to be back in the hotel; if he was missed, it would be over. They hadn't finished their preparations, the plan was still little more than fragments, but it would have to be enough.

It was almost first light, grey fingers of dawn stretching from beyond the mountains, when Harry sneaked his way back in. The old woman was asleep in her chair, steadily snoring. He slipped into his room without disturbing her. He found Martha asleep in his bed, waiting. She was lying half-covered by the rumpled duvet, her dressing gown twisted. If her dress sense was usually a little too brash for Harry's taste, her sense of undress was from a different world. The skin of her exposed breast was pale, with a cascade of freckles falling gently from her neck. He found it inspiring, even in his exhausted condition. He sat down on the bed beside her. She opened a sleepy eye and yawned.

'Dirty stop-out,' she muttered. Then she noticed her exposed breast. 'I could get you locked up for this.'

'I'm sure Major Sydykov would be happy to oblige.'

Calmly and without undue haste, she covered herself.

'Martha, I need a very big favour.'

'Oh, you dreary, predictable man,' she said, sitting up in bed and adjusting the pillows. 'Can't you come up with something a little more original?'

The adrenalin that had been sustaining him through the night was now rapidly fading and he found himself desperately weary; he hadn't slept properly for many nights and this past night not at all. 'I think we can do it,' he said, 'but it all rather depends on you. Sydykov and his chums do everything by numbers, you see, they've no bloody imagination. And it's those numbers we've got to rely on.'

'Hang on, Harry, you're not making much sense.' She leant across and switched on the bedside radio. 'Come here and tell me if this big favour you want of me is any more interesting than the one Roddy Bowles suggested.'

They made it down to breakfast, a little late. Malik was sitting in a corner on his own, reading, and there was no sign of Sid Proffit. Roddy Bowles was at a side table with Sydykov, and his eyes followed them like shadows all the way across the room. He smiled, too broadly.

'Morning, you two.' He had the knack of making an ordinary greeting sound like an indictment. 'Glad you're up.' That moist wriggle of the lips once more. 'We've got a small change of plan to discuss. Get some breakfast, I'll join you in a minute.' He went back to talking with Sydykov.

By the time he sidled over, Martha and Harry had got their food. Her meal was light, like a sparrow, all nuts and berries, while Harry had a plate loaded with calories. He thought he might need them. Uninvited, Bowles drew up a chair.

'Look, we've rejigged things a little,' he announced. 'They've managed to open up the road to the hydro-electric project and from their point of view it's an important part of this trip. Just the sort of infrastructure project we ought to be encouraging. So we're going up there this afternoon. It'll mean us staying there overnight, but otherwise we keep to the rest of our schedule.'

Tonight? Martha froze. It couldn't be. What streak of wretched fortune was this? Up in his room, Harry had just spent the best part of the last hour explaining that this was to be the night . . .

Beneath the table, Harry nudged her shin. 'Sounds like a good idea, Roddy,' he said, taking control. 'When do we leave?'

'Back here for a quick lunch after our morning visits, then pack our bags and off we go.'

'Fair enough. I've wanted to see that plant, and I think by then we'll have had enough bloody lectures, don't you?'

'Excellent. And it'll keep that old idiot Sid Proffit out of the reach of temptation. Went off on the prowl last night, apparently.'

'Good lord.'

'Silly bugger. Said that the beer had given him wind so he needed to find a proper drink. Preferably served by improper women.'

'What was it, a pole-dancing club?'

'Without the poles. They don't encourage such things in these parts.'

'Sly old dog.' Harry couldn't hide a hint of admiration. Seventy-two and still not giving a damn.

'And now chained to the kennel. If he goes wandering tonight he'll freeze his bloody balls off, I tell you. And come to mention it, Harry, you're looking a little grim around the gills – as if you've been up all night, too. Weren't out on the tiles with Sid, were you?'

Bowles leered, suggestively. Harry responded with a sigh and pushed his plate away. 'Got to admit, I am feeling a little rough. Bit of an upset stomach. Was hoping a good breakfast might fix it, but . . .' He smiled, wanly. 'It's a touch of jet lag, nothing more.'

'You sure?' Bowles replied, casting an eye on Martha in the hope of discovering signs of some compromising blush.

'I'll be fine,' Harry reassured him.

'You OK with the new plan, Martha?' Bowles asked.

'Last delegation you led, Roddy – to Berlin, wasn't it? I understand some of the members spent every single night in dubious clubs. I heard one even ended up needing treatment for flesh wounds. To his buttocks. A hydro-electric plant's got to be safer.'

'Good. Well, er . . .' Bowles muttered, searching for a riposte that eluded him. 'I'll see you later.'

They watched his odious figure retreat until he had sat down at his own table once more. 'Does he know?' Martha whispered in alarm to Harry.

'Roddy? No. Not Sydykov, either. He only suspects.'

'But how?'

'He's a policeman. He suspects everyone.'

'What the hell are we going to do, Harry?'

'You're going to look at me in the manner of a concerned mother hen, then put your hand on my brow. Check if I've got a fever.'

'And have you?'

'Only when I start thinking about you in that dressing gown.'

Harry threw up, right on cue, directly over the wheel of their minibus.

They'd spent the morning with the Minister for Transport and Communications, during which Roddy had shown himself surprisingly well briefed and had grown very enthusiastic, dominating most of the discussion. Nobody objected, certainly not Sid Proffit, who joined them late and sat looking morose. Then it had been Trade. The minister, through a torrent of fractured English and mind-numbing statistics, had explained the plight of the country since the Soviets had left, taking most of their sweetheart trade deals with them.

'In Soviet time,' he had declared forlornly, 'we had many favourable situations. Our munitions factory worked at full capacity, making bullets for Kalashnikovs. Now output is only ten per cent of what it once was. A tragedy. So sad.'

It was as they were leaving that Harry leaned against the bonnet of their vehicle and vomited. He'd been quiet all morning, like a wounded bear, then as the time came for them to leave he had rushed out, put his head down and brought up what little of his breakfast he had been able to eat. No one saw the two fingers down the back of his throat that had forced the issue. Martha ran over to him, full of concern, followed at a more cautious pace by Bowles and Sydykov.

'I thought you were sickening for something,' Bowles said.

'Sorry,' Harry muttered, wiping his mouth with his handkerchief.

'It is not the food,' Sydykov insisted, clearly feeling the need to defend his nation's honour.

'No,' Harry replied, peering up through weeping eyes, 'I think I picked up a bug. There's a lot of them doing the rounds in London.'

The Ta'argi seemed relieved. 'We will get you back to your hotel.'

'Yes, thanks. Don't think I'll be up to travelling this afternoon. Sorry, Roddy.' His chest heaved again, threatening a repeat performance, and Bowles took a rapid step backwards.

'I think I'll stay with him,' Martha declared, 'just in case it's a bug.'

'I shall get a doctor,' Sydykov said, staring into Harry's tearful eyes.

'No need,' Harry whispered limply. 'All I want is a little rest.'

'Oh, but I insist. I do insist. We can't take risks with someone like you, Mr Jones,' Sydykov said, taking Harry's arm and guiding him into the bus.

*

Forty minutes later the doctor summoned to the hotel room by Sydykov examined Harry's grey complexion and bloodshot eyes. This wasn't a part of the world where health services or medical diagnosis were particularly refined; he wasn't to know these symptoms were merely the result of exhaustion. He prodded his patient's stomach, found it undeniably sore, still suffering from the blow of the gorilla's fist. The doctor prescribed codeine and bed rest. It was also agreed that, unless his condition improved, it would make sense for Harry to get the next flight home, at six the following morning. Sydykov came up with the suggestion himself; in fact, he all but insisted. The pieces, in the haphazard manner of all such things, began to fall into place. Martha said she would stay to monitor Harry's progress and, if necessary, accompany him home. There was no need for the rest of them to have their plans disrupted.

And just in case of any further unforeseen eventualities, Sydykov said he would arrange for an armed guard outside the hotel room.

'Thank you but – that's not necessary,' Harry sighed, waving the suggestion away.

Yet once again Sydykov was adamant. 'In Ta'argistan we leave nothing to chance, not when it comes to the welfare of our guests, Mr Jones,' he said. 'He will be there. Just in case.'

Harry couldn't protest, he wasn't supposed to have the energy. But an armed guard on his doorstep? He went cold, felt genuinely sick. That wasn't in the bloody plan.

As Sydykov's footsteps faded along the corridor, Harry settled back on his bed, very still. He lay there for some time, before suddenly snatching a pillow and hurling it at the door. He also swore profoundly. When he turned to face Martha, his expression was flooded with confusion.

'It can't be done,' he whispered. 'Not with an armed guard outside the bloody door. How can I come and go when I'm supposed to be in my sick bed? They'll know!' His eyes screamed out that he needed help, needed her, that Harry Jones couldn't do without Martha Riley. It touched something inside her; she caught her breath.

'Christ, this is a mess,' he muttered.

Ah, just business, then. 'That's why you've got me,' she said.

'No, Martha. I can't let you, not now.'

'Patronizing bastard. I think I'll make up my own mind.'

'There are too many risks in this.'

'I never thought it was a game.'

'Look, they say Zac doesn't even exist. So if we get him out and he gets paraded in front of every human-rights commission on the planet, it'll cause them tremendous damage. They'll do anything to stop that.'

Anything. The word hung between them.

'And being a woman, being a Brit, won't protect you,' he continued. 'The gunboats will never make it this far up the mountains.' He had to tell her, make sure she understood.

'We still have gunboats?' she enquired. 'How sweet. Anyway, I'm an American, only a Brit by adoption.'

'Martha, this is your chance to bow out gracefully. It's getting much too dangerous.'

'Have you forgotten? I don't do graceful, Harry. And you can't do this on your own, can you?'

His silence told her she was right. She retrieved the pillow and tossed it back to him. 'You're going to need more than pillows for this one, Harry. And right now I'm the only alternative you've got.'

Martha knocked urgently at Sid Proffit's door. She didn't have much time. She found him packing for his trip to the dam, throwing his clothing distractedly into his battered and much-travelled suitcase.

'Damn you, Martha,' he said. 'I was comforting myself that at least I'd have you to look at on this ridiculous trip up the mountains, but now you've decided to play Florence Nightingale I'm left with nothing but that wanker Roddy.' He was being deliberately provocative; he enjoyed it, in his nature, a moment of mild revenge for the times he'd scraped up against the rough side of Martha's tongue. He threw a couple of pairs of faded and overstretched underpants onto the heap.

'Sid, I want to ask you a great personal favour.'

He stopped fussing over his underwear and turned slowly to her, tugging thoughtfully at his beard. 'There was a time, my dear, when those words would have reduced me to a state of total servitude. But that was before the afternoon in the Tea Room you referred to me as a ludicrous old wreck. Very loudly. Over baked beans on toast, I seem to remember.'

'That was in jest,' she protested, a little feebly.

He raised an eyebrow, and continued with his packing. It hadn't been one of her more memorable moments, even she had to admit to that, but she was surprised to discover that the words still rankled; she'd never thought he paid much attention to anything she said, which was perhaps why she sometimes went over the top. Now she felt awkward.

'Sid, this is really important. I need your help. I want to ask you not to go on this trip. To come home on tomorrow's flight.'

'An early bath, away from Roddy? With you?' he teased.

'With Harry and me.'

'Oh, Harry, is it? Pity. Always thought that three's a crowd.' He was hamming it up, he owed her nothing.

'I'd be so very grateful.'

He closed the suitcase lid with a thump. 'Sorry. Just finished packing for the mountains.'

'Please!'

He sighed. 'Look, Martha, I don't know what this

is about, but I do know that you don't much like me. It's all very well tramping round the corridors of Westminster denouncing me as you do, but what have I ever done to offend you? You want to get up on your high horse, that's your business, but don't expect me to follow behind you with a bucket and spade clearing up your mess.'

'Have I been that much of a pain?'

'Yes.'

She chewed on her lip. 'Well, things have changed.'

'Oh, really,' he muttered, disbelieving.

'Can't do without you.' She attempted to appear playful, even a little coquettish, but she was desperately out of practice. She was making a mess of it.

He snapped the locks shut.

'Sid, it's really important.'

'Which is really sad.'

'Give me five minutes to explain.'

'Roddy is already waiting downstairs.'

'What do I have to do, offer you my body?'

His eyes fastened on her, like an angler with a sudden bite. Any trace of humour had gone, replaced by an air of quiet sorrow. 'Twenty years ago, for sure. Maybe even ten. But now . . . I have to leave things to my imagination, dearie.'

'I wish you wouldn't call me that.'

'Given what you've just offered me, I think I'll call you what the bloody hell I like.'

'I'm sorry, I'm making a mess of this.'

'And since you are the one who raised the subject, I'll tell you something. I think a few good nights of rumpty-tumpty' – God, he was showing his age – 'would do you good, woman. You go around the place casting aspersions like the Spanish Inquisition. Relax, for pity's sake. Give yourself a chance – give a man a chance! Don't waste your entire life poisoning the well just because at some point in the past one or two miserable specimens have run off with your bucket.'

'Don't judge me, Sid.'

'Don't have to, Martha. It's written all over your face. You accuse a man with your eyes before he's even opened his mouth.'

He expected to unleash a whirlwind of rebuttal, but instead he was alarmed to see her gasp, bite her knuckle, clearly distressed by what he had said. Her vulnerability trickled through, and as he saw her suffer, he softened.

'No reason why I should say this, Martha, no reason at all,' he muttered, 'but you're better than that. In my opinion.'

She hung her head in silence. It was an unusual condition for her, and he knew it. 'Why do you want my help?'

'A friend of Harry's, here in Ashkek. He's in trouble. Right up to his neck, and almost beyond. We don't have much time. We're trying to help.'

'What would I have to do?'

'Just be ready to come home with us tomorrow.'

'Is it worth that much to you?'

'I offered you my body, didn't I?' she replied, attempting a weak smile.

'You're an aggravating bloody woman, Martha Riley. So what if I pretend to be a bit if a rogue? A woman like you should be able to see through that. I'm nothing but a harmless old idiot whose bits are falling apart but . . . well, who likes to take his imagination for a stroll around the block occasionally.' He wiped his moist nose. 'Beats going straight back home to a lonely supper.'

Suddenly she saw not the sulphurous predator that lived in her mind but a rather frightened, lonely old man.

'I'm so sorry, Sid.'

His beard bristled once more, as though attempting to frighten off the enemy. 'I'm way north of seventy, I've got varicose veins and an enlarged prostate. And you think I can help.'

'Yes.'

'Well, if it's a choice between you and bloody Roddy . . .' He paused. 'He made it plain to me this morning that I had rather overstayed my welcome here.'

'So . . . you'll help us?'

'I do so love a dominatrix.'

'Thank you!'

'I'm not helping you, mind, nor Harry either. I'll be helping myself. Sounds like a bit of an adventure, and

I can do with a bit of adventure at my time of life. Need to feed that imagination, you see.'

'You're wonderful.'

'Oh, and that offer of yours? Well, give me a few days and a new doctor – and who knows?'

Martha walked out of the hotel with a shopping bag over her shoulder. The guard outside Harry's room didn't try to stop her, just watched all the way down the corridor.

It was her first chance to see the city of Ashkek from any viewpoint other than the back of a speeding government car or minibus. As she walked from the hotel, the Union flag was fluttering in the car park, along with the Stars and Stripes, and the Russian, Chinese and several other flags. Yet the car park itself held no cars. It had been dug up, the crumbling tarmac and concrete left in untidy piles where the architect's plans had called for trees and bushes. As she found her way across uneven pavements, taking care to avoid the open storm drains, she discovered a different world. Ashkek was a city still only half completed, yet already half destroyed. Those parts that had been built during the near-eighty years of Soviet rule had, in the twenty years since, been under attack from a combination of natural forces and human neglect. She came across construction sites, abandoned for so long that trees were growing through the empty windows. Everything seemed covered in a blanket of brown winter dust. She passed a motorist leaning wearily over the wing of his old Moskvitch, the bonnet up, looking forlornly at his engine, his slumped shoulders suggesting this wasn't the first time, his sighs of frustration condensing around his head. Meanwhile, along the road behind him came a Mercedes SUV, all black and chrome, freshly cleaned, darkened windows, glossed tyres. It rushed past in the direction of the Presidential Palace.

As she walked, the solid tin sky squeezed lower, as though it had become too heavy for whatever was supporting it – the air had grown bitterly cold, too cold for snow. Martha hurried along on her errand. She followed Harry's directions and found the Fat Chance Saloon without difficulty. It was as he had described it – a basement jazz club filled with old smoke and worn sofas, but no clients, not at this time of day. Instead, youngsters huddled round computer monitors in the alcoves, deep in conversation, tapping away or excitedly sharing some new idea or nugget of information. Martha sensed their enthusiasm was infectious but it didn't seem to extend as far as Bektour and his mother, who she found arguing ferociously in a corner by the tiny, overstocked bar. They stopped when they saw her. The mother was red in the face.

Harry had already agreed with Bektour the means by which they might get Zac out of the prison; it was Martha's job to explain how they intended to get him out of the country. As Harry had set out the plan to her, it seemed so simple it was almost laughable – in fact,

Martha had laughed, until she looked into his eyes and saw only total focus, and behind that, as though reflected in mirrors, a fleeting glimpse of something she thought was fear. Now she, in turn, told Bektour and his mother, and they looked at her in similar disbelief. 'Harry says he's sorry, but he hasn't had time to think of anything more complicated,' she explained. Bektour smiled, but the irony seemed to pass Benazir by.

There were other things he had thought of; clothing was needed, boots, too. Harry had given her a list that she had memorized. And the timings. *Everything depends on the timings!* he had told her, grabbing her wrists as though she might run off and tell Sydykov. Not that there would have been any point. He wouldn't believe what they were planning.

When she was finished, and was sure they understood, Martha thanked them, and told them that when she and Harry returned to Britain they would do everything in their power to make sure that Bektour's cyber group was placed on a sound footing. He needed money, and they would make sure he had it, along with other things that money couldn't buy in a place like Ta'argistan. Like a fully qualified systems administrator, and encryption software so good it would leave the authorities in Ashkek drowning in their wake. Plus the latest hardware, subscriptions, and any satellite access they might need. Harry and she had money, backed by friends in universities and foundations who would be willing to sustain them.

'I know what we're asking,' she said, 'but it's only for a few hours. Tomorrow we'll be gone. I know it will take much longer than that to change Ta'argistan, but this is the sort of thing that can tip everything in your favour.'

Bektour bounced with excitement. 'Mother, this is what we've been waiting for, what we've dreamed about.'

She brushed aside his enthusiasm with a scowl, yet he wouldn't be beaten down.

'All those years you and Father fought, all the times you've suffered. But at last we can make it worth while. Now it's possible to bury their lies, sweep them away in a tidal wave of information. We can beat them with weapons they don't even understand!'

But Benazir didn't seem to understand, either. She sat behind her bar looking sullen and suspicious. 'It's too risky,' she insisted.

'Wasn't it Father who said it was a greater risk to do nothing? Much like Mr Jones.'

'How can you trust these people?' she spat.

'Distrust is Karabayev's weapon, not ours,' he replied softly.

She would not be comforted. As Martha walked up the steps to the street, night was already falling, and Bektour and his mother went back to arguing.

Karabayev looked from the window of his presidential home towards the outline of his capital several kilometres in the distance. Before him stretched a path of lights, like an airport runway, that led to his palace in the city centre. The Avenue of Heroes, it was called. The trees that bordered it were immaculate, its paving fresh, its kerbs and signage cared for as though they were prime livestock. It was the only adequately lit road in the country, but soon there would be more lights. Close to the city, but out of sight of Karabayev's windows, they were building three new casinos. Ten per cent of the action would find its way into the President's pocket as a guarantee of official favour. And from somewhere, somehow, there would be those who would find the money for the tables – visiting Kazakhs and Uzbeks, mostly, particularly when the recession had paled and their oil wells were pumping at full capacity again, but some Ta'argis, too. Then the foreigners would restart their building programmes, new houses in specially created suburbs where they could escape with their money from the prying eyes of their own countrymen. A tax haven. Ta'argistan would become the Switzerland of Central Asia. Well, somebody had to plan ahead. What else could you do in a country that had fuck-all except irradiated rock?

He took the glass of orange juice that had just been presented to him on a beaten metal tray and raised it to his nose. He could smell the orchards. He sipped it carefully, but methodically, until it was gone, and held out his hand for more. From beside the fireplace, Amir Beg waved away the offer of a second glass.

'So what are they up to, these Britishers?' the President demanded.

'Some are off to the dam to play with the water pumps. The others are going home.'

'May devils pursue them.'

'One of them has brought the devil with him. Causing trouble. Keeps asking about our American guest.'

'So what have you done?' Karabayev asked, suddenly cautious.

'I told him that we know nothing. And I have put an armed guard outside his door until he leaves.'

'Double it.'

Beg nodded, taking care not to let his anger show. Damn him! Why was it that Karabayev always interfered, as if he knew better, wouldn't trust him, even after all these years and everything Beg had done?

'So why didn't he try to bribe you?' the President asked.

'He did.'

'How much?'

'I never asked.'

For the first time the President turned from the window to face the other man. 'You did well to refuse.'

Once again, Beg nodded.

'But you should have told me,' the President added.

Criticism. Always criticism. A man who piled his insecurities so high that one day he would surely stumble over them . . .

'It's under control,' Beg replied.

'It had better be.'

It sounded like a warning. Beg struggled hard to swallow his resentment. Regular practice made it no easier.

'So what have you done with that piece of American shit?' The President couldn't bring himself to utter the name of the man who had screwed his wife and made such a fool of him.

'We have fed him, brought him round. As you instructed.'

'Good – excellent! I want the bastard to know what's happening when we string him up.'

Martha had stopped on her way back to the hotel to purchase a couple of sweaters – made in China, presumably from recycled plastic bottles, cheap but bulky, which she shoved into her bag. She was, after all, supposed to be on a shopping trip. She also bought two bottles of very fine Russian vodka. Pshenichnaya. Forty per cent alcohol.

When eventually she returned to the hotel, she was dismayed to discover that there was now not one but two guards in the corridor outside Harry's room, although the old crone appeared to have been given the night off. Martha put on a smile for the guards as she walked towards her own room. They were young, probably conscripts, seemed uncomfortable, and kept their eyes fixed firmly to the front until she had passed, after which she sensed their eyes had glued themselves firmly to her disappearing arse.

As soon as she had closed her door she lifted the phone and asked for four glasses to be brought to her room. She also ordered two meals, and a couple of DVDs – a comedy and a biopic, only recently released in the West and almost certainly counterfeit. While she waited, she began to pack her suitcases, all the time glancing at her watch. Harry had emphasized, timing would be everything.

The room service took ten minutes longer to arrive than she had anticipated, on a trolley under the command of a youth with a lopsided grin. She jumped at his knock; she couldn't suppress the tension building inside her. It was twelve minutes to seven by the time she began pushing the trolley, now complete with the bottles of Pshenichnaya, out of her own door and down the corridor towards Harry's room. She had changed into one of her new sweaters, brightly coloured and filled with static electricity so it clung closely to her body, a fact which the guards couldn't fail to notice. She smiled at them once more, broadly, full in their face; this time their eyes faltered, stumbling in distraction between her sweater and the bottles of vodka. They even helped her open Harry's door.

'Harry!' she called out. 'You feeling better?'

A wan smile delivered from his bed suggested there had been some marginal improvement.

'I've brought you dinner.'

One of the guards even pushed the trolley into the

room, saluting them both, his gaze lingering a little too long on Martha before he turned and left. As the door closed, Harry nodded in appreciation. 'Ah, food.' He nodded after the guard. 'And I see you make a very good tart.'

A couple of minutes later Martha was back in the corridor, carrying one of the bottles of vodka and three glasses. She set these down on a hallway table beside a vase of faded artificial flowers and, looking at the guards, held her thumb and finger an inch apart. They shook their heads in denial. Then she filled the glasses. The young men watched her as closely as if she was priming a bomb. She took one of the glasses for herself, and nodded for the guards to take the others. For a moment they hesitated, flustered, but she raised her glass to her lips. 'To the revolution!' she toasted, and drank. It tickled like butterflies on the way down, but about three seconds after reaching her stomach turned into a nest of squabbling polecats intent on testing their claws. Twenty years earlier, back in her white clapboard sorority house, she had downed buckets of tequila with salt and lemon chasers. She winced. God, she was out of practice.

The guards glanced up and down the corridor, as though expecting the arrival of a punishment unit led by their dog-breath of a captain, but everything was silent, particularly now that Bowles and the others had left for the mountains. Their eyes were drawn back to the encouraging smile of Martha, and the vodka, which would have cost each of them a week's wages. They wavered in indecision. It was bad manners to refuse a foreign guest, especially a woman, and this one was not only well connected but also particularly well constructed. The decision was made. Screw the captain, even better his wife. They drank.

Fifty kilometres away, up in the mountains, Roddy Bowles was also raising his glass along with Bobby Malik, who was showing little of the Muslim orthodoxy he was prone to preach around his constituency and was well on his way to a state of alcoholic serenity. They were in a rough wooden chalet, more guest house than hotel, with huge log fires and subdued lighting – even here, beside the dam, the power supplies seemed stretched. The darkness and the warmth wrapped around them like a cocoon, an impression of comfort enhanced by the solid food they had eaten, and the ubiquitous vodka. Sydykov was there, too. It was he who poured.

'Well, if you absolutely insist, perhaps one more,' Malik said, affecting reluctance, settling in an armchair beside the fire.

'But Mr Malik, in my country it is an insult not to finish the bottle. Please – relax. Enjoy a little Ta'argi hospitality.'

'When in Rome,' Bowles joined in, chortling, a throaty sound, as though coughing up his innocence. He raised his glass; the vodka was cold, as though it had slipped from a mountain top all the way down a glacier, and tasted of lemon.

'It's a pity your other colleagues could not join us,' Sydykov said, refilling their glasses, 'but at least it will allow us to make faster progress.'

'*Much* faster progress,' Bowles replied, arching an eyebrow in emphasis.

'I shall be sorry in particular to see Mr Jones leave,' Sydykov lied. 'I think I would have enjoyed getting to know him.'

'That I very much doubt,' Bowles muttered, his voice dripping in scorn. He held up his glass, inspecting its contents by the light of the fire as if they held the answer to all things. 'You know, wherever that man goes he has the uncanny knack of leaving a long trail of trouble behind him. Bull in a china shop, as we say.'

'I understand.'

'The man still thinks he's in the SAS.'

'I beg your pardon?'

'The SAS. The Special Air Service. It's one of our wilder military units. He was an officer. Didn't you know?'

'No,' Sydykov said, his glass pausing halfway to his lips. 'We knew so very little about Mr Jones. We were expecting Mr McKenzie.'

'See what I mean?' Bowles said, turning to Malik. 'Harry Jumped-up Jones. Nothing but trouble.'

He tried to pass off the remark with a lighthearted chuckle, but a log on the fire spat in confirmation.

'I had no idea . . . that Mr Jones was a soldier,' Sydykov said softly.

'Well, that was twenty years ago. But he's the type that doesn't seem able to leave it behind – you know the sort. Best time of their lives, all that stuff and non-sense. Glory-hunters, really.' Bowles knew he was going too far, and glanced at Malik, but the younger man didn't seem ready to contest the point, rolling the glass between his palms and staring into the fire.

It wasn't often Bowles could relax like this, let his hair down, be totally frank, and the smoky atmos-phere encouraged informality. The vodka helped, too. 'Jones has been lucky, managed to help the Queen out of a bit of a scrape during the State Opening of our Parliament a couple of years ago. Got himself a George Cross for his pains – not that he really deserved it, just happened to be in the right place at the appropriate time, if you ask me. Ended up killing a man, though. A rough bugger, is Harry Jones, 'scuse my French. Unpredictable. Unreliable. Unelectable, too, in my book, and goodness only knows how he manages to hang on. Frankly, as head of this little del-egation of ours, I didn't want him with us in the first place, and I'll be as relieved as a dog at a lamppost when I know he's aboard the plane and on his way back home.'

He sat back, feeling better for his outburst, as though he had purged himself of a secret that had long been bothering him. He drained his glass and let his head sink into the back of the chair, enjoying the moment. He was startled to see Sydykov rising to his feet.

'Mr Bowles, please forgive me for just a moment,' the security man apologized. 'I have just remembered. I have to make an urgent telephone call.'

CHAPTER SEVEN

The DVDs were pirate copies, fuzzy, inferior, the art-work on the sleeve run off on a photocopier, the sound emerging as though through a sock, but it gave Harry and Martha cover while they talked.

'You look different,' he said, as they huddled close together on the bed, backs against the pillows.

'How?'

'I miss the dressing gown.'

'Keep your mind on the job, Jones,' she said, but a reluctant smile turned up the corners of her mouth. The vodka had had its effect.

'A soldier's perks. Before the hour of battle. Alcohol and sex,' he suggested.

'In my experience, that's what every man regards as his perks, whatever the circumstances,' she countered.

He turned on his elbow to look at her from close quarters, his tone no longer flippant. 'Your experience, Martha. What's it been?'

She flustered, discomforted by such a direct question, but perhaps it was another of those soldier's perks before the hour of battle, the right to dig for the truth.

'My experience? Like most women. Too broad,' she replied.

'Then why are you doing this?' he asked softly.

She hesitated, studying her knees. 'I'm not entirely sure. It's a question I've been asking myself.'

'Doubts?'

'No, not that, it's . . .' She seemed to be on the point of a conclusion before habit drew her back behind her defences. 'Anyway, what about you? You gave me all that bullshit about friendship and loyalty.'

'No bullshit.'

'But it's not just that, is it? This sort of thing keeps happening to you, Harry, putting your neck on the line, finding trouble. You go looking for it. It's as though you're always testing yourself, having to prove yourself to others.'

So, she'd noticed. Not so much a stranger, after all.

'Something in me, I guess,' he replied. 'From my father. He was a tough bastard – at times too damned tough.'

'You, too?'

The heat that had crept into Harry's voice was as nothing compared to the pain that suddenly flooded into hers. She had to gasp for breath, the room went cold. She lowered her head in embarrassment, and in shame.

'My father was rich,' he continued slowly, giving her time to recover, 'some would say excessively so. A bit of a financial gangster. He worked hard and played hard.

Too hard. When I was a kid he told me there were no rules and gave me no limits. He let me live the high life. It was guilt, I guess, for the way he had treated my mother. I look back and I remember room service all the way, everything first class. Holidays. Parties. Sports tickets. And women. He took care of that, too, when I was still only sixteen. Then I grew up and he decided my childhood was over, so he dumped me. Forced me to stand on my own feet.'

'You hated him?'

He shook his head. 'No, not really, except about Mum. I loved him, most of the time. I just didn't respect him very much.' He took a deep breath, as though he had run a long way. 'And you, Martha?'

'I hope he's rotting in hell, where he belongs,' she whispered. The words came like old dust escaping from an opened coffin. 'He wasn't interested in me standing on my own feet. He wanted me on my back.'

'You serious?' And as he looked into her eyes, a door opened, just a fraction, but enough to allow him to peer inside and catch a glimpse of things that were hidden deep away. He saw a different woman, lonely, cautious, pitifully damaged, one who had more in common with him than he cared to admit. 'So that's why . . .' As soon as he had uttered them, he bit the words back, but it was too late. They both knew what was in his mind.

'What?' she demanded defensively.

He shook his head.

'Why I'm a professional man-hater. Is that it?' Her tone was suddenly bitter, full of resentment, as it so often had been.

'Martha, I have no right to judge . . .'

'From the age of ten until I was seventeen, Harry. While you were on your yachts and . . .' The hazel eyes were melting with resentment. Why the devil should he have had it so easy? 'Until I found another man to run away with. He was almost as old as my father, and barely any better. In the years since, none of the bastards have been. As far as I'm concerned, they should all burn!'

'You know that's not true.'

'What? You expect me to be fair? Offer some smug homily about give-and-fucking-take? With my legs up in the air? Turn over, girl, and take it?'

'No, not at all . . .'

'Alcohol and sex. A soldier's perks,' she sneered.

'Look, Martha, I was wondering. When we get back to London—'

'*If* we get back,' she snapped.

'Maybe we could spend a little time together?'

She snorted in mockery. 'You think I'm a charity job?'

'Get to know each other better,' he said, softly, doggedly, like rain falling on a fire. He saw her dig her nails deep into her palms, trying to regain control. God, she was a fighter, with one whole half of humanity, of course, but most of all with herself. He watched while the battle within slowly subsided.

'That's what this is all about, isn't it?' she said eventually. 'Getting to know ourselves better. Testing ourselves. Finding out who we really are.'

'I don't understand . . .'

'Don't try to kid me that you're doing this for friendship, or from a sense of duty, Harry. At the end of the day, this is really just about you. It's who you are, something in you that never looks for the easy route, always takes that extra step no matter what the consequences for others. Because if you stop, you think you'll die, something inside you will suffocate, like a shark that can't swim. This isn't about Zac, for God's sake. It's about you.'

Her words hurt. They should have been easier to deflect, to ignore, but he hadn't looked at things like that before. 'Perhaps you're right. Maybe you understand me better than I do myself,' he said sadly.

'How the hell can I understand you when I'm so God-awful at understanding even me?' she cried out, determined to contradict him at every turn. Yet now her anger with him was washing away in tears of self-recrimination. No matter how she might try, there were some things she had never been able to deny. Her life was her own fault. As much as she frequently blamed others, she always blamed herself. Her head sank down to his shoulder.

'That's why I wondered,' he said gently, 'when we're back home . . .'

She wiped her tears on his shirt, looked up into his

eyes, very close. 'I'd like to, Harry, more than you can imagine. But I don't think it would work, you and me.'

'You said we were alike.'

'Too much so. Doing things our own way.'

'Too selfish, you mean? In too much of a hurry? We could maybe learn to slow down a bit.'

'Slow down? I can't, Harry.'

'Why the hell not?'

'I'm thirty-eight. Divorced. No kids. You work it out.'

'Well, hare and tortoise time, then. You know, need to take it easy in order to get to the finishing line first.'

She nestled back into her pillows, her eyes focused on something a million miles away. 'I don't think I can do that, Harry. I can't forgive, you see. I'm just too bloody angry all the time.'

'We could talk about it, maybe? Later?'

She sucked in a deep breath. 'We need to think about now,' she said, glancing at the bedside clock, moving from one reality to another and slamming the door behind her. The moment was over.

He took her hand, knotting his fingers through hers and massaging them tenderly. 'OK, Martha Riley, one step at a time. But there's one thing you must promise me.'

'Which is?'

'Thanks to you I don't know any more whether I'm trying to save Zac or simply save myself. But whatever happens to Zac and me – *what ever happens*' – he picked out the words with great care – 'you'll be on that plane tomorrow morning. No excuses.'

Her fingers tightened around his. The blue neon figures on the clock insisted that the night was moving towards ten. They had barely eight hours.

Martha stepped back out into the corridor again. She had recovered her composure – a necessary tool for a woman in politics – and she smiled in conspiratorial fashion at the young guards, who were now relaxed, a gentle flush covering their cheeks. One was leaning idly against the wall, the other sitting on the floor, smoking. The glasses were near at hand, the bottle almost done.

She passed them by, disappearing into her own room. Five minutes later she reappeared, changed into her dressing gown. It had been tied clumsily, too loosely for decency. She beckoned towards the guards. 'Come here, you two total losers, and see what Mama's got for you.'

They shook their heads dumbly, not a snatch of English between them. She waved her hand again, more urgently; they looked at each other in uncertainty. They might not understand her words but they read much in her gesture, and imagined more. The guard who was propping up the wall sauntered over. She beckoned him to her bathroom. He took a tentative step forward, then another. She was leaning over the basin, her gown cascading down, revealing much and suggesting still more, while she struggled with her tap. It responded with a reluctant dribble. It had been like that ever since she'd arrived, the management had offered their sincere regrets but absolutely no form of practical assistance. She twisted it one way, then the other, before turning to the guard. 'Hello, there, are you from Jerksville, like the rest of them?'

He nodded enthusiastically.

'So can you help me, you useless, bad-ass bogey-man?'

The other guard had now joined them, his caution overwhelmed by curiosity as he peered over his colleague's shoulder, and the pantomime began. She leaned over the basin, they stared; she turned the tap, they muttered to each other in appreciation; she turned it off and pointed helplessly. Then the performance was repeated. One of the guards started fiddling with the tap himself while the other made a suggestion in Russian that Martha sensed was profoundly vulgar. The guard laughed. So did she. They inched closer. She began to fear she'd overdone the exposed flesh.

'Alcohol and sex, you primitive bastards,' she said with bravado, trying to appear amused. 'What the hell, you really are all the fucking same.'

They roared.

Then, on cue and much to her relief, the solid figure of Sid Proffit appeared in the doorway. 'Hullo there, Martha. You finished packing?'

The guards jumped back in alarm.

'These bellboys of yours, are they ready to take the cases down?' Proffit bawled.

The pantomime in the bathroom broke up in confusion.

By which time, behind their backs, Harry had slipped out of the hotel and was on his way.

The temperature had dropped several degrees since Harry had last been outside. He would have preferred snow, large, overblown flakes that would have given him cover, but instead the night was clear. The world had become a monochrome print, like an engraving from Oliver Twist, a place of black and grey, and shadows, and fears. He passed the monument to Lenin with its rotting plinth; moonlight bounced off the monster's skeletal head while his outstretched arm pointed towards the stars, yet the eyes seemed to follow Harry's every step. He hurried on.

He met his team at the rough shelter beside the railway station. Just three of them. The man with the moustache, who turned out to be called Aibeck, the young gorilla who had thumped him, named Mourat, and Bektour. None of them appeared as confident as the night before. They looked at him nervously, in silence. No greeting. Harry went round them all and took their hands, one by one, reassuring them, and their faces slowly relaxed.

'Is everything ready?' Harry asked.

Bektour nodded, but Harry insisted on inspecting

each item. The equipment had been gathered from sheds and car-body shops, the clothing from wherever they'd been able to scrounge it. None of it as new, some of it was ancient, but it would have to do. There wasn't time to change it.

'And no weapons,' Harry demanded. 'Remember, this is silent-in, silent-out. Otherwise we're dog meat.'

'Mourat and I aren't gangsters, Mr Jones, we're geeks,' Bektour replied in soft reprimand. 'We hate any noise that hasn't come through an amplifier. And Aibeck here drives a taxi, not a tank. He's not even very good at that. Weapons? I doubt he could operate the cigarette lighter.'

Harry couldn't resist a smile; he liked this kid. Bektour had his spectacles taped to his head and his long hair tied back in a knot, just as Harry had told him to. Ninja geek.

'You all up for this?'

'I think we should get on with this before my glasses start misting up and Mourat's manhood freezes,' Bektour replied.

'I don't suppose you'd win prizes as the prettiest regiment in the world,' Harry said, his words leaving clouds of vapour condensing in the stiff night air, 'but you'll do. So let's start the party.'

They clapped their hands, to summon up the blood, to keep warm. Aibeck led the way to a dilapidated Datsun truck with canvas sides, the type of vehicle that could be found anywhere in Central Asia, the threadbare camels of the new Silk Road. While he climbed up to the driver's cab, Harry, Bektour and Mourat hauled themselves into the back. As they settled down on the bare boards the engine spluttered into reluctant life, drenching them in a cloud of oily smoke, and Harry began changing his clothes, swapping his overcoat for a dark sweater, throwing aside his unrealistic hand-stitched leather shoes and squeezing into a pair of old trainers. The trainers were too tight, pinched his toes, which would soon blister. He used to tramp all over Wales with much worse, although that had been twenty years earlier . . .

The truck jolted forward, its gearbox groaning wearily, slowly leaving the stench of overcooked engine oil behind as it made its way through the city, keeping to the lesser streets, as they headed towards the Castle.

Sidney Proffit was a man not only of legendary whiskers but also of long experience, which had left him with a variety of talents. He knew how to drink, was a master of the art of bullshit, and even understood a smattering of Russian from his university days, which had been spent soaking up all sorts of radical passions at the start of the Cold War. These talents were proving useful as, with the assistance of the second bottle of vodka, he engaged the attentions of the two guards. Theirs wasn't much of a conversation, Sid's Russian creaked more than his joints and the guards themselves weren't accomplished raconteurs, but the 80-proof spirit filled the gaps. The three of them squatted on the thin carpet of the hotel corridor, their faces flushed, their tongues thick. They had toasted many things: first, the revolution, then their mothers, each one by name, and after that international solidarity, the manufacturers of Ferrari racing cars and almost the entire first-team squad of Manchester United – they had even raised their glasses to Britney Spears, which had caused one of the guards to chuckle until he choked. The Englishman knew he was winning when he was able to push plastic flowers from the hallway vase into the breast pockets of their uniforms, where they protruded and drooped like an ageing vicar's lust.

Martha had long since retreated to Harry's room, now far more modest, hugging her gown around her. Sid waved vaguely in the direction of the door. 'Stick it up the enemy!' he cried in schoolboy Russian, and made a crude copulative gesture. The guards roared in approval, and levered themselves onto elbows while holding out their glasses for refills. They didn't notice that Sid had stopped drinking some while ago.

The moonlight had become more intense. It didn't help. To get inside the prison, Harry and the others planned to steal their way into the sewers, and the only practical access point was in a modest square tucked up beneath the Castle walls. Miserably for the fulfilment of their plans, it was overlooked by the guardhouse at the side gate. They desperately needed distraction, yet Martha was otherwise engaged, so as the truck crept into the square, crashing through its gearbox, it gave a chassis-rattling shudder and came coasting to a halt as the engine died. No amount of abuse poured on the starter motor would persuade it to cough back into life. Wearily Aibeck climbed from his cab, slamming the door shut in irritation, and unhooked the engine cowling. Its worn hinges groaned in despair. He gazed mournfully at the engine, then began testing components with his fingers, twiddling here, tugging there, before wiping his hands on an old rag and kicking the tyre to vent his frustration. He returned to his cab and retrieved his tool box. Soon he could be seen, and heard, leaning over the engine compartment, cursing.

The game went on for several minutes. No one came to investigate. A truck had broken down – so what? Big deal. The situation was a good fifty metres from the Castle walls, and the weather was cold enough to freeze camel spit. It was no one's problem but the poor bastard who had his butt poking out at the moon. So the guards in their warm guardhouse failed to spot Harry and the others dropping from beneath the canvas on the far side of the truck and levering open the manhole cover that lay directly beneath their feet. As they struggled with cold fingers, it slipped, fell with a clatter; Aibeck began hammering heartily on the engine. It was Harry who went down first, followed by

Bektour. Mourat took the rear, dragging the heavy metal plate back into place above them. Not until they heard the clunk of the cover locking into position did they switch on the LED camping lights that were strapped around their heads.

The stench was gut-wrenching, left them reeling. While the Castle was built on the highest point of Ashkek and gravity dealt with the contents of the sewer, the prison facility didn't use much water, there wasn't much washing, and the passage of the shit through the sewer was slow. Human and other waste was left to fester, and the resulting process of decomposition released gases that attacked Harry and the others with the ferocity of an artillery barrage. They had brought scarves with them and they tied these across their mouths and nostrils; it didn't make much difference. Even the rats knew better, fleeing in search of safer ground as the three men approached, the light from their lamps glancing off all manner of dark vileness. Crystals were growing down the walls, stalactites dangled from the roof like witches' fingers. The effluent formed a foul, sluggish stream about two feet across and half as deep at the lowest point, and they tried to find footholds on the slippery walls either side of it all. The sewer had been built with bricks, now well past their prime and crumbling in many places, and the height was about five feet, which forced them to stoop. They made their way cautiously along the tunnel, feeling uncertainly for every step, their hands and elbows knocking lumps of dark, sweating slime from the walls. Then Harry stumbled. He lost his footing on a section of broken brick and went tumbling, head first. He managed to keep his face out of it, but as he spun like a cat to protect himself he was covered from shoulder to shin in the stuff. He couldn't even curse, not daring to risk any unnecessary mouthful, but inside he exploded with disgust, and he spat, trying to rid himself of the awful bitter-sweet taste in his mouth. As quickly as he could, he hauled himself to his feet. That was when the narrow beam of his torch picked out the glistening bars that were blocking their way.

The bars were of steel, and ran from top to bottom of the tunnel. They were designed to be wide enough for sewage, but not a man. The intention was clear; there was to be no repeat of the previous escape. And that is why Mourat had brought a hydraulic spreader with them, nearly forty pounds of it, slung across his broad shoulders, the type of equipment used to bend broken car frames back into shape and repair accident damage. Useful kit on the roads of Ta'argistan, and which, with Mourat's muscle behind it, was capable of concentrating four tons of pressure through its jaws. Yet it was hard work in the stench and darkness, with everything covered in slime. For a moment, as the jaws slipped on the bars for the third time, Harry thought they might not make it, but Mourat was not only strong but also persevering. The steel was poor quality, and once he found a grip on the two longest bars, they bent, then burst from their mountings, showering ancient brick dust in every direction.

When the dust settled, they could see. They were through.

It had taken some time for Sydykov to get hold of Amir Beg on the telephone. He had to go through the security services' control room, and late at night there were always delays and incompetence – and outright obstruction, of course. No one wanted to bear the responsibility for disturbing him; men had been known to disappear for less.

'Sir, I apologize for troubling you.'

'What is it?' Beg muttered, shaking the sleep from his voice, not yet annoyed. Sydykov was a sound man, not prone to panic or excessive enthusiasm. There would be a reason.

'I have learned something I thought I should report. The British SAS. That's—'

'Yes, yes, get on with it.'

'Sir, Mr Jones was once a senior member. An officer. I thought you ought to know.'

'We should have known sooner.'

For a moment Sydykov thought his boss might be accepting some of the responsibility for this lapse, but quickly put such thoughts aside. Sydykov would have to accept the blame himself, or shove it further down the line. 'It seems Jones has a reputation for trouble. I don't think we can afford to trust him.'

'Trust him? I'd sooner trust a Turkish whore.'

'He's sick, I know, but even so. I thought . . .'

'You thought right, Major. We should take nothing for granted, not even his indisposition. I think we'll check on Mr Jones, make sure he's tucked up safely in his bed, right where he's supposed to be. Nailed to it, if necessary.'

'Should I—'

'No. Leave him to me.' He jabbed a carefully manicured finger at the phone, closing the connection, and immediately started redialling.

They came up through a manhole in the floor of the kitchens, pushing aside the thick wooden lid, scrambling out of the sewer, on the point of retching. All three lay on the cold, uneven flagstones, gasping as they filled their lungs with fresh air. Only slowly did Harry appreciate how disgusting his condition had become, covered in sewage that clung stubbornly to him and soaked through his clothes, and beneath them. He had to fight the temptation to vomit as he scraped himself down as best he could with a wooden spatula he found on a counter.

It was close to midnight. In some distant part of the building a door slammed, but other sounds were hidden by the thick walls of the fortress. All seemed quiet, except for the rasp of their own breathing and the ancient refrigerator that kicked into life in a corner.

'So far, so very unpleasant,' Bektour muttered as he

inspected Harry's condition and pulled a face. 'Perhaps you should wait for it to harden, then peel it off like an eggshell.'

'Thanks for the advice,' Harry replied, not meaning it.

But Bektour had been of enormous help. He was a young man of quiet yet irrepressible enthusiasm that managed to fill the holes left by Harry's own misgivings. From a pocket that was now damp with soil, Harry brought out the map they had prepared the night before and spread it on the stones of the kitchen floor, tracing their path with a filth-covered finger. Bektour knelt beside him, studying it in the pool of light thrown by his lamp.

'If I'd known this way was going to smell so bloody awful, I'd have knocked on the door,' Harry said.

'Don't worry, Mr Jones,' Bektour encouraged, 'I think there's enough shit waiting ahead of us that you'll soon feel right at home.'

The party in the hotel corridor was proceeding under the indulgent and increasingly watery eye of Lord Proffit when the guards' radio spluttered into life. It was as though a live grenade had been rolled into their midst. One moment the guards were in a state of inebriation, the next they were transported to a condition of intense if ill-focused alert. Proffit had enough Russian to follow what was going on. They were being instructed to check that Harry was in his room. Dear

God, something was up, someone was growing suspicious. It was only the soporific effect of his own intake of alcohol that prevented the peer from falling into a panic.

The guards began to stir, levering themselves to their feet, stretching their arms, swimming through their sea of confusion, but Proffit, even with his old bones, was ahead of them.

'You can't go in there!' he cried in a profound bass voice that stretched not only as far as Harry's door but, he fervently hoped, also beyond it. '*Eadi otsuda! Not go in!* Not while those two are – do I have to spell it out for you blithering heathens? – engaged in a little horizontal electioneering? A bit of Boris and Brenda?' He didn't attempt the translation, which in any event would have been beyond him. Instead, he burst into merriment as he grabbed his crotch and began gesticulating towards the door.

The guards stepped forward, yet their expressions were awash with uncertainty. What *precisely* was it they were supposed to do? Break down the door? Burst in on two British politicians? Cause a diplomatic incident? Kick the Cold War back to life? The order, when it was given, had sounded simple enough, but with every shake of their heads the matter seemed to be growing increasingly complicated. The only thing they could see for certain was that if it all went pig-shaped, it would be their balls on the block.

The elderly peer made sure he got to the door first,

pressing his ear to the panel, a frown of concentration imprinted on his face. Then, slowly, his expression began to transform to one of wonder, which was followed by lewd gloating. He motioned for the guards to listen; they did so, at first cautious, then increasingly boldly. They began to nod to each other. It seemed the patient was recovering fast. Perhaps it was the vodka – or maybe a little mouth-to-mouth resuscitation? They sniggered, and began to relax. Whatever the cause of the enquiry, they were now in a position to confirm that the foreign visitors were both cosy and accounted for – enjoying themselves, even, loading up on a few precious last-minute memories of their stay in Ta'argistan. Because, from inside the room, the guards could hear the strains of a creaking bed and the unambiguous sound of Martha slowly working her way up to an elemental, earth-moving orgasm.

With the help of their sources on the inside of the Castle, they knew where Zac was being held. They also had a pretty good understanding of the security system, which was elementary and based mostly around men and metal. Harry had a lifetime of experience with security systems. They had a chronic susceptibility for looking in entirely the wrong direction, a bit like the Maginot Line. Almost every military strategy Harry had ever encountered had focused on winning the last war rather than the next, just as security inside the prison was designed to deal with the last escape rather than what Harry and the others had in mind. That's why the sewers had been blocked, to stop those trying to get out. No one had paused to consider that someone might try to get in. After all, who'd be insane enough to do that, break into a place like this? As Harry tried to wash the shit from his hands and face, it seemed a perfectly reasonable question.

The prison kitchen required regular deliveries of supplies, and so it had ready access to the courtyard and the gate through which Harry had first entered. The same went for the governor's office and other sections of the administration block. There wasn't much call for tight security there; the system had been concentrated on the prisoners' quarters. From the kitchen, therefore, there was easy entry not only to the courtyard but also to everything that ran off it.

That's what had caught Harry's attention. There was something else he had seen on the plans, a door from the courtyard that opened into a long basement corridor. 'What's that?' he had enquired as they had made their plans, jabbing his finger at the point where the corridor came to an end.

There had been a moment of unease between the prison officers, who looked at Bektour.

'Go on, tell him,' Bektour had whispered.

'It's the Hanging Room,' they had told Harry. 'Where they . . .' The sentence had been left unfinished. There was no need.

There had been progress in Ta'argistan, of sorts. Gone

were the days when victims were dragged behind horses across the steppes for the passing amusement of ruling lords and the further instruction of the masses. Nowadays the bodies of the executed were taken out quietly, along this corridor, through the door and into the courtyard, to be disposed of along with the rest of the prison's rubbish. And at its other end, beyond the Hanging Room, lay the Extreme Punishment Wing. That was where they would find Zac.

There was no formidable security on the route that led from the execution chamber, they had been told. Only corpses came this way. The difficulty, of course, was the courtyard, which was lit, albeit like the rest of Ashkek in a desultory fashion, but well enough for interlopers to be seen. Harry would need to cross the courtyard and a hundred feet away, in full view, were the armed guards at the gate.

He tapped his watch. 'The bloody sewer took longer than we bargained for. We haven't got much time. Come on.' He moved to the kitchen door that would spill them out onto the courtyard. It wasn't locked, merely closed, and here they stood, Harry tapping his toe, marking the seconds as he stared intently at the face of his watch. It was no ordinary timepiece but a Rolex Yacht-Master, made from yellow gold, one of two identical watches that Julia had bought and engraved on the back with a simple message. 'Thank You. J.' The first she had presented to Zac, the other to Harry. He had worn it ever since, for luck. And, as he had repeatedly told everyone to the point of their witlessness, on this job, timing was everything. So they waited.

And waited.

Eventually, Harry clenched his hand until it made a fist. 'Bollocks. Something's wrong.'

The plan had called for a power cut at 12.20 a.m. that would knock out the lights and drown the courtyard in darkness, courtesy of another friend of Bektour's group who worked at the local power station. Easiest thing in the world, to trip the supply, happened all the time, most evenings, in fact, even with teams of engineers toiling to stop it happening. But not, it seemed, tonight.

Three minutes passed, five, then eight.

Nothing.

Most of Ashkek slept.

In the hotel, Sid Proffit was pouring the last of the vodka into the glasses of the guards, who were in the state of relaxation that comes only when a man knows his duty is done and there is free booze for the asking. They sat in the corridor with their backs propped up against the wall. One was almost asleep, his eyes glazed, his chin drooping towards the plastic flower that still protruded from his breast pocket.

Yet as one cog in the system ground to a halt, another was stirred into action. In the square outside the prison, a guard, considerably more alert than Sid Proffit's companions, at last emerged from the gatehouse to inspect the problem with Aibeck's truck.

'What's up?'

'How the fuck do I know?' Aibeck replied. 'My boss pays me to drive, not piece back together this load of Japanese junk.' He spat in the snow, professing anger, trying to stop his fingers from shaking with fear as he scraped at a spark plug with a strip of emery paper.

'Bosses? Tell me about them,' the guard muttered goodnaturedly. 'You want to try working in this shit hole.'

'No thanks. Too reliable. It means I'd have to go home every night to the wife. I'd rather stand here and freeze.'

The guard laughed, while Aibeck's trembling hands dropped the spark plug in the snow. 'So bloody cold I can't feel my fingers any more.'

'You want tea?'

Aibeck glanced at his watch. 12.32 a.m. The others were due out at 1.20. He had to keep this going, and tea would give him cover, fill the time. And he was fucking freezing, ice collecting on his moustache. 'Thanks. Can I have it here, though? Need to get this bathtub back on the road.'

'What, you think I'd let you into the prison? I'd have to shoot you first! No, you wait here,' the guard instructed over his shoulder as he walked back to the guardhouse.

Aibeck thrust his hands deep into his pockets to stop them shaking. It was several minutes before he dared even try to pick up the spark plug from the snow.

Meanwhile, on the other side of the prison walls, Harry had come to a decision. 'We'll have to risk it.'

'What, beneath the lights?' Bektour protested. 'They'll see us for sure.'

'I don't think so. I've been watching. None of them have looked this way in five minutes. If they're not scratching their balls or making tea they're looking at what Aibeck's up to in the square.'

'I guess we're going to have to take this game up a level,' Mourat muttered, flexing his shoulders, trying to spit, pretend indifference, but nothing came, his mouth was dry.

Suddenly Harry knew he was taking advantage of these young men. Perhaps he'd known it from the start and simply hadn't bothered about it. He was leading them on, allowing their inexperience and youthful enthusiasm to take them further, step after step, disguising the danger behind a web of adventure. But it was the same with all military service, wasn't it? It was a young man's game, had to be, not simply because of factors like speed, and strength, and resilience, but because old men didn't appreciate the joke, knew when to duck and run. Harry was old enough to know better than to wade through a tunnel of shit in order to break into a prison, but he knew he'd come too far to turn back. What had Martha said – a shark that had to swim? That hurt, too close for comfort, but he'd worry about that later. For now, he had a job to do. He picked up a broom and thrust it at Mourat, then grabbed a bucket and mop for himself.

'Look, we don't run, we walk,' he instructed. 'Slowly, as if we own the place. If they spot us, they'll assume we have reason to be here.'

'And if not?' Bektour asked.

'Then I guess it's a race for the sewers. Which we will win.'

'How can you be sure?'

'Because we've got so much more to lose than they have.'

Bektour looked pale in the light of the torch. He stared at Harry for a while, uncertain, then he sighed. 'You'd better put on one of those kitchen coats, Harry,' he suggested. 'You smell like shit.'

Amir Beg lay back on his pillow, sleepless. The report had come in from the hotel that Jones was safely abed, but that hadn't been enough to satisfy him. He was a man with a restless nature and mistrustful mind, and this business seemed to him to be just too neat, overly simple. Neat and simple didn't fit comfortably with Amir Beg's view of life, which stated that the shortest route to hell was in the company of someone you trust. Anyway, it wasn't the hotel, it was the prison he had to worry about, that's where all their unpleasant little secrets were buried. He lit a rare cigarette, and as the smoke drifted away, it took with it any temptation he might have had to complacency. He rolled over on his side and stretched for the phone, dialling his duty officer.

It rang, several times, then some more before it was answered, while Beg ground out his cigarette in impatience.

'You know who this is?' he demanded, when at last a voice appeared.

'Yes, sir!'

'Have you been sleeping?'

'N-no, sir!'

'Then you have been idle.'

Beg didn't raise his voice, didn't need to. There was a damning hesitation at the other end. He could almost sense the mug of coffee being put aside, the magazine being closed, the mouth turning suddenly dry.

'I'm sorry, sir.'

Ah, at least the man hadn't lied and invented some ridiculous excuse. An honest malingerer. The service was full of malingerers, but so few of them were honest. This one was a rare bird. It meant he might survive.

'Stop filling your pants,' Beg instructed, 'and get Governor Akmatov out of bed for me.'

Every step felt as if they were dragging dead horses behind them. They needed to cross thirty yards of the courtyard before they would be out of sight of the guard room. They hadn't covered twenty when a voice rang out.

'Hey! What's going on?'

Harry brought up his hand and waved, very slowly, but kept walking.

'Come here a minute!' the guard demanded, his tone a little sharper.

'We've got blocked drains to clear,' Bektour shouted back. 'Make us some tea, we'll be back in a few minutes.'

The bluff wasn't working. The guard took a pace towards them. 'I wasn't told about any night work.'

'Now, may God help us,' whispered Mourat.

That's when the lights went out.

CHAPTER EIGHT

It had been agreed, during the previous frenetic day of planning, that one of Bektour's young friends in his Internet group would take care of the lights. Anna was only twenty, and was the in-house web designer who also wrote, with a decidedly radical edge, about women's issues. Wife-beating was still commonplace in Ta'argistan, and wife-kidnapping far from exceptional, so she would never suffer from a shortage of copy. Anna was a woman of both opinions and interests, and one of her many interests was Volkov, an engineer at the municipal power station where the tall chimneys soared above the eastern suburbs of Ashkek and belched dense clouds of steam and smut into the mountain skies. Volkov was the passionate type, and Anna had little difficulty in persuading him to tamper with the control systems at the station. She spun him a story about using a power cut as cover for a raid on the server at the Ministry of Justice, where she wanted to wipe out a backlog of traffic convictions. Cutting the electricity supply would be a simple task in such a rickety system, the work of a moment, with the responsibility entirely undetectable by Volkov's bosses.

But Volkov was not only passionate, he was also intensely jealous, and during the afternoon he had changed his mind. He was twelve years older than Anna and had difficulty in keeping pace with her uncompromising lifestyle. They had rowed on the phone, and he had reneged on his promise. So the lights had stayed on.

She had called him, he had sulked. She had threatened. She would inform his wife, she said, as well as posting compromising pictures of him on all sorts of websites – a task, she reminded him, which wouldn't require foreshortening any of the images in order to leave him squirming in humiliation and forever after being known around Ashkek as Needle Dick. She even emailed one to him as illustration. Only then did he relent.

By which time it was 12.37. Seventeen minutes late.

The confusion caused within the prison by the power cut didn't create chaos, it was too common an occurrence for that. But it distracted the guard, made other demands on him, and in the sudden darkness Harry and his team got to the door. It was just as he had been told, secured on the outside with nothing more than a simple heavy-duty barrel bolt. He drew it back, had to hit it hard to persuade it to move, but the noise was more than covered by the agitation of the guards. Before he ducked inside, Harry looked over his shoulder at what they were leaving behind, a landscape of silhouettes and shadows, and eyeless prison windows, and bars, a claustrophobic world lit only by a pale, half-hearted moon. From where he was standing, whatever else lay beyond the prison walls had ceased to exist.

They had prepared for what they found at this point. Once inside, Bektour placed wooden wedges beneath the door to make sure that although it appeared closed, it couldn't be locked on them. This was not only the way in, but also their way out. Ahead of them the passageway stretched beyond the reach of their torches, and even a single pace inside the air was stale and dank. The paintwork bore the signs of endless neglect; great chunks were flaking off, and what was left was badly scratched. Harry imagined this as the marks of desperate hands and feet. It couldn't have been like that, of course. Corpses don't kick.

The passage was littered with ancient, dangling cobwebs and patrolled by cumbersome woodlice. Two red eyes peered out at them from the distance before scurrying off into the darkness, claws scratching along the rough concrete floor. They followed, every step taking them deeper inside, every sense on alert, fighting their instinct to turn and retreat. Near the end of the passage they discovered an old gurney, a stretcher on wheels that blocked their way. Bektour sighed sadly, from somewhere deep within, brushed it with his hand, as though his father was still lying on it. The others let him stand for a moment, lost in remembrance, before they squeezed past to the door that lay beyond. Another simple barrel bolt, this time much stiffer; it gave way with the sound of a hammer on an anvil, or perhaps a falling trapdoor. The echo shot back from the walls like alarm bells, but no one came. The door opened slowly on tired hinges.

The Hanging Room, was, Harry thought, probably the most pitiless place he had ever seen. He was no stranger to death or judicial executions, and even executions that hadn't bothered with a judge, but nothing he had seen was more immediately offensive than this. Everything in it stank of death. It was a square room, twenty feet across and almost as high. Their torches picked out the dull glint of scaffolding poles that formed a structure nine feet high, a construction so haphazard it seemed as though two men might tip it over with their bare hands. By contrast, the steps that climbed to the top were solid, wide, with substantial handrails on either side in case anything needed to be hauled up them. They led to a platform of wooden planks, and in the middle of it, square and a little warped, was a trapdoor. Harry's eyes were dragged upwards with an irresistible force. Almost at ceiling height was a discoloured steel joist stretching from wall to wall. From this, staring at them in the torchlight like a one-eyed goddess of vengeance, hung the noose with its huge hemp knot.

Bektour stood, gazing, his lips moving silently, holding

out his hands in prayer. As he finished, his entire frame gave a terrible shudder.

There was worse. Harry saw old, evil stains beneath the scaffold, signs not just of death but of botched executions, too long a drop, too much twisting, too great a force for fragile necks and skin and tissue to withstand. Damn these people, they couldn't even kill properly. But perhaps that was the point of this crude machinery. Its message was that those who built it simply didn't care. Life was of no significance, scarcely worth the bother it took to finish it, so if they butchered you like a chicken it was of no consequence. If they didn't get it right first time they'd simply try again until the job was done. There was no dignity in this place, death was little more than a crude game, played out for the passing gratification of others. Little wonder some struggled as they were dragged up these steps.

Harry turned away in disgust, but the horror wasn't over. His light fell upon the wall by the far door, the first thing that would catch the eye as you entered. Photographs. Crudely stuck to the wall with pins and tape like shopping lists. Some were new, some much older, stained, or curling at the edges. Dozens of them. Of executions. Of men standing, of men falling, of corpses dangling. Of heads being held up by the hair where the execution had gone so gruesomely wrong. Of empty faces with their torn, twisted necks. Of faces being forced back in their proper places by boots for the benefit of the photographer. In one, a man was kneeling between two corpses, their lifeless heads propped up in his hands. A man and a woman, stripped to the waist. The man clearly had a death erection. Husband and wife? Harry wondered. But it was a redundant question. Here they were nothing but trophies. No better than pigs' heads on a plate.

These images were the last things a prisoner would see, the images they would die with, knowing that in death they, too, would be nothing more than pieces of pornography stuck to a peeling wall.

It's what they planned for Zac.

Harry had to get him out. There were no more doubts. Silently, he yelled Zac's name. *Fuck it, Harry, get on with it*, came the reply.

He scolded himself for his distraction and headed for the far door.

Governor Akmatov arrived at the main entrance to the prison shortly after the power supply had failed. The confusion he found did nothing to improve his mood. He was a man who slept heavily and resented disturbance, but he was also an adept player of the game necessary for survival. It was inevitable that fortunes amongst the elite in Ashkek would ebb and flow, but one of the constants was that you did not cross Amir Beg. Now Beg had sneezed, so Akmatov had sprung, and the governor was not in a mood to tolerate any underling who stumbled in his way.

He arrived looking as though he had put on a few

pounds, still in his pyjamas that were tucked away beneath his suit. Comfort clothing. He felt in need of it.

'What the hell's happening?' he snapped at the duty captain who had rushed to meet him at the gate. Akmatov hadn't been told that anything was happening, not for sure, but his staff had a multifaceted talent for screwing things up. Give them an egg and they'd end up with an outbreak of dysentery.

'Why, nothing, Governor,' the captain answered, hesitantly. 'All's quiet.'

'No alarms?'

'Well, no, sir, I mean . . . the power's gone. The alarms aren't working.'

'What? You moron. Why the hell wasn't I told?'

This last exchange was a well-practised dance, a formal two-step conducted for the benefit of the record. They both knew the alarm system wasn't worth a damn, with or without the power. They also knew whose responsibility it was, but the captain didn't dare rub the point home. The system within the Castle was basic to the point of obsolescence – magnetic contacts on some of the main doors and exits, rudimentary CCTV, and motion detectors in a few of the important locations, all of which were designed to be fed into a computerized monitoring operation that wouldn't have been out of place in a backstreet grocery shop. It had been installed under the auspices of the European Union's humanitarian-aid programme with the stated objective of preventing the abuse of some prisoners by others, and of making sure the prison officers, too, followed the rules. Yet the elementary nature of the system had scarcely been reflected in its expense; the installation had been budgeted for around €800,000 but had ballooned beyond the two million mark, the contractor arguing that cost inflation was inevitable because of the ancient nature of the structure and the extraordinarily damp conditions in some of its areas. It was those conditions, too, he said, which caused the notorious lack of reliability.

There were some obvious flaws in the contractor's argument. After all, the Castle hadn't changed much in fifty years; it might be argued that he should have foreseen these difficulties. There was also the point that the contractor was Governor Akmatov's brother-in-law so there were no grounds for surprise. Yet the EU paymasters in Brussels were a long way away, and foreign-aid programmes come with their inevitable clutter. However, no one was willing to let such an unsatisfactory situation stagnate. A further submission had recently been made to the EU for a full refurbishment and upgrade programme. The governor had given it his full support. Everything would get fixed. Tomorrow.

But, tonight, it failed. Part of the basic CCTV system operated in the Extreme Punishment Wing, where conditions were too taxing for guards to remain on full-time duty, and where the cameras were supposed to fill the gaps. Yet, for now, the Castle was bathed in pale moonlight, the gloom pierced by nothing more than the occasional flash of a torch. It wasn't the first time Akmatov had found his prison in this state, the condition was almost normal, nothing to worry about, except for the fact that Amir Beg was on the phone. That was one hell of a coincidence, and the governor hated coincidences. He hurried on his way.

The stout wooden door on the far side of the execution chamber had no lock. That made a sort of sense. Who would want to break in here? Harry knew what was on the other side, from the details of the governor's map imprinted on his brain: three corridors that made up the heart of the Extreme Punishment Wing, running parallel like the tines of a fork, with a control room at the far end where the guards sat.

There was no mistaking the nature of this place, even without light. It stank, not just like the sewer but worse. Mixed in with the mire there was fear, despair so strong they could smell it. There was little sound, apart from the soft pad of their footsteps, but the air was thick, uncompromising, the ceilings low, supported on walls of old stones that ran with moisture and slime, the passageways narrow and claustrophobic. And it was on one of these passageways, the one on their far right, and four doors along, that they found Zac.

At first, when Harry peered through the grille on the door, the cell seemed empty, but as he searched, his torchlight fell upon what seemed to be a pile of rags thrown into a corner. A bare foot was peering out from beneath them.

'Zac?'

Nothing.

'Zac!' Harry whispered, a little more loudly, but desperate not to disturb others.

The foot stirred. Then, from the darkness, two eyes slowly emerged that stirred some distant memory for Harry. Zac's eyes had been one of his most attractive and prominent features; they had spoken of adventure, ambition, mischief, wit, defiance, lust – yes, lust even for Julia, too, Harry had always known that, and had wondered whether Zac had ever tried to claim what on other occasions he had called salvage rights. Yet these eyes were not like that. They were withdrawn, empty. But undeniably Zac's.

Even here, at the heart of the Extreme Punishment Wing, the door security was unimaginative. There were two heavy-duty barrel bolts, top and bottom, but it was the work of a second to slip them back, and quietly. The lock offered a different challenge. It was large, to be sure, and solid, a deadlock, and the door itself was metal, cold, unyielding, like the stone walls that surrounded it but, with the usual Ta'argi eye for skimping, the frame was wood. A job for Mourat and his hydraulic spreader. The wood groaned and resisted as the jaws of the spreader got to work, but the frame couldn't withstand the sorts of pressures that the gear exerted. The door jamb bent, was forced back into the mortar. A rivet popped. A small avalanche of dust began to trickle to the floor. The timber began to splinter and groan, but still the lock wouldn't slip its catch. The noise of their exertions began to echo along the corridor; beads of sweat tumbled from Mourat's forehead, he was panting, his breath rasping.

Then it happened, with a nudge from Harry's shoulder. The jamb twisted back far enough for the lock to be forced, and the door swung open. There was no crash of falling stonework, no scream of splintered timber, nothing but a low groan of complaint from the hinges and Mourat's muffled curse.

Harry rushed inside the cell, his torch picking up only shades of darkness, even as he knelt beside the huddled form of his friend. A hand appeared, slowly, stiffly, filthy, to shield the eyes. With his sleeve Harry tried to wipe the grime from around the face.

'Harry?' Zac's voice was weak, hesitant. 'Is that you?'

'Yes, Zac.'

'Been expecting you. He said you'd come for me.'

'Who?' said Harry, startled.

'Amir Beg. Nasty bastard. You know him?'

It wasn't the greeting Harry had expected. Suddenly the hair on the back of his neck bristled in alarm. His instinct kicked in. It told him he was in more trouble than he'd thought. Much more trouble.

Akmatov wasn't a frequent visitor to the more distant or dubious parts of his prison. He preferred his office in the administration block, where it was warmer, sheltered from any commotion and away from the crap that flowed incessantly through his facility. It also enabled him to look visitors like Martha in the eye and tell them that he knew of no abuses in his prison; he made a point of not witnessing them. Yet now Amir Beg was on the case and Akmatov wasn't about to leave his future security, let alone his manhood, in anyone else's hands. He was going to see for himself.

The sudden appearance of the governor, pounding his way down the steps to the Punishment Wing's control centre, took the guards completely by surprise. They had no time to extinguish their cigarettes or hide the bottle that had been keeping them company, leaving it standing in a pool of light thrown by the duty captain's torch. Akmatov swore with surprising passion for a man still in his pyjamas. The guards leapt to their feet; one of the chairs went clattering.

Then Akmatov cursed them some more. He abused them and their mothers, and recited a long list of charges they would face before being thrown into the deepest cell while he spent his afternoons fucking both their wives. They had, of course, done nothing that wasn't normal practice within the Castle, but Akmatov needed a scapegoat, preferably two, just in case. Amir Beg had made him nervous.

'You bastards have been here all night?' the governor demanded.

'Yes, sir!' they cried as though on the parade ground.

'No piss breaks, even? No screwing off? You sure?'

'No, sir!'

'Has anyone – *anyone* – come in or out of here?'

'Not since we relieved the last shift, Governor. It's all been quiet.'

'You arseholes had so better be right or you'll be swinging along with the others,' Akmatov spat, staring them in the eyes, so close that his spittle streaked their cheeks. 'Open up!'

The control centre was merely one half of a room located at the top end of the cells and separated from them by a barrier of bars. As the guards rushed to the gate that gave access to the corridors and cells, one of them fumbled the keys and dropped them. He blanched in fright, expecting an avalanche of abuse, but the governor was done with screaming, the foul air was already getting to him. He tugged at the sleeve of his pyjamas, holding the cotton fabric to his face.

The captain stepped into his stead. 'You imbecile!' he screamed in encouragement as the guard scrabbled on the floor to retrieve the keys. Then, eventually, the gate swung open and Akmatov burst through.

There is always a point in a man's life, and sometimes several, which marks it forever – sends it off in a new direction, perhaps scars it, maybe even begins the process that will bring that life to its end. Harry knew he faced that moment.

The commotion, of new arrivals, of shouts and

abuse, of urgent, jangling keys, from not very far away, told him that they were about to be discovered. It was over. None of them would be getting out of this place. Ever.

As he stared into Zac's eyes, he was back on the side of the mountain. With Julia. Staring into her eyes. That last time. They were about to be swept away, and this time there would be no escape for any of them.

He wasn't afraid of death, only of the frustrations that came with it. There was so much he still had to do. Harry had enjoyed a life that some would say had been filled not simply to the brim but to overflowing. Wealth, fame, acclaim, success, he'd known them all, they had become good friends, but from Harry's point of view none of it had been enough. His life had barely started. Some ancient Chinese dreamer had once said that it wasn't how far a man had travelled but how much he had seen on the journey that was the making of him, and although Harry had travelled further than most men ever would, he still felt he'd barely started on that most important journey of all, the one inside himself. In some ways it was the shortest journey a man could make, yet its challenge was greater than trekking to the ends of the world. To understand himself, to know truly who he was, was a challenge he felt he still had to undertake. A little like Martha, perhaps. The greatest contest is always with the enemy within, and that battleground can be the loneliest place on earth.

That was one of the many reasons why he missed Julia so much. She had been his guide, the one who saw deeper inside him than he did himself. Without her he had run so fast, away from the pain, and lost his way, stumbled into a life that he found all but pointless. And that's what he was doing here, in this piss hole of a prison. Trying to find himself. He'd tried to pretend otherwise, but who was he kidding? Martha had seen it. This hadn't been about saving Zac, it was about finding Harry.

There was still so much more for him to do; mountains to climb, seas to swim – yes, and slopes to ski. Time to find another Julia, if he could. But for all his wealth, this was the one commodity he could not buy, not a single extra second of it. His time was about to run out.

Bektour and Mourat were staring at him, eyes dancing with fear.

'Mr Jones?'

That's when Harry knew what he had to do. 'Take Zac,' he instructed, hauling him to his feet and handing him into Mourat's strong arms. 'Go!'

'Mr Jones—'

'You know the plan. Take him to Martha. Get them on that plane. Tell her to do everything as we discussed.'

'But . . .'

'You have to leave me here. Lock me in.'

Bektour was shaking his head in confusion.

'Look, if they find the cell empty they'll sound the alarm. None of us will make it. We won't even get across the courtyard, let alone out of the prison. But if they find the cell locked with the prisoner inside . . .' And already he was ripping his clothes, turning them to rags.

'Mr Jones, you can't—'

'I have a better chance than Zac.'

'There must be some other way.' Bektour tried to interrupt; Harry rode straight through him.

'There's no time. Listen!'

And from far too close at hand they could hear the security gate creaking open and crashing into a wall.

'You have less than a minute. For the sake of whichever God you believe in, get out of here!' Harry hissed.

He was already half-covered in shit, now he was blackening up his face, his hair, the rest of him, with dirt scraped from the damp walls of the cell. As they watched, Harry was transformed. He became the prisoner.

'Go!' he snapped.

Zac reached out for him, grasped his hand with surprising strength for a man who couldn't properly stand, and clung to it. His eyes were glazed with confusion, and fear. Harry froze. The fear was infectious. Then the others dragged Zac away. As their hands parted, Harry found that Zac had pressed something into his palm. It was a chess piece. A black horse.

They stumbled from the cell, Zac's feet dragging behind. The door, with its loose lock and a little encouragement from Mourat's shoulder, clicked back into place. The bolts were slid quietly home. And they were gone.

The duty captain made it to the cell door first, shining his light through the grille. 'He's here!' he called out. There was no mistaking his relief.

Akmatov shoved him roughly aside. The beam of his own torch lashed across Harry, who stirred, and blinked bewildered into the light, his hair stuck to his scalp by filth, his shirt hanging from one shoulder.

'Shall I open the door, Governor?' one of the guards enquired, his voice rattling with unease.

But Akmatov drew back, his pyjama sleeve clamped to his face. The reek of the Punishment Wing was bad enough but it was rose water compared to the stench issuing from the cell. He'd done enough, covered his arse, kept Amir Beg off his back, there was nothing more to do and no need that he could see for getting his shoes covered in any more crap than they already were. 'No,' he instructed. 'No need.'

He turned and hurried back down the passage, leaving Harry a prisoner, locked away, alone in the darkness.

PART TWO

The Captive

CHAPTER NINE

Their margin of survival was terrifyingly small. They only just made it out of the Punishment Wing in time. Zac kept stumbling, his feet dragging, as though he had to relearn every step, but they had Mourat's strength to carry them, and their fear. They could hear the posse behind them, drawing closer, the governor's heavy feet pounding along the stone floor, the guards scurrying in pursuit, jangling their keys. They dragged Zac behind the door of the execution chamber in the nick of time, as the guards' torches hunted them.

For a short while they sat slumped, panting in fear, afraid their rasping lungs would give them away, listening for the sounds of pursuit, but none came. Slowly they began to recover their wits, but it was only a fleeting respite, for ahead of them stood the gallows with its beckoning eye. The sight drove them on, across the chamber, past this awful contraption of death, and through the door on the far side. By the time they were back in the passage, sweating despite the cold, they were glad of the gurney. They placed Zac on top and wheeled him all the way to the end. Their wedges were still in place under the door; they eased it open. Ahead of them lay the courtyard.

They would never have made it across if the lights had been on, not carrying Zac. His early flickers of response had faded as they had sat gasping for breath in the chamber, the sight of the noose seeming to drive him into a still darker world, so that he became dead weight. As they entered the courtyard, Mourat carried him over his shoulder, through the moonlight that seemed to glow more brightly with every step, knowing they would be dinner for every dog in Ashkek if but one of the guards happened to glance in their direction.

But somehow they made it, into the kitchens and then down into that awful sewer. Zac's weight became ever more of a problem in the confined space. It was while they were easing him through the barrier of bars that suddenly he cried out – screamed. His eyes had opened to discover a world even worse than the one he had been taken from, a small hole deep underground and immersed in so much squalor that even the rats refused to stay. He screamed again, started to struggle. Mourat slapped him in the face; suddenly Zac's eyes were more alert, he stopped screaming, even taking one or two faltering steps for himself.

They couldn't know it as they were struggling in the sewer, but that was when the power kicked back in and the lights came on. On the other side of the prison walls, Aibeck was still glancing nervously at his watch.

Harry and the others should have been out at 2.20 a.m., but the deadline had long since passed. He continued to lean over the truck's engine, listening for the first signs of alarm from within, ready to flee, but all appeared calm, so he stayed, and sipped the tea the guard had brought. He replaced all the spark plugs but switched two of the leads from the distributor, so that when he turned the engine to offer the guards some sign of progress the cylinders fired out of sequence. It sounded as if someone had dropped a match into a box of firecrackers. He quickly let the engine die once more. At 2.40 a.m. he repeated the process, then returned the empty mug of tea to the guardhouse. At 2.42 a.m., when the lights flashed back into life, Aibeck began to shake all over again. Not until 2.53 a.m. did he hear the scraping of the sewer lid from the far side of the truck. It took him two seconds to switch the leads back to where they should have been. By 2.55 a.m., they were gone.

The streets of Ashkek were dark and almost deserted as they headed for the suburbs. The crumbling monumental extravagance of the city centre soon gave way to more blatant poverty. Decaying houses were interspersed with hovels, the landscape held together with little more than corrugated iron and stray sheets of wooden panelling. Nothing was meant to last. Only dogs prowled the broken streets.

Eventually they turned off the highway and drove into the parking area of a truck-repair shop, out of sight of the road. An empty taxi was waiting. With only a fleeting farewell to the faithful Aibeck they started off again, with Bektour driving, until they approached a complex of tall buildings that stood out against the night sky like the trees of a dead forest. These were apartment blocks, towering above everything else that stood around. In Soviet times these had been Moscow's answer to the housing shortage, a micro-city, for worker ants. It had been built to a blueprint devised almost two thousand miles away in the Soviet capital that had handed down inflexible prescriptions for the most elementary details of the design, every leaking tap, every loose door knob, every faltering light switch, every corner of crumbling concrete. By order. Nothing seemed to have escaped the imagination of the bureaucrats, except how people could live in these conditions. Those who slept here were almost grateful for the work that required them to be elsewhere six days of every week. As the taxi drove past the dilapidated store sheds and garages that cowered in the shadow of these behemoths, plumes of rubbish leapt up behind them, dancing in the air before giving up the struggle and falling back to the frozen earth. Dogs barked at the disturbance. The taxi heaved as it fell down yet another pot hole. That's where Bektour stopped.

They had drawn up outside Block 11-C. If that sounded like a factory complex, the comparison was not misplaced. The entrance door was dimly lit, its glass fractured. The stairwell that led from it was damp and smelled of cabbage. There was no lift, and as they climbed to the second floor, they found Bektour's mother was waiting for them at an open door. She offered no word of greeting, nothing but a scowl, stepping back with a show of unblemished reluctance to allow them inside. Her apartment was no more than a single main room, with the barest of kitchens in one corner, bookshelves against one wall, a sofa bed against another and one solitary window that stared out into the darkness beyond. As they helped Zac inside, Benazir grew more distressed, as if at any moment she expected armed men to come charging up the stairs. She began an argument with Bektour, one they had clearly rehearsed before, and he brought it to a rapid end. She bit her tongue and stepped away, her face set and sullen.

They stripped Zac. Then Bektour and Mourat helped him into the miserable bathroom and attacked him with a hand-held shower, reviving him as they cleansed him, washing away the signs of their own immersion in the sewer while they were about it. They sat him on a stool, trimmed his hair, then he was shaved. Just as they finished, a gentle knock on the door announced the arrival of a doctor. He was elderly, a little stooped, seemed nervous, as though he wanted to be away. He made a rapid examination of Zac, who still had difficulty in standing and could do little more than mumble. The marks on Zac's body further distressed the doctor, who muttered to himself.

Zac was chronically dehydrated. The doctor produced a hypodermic, filled it with a yellowy fluid, and stuck the needle in Zac's arm; Zac didn't flinch, he barely seemed to notice.

'This man needs to be in hospital,' the doctor said. 'I don't suppose . . .? No, well, give him as much to drink as he can take,' he instructed, quickly repacking his bag. 'Then give him some more.' He made a final inspection of Zac's pupils and pulse; the patient already seemed to be reviving. It was all he could do in the circumstances. With a quick word to Benazir, he disappeared the way he had come.

The doctor had injected glucagon, which poured glucose into the bloodstream, and after they had given Zac a drink of hot, sweet black tea, he began to show signs of improvement. Within a few minutes he was able to stand and give them a little help as they dressed him in a new set of clothes. Meanwhile, Benazir stationed herself at the window, repeatedly pulling back the curtain and glancing down anxiously at the street below. Mourat searched the apartment for signs of their presence – Zac's stained clothes, his hair clippings, even the towels used to rub him down – and threw the lot into a plastic bag for burning. They stood Zac up for inspection. He had become a different man, not one likely to pass muster on the streets of Michigan but who, in the half-light of Central Asia, might just fade unnoticed into the margins.

As they left, Benazir stood framed in her doorway. Tears trickled down her cheeks. Bektour turned from the stairwell in reproach, but could only wave forlornly. She was not a coward, she had taken her own share of risks over the years, but this was different. This was Bektour. Her only child. Everything she had. And she found it impossible to accept that he was in the line of fire, even more so because the man with him was a foreigner, a stranger who would disappear, never to be seen again, while her son was left behind to face whatever consequences might follow. Her head might listen to his words but her heart cried out for survival – her own, for she was afraid, but above all for the survival of her child. Her determination in that matter would never fail. And she would never forgive those who had put him in jeopardy.

Yet now, at last, they were gone. Mourat crept away in the direction of his own home, where he would incinerate the clothes and destroy any trace of the night. Meanwhile Bektour and Zac climbed into the taxi and drove off. They headed for the hotel. It was 4.05 a.m. They were late. The plane left in less than two hours.

Martha had come to the conclusion that the worst part of this enterprise was to be forced to wait. She was a woman who was used to speaking her mind, giving 'em hell and getting on with things; instead, she was reduced to staring at suitcases. It was a task for which she was spectacularly ill-equipped. It was like being stranded at home, waiting for a man to return, and suspecting the bastard wouldn't.

In the early hours she had gone back to her own room. As she crossed the corridor one of the guards, still slumped against the wall, had opened an eye. She had smiled, he had gone back to sleep. Once inside her room she had showered and changed her clothes, finished her packing, found herself checking every drawer and cupboard corner a third time, and grown ever more nervous. She couldn't escape the feeling that something had gone horribly wrong, a woman's instinct, it rarely let her down. It brought back memories of her husband, away, allegedly on business, which he wasn't, promising he would return, which he didn't, leaving her to imagine the worst. And after years of sleeping in a cold, deserted bed, Martha had developed a formidable imagination.

Shortly after four she called down to the reception desk for help with her suitcases; as they had arranged, at almost the same moment, Sid Proffit did the same. Shortly afterwards, and much to the consternation of the stupefied guards, the corridor suddenly filled with activity as doors opened and luggage trolleys came wheeling in and out of every room. Bodies dashed back and forth, while Proffit descended on the guards to shake their hands and shout his thanks in their faces. Almost before they could wipe the fog from their eyes, the guards found the guests were on their way down.

So they relaxed once more. They had done their duty, the foreigners were gone, the rooms empty. They would particularly miss Martha.

There was no need to sign bills, which were being taken care of by their hosts, even the bottles of vodka, and with Sid Proffit still providing as much distraction as possible, they were soon on the forecourt watching their bags being loaded into a taxi.

It was fortunate that Harry and the peer had travelled light; even so, it was only with considerable difficulty that their bags were squeezed in the boot of the taxi alongside Martha's. She was forced to carry the smaller one on her lap. The staff rolled their weary eyes in despair as they were sent scuttling back and forth on yet another errand. Early morning confusion took hold as doors opened and closed, with the passengers climbing in, then out again, as Proffit began arguing about his luggage before finally settling in his seat up front. No one took much notice of the third passenger in the taxi, sitting in the darkness of the back seat. Three rooms, three lots of luggage, three passengers. It all made sense as the taxi pulled away.

No one spoke until the hotel had disappeared from sight behind them. Then Martha turned. 'Mr Kravitz?' she asked.

The figure beside her turned his head, stiffly, his features lit sporadically by the passing light of the street lamps, but he said nothing.

'Is everything OK?' she persisted.

'Mr Jones. He didn't make it,' Bektour whispered from the driver's seat.

'What?'

'He's still inside the prison.'

'That can't be . . .'

Her voice faded in despair. Harry was supposed to be heading west, that's what the plan said, towards that porous line on the map that passed for a frontier. Within a few hours he was meant to be across and out of reach.

'He said you have to do exactly what he told you to do,' Bektour continued, his voice tight.

'How—'

'He says you must take Mr Kravitz on the plane.'

'But what the hell is Harry going to do?' she gasped.

'I don't know,' Bektour replied mournfully as their car rolled over the bumps of the dual carriageway taking them towards the airport.

'But we can't just leave him.'

'He says you must. Otherwise we'll all end up –' Bektour paused; he wouldn't repeat the colourful expression Harry had used, not to a woman – 'in very deep trouble.'

'The poor bastard,' Proffit sighed from the front seat. 'Poor bloody Harry.'

'We've got to do something,' Martha pleaded.

The peer turned to face her, his voice hoarse with pain. 'Nothing we can do, old love. It's Harry's choice. All of it. Harry's choice.' He looked across at Zac. 'I do hope you're worth it, Mr Kravitz.'

Through all of this Zac had been silent, gnawing at a bar of chocolate, instant energy. He swallowed stiffly; his lips parted, but even after several attempts, no words came. He went back to his chocolate.

A small group was waiting for them at the airport, courtesy of the distant Sydykov. When the taxi drew up, four men descended on them, three to take care of their luggage while the other, wearing a suit as a mark of his higher status, guided them through the concourse to the VIP suite. It was a small airport, not busy at this early time of morning, and their progress was rapid. Their guide chatted as they went, enquiring about their stay, their comfort, asking if Mr Jones was feeling better, declaring his regret that their visit should be ended so soon. Every time he began to pay attention to Zac, Proffit manoeuvred himself into the conversation, his voice bellowing, his tongue thick, his speech faltering just enough to suggest an over-indulged halfwit.

And soon they were at the door of the VIP lounge. Back where they had started, a lifetime ago.

Once inside, the guide continued to fuss, asking for their passports, explaining they had arrived a little later than expected, they hadn't much time. Martha, in her role as group leader, scrabbled in her handbag and handed across all three. He hastened away, leaving them on their own.

'Oh, bollocks, I need a drink, I really do,' whispered a suddenly sober Proffit.

Otherwise, no one spoke. They all knew this was the most critical time. It would take only one curious official to notice that Harry's passport was being used by a man with different-coloured eyes and a broken nose, a man who could scarcely speak and who had surprising difficulty walking, even for a sick man. If that happened, they were lost. Here, in the VIP lounge, they had nowhere to run. Yet it was the lounge itself that kept them away from such curiosity; with luck, it was to be their route through the system. But luck had been a poor friend this night.

The guide returned; he was alone, no guards stampeding behind him. He had a courteous smile and was clutching three passports. Their exit visas were stamped and their boarding passes enclosed.

'I wonder,' Martha said, descending on him to take back the documents, 'whether there's a chance of a cup of tea.'

'Tea?' Proffit declared in the astonished manner of a motorist who had returned to his car to discover a parking ticket on his windscreen, 'we'll have no bloody tea. What about a little vodka, eh?'

He offered up a little prayer to the mother of God, wondering how much longer they could continue with this act, but it was working. The guide gazed round in confusion. 'I'm so sorry,' he began, 'but . . . I fear there is no time. You must go straight to your plane. Please.'

He indicated the door on the far side of the room, near which Zac was sitting quietly, pale, brown eyes down.

Even as the Ta'argi spoke, it opened and an airport official, a broad, middle-aged woman in an overly tight uniform, stood on the other side waiting to escort them.

Proffit made a grab for their guide's hand, wringing it overlong until it hurt. 'Shame about the vodka, but it's a damned fine reason to come again one day. Yes, already looking forward to the return match. Your hospitality's been like nothing I've ever experienced, take my word for it. Goodbye!'

And they were gone.

No one talked as they made their way, slowly because of Zac, to the aircraft, skirting all the remaining formalities. No further passport checks, no inspection of their hand luggage, no prying eyes. It was only a short walk, and their female guide spoke no English.

'*Spasibo. Do svidanya,*' Proffit declared as she delivered them directly to the cabin door. The other passengers had already taken their seats.

The moment she set foot on the plane, Martha asked to speak to the captain. The prissy flight attendant would have none of it; the captain was busy with his pre-flight checks and couldn't possibly be disturbed. The escalation that ensued was swift and short lived, Martha versus an unsuspecting attendant was simply no match. She was shown through to the cockpit.

The captain was, as Martha had been told, signing off on his load sheet that recorded fuel, weight and passenger numbers on board. The only other person

present was the co-pilot. The captain appeared distracted, head down, not best pleased at the interruption,
but when he looked up, his expression softened.

'Mrs Riley, isn't it?' he asked, his accent suggesting
that home was somewhere near Bristol. 'Saw you on
the box the other week. You didn't take any prisoners,
I seem to remember.'

'Then you'll know I don't dick around, Captain.'

The smile faded. This clearly wasn't a courtesy call.
He shifted in his seat. She had his full attention.

'There are a couple of my parliamentary colleagues
seated in first class. One is Harry Jones . . .'

The captain's eyes indicated he recognized the name.

'So there are two things you need to know, Captain.
The first is that Mr Jones has made himself deeply
unpopular with the Ta'argi authorities.'

'I seem to remember he has something of a reputation for getting himself into scrapes . . .'

'More than that. I think someone has tried to poison
him. He's not at all well. Whatever happens, it's imper-
ative that he leaves on this flight and the Ta'argis aren't
allowed to take him off.'

The captain's brow creased. 'Once he's on board, Mrs
Riley, he's pretty much legally on British territory.
They'd have to use crowbars to get him off.'

'I don't think that's likely to happen. I just want to
get him home.'

'Well, we're almost done with our pre-flight checks.
Another ten minutes or so, we should be on our way.'

'Thank you, Captain.'

'Poisoned, eh? Sounds like you've had a lucky escape.'

'Not quite.' She took a deep breath. It was the moment for decision. She hadn't been certain that she was capable of carrying through with what she had in mind. She stood on the very edge, suffering from vertigo, trying to ignore the nausea rising in her stomach, remembering Sid Proffit's words that everything that had happened had been Harry's choice. She also remembered she had a life and a one-eyed cat to feed back home, but – what the hell, where had playing everything straight got her? And that's all she had back home, a cat. So she jumped. 'There's the second thing you need to know.'

'Which is?'

'I'm not coming with you.'

The captain couldn't hide his surprise. 'Can I ask why?'

'Unfinished business.'

'Well, that's your choice, I suppose. But it'll delay things. We'll have to unload your baggage first.'

'Not necessary. I have none.' And it was true. Sid Proffit had taken care of it, all the baggage receipts were on his boarding card.

'I see.' The captain fell silent, ransacking his memory for the regulations covering this situation and pondering the downpour of corporate crap that awaited him if he got it wrong. 'I can't force you to fly with us, Mrs Riley.'

'Some other time, I hope.'

'But if the rest of us are to get underway on schedule, I'm going to have to ask you to leave. We're about to close the doors.'

'You don't need to inform the Ta'argis that I'm getting off, do you?' It was more plea than question.

'I have to fill out an LMC – Last Minute Change – on the load sheet. But that's all. The Ta'argis are notoriously poor with their paperwork, and my handwriting's rubbish. It might be days before they decipher it.'

'Thanks.'

He nodded. She turned to leave.

'Mrs Riley.'

'Yes?'

'On this plane, you're safe. But the other side of that cabin door isn't. You're a long way from home. Please take care.'

Beg slid beneath the water in his bath tub, so slowly he caused barely a ripple. He let out a long sigh as the water closed around him, carrying him away from the weariness that had seeped into every one of his bones, and from the fug of cigarette smoke that had taken over in his bedroom. That was unusual for Beg, he'd often go days without a cigarette, yet sometimes his dark moods would gather and he was a man who preferred to keep his comforts close at hand, totally private. But he'd been surprised to discover there had been a continuous stream of cigarettes in the last couple of hours, ever since the phone call. He'd lost track somewhere along the way. Too much to think about, too many concerns. And his hands hurt so.

Through the window of his bathroom he looked east, to the Celestial Mountains, where the embers of time were being fanned gently back to life. That's where he was from, the mountains, with the villages and communities huddled beneath the peaks, where the herds were still driven up to their summer pastures and where, during winter, when the snow reclaimed the earth, the mountain people gathered round their fires and the *akyns* sang their songs of long ago. Amir Beg had promised himself that one day he would go back there, for good, leave the corruption of the city for the simple wooden chalet he had built beside the Shimmering Lake, where, during the summer months, he would sleep in a felt-covered yurt, like his father had done. No TV. No telephone. Just old ways and enduring loyalties. Leave Karabayev, his casinos and his petty conquests far behind. Slowly he lowered his hands into the water, but quickly lifted them again as the water seemed to scald. The pain was getting worse.

It hadn't always been like this, with Karabayev. There had been a point when they had shared their lives, studied at the Lenin University together, in the Soviet time. It was when the Russians had got stuck in Afghanistan, getting their eyes gouged and their balls hacked off, and the terror had spilled over the mountains into Ta'argistan. Beg and Karabayev had been part of the nationalist movement, kids' stuff, really, but that hadn't saved them. They, and many more, had been rounded up and fed into the vast machinery of retribution and repression that Moscow had kept oiled almost to perfection. Beg had had it worst, three years of it, to the point where he would fall asleep every night praying he wouldn't wake up in the morning. He'd lost count how many times they'd crushed every one of his knuckles with hammers, but he wouldn't submit.

Karabayev's passage through the machine had been altogether smoother, and substantially shorter. Somehow he'd managed to talk his way out, done some sort of deal, so it had been rumoured. He was always doing deals. But what could you trade to get out of a prison cell, except, of course, other lives? And by the time the Russians had retreated from Afghanistan and their empire came crashing down, Karabayev had transformed himself into a symbol of national resistance, while Beg was left to pick up the pieces of his life – not that he could pick up much at all. So Karabayev slept in the Presidential Palace, while Beg chain-smoked through the night.

Through the window, Beg could see the light slowly building up behind the mountains. That was another of his concerns. Something was going on up there, in the shadows of the peaks. In the last few months there had been a noticeable rise in the number of foreigners visiting Ta'argistan – it was officially encouraged, since visitors brought with them vital foreign currency, but too many had been making the trip to the mountains for Beg's taste. They weren't tour operators with an eye to a new market or backpackers chasing spiritual salvation and cheap drugs, these were businessmen with mining connections. The excuse was the old mines down which the Soviets had tipped all their radioactive garbage, and which in the minds of some nervous observers now threatened to turn into some sort of ecological doomsday whose every rad and roentgen would be the match of Chernobyl. So an international consortium had been created to tackle the situation, paid for by international busybodies like the UN and European Union, and administered by foreign companies. That was the obscenity of such projects; fabulous sums of aid were promised by the West, but all of it seemed to end up in the pockets of companies back home. And what in the name of God did thick-necked thugs like Kravitz know about nuclear waste? No, there was something else going on, Beg could feel it in his aching bones. Foreigners had never brought Ta'argistan anything other than death and despair, and those huge dumps of irradiated trash. They came and helped themselves to everything, including the President's wife, then left. Well, not this one. That bastard was going nowhere. Ever.

God help him, but his hands hurt! It was as much as he could do to hold the cigarette that, to his surprise, he was smoking. Here in the bathroom. He shook his head in self-mockery. There was too much going on. Time to sort it. Starting with the foreigners. Well, one, at least.

Martha had to force herself not to run. She paced herself as she walked from the plane back to the VIP lounge. No one was there to stop her, no security to shout foul, no men in well-pressed suits demanding to see her passport. They had all gone to other duties. On the other side of a glass wall the airport was beginning to grow busier, with people milling around waiting for a flight to Istanbul. She could see passengers lining up to have their hand luggage checked; one elderly woman in an embroidered native headdress was quarrelling furiously with an official about her oversized bag that seemed to be stuffed to bursting point with thick *nan* flat breads. Didn't they bake bread in Istanbul, for pity's sake? The cautious customs man was beginning to tear one apart, anxious about what might be inside. The woman screamed in objection, almost in tears. No one looked in Martha's direction.

The door to the VIP room was as she had left it, locked open, when their host had left them alone. She drew it back, very slowly, expecting to be accosted by accusing eyes, but the room was empty and she scurried across to the door on the far side. Then she was through, into the main concourse. No one challenged her. Those in the growing crowd had their own distractions with their unruly children and aged parents, tickets, Tannoy

messages, luggage, or had their attention fixed on the
TV monitors in the waiting area that were showing an
ice-hockey match. A Russian league match. It seemed
the empire wasn't yet dead.

Suddenly she stopped, flooding with alarm. Barely a
few yards away, talking to a security guard with a
dinner-plate hat and a Kalashnikov hooked over his
arm, was the official who had said farewell to her only
minutes earlier in the VIP lounge. It would take only a
turn of his head and she was undone. But he didn't.
She hurried on, through the swing doors and back into
the freezing dawn of Ta'argistan.

The power came back on and the single bulb in the cell
snapped back into life. As his eyes grew accustomed to
the dim light, Harry looked around him. He was in a
space no more than ten feet square, with walls and
floor constructed from rough-hewn stone and substantially older than the Soviet-era prison built above it.
There were no windows, only a small funnel that led
upwards from the ceiling and was connected, he pre-
sumed, to a primitive and spectacularly inadequate
ventilation system. There were bars across the funnel,
which in any event was too small for a man to slip
through.

This had once been a storage cellar, Harry guessed,
and he was surprised how damp it seemed and how
much moss and slime grew on its walls, until he realized that the damp was condensation created by the

prisoners, whose bodies provided the only source of heat. The cell was entirely devoid of furniture except for a rough wooden pallet six inches off the floor, on top of which lay a thin straw palliasse stained so deeply that it was impossible to tell anything about the colour of the original covering. It was riddled with holes where the rats had gnawed. A slop bucket glowered from the far corner. Apart from that, and the solitary bulb, there was nothing else, except for the pervading stench of things rotten from which he couldn't escape, even when he closed his eyes. It was like being buried at the bottom of a medieval garbage pit. Harry had been in worse places – always when he found himself in difficulties, he reassured himself that he'd seen worse and survived. Only problem was, right now, that he couldn't remember when. Now he realized why Zac had been so determined to press on him the chess piece; it was a connection with the world outside, fuel for the imagination, something that might sustain hope. A few hours in this place and that tiny horse would grow to almost mythical dimensions.

But Harry wouldn't be here long. Already he was forming a plan. The prison's security had been tried and found wanting, the bolts on the door were disgracefully ill-fitting and the battered lock was loose. What more did he need, apart from a little luck? He had a way out, by the same route he'd broken in, and although the lighting and CCTV had been restored, they would only prove a problem if the guards lifted their heads from their trough. Yet they were bound to be dozy, and he would be quick, like a rat in the shadows. He would be out tonight, once it was fully dark, so long as no one looked too closely in the meantime and they left him alone. Why, he reassured himself, once he was on the other side of this door he was already halfway there!

The sound of approaching activity echoed along the passageway, interrupting his thoughts. The morning breakfast inspection was underway, but not yet close at hand. Harry hated simply sitting still, waiting, while his mind was agitated and his imagination on fire. He had a little time before the inspection arrived with its inquisitive eyes, so he crossed to the door, the barrier between him and his escape route, the door that had swung open so easily during the night. Too easily, perhaps? He couldn't afford for a loose lock to arouse suspicion. On the other hand, he needed to be able to break it once more.

He nudged the door. It was satisfactorily tight. He put a shoulder to it, with the same result. A flood of uncertainty began to leap around him. He squeezed his body between the doorjambs, placing his back against one and his foot against the other, and heaved with all his strength, then heaved again, and again, until his heart began pounding in his ears.

Nothing.

Without Mourat's persuasive talents and four tons of

pressure from the hydraulic spreader, the lock was going nowhere.

And neither was Harry.

Martha stood in the shadows of the airport car park beneath the branches of a leafless tree, struggling to come to terms with the enormity of what she had done. God in Heaven, it was cold. She wasn't prepared for this, had rushed, been impulsive, was wearing clothing that was entirely inadequate for standing in a car park, let alone anything else. She had brought nothing with her, apart from the contents of her handbag.

As she cowered beneath the tree, shivering, trying to struggle through the thick mud of uncertainty oozing into every corner of her mind, she heard the whine of aircraft engines. Two Pratt & Whitney turbofans were roaring, rising in pitch until the air around her started to shake. As she watched, the flight to London rose into the early morning sky. Within twenty minutes it would be out of Ta'argi airspace. Zac Kravitz was on his way home.

She found no sense of exhilaration. An icy wind bit at her ankles and carried away with it the courage that had bubbled through her only a short while before. She was standing in the corner of some foreign plot, freezing, and suddenly frightened of her own stupidity. It was all very well being carried off in the heat of the moment, but there was work to be done. Harry's life might depend upon her. She realized that she hadn't the slightest idea what she should do.

He sat on the filthy straw, his mind brimming with despair. If he couldn't get out of this putrid cell, Harry knew he was lost, totally and most comprehensively screwed. On this side of the door, there was nothing for him but disaster.

He scanned the cell once more, desperate for something he might have overlooked, but he found only scratchings on the wall. A date, from seven years ago. A phrase in Russian he couldn't translate but which looked like a prayer. And a name. Polina. With a single word beside it. *Proshaite.* Farewell.

He dragged his thoughts away from what these marks implied; he had other priorities. He could hear the morning inspection drawing closer, and he began to reassess his own situation, realizing how vulnerable he was, particularly with the light back on. He cursed his idiocy – he still had Julia's watch on his wrist. His lucky charm. Yet it seemed to have lost its magical powers, had even become dangerous, was something that could betray him. It had to be hidden, the head torch, too, which had been tossed into a corner during the chaos of Zac's departure. The only hiding place was in the straw palliasse, and he quickly stuffed them into one of the rat holes, just in time. There was a clatter outside the door; he curled himself into a ball, like a hedgehog, back to the door, and stirred only enough to show that he was still alive.

There was a crash as a hatch at the bottom of the door was swung open and a metal bowl pushed through, scraping along the floor. Suddenly, Harry tasted fear, a cold, metallic sensation in the back of his throat that persisted, no matter how hard he tried to swallow. He became aware that the guard hadn't gone, and was watching him through the grille.

'Food, you bastard. Move!' the guard growled, kicking the door.

Harry had to obey. He rolled over, very slowly, tried not to catch the guard's eye, hung his head, collected the bowl, crawled back. The bowl contained a foul mess of porridge with some form of animal fat mixed in, coagulated, cold, made from oats milled so roughly that the husks came along too. No spoon. He tipped the bowl, took a mouthful, had to struggle to force it down; it tasted of soap. The guard was still watching. Harry took another small mouthful. Only then did the guard disappear.

Dejectedly, Harry climbed from his mattress, moved across to the slop bin, and poured the rest of the mess away.

Martha wasn't the sort to dwell on her misery. Dealing with her father had taught her that. She sat in a taxi making the trip back into town, past the power station, its chimneys belching new smoke into the skies. Around her the people of Ashkek were stepping out to their daily grind, wrapped in caps or headscarves against the cold, waiting for clapped-out buses with grimy windows and dirt splashed up their sides. At an intersection the taxi drew up alongside a police car, an aged Lada, and she had to struggle against the temptation to give herself away by sinking down into her seat and revealing her guilt. Already the driver was studying her in the mirror, a frown scratched across his face; did he suspect?

'Where?' the driver asked as the taxi drew away, its exhausted suspension giving a heave as it found yet another pothole. Martha merely waved down the road towards the city centre. She didn't know where to go.

She desperately needed help. Yet Britain had no embassy in Ta'argistan. There was an honorary consul, should she contact him? Or the US Embassy? But they would be able to do nothing except ask questions – questions that Harry could ill afford to have answered. She thought about trying to phone the Foreign Office in London, but back there it was barely past midnight and by that time of night the princes had turned back into frogs. For now she was stranded in a strange place with no man to shout at, other than a taxi driver who understood scarcely a word of English. She was helpless. She felt fear closing around her like a fist, just as though she were still waiting for the creak of her father's footstep on the stairs. Somehow now, as then, it felt as though it were all her fault.

'Where? Where?' the driver demanded yet again as they started hitting the suburbs.

Suddenly she realized there was only one place she could go.

'The Fat Chance Saloon!' she shouted in the driver's ear, as though sheer volume would force its way past any lack of comprehension.

He scowled, waggled a finger in his abused ear, and put his foot down.

Amir Beg was also being driven through the capital. He no longer saw the huddled masses and the decaying streets that in his youth had fuelled his passions and screamed to him of injustice; nowadays his cares were more directly personal. He knew he was obsessive, couldn't let things go, wouldn't delegate or trust others. It was a fault, but it was his nature. That's why he'd been alarmed by Harry Jones. Beg had recognized in him another remorseless soul who wouldn't pass things by. But now he was gone, and Beg was relieved. Time for unfinished business. The American, Kravitz.

He wouldn't be the first to die at Karabayev's insistence. Wasn't it an indisputable fact that the entire wretched country was dying? The President was a dangerous and vindictive man, and Beg was in no doubt that if he put a foot wrong, it would be his turn, too. The dreams he and Karabayev had once shared together had long since burned in the fires of the other man's ambitions.

Beg had new dreams. In them, the President was strung up beside the foreign prisoner, his neck bent, his body swinging lifeless. In one snap of the trapdoor Ta'argistan would have been cleansed of two sources of infection, the years of growing humiliation that Beg had suffered at the other man's hands set aside. Yet, for the moment, at least, it was nothing more than a dream. Today, only one would die.

The sun was rising above the streets, the day moving forward. It was time.

'The Castle,' he snapped at his driver.

CHAPTER TEN

The guard, whose name was Bolot, turned from Harry's door and began retracing his footsteps, his mind whirling as he tried to decode the meaning of what he'd just seen. It made no sense. He was barely nineteen, had only been in the job a few months, yet he wasn't an idiot and knew that surprises weren't welcome, least of all down here in the Punishment Wing. His anxiety quickened his pace, and soon he was running, his footsteps echoing back from the stones until he had reached the security gate. He began rattling the bars, demanding he be let through.

'Who put the bee up your bum?' his colleague on the other side muttered, dragged from his magazine and reaching lazily for the keys.

'Come on, camel breath!' Bolot spat in impatience.

'What's the matter, your sister caught crabs or something?' the other man replied, making a point of fiddling with the keys, very slowly, taunting. When at last he unlocked the gate, he was almost bowled over as Bolot rushed through and past him.

'She didn't have crabs the last time I fucked her!' the

other guard called after him, but in vain. Bolot didn't stop, vaulting up the steps to the main level two at a time.

Bolot was a straightforward, unimaginative soul, a minor link in the chain of command. It was his intention to report to the duty captain. The captain was a sanctimonious prick, to be sure, married to Bolot's cousin, on whom he cheated regularly, but he was the one who had provided Bolot with the job in the prison in the first place, and he was the one in charge of the duty roster. With luck, after what he was about to report, Bolot reckoned he might get a promotion away from the breakfast slop duty, and maybe even extra leave. The thought drove him on, too impetuously, for as he flung himself into the officer's room he found not the captain but no less than the deputy governor, his balding head bending over his breakfast.

The deputy governor looked up, a face ready to spit bullets. 'This had better be good,' he growled in warning, his lips dribbling crumbs of bread.

Bolot hesitated, panting from his exertions and the excitement. 'It's . . . it's . . .'

'Get on with it!'

'The American, sir.'

The deputy governor's eyebrow rose, suddenly cautious. 'What about the American?'

'I think he's wearing sports shoes . . .'

Martha had always been impetuous, ever since . . . well, ever since she'd left home. One of her first lessons in life, get your retaliation in first, girl, while their minds are off duty, halfway up your thighs. Never stand still long enough to encourage them, always move on, and that's what she'd done, from every relationship she'd ever formed, even from her marriage. No sticking place. That's why men, even her political masters, had so much difficulty dealing with her, and why she'd never made it to the ministerial corridor; she pretended it was prejudice, glass ceilings and all that misogyny crap, but it was also partly down to her. She growled at them like a Rottweiler even while she was running, kept ducking responsibility, never allowing anyone to know how scared she was.

So why was she still here? She could simply have kept running, stayed on the aircraft, as they'd agreed, but something had got to her.

Harry. Bloody Harry, that's what. Turning her world on its head.

Yes, she'd like to be back on his bed, making a mess of his sheets, no denying it. She might distrust a man's intentions but she still had her needs. Yet it was more than that. She'd found herself being drawn not just to the muscle but also to the man inside. She recognized a fellow sufferer, another wanderer in the desert, someone who would understand. Why else had she blurted out all that stuff about her father?

She was tired of running away, putting on a front, smiling when she hurt, pretending it didn't matter all the nights she was on her own with no one for company, still waiting for a creak on the stair. Yet now, as she stood freezing in front of the Fat Chance, she found herself growing ever more confused. She'd stayed behind, for Harry, but Harry wasn't here and she didn't know what to do. The place was shut tight, the door locked. Silent. She chided herself. What else could she have expected? This was a club for middle-aged jazz freaks and spotty Internet junkies, assorted insomniacs who wouldn't be crawling back into circulation for hours yet. God, she was acting like a teenager.

Damn you, Harry, for messing around with my life.

She'd had a teddy bear, when she was young, with grazed fur and a torn ear, that she used to hold, and talk to while her father sweated onto her chest. She still had it, tucked into her bed, waiting for her. How many nights had she run back from the Parliament, with both praise and protests ringing in her ear and the world thinking she was made of polished glass, only to cry into a pillow alongside her precious toy? If only the world had known the truth. For some reason, she wanted Harry to know.

A policeman stood on the street corner, idly watching her. He didn't seem suspicious, not yet, saw nothing but legs and well-cut clothes, but soon his idle curiosity might breed questions. She couldn't run that risk, because she could give him no answers. So she hurried on.

The deputy governor, Sergei Anisimov, was in no mood for distractions. He'd just been told that Amir Beg was on his way, which was why he was trying to gobble down the last of his breakfast. God knew when he might next eat, could be hours. He'd already completed a rapid tour of inspection, checking that nothing had burned down during the night, and he'd found everything in reasonable shape, and better shape than usual after being spruced up for the visit of the foreign politicians. But sports shoes? The guard was clearly drunk, or had spent too long sniffing up the atmosphere of the Punishment Wing; there could be no other explanation, unless while Anisimov had been off duty they'd drifted into some parallel and entirely ludicrous universe. Being off duty wouldn't save him if something was amiss, of course, the governor would make sure of that. Yet Bolot's report made no sense. Prisoners didn't wear shoes, not on the Punishment Wing. How the hell were you supposed to beat a prisoner's feet or extract his toenails until he poured out every last bit of information if he was wearing bloody sports shoes? That wasn't the way things worked, it made no sense, but Anisimov could take nothing for granted, not with Amir Beg descending. He looked despairingly at his unfinished breakfast, then turned angrily on Bolot, who flinched, but there was no option. He'd have to see for himself. With a sigh, he scraped back his chair and set off for the Punishment Wing.

Harry heard them coming all the way along the passage, men in a hurry, their boots noisy as they clipped the stone floor. He sensed trouble, curled himself up into a ball once more, making himself as inconspicuous and anonymous as possible. He couldn't make out what they were saying from outside the cell, but he felt their eyes on him. He lay totally still, trying to ignore whatever had crawled out from the mattress and was biting him.

Anisimov, like Governor Akmatov a few hours before him, didn't enter the cell. He didn't need to. He saw not only sports shoes but also a belt, and despite the dirt and the rents that Harry had torn in his clothing they were of too good a quality for any inmate in this wing. Harry had dealt with the wristwatch and the torch, but in the dark, and in the rush, it hadn't been enough.

There was another reason why Anisimov wouldn't go in. He was afraid. He was the creature of a System that required an order to things, everything in its proper place. The System didn't welcome surprises. Yet something extraordinary had happened in this cell, and that spelt danger.

'Who's been here?' he demanded.

'No one, sir,' the guard replied, 'apart from you and me. And the governor, last night.'

The deputy's heart missed a beat, then another. 'The governor was here, you say?'

'Yessir.'

'Why?'

'I don't know, sir.'

'And what did he do?'

'Nothing. He didn't even go in. He just made a quick inspection and left.'

The words effected a miraculous cure upon Anisimov's faltering pulse, which now began to race like a galloping horse. The matter grew murkier with every minute, and he knew he was best out of it. There was a fundamental rule of survival, one which towered above all the others. Don't get involved. Stand too close and you were certain to get spattered. He was glad he hadn't gone into the cell, because he sensed that this particular puddle of shit was so deep that a man might disappear in it entirely. This was a problem he should pass to those higher up the food chain – and they didn't come better fed than Governor Akmatov. His boss was a man who, up to now, had played the System to perfection, much to his deputy's frustration, but he had grown long in the tooth, idle from office, was slowing up. In other words, victim material. And in this world a man's future could change overnight, especially after a night such as this.

The System wasn't sophisticated, its pleasure lay in its simplicity. It didn't demand undue competence, merely that you didn't get caught – either with your hand in the wrong pocket, or standing too close to someone else's disaster. When boats rocked, it was necessary to throw some of the baggage overboard in order to restore the balance, and Akmatov made such splendid ballast. Anisimov didn't view it as betrayal, merely business. Get this right, the deputy concluded, and he could be sitting in Akmatov's chair by nightfall, enjoying all the privileges that attended the job – an almost new Volkswagen, a share in a *dacha* in the mountains, his own lavatory. He might even be able to get his wife's younger and far more adventurous sister on to the payroll, with all the daily distractions that would offer. Keep it in the family.

He hurried back down the passage, his imagination harvesting the possibilities. Why, he and the governor shared the same initials, the change wouldn't even give the System wind. For the first time that morning, the deputy broke into a broad smile.

She had to stop wandering pointlessly. It wasn't just that her shoes were impractical and her feet were frozen. This was a moment in Martha Riley's life that would mark it forever, measure her as both a friend and a woman, and right this minute she was failing on both counts. She sat in a coffee shop with her third cup of cappuccino, staring at the bill, trying to pretend she was as tough as everyone thought she was. Yet she had only her handbag, a small amount of local currency, and still no idea what she should do next.

She paid the bill and took a tissue from her handbag to wipe her nose, damp from the cold outside air. She made an inspection of the bag's other contents, because it was all she had. A hairbrush and makeup to wipe away the signs of worry. Her reading glasses, which she used as rarely as possible, and usually only in private. Perfume. Mints. Panty liners. Her purse and her credit cards. There was also her MP's pass; it was of no use here and might even compromise her, but it also reminded her of what she was supposed to be about. This handbag and its contents would have to be her armoury. So where to start? Silly question. Credit cards, of course.

A brisk walk through the late morning air and she was in the local department store. It was unlike anything she was used to back home. Outside it boasted a big neon sign, but inside its four floors were filled with individual stalls, boutiques, single traders, like a street market, except many of the pitches were abandoned and most of the space on the fourth floor was empty, echoing like a hollow tunnel. Even here, tucked away in a far corner of the world, the recession had sharp teeth. The stalls were piled with everything from cheap leather goods and children's wear to mobile phones and mementoes of the Soviet time, bric-a-brac, and bargains even at the official exchange rate. She could have picked up hand-woven silks and a fur hat, but her attention was drawn to a Red Army medal commemorating the Battle for Berlin, its striped ribbon stained, the metal dull. *Berlina.* 2 May 1945. Less than ten pounds. She haggled a little, bought it. For Harry. A homecoming present, when he got out . . .

She moved on, knowing she must be more practical. What she needed much more than a medal were stout new shoes, and a ski jacket in case she was forced to spend more time out on the streets. Yet her thoughts kept coming back to Harry. When he got out, however he got out, he would need new clothes, particularly after swimming through the sewer, so she bought a large rucksack and filled it with what she thought would be appropriate, conjuring up his body in her mind, guessing his size. Part of her enjoyed the process. It filled a couple of hours, while she waited.

Amir Beg listened carefully to what the deputy governor had to say. He didn't understand everything that had happened, any more than Anisimov did, but he was in no doubt as to the potential fallout. Somehow, it seemed, the prisoner in the cell was not the American. Beg's mouth went dry as he considered the possible consequences. For this failure he would skin every guard in the place, if necessary, and Akmatov in particular, but he was under no illusion that the skin most under threat right now was his own, because less than an hour earlier he had told his President that the man they had caught for screwing his wife and making such a fool of him was about to get his neck stretched all the way to the highest point in the Celestial Mountains. Karabayev had demanded photographs, as usual.

Anisimov stood close by, expectant, but his hopes of gratitude and immediate elevation were to be disappointed. He'd expected Beg to lead a charge down to the cell, break a few of the prisoner's bones and drag the truth from him, uncover some conspiracy for which the governor would bear the blame, but instead Beg seemed to draw in upon himself, lost in thought. There was no excitement, his apprehension unmistakable. Anisimov sensed the moment had moved away from them both. 'May I ask what's wrong, sir?' he asked tentatively.

'I came here to hang him,' Beg replied quietly.

Now Anisimov understood. The System was uncompromising, totally unforgiving. It must win. It neither made mistakes itself, nor permitted mistakes in others. He had brought disastrous news, news of failure, which therefore became his news and now placed him in the line of fire. He had gambled and lost. His ambitions began to collapse around him like a snow face in spring.

'Who else knows about this?' Beg snapped, ripping off his glasses.

'Why, no one, apart from the two of us, and the guard.' He watched in growing alarm as Beg's teeth bit into one of his white knuckles in a fusion of concentration and pain. 'I'm sorry, sir,' Anisimov blurted, 'if your plans have to change.'

Beg glanced sharply into the face of the deputy governor, his dark, naked eyes bright, burning in desire, like a hunting stoat. 'No, nothing changes. We carry on.'

It was gone midday by the time Martha returned to the Fat Chance. She had eaten, felt warmer in her new jacket, more confident. The door was still shut but she could see a light shining behind it and the sound of someone cleaning coming from below. There was no knocker, no bell, so she pounded on the wooden panel.

It was some time before she heard the footsteps. The lock rattled, the door swung slowly open. It was Benazir. Her tired eyes flooded with surprise as they saw Martha, then quickly darkened and she began to close the door. Only Martha's foot prevented it. She had to use her full weight to force her way in.

'You're not wanted here. Get out!' Benazir spat as she was forced backwards.

'I need your help,' Martha said, trying to fathom the reason for the outburst of fury.

'But we need none of yours. Now go!' The older woman pointed with a trembling finger.

It is one of the aspects of politics that those who choose to practise it have to grow accustomed to abuse. It arrives as regularly as rain and they must weather the storm. Martha didn't flinch. Instead she pushed past the mother's restraining hand and ran down into the cellar. For a little while Benazir didn't budge, trying by force of will to get Martha back out onto the street, but eventually she realized it wasn't going to be quite as simple as that; her unwanted guest was just as stubborn and no respecter of manners. As Martha sat herself down at one of the tables, its top still stained and sticky from the night before, she heard Benazir bustling down the stairs after her. When she appeared, her face was contorted with fury.

'You almost got my son killed!' she spat.

'He is a brave boy.'

'He is *my* boy!'

'We need to get Harry out,' Martha replied, shifting the ground, determined to remain calm.

'Then you go and do it, but you'll not get a finger lifted here to help you.'

'Why are you so angry?'

'Bektour. You put him in great danger, almost got him locked up with your friend. And no one gets out of that place.'

That wasn't entirely true, as she'd only just put Zac on the plane, but there seemed little point in getting pedantic. 'We were unlucky,' Martha said.

'And your rotten luck is staying with you, no one else. No one asked you to come here, so now I tell you to go.'

'We can't just leave Harry to rot.'

The woman's thin lips twisted in contempt, every furrow on her face growing deeper, making her look a hundred years old. 'He's not going to rot, he's going to *die.*'

The word sang out, freezing Martha as though she stood in a mountain wind, despite the new jacket.

'And he's going to do it on his own,' Benazir continued, 'not with my son!'

And Martha knew, not so much from the words but from the strength of the passion, that she would never change this woman's mind. Even so, she shook her head in defiance. 'I can't leave him.'

'You can get on a plane and fly.'

'No, it's . . . not as simple as that.' Damn it, she was

supposed to be at 35,000 feet on a flight to Heathrow right now. 'It's not as simple as that,' she repeated, more softly, her voice falling, betraying her confusion. Benazir recognized it for what it was, and her own tone softened a fraction. She wiped a greying lock of hair from her eyes as she bent over Martha.

'You love him. I pity you. All love is madness, which in the end betrays a woman, leaves her in pain. But we cling to it while we can, so you will understand why I will not help you. I love Bektour, he is all I have, and I will not give him up to you and your madness.'

'But Harry will find some way out, I know he will.'

'He will die in there.'

'Either way, until we hear, I'm staying. And this is the only place I have, the only place he knows.'

'I will not let you stay.'

'Then you'd better call the police and explain what I'm doing here,' Martha said, struggling out of her new coat, setting up camp in order to make her point. 'I'll just sit here and wait for them, shall I?'

Benazir stared defiantly, locked in a clash of competing loves, but she knew that Martha had won this round. The wretched woman was right, she couldn't afford to make too much of a fuss and risk drawing attention to what had gone on, least of all to Bektour's role in it. With a snort of frustration that indicated the matter was far from settled, she went back to her cleaning, confident that her love as a mother would far outlast the feelings of this woman.

She wasn't the first to have underestimated Martha Riley.

Harry began to make a meticulous search of his cell. He checked every corner, every crevice. The mortar was old but had been used sparingly, since the stones were well faced and tightly laid. None of them was going to leap into his hands and offer him a way out. He peered particularly closely at the bars on the ventilation flue, even hanging from them to test their strength. It was while he was hanging that he noticed another scratching on a stone, high up on the wall. He brushed a finger across it to wipe away the damp and reveal its message.

Dmitri Panov. Hanged Himself. Fuck Them All.

The date was indecipherable. Harry reckoned it might have been scratched during any of the past hundred years. Perhaps he'd used a shirt or his trousers as a ligature, maybe his belt, even shoelaces. And, in the process, Dmitri had proved that these bars weren't going to shift.

Harry had tried to resist, but he'd been forced to use the slop bucket, which was full almost to the point of overflowing. Zac's bucket. By now he'd be touching down at Heathrow, explaining to bemused immigration officials what it was all about, with the help of Sid Proffit. They'd be a fuss, of course, in a typically quiet and restrained British way. Discreet enquiries over tea in the Foreign Office. Harry hoped they'd hurry about it; he wasn't getting out of here on his own any time soon.

Or they might simply crawl away in embarrassment at this foul-up he had caused, just as the Americans had with Zac. Bloody Harry Jones. Not their problem.

When he was finished with the slop bucket Harry wrenched off its handle and used it to attack the door, but the primitive tool bent pathetically. Over the course of the next couple of hours he tried several times to shift the lock, at first wedging his body between the door jambs in any number of imaginative ways, even tearing a length of wood from the pallet on which his mattress was spread, using it as a crowbar, then a battering ram, and finally a hammer. The result was always the same. Nothing. Eventually the wood splintered and fell apart, yet his growing sense of doom forced him on, his mind trying to conjure up feats of Herculean proportions that would rip the lock from its housing. He'd be happy if it shifted even a little, but soon he began to tire, and as his strength seeped away, so did his sense of invincibility. He was no longer the young warrior who could never die. That was years ago, and anyway it had never been true.

He found himself drawn back to the wristwatch, Julia's gift, hidden in the verminous straw, rubbing its face for encouragement, but it soon became like an hourglass whose sand was trickling inexorably away. He had no choice. Somehow, he'd have to get them to open the door for him. He sat back and waited.

His mind wandered back to Dmitri Panov. Who was he? Had he a family? What was his crime? And what had driven him to kill himself? What horrors had he known? It was thinking about Dmitri that made Harry realize he'd made a most terrible mistake. Whatever the poor bastard had hanged himself with, it wasn't a belt or his bloody shoelaces. No, they would never have made it that easy for him, Dmitri wouldn't have been allowed to keep such things. And, as Harry looked down at his trainers and Bond Street belt, he knew he must have given his own game away.

He cursed himself violently. He was undone.

He heard them coming for him, down the passageway, their feet pounding out their purpose. Four of them. Very official. In step. Like a beating drum. And suddenly his wish was granted, the cell door was thrown open, but it did him no good. They hauled him to his feet, and almost before he knew it they had manacled his hands behind his back and secured a leather strap around his chest, so tight it made breathing difficult, then used it to drag him into the passageway.

His mind was racing as he tried to keep up with the guards, but his feet were suddenly treacherous, stumbling. The guards took his weight and dragged him on. Everything was a blur, the pale corridor lights flashing past him, and he tried to scream in protest but he couldn't get his breath. He desperately needed to tell them. They were going the wrong way! Turned left out of the cell, not to the right, and he knew that way led only to one place.

The Hanging Room.

*

The aircraft was less than an hour from Heathrow when Sid Proffit waved for one of the cabin crew. The flight path had taken them over Russia so he'd left matters late, wanting to make sure they were over familiar territory. The young attendant tried to ignore the summons; she was busy with the pre-landing checks, and he'd had more than his share of the wine, drinking not excessively but mechanically, methodically, not for pleasure but, it seemed, from need, ever since they'd started serving breakfast, as though he needed to deaden some deep seated pain. But he was insistent. He even took the handkerchief from the breast pocket of his suit and flapped it in the air. She bent warily over his seat.

'We have a little problem,' he announced.

She said nothing, her eyes defensive, hard, but they began to melt in disbelief as he talked. The passenger flying under the name of Harry Jones wasn't him at all. He wasn't a criminal, but it was a delicate diplomatic situation. All a bit of a tangle, really . . . Not until Proffit had produced his parliamentary pass did she even begin to take him seriously, and still she suspected the old goat was trying to proposition her, but a lord was a lord, no matter how much he'd had to drink. She knew she needed to talk to the captain.

The captain left his flight deck and came back into the cabin with considerable reluctance, but the cabin attendant's story and his own earlier encounter with Martha were enough to ring alarm bells. He listened as the peer recounted his tale, which by the time he'd finished seemed to involve a head-on collision with almost everything that was solid and immovable: the criminal law, human rights, airline protocols, passport controls, parliamentary privilege, diplomatic relations, not to mention his own company's rulebook.

Yet whatever doubts the captain harboured were pushed aside by the sight of the man sitting next to Proffit. Whoever he was, he needed help. The strain of his imprisonment and escape had caught up with Zac, the shot he'd been given had long since faded, leaving him scarcely conscious and barely coherent, drifting in and out of sleep even as the captain tried to talk to him. Truth was, he was probably unfit to travel and shouldn't have been allowed on the aircraft in the first place. Neither did he look much like the photo in his passport. Something else they'd probably throw at the captain. He was regretting getting up that morning.

'He needs medical help,' the peer said.

'I'll see to it. Have it waiting when we land.'

'And the police.'

'By the sounds of things, you'll be needing the entire British army.'

'I fear it's too late for that,' Proffit said, his voice cracking with concern.

He was being dragged along the passageway, head down, the sweat running into his eyes. He couldn't see much, only shapes. Suddenly Harry was blinded by a shaft of brilliance spread from a door that was opening up ahead of him, and he was being kicked and man-handled up the short steps leading to it. He blinked, tried to clear his vision. Through the blur and haze a face came into view, standing in the light, blocking the way. It was Amir Beg.

There was no mistaking the disbelief that stretched across the Ta'argi's normally impassive features. Whatever, or whomever, he had been expecting, it wasn't this. And Harry's heart leapt.

'You've got the wrong man! You know me. I'm Harry Jones!'

Beg stared at him, a long while, his face slowly reforming itself before he replied. 'In this place,' he said quietly, 'there are no names. Only numbers.' And he stepped aside.

Harry stumbled. When he raised his head from the floor, he saw the unblinking eye of the noose, staring down at him. It must be a joke, they couldn't be serious, but he wasn't appreciating the humour. 'This is a mis-take!' he cried out. But they were bundling him towards the steps of the scaffold.

Harry tried to resist, was desperate to struggle his way free, but they bound his legs, too, guards pressing down with their knees upon his back as he lay spread-eagled on the rough wooden treads. His resistance faded into nothing more than a pathetic wriggle. They dragged him forward, his face scratching raw across the final steps, then they hauled him to his feet, trussed like a chicken.

He was standing at the centre of a crude trapdoor, his feet on a roughly painted white cross. Three men beside him. They jerked his chin up. He felt the noose being lowered around his neck.

It was coarse, scratched him, he could feel stray fibres of hemp sticking into his neck.

Come on, guys, this is a joke. Gone far enough . . .

Beneath him, he saw a guard with a camera, pointed at him, already taking photographs. Harry remembered the display spread across the wall.

'You're making a mistake!' Harry shouted, but the words caught in his throat. 'I haven't even had a trial.'

One of the guards, who understood a little English, burst into mocking laughter. Then he pulled at the rope, tightening the noose. Harry could feel the heavy knot nestling behind his left ear, smell the guard's sour breath.

God, forgive me, for whatever I have done . . .

The seconds that had dashed past at the gallop now seemed to stand still. All became quiet. The guards stepped away from him. In the middle of the floor, staring up at him, stood Amir Beg. Harry could hear the camera shutter clicking. And his heart pounding.

He had been close to death many times before, but never like this. In an abattoir.

Death is a soldier's profession, and Harry had never complained. He'd always hoped he would die like a man, even though he had no idea what that meant. Except this wasn't it. Look Death in the eye, spit in his face, but all Harry could see was Amir Beg, a tight, thin smile marked on his face, like a scar.

He seemed to have been standing there for half of eternity. Harry wondered if that was it, if he had already died and Death was simply the last image of life captured and preserved forever, so that he would be left staring into Amir Beg's eyes for the rest of time. Yet when he shook his head, he felt the noose scratching, and knew what was still to come.

They were about to kill him. Part of him wanted to scream, to offer them anything they asked, if only they would let him live, but they wanted nothing, except to see him hang, even better if he broke to pieces.

Yet who gives a fuck about them? Do it your way, Harry. For you!

He stood, as tall as he could, struggling to keep his balance despite his bonds, his mind now uncluttered, his thrashing heart suddenly slowing.

Do it your way, Harry . . .!

Life's most closely held secret was what followed, when living was done, and he was about to discover the truth.

Amir Beg had lifted his right hand, raised his crown of crippled knuckles. It was the sign.

CHAPTER ELEVEN

Beg stopped the execution. Harry had braced himself, trying to pretend he didn't care, when Beg's voice rang out. One word.

Stop.

Harry was only half aware as the guards dragged him back to his cell, undid his bonds, took his belt and trainers, and threw him into a corner. Then they gave him a bloody good kicking. That woke him up. When they had done he lay there shivering, and not just from the damp and cold. It was some time before Amir Beg appeared.

Harry hadn't noticed before but the other man was dressed as though for a wedding, in a neat suit, white collar and colourful tie. He stepped into the cell with a cautious foot, anxious not to get his polished shoes caught in anything too unpleasant. He held a white handkerchief to his nose to stifle the stench – a stench Harry had long since ceased to notice or care about.

'Mr Jones,' Beg said, from the far side of the cell, 'this is not what I expected. Not what I expected at all.'

Harry propped himself up against the stone wall.

'I'm delighted to have brought a little interest to your dull day. You must get bored with nothing better to do than hanging innocent men.'

'It should have been your friend, Mr Kravitz, and he can scarcely be accused of innocence. Not when he was discovered in bed with the President's wife.'

Harry moaned and banged the back of his head against the wall in despair. So that was it. A woman. The man hadn't changed. Fuck you, Zac.

'So he was in the wrong bed. And you're in the wrong cell, Mr Jones. Most unfortunate.'

'We all have our weaknesses,' Harry muttered through clenched teeth as his hand inspected his battered ribs; he thought he'd probably cracked a couple.

'You are right. I myself have a weakness, a great one. A need to understand. I suspect you share that weakness. We both have enquiring minds and an inability to pass a problem by. That cost me dear in the Soviet time, just as it has now cost you.' He coughed, cleared his throat. He needed both hands to wipe the handkerchief across his lips. 'Even today I have not learned my lesson,' he continued. 'You see, I could simply have let you hang and the world – my world – would be content. Everything would add up. One crime committed, one prisoner suitably punished. But that wasn't enough for me, you see. I realized that you would have taken with you too many secrets, left behind too many mysteries. How you ended up here. *Why* you ended up here – I am most curious about that, Mr Jones. And, of course, who helped you in all this. I am intrigued. I would like to know. So I have spared you.'

'Sorry to give you sleepless nights.'

'Men with minds like ours often have difficulty sleeping.'

'I suppose it's easier if you've just done a heavy day's work with a noose.'

'We live in an uncertain world. And it is with clearing up a few of those uncertainties that I would like your help.'

Harry stared at Beg, into the dark, pitiless eyes, at the weak, rounded shoulders and the crippled hands. He had to make a judgement, to take the measure of this man and his intentions, and every instinct told him it was pointless. Harry knew he wasn't being spared, he was merely being used. To resolve Beg's uncertainties.

'You're not going to let me walk out of here, are you?'

Beg inclined his head. 'I'm afraid that's not possible. You see, my President . . . like us, he has a weakness, too. An inability to let bygones be bygones. He is a simple, unsophisticated man. He prefers revenge.'

'But you are offering me a deal?'

'In a way.'

'I'm fascinated,' Harry replied drily.

For the first time, Beg took his eyes off Harry in order to compose his words. 'We will all die, Mr Jones, and few of us are allowed to know the moment of our death. But some of us, at least, can determine the manner of our death.'

Harry knew where the other man was headed.

'It's a privilege which not everyone enjoys, to die without pain. A man can suffer so much.'

So that was the deal. Tell Beg everything, so that death would come quickly. Or stretch the process further than his neck and suffer horribly, a process which, in Beg's experienced if mutilated hands, would almost certainly result in Harry telling him what he wanted to know anyway. Harry's eyes wandered up to the bars across the ventilation flue, and the marks on the wall. What had that man been through, before he decided he would end his own life?

'You are a man of considerable experience, Mr Jones. You understand what I mean, I think. A man might die a thousand miserable deaths in a room like this. I offer you the chance to die only once.'

Harry looked around him. He couldn't think of anywhere worse, dying here, like a rat.

'You won't get anything out of me.'

'Oh, I think I will.'

Harry knew he was right. Everyone broke, eventually. At first you gave them only your name, rank and number, but then a little more – controlled release, the NCOs at Hereford called it, but men like Beg were never satisfied, would persist, find the sort of pain that was unendurable, and so you would end up giving them your guts, every yard of them. Anyway, Harry suspected that Beg was the sort of man who would want to make him suffer, for the pleasure he gained of watching a better man cringe and fall apart. His way of showing off his superiority, to himself.

Harry would die. He might not be able to decide when or how he died, but perhaps he might yet be able to decide where he died. It might be the last thing he ever achieved. And he didn't want it to be here, not in this stinking pit, the most wretched place on earth. So, slowly, hurting from his beating, he crawled his way up the wall until he was standing several feet from Beg. His tormentor still had his handkerchief clasped to his face, and was showing a substantial stretch of stiff white shirt cuff.

'I won't die here, not in this room,' Harry said defiantly.

'I don't think you have much choice in the matter, Mr Jones.'

'Let's see, shall we?' And with dexterity and speed that surprised him, given the pain his ribs were causing, Harry picked up the brimming slop bucket and threw the contents full over Amir Beg and his stiff white shirt. The man, and the cell floor, were covered in excrement.

Beg fled through the door, vomiting.

Harry would die, the other man was certain to insist on it. But not here.

Martha made herself comfortable in one of the alcoves, out of sight of Benazir, not wishing to aggravate her any more than was necessary. There she sat, and waited.

It wasn't in her nature to be patient, yet she was discovering many new things about herself on this trip. The reawakening of her emotions. Her ability to improvise, and to trust her instincts; to trust Harry. Her previously unknown capacity for being brave, rather than simply bellicose, and finding the strength to swallow the fear and get on with the job. She had been afraid, terrified, still was. Not the sort of fear that comes because you hate someone, but rather the opposite – the fear that is there because you care, and are afraid of losing what it is you value and love. Harry.

Neither was she the type of woman who would normally remain silent. Every fibre in her body screamed for her to do something, to shout out her lungs and create the most spectacular fuss. The politician's way. But that wouldn't be Harry's way. Sit on the bank of the river and wait for the body of your enemy to float past, he had once said to her, she couldn't remember when. An old Chinese proverb, but it had stuck, so, not knowing what else to do, she waited.

No woman can sit still forever. She needed the toilet. And on the way she discovered a waist-high bookcase, its top covered in globules of ancient candle wax, its shelves crammed with paperbacks, mostly Russian, but to one side she discovered a copy of a novel entitled *Jamilia*, written by Chingiz Aitmatov. The back cover announced that he was a Kyrgyz and the winner of many things, including a Lenin Prize, and that the book was 'the most beautiful love story in the world'. She was in the mood for distraction and it would while away the time. It might even help her understand these strange impenetrable people. She returned to her alcove, the book in her hand, to discover a mug of tea and a plate of bread and jam on the table. Perhaps the other woman had begun to soften. She sat down, sipped, nibbled, and began to read.

It was Bektour, not his mother, who appeared at her side a few minutes later.

'I didn't think I would see you again,' she said.

'Me, neither.' He tried to offer a smile, but it was a tired attempt that couldn't stretch as far as his eyes. His long hair, usually carefully groomed, was tangled.

'Have you heard anything?'

'Something's going on at the prison, something unusual. Amir Beg has arrived. That's not usually a good sign.'

'We have to find out about Harry,' she said, reaching out to squeeze his hand in concern.

'We will. We have a saying. A house with too many draughts can hold no secrets. By this evening our friends in the Castle will be able to tell us what's happening.' He frowned, pushed his tinted glasses back up to the bridge of his nose, as though his eyes might betray him. He was trying to be brave, for her, but his weariness made him clumsy. 'I hope it's not too late,' he said.

Harry got his wish. He wasn't going to die in that cell. Soon after the spluttering form of Amir Beg had disappeared, three guards came in and set about kicking him again. Yet they did it quietly, with no taunts, and without undue force, beating him almost with respect. It wasn't every day a prisoner covered Amir Beg from head to polished toe in total humiliation. This was a man they would remember.

Harry did his best to protect himself, pushing himself into a corner, going limp, trying to ride the blows, hands around his head, but another couple of ribs went and his left eye would be closed for days. While they were laying into him, the boot tips slamming home, he tried to get away from them by withdrawing into himself, focusing his mind on anything but the beating, and he found himself clutching Zac's chess piece. The horse. He hadn't realized he'd been carrying it all this time, even on the scaffold, clutched so tightly in his hand that it had all but sunk into the flesh. Now he understood what it had done for Zac, and what it could do for him. Harry began to ride the horse, away from the straining boots, beyond the cell, right out of this world, until his mind floated into darkness and he could no longer feel the pain.

The guards stopped as soon as he slipped into unconsciousness, and left him, lying in the shit.

It was several hours later when they came back for him. They hauled him back to his feet and dragged him out of the cell. Harry allowed himself a grim smile of satisfaction as he realized they weren't headed for the Hanging Room but in the other direction. He was in so much pain and confusion, and had only one eye open, that he had little idea where they were taking him, but he remembered a short flight of steps, they were dragging him upward, to another level, out of the Punishment Wing. Amir Beg had clearly had enough of the rat's nest of cells for one day. Harry even managed to laugh a little. He might yet die in daylight. One of the guards shook his head in pity. 'Crazy man,' he muttered, as they dragged him on.

An electric buggy was waiting for Sid Proffit and the barely conscious Zac when they got off the plane. An immigration officer stood beside it. He demanded their passports.

'It's not him,' Proffit blurted out in explanation. 'Not Harry Jones.'

'I know that, sir,' the immigration officer replied as they assisted Zac into the buggy. 'I met Mr Jones once, several years ago, when he was a minister in the Home Office. I've even seen you on your hind legs a couple of times, on the telly in the House of Lords.'

'Oh, really. Was I at all interesting?'

'No idea, to be honest. We remember faces more than facts. And yours is an easy one. Not too many who go round looking like Karl Marx nowadays.'

'Karl Marx didn't have his suits made in Savile Row,' the peer huffed.

'He lived just round the corner, sir, in Soho, while he was writing *Das Kapital*.'

'Did he? You seem remarkably well informed.'

'Used to be Special Branch, in my early years.'

The buggy was approaching passport control; the immigration officer nodded to a colleague and they were waved straight through. Shortly after they drew up outside a sick bay. A doctor and nurse were waiting for Zac, who was laid on a cot while they began an immediate inspection. He barely stirred. The immigration officer took Proffit to an adjoining room where cups of tea were waiting. The peer piled in three sugars and sipped greedily; he needed the energy, he was exhausted. Yet as his strength was restored, he grew agitated. 'You must do something about poor Harry,' he insisted.

'Sorry, sir. Not my part of the pitch. Someone will be along soon. But what can you tell me about Mr Kravitz?'

'Not a lot, really. He's simply a friend of Harry's.'

'Then he's a lucky man,' the immigration official replied, and went back to his tea.

It was some while before a police inspector arrived. She was accompanied by a sergeant, and once again Proffit began to recount his tale. There were moments when he struggled to contain his impatience, tempted to pull rank or lean on his many years and demand they take immediate action rather than sitting around in an overheated room sipping hot drinks, but events had taken their toll on his old limbs, and he had no suggestions as to what precisely they should do. What could anyone do for Harry now? So he sighed, answered their questions, told them what he could, while the immigration officer chewed his lip, the inspector leaned forward attentively in her chair, and the sergeant scribbled notes.

'There's Martha, too,' Proffit said. 'Heaven knows what she's up to. She stayed behind to help him, you see. Ran from the plane as the doors were closing.'

'And Mr Jones – what happened to him?' the police inspector asked.

'I don't know! All I know is that Harry went into the prison, and he never came out.'

'A little rash of him, if you don't mind me saying.'

'I do,' the peer protested. 'I regard what he did as an act of singular bravery.'

'Well, we'll see.'

Proffit looked with beseeching eyes towards the immigration officer, but he merely shrugged. As he had said, not his part of the pitch.

'You must help him, quickly,' Proffit pleaded.

'We need to know as much as possible before we can do anything. Can't go blundering in. You understand that, don't you, my lord?' the police inspector said.

'Of course. But only his American friend can tell you more.'

'And the doc says he'll not be fit for questioning for another twenty-four hours,' the immigration official said.

'Ah . . .' The police inspector sighed in resignation, while the sergeant snapped his notebook shut.

'You have to stir yourselves. Pull your fingers out or whatever it is you people do!' Proffit burst out in impatience. 'I fear something terrible is happening.' But his protest was like the last guttering of a candle. He fell back in his seat, exhausted, his beard slumped on his chest.

'We've got to wait for the American. Hang on until then,' the police inspector replied.

'I only pray Harry can hang on, too,' Proffit sighed mournfully.

Martha began reading *Jamilia*, at speed, as she had become accustomed to in her job. It was a story, recounted by a young boy, of frozen hearts, indifference, and family cruelty, of people looking the other way, refusing to see the pain, of the abuse of a young woman, for the reason that she was young, and a woman. Martha's story, too.

Suddenly her tears were blotting the pages.

'Are you all right, Mrs Riley?' Bektour asked as he passed.

She shook her head. 'It's just this stale tobacco smoke,' she lied, wiping her eyes with the back of her hand. 'We don't do this in Britain. I'm not used to it.'

'Get some fresh air,' he suggested. 'I'll be here.'

'I can't. In case . . .' In case Harry turned up. A ridiculous notion, but one she had to cling to.

'Here, take my mobile phone. I'll text if anything happens.' He pushed it across the table.

'You're very kind.'

'And my mother's very frightened. I hope you'll forgive her.'

'I'm frightened, too, Bektour,' Martha whispered, picking up the phone and heading for the door.

The guards threw him to the floor. His hands reached out to cushion the impact of the fall on his cracked ribs; still he gasped in agony. When he looked up he found himself in a wet room, with tiles on the walls as well as the floor, which had a large drainage hole in its middle. Many of the tiles were cracked and others had been replaced in varying shades of off-white. A collection of buckets, brooms, mops and other cleaning paraphernalia stood guard in one corner. There was also a third guard. He was holding a hose.

They instructed him to take off his clothes. Even flexing his shoulder to slip off his shirt made him wince. Soon he was down to his underwear. Boxers, and still remarkably white. 'Mr Klein sends his compliments,' Harry muttered as he dropped them to the floor. The guard with the hose turned on a tap, and Harry braced himself for the barrage of water that was about to come.

Yet it was an anticlimax. Instead of erupting in a gushing fist of water, the hose dribbled and had difficulty in reaching across the room. The guard had to place his thumb across the end to create more pressure, like a gardener watering flowers. Harry laughed gently at yet another absurdity in this clapped-out country. 'Marshal Stalin's compliments, too, I see.' The guard with the hose, hearing the dictator's name, got the joke and nodded ruefully. Harry stepped forward, made the job easier for him. He knew that washing all the crap off wasn't for his benefit but somehow, even at this time, he preferred to be clean.

A little further down the corridor was another room. They escorted Harry there, still naked, dripping wet. They didn't kick or abuse him, but instead grew quiet, as though they were the ones who should be nervous. Harry's heart sank as he stood at the entrance. It was a room about twice as large as his cell, and although it had no windows it was brilliantly lit. At first blush it seemed like an office. There was a large desk with a plain wooden top completely bare except for a glass ashtray, and a comfortable captain's chair positioned behind it. Standing in front of the desk was a simpler, stouter chair. There was a large cupboard against one wall with double doors, a map of Ta'argistan on the opposite wall, and even a coat stand in one corner. There was also a hand basin with a towel hanging beside it. Yet if this was a place of work, it was work of the most appalling kind, for above all the other impressions that Harry was taking on board hovered the sharp smell of antiseptic, not the carefully disguised scent you might find in a place of healing but the sweet-sour, astringent reek that came when the stuff was used in industrial quantities. He looked at the floor. No rug, just bare concrete, painted with thick gloss grey, like a garage. And every leg of the chair in front of the desk was bolted to it.

So it would be here.

Harry was still naked and damp. The guards pushed him forward, sat him in the chair, secured him to it with thick leather straps at his wrists and ankles, and one right around his chest. He groaned as they tightened the strap, above the cracked ribs. When he opened his eyes once more, Amir Beg was there.

He perched on the desk, in front of Harry, sipping a mug of steaming tea. Different glasses, the usual pair still being cleaned of shit. He was staring at Harry's body, his eyes wandering slowly across it, sizing the man up. There was a peculiar passion in his expression, one that made Harry feel desperately uncomfortable, want to cross his legs, hide himself, if only he could. He wondered it there were something sexual in it all. Harry knew what he had to do, try to knock the bastard off course, deflect him, distract him, because there could be no doubting that his intentions would take Harry through the most excruciating moments of his life.

'I see we've both managed to change out of our old shirts,' Harry said.

Beg didn't react, knew Harry's game. 'Please, Mr Jones, let us not quarrel about the past.'

'Agreed. Come on, let's go down the pub and have a beer.'

And the scene was set. They both knew what they

were about. Amir Beg was going to inflict his will upon Harry, in such a manner that what had gone before would be of no consequence. Put the past to rest, and along with it, Harry's future.

For Harry, this was no longer a game of survival. He was going to die in this chair. His only choice, if it could be thought of as a choice, was to see whether he could die on his terms, terms that weren't entirely Amir Beg's. It would be a victory, of sorts. Beg would win the physical contest, of that there was no shred of doubt, but there was another battle, that of the mind, and of the soul, that Harry was still determined to fight, as long as he could.

'I hope you will understand,' Beg said, 'that I admire you, Mr Jones. We have a lot in common.'

'You learn something new all the time.'

'You are a most extraordinary man – no, really. Those scars on your body, they are proof of that. And your willingness to give up your life for a friend.' As he sipped his tea once more, his spectacles began to steam. He polished them with another of his spotless white handkerchiefs. 'A noble gesture. I congratulate you. I assume you succeeded and Mr Kravitz is now out of the country.'

It was a question, not a statement, and Harry knew he was fishing.

'Harry Jones. Member of Parliament. London SW1A 0AA. Sorry, I don't have a serial number any more, so I've given you the post code.'

'Don't underestimate me, Mr Jones. We are both experienced at what we do. You know I will get what I want eventually. And the sooner you cooperate, the sooner it will be over.'

'My life, you mean.'

'Your suffering.' Beg rose from his perch and moved across to the cupboard. Taking a small key from his pocket, he inserted it into the primitive lock, and the doors swung open. As he saw what was inside, Harry felt his stomach trying to escape through the back of his throat. Every shelf was packed with items that had been gathered for one purpose, to inflict so much horror upon whoever sat in this chair that they would do whatever Amir Beg asked.

The Ta'argi picked up a hammer, the sort with a heavy head that was used to crush rocks or bricks. 'I know what's going through your mind, Mr Jones. I've been in your position, remember. Waiting. For whatever happens next.' He cradled the hammer in his hands, like a father inspecting his newborn child. 'They broke my hands, you see, the Soviets. Knuckle by knuckle. And when they had healed, they broke them all over again. I'm reminded of that every day of my life. So much pain. But what you remember most, even more than the pain of the flesh, is the pain of waiting. The fear of the unknown. Simply not knowing what's going to happen to you. You understand that, don't you? Your imagination fills with all sorts of horror.' He looked at Harry, could smell his fear. 'You see, I meant what I said. We have a lot in common.'

'You cracked. You gave the Soviets what they wanted.'

'But of course. Everyone does. In time.'

'I guess Mr Karabayev must have cracked a whole lot sooner, then. Clever man. He seems to have got out with much less trouble.'

Harry could see he had hit a target. Beg's face darkened, almost flinched, the anger bubbling through like a mountain spring. 'Our President is a parasite,' he whispered.

'Yet you do his dirty work.'

'I do *my* work!' Beg snapped. 'And one day I shall dance and sing on his grave.'

'You sound as if you might volunteer to dig it, too.'

Beg's body stiffened in passion. 'You know, we have a law, passed after the Soviet time, that any man seeking to be President must show he can speak a little Ta'argi. A marker, a sign that we have grown up. That we are free in our own land.' He ran his tongue along lips that were thin, dry. 'Can you imagine what he did?'

'My imagination's pretty stimulated right now.'

'One thirty-second television broadcast. That *I* wrote for him. For which *I* rehearsed him.' He pounded his chest with a crooked hand, claiming his credit. 'It took more than three weeks before he even came close to getting it right!'

'And now you're going to kill me for no better reason than that my friend fucked his wife. Let me go, Beg. I could help you do much more damage to him alive.'

'I need no foreigner's help to get rid of him!'

'My enemy's enemy is my friend.'

'You Westerners have no friends in this part of the world, have you not yet learned that lesson?'

'Nevertheless, we still have our uses.'

'And you have uses for me, Mr Jones. Dead. As a message to all other foreigners who intend to come here and rape Ta'argistan.'

There was an edge of madness in Beg's eye, so Harry thought, and a little trickle of spittle falling from the corner of his mouth. Harry knew he was never going to argue his way out of this corner.

'So that's what you intend to do. After you have broken my hands. For fun. Just like the Soviets did to you. You know, you're still their puppet.'

Beg wrinkled his nose in puzzlement. 'Oh, no, Mr Jones,' he said, putting the hammer aside on the desk. 'I have entirely other plans for you.'

Martha didn't intend to wander far. She had no wish to find herself lost in a strange city, let alone have any difficulty in getting back to the Fat Chance, just in case. Yet she knew she had to spend a little time away from the cellar. It had become like a crypt.

She wandered distractedly along unkempt, snow-crowded streets, catching glimpses of a strange woman staring back at her from the reflections in shop fronts and restaurant windows. The new Martha Reilly. A puzzling woman. Was she in love with Harry? If that was so, it was proving a pitifully tangled experience, yet love had always been that way for her. She'd not even liked Harry, at first, thought him too rich, one of those privileged Englishmen who'd had it all too easy, for too long. Just the sort of man who prevented her from getting where she thought she wanted to be. But that had been a superficial judgement, she knew that now, she'd seen the scars on his body that told her his hadn't been a life spent between satin sheets, even if he could afford them. He was a restless soul, discontented with his life, looking for something more. They were a lot like each other, and perhaps that was why they fought. Her feelings about all men were twisted, filled with searing memories that had all been glued together, and she'd never succeeded in prising them apart and dealing with them, hadn't even wanted to, until now. Harry could help, and she wanted his help. Perhaps that was what love was about.

Yet what a terrible place to find love. She gazed around her, searching above the skyline of Ashkek, beyond the belching chimneys of the power station, to the jagged line of mountains in the distance. They seemed cold and unforgiving; give her the surf of Cape Cod any day. She shivered, despite her new jacket, which was proving less adequate than it looked. Yet those old women squatting on the pavement wore considerably less, their bare arms reaching out from beneath shawls to plead with her to buy their wares, or simply to beg. '*Ya vas umolyau*,' they whispered, *Please,*

please, their lips cracked, their round eyes filled with tearful memories of better times. Martha hurried on.

She was lost in her own world of troubles, thinking of Harry, when she looked up to discover that two policemen were standing on the street corner not twenty yards ahead. She grew nervous, sure they would spot the guilty blush on her cheeks. She wanted to take no chances, so cast around for shelter. A few steps away were steps that led beneath an arch to a set of polished wooden doors – a church, Russian Orthodox, its onion dome towering above her head. She recalled her briefing – so many religious remnants had been left scattered along the Silk Road; it might just as easily have been a Buddhist or Hindu or Shamanist temple, even more likely a mosque. The new System, unlike its ardently atheistic Soviet predecessors, didn't mind very much to whom you prayed, so long as above all else you remembered to worship It. She lowered her head and ducked inside.

She hadn't been in a church since her marriage, except for Remembrance Sunday, which was inescapable duty. And they hadn't been churches like this, so overpoweringly ornate, filled with mysteries and flickering candles and polished woods, and relics waiting for the lips of the devout, and the overpowering waft of incense. An old *babushka* in dark widow's weeds was bent over the steps before the altar, worn polishing cloth in her hand, while close by another woman trimmed candles in their glittering brass holders. Martha slipped into a pew at the back of the church, trying to make herself invisible amongst the congregation of gilded saints that stood on all sides. From the mosaic of the vast domed ceiling, the robed figures of Christ and the apostles stared down on her.

She hadn't tried prayer, not since she was eleven and wanted a pony, but as she sat on the hard wooden seat she envied the simple faith of the elderly women who toiled in front of her. Yet strange things had been happening to her, deep inside, and she had never wanted anything more in her adult life than what she sought now – Harry, and his safety. She slipped to her knees. It couldn't hurt.

She bent her head, closed her eyes, focused her mind, summoned all her energies and willed him to be free. 'Please, God,' she whispered.

When she raised her eyes and sat up once again, she felt a surge of comfort. She still had no idea about God, but she knew for certain that something special had happened in her life through meeting Harry and coming to this place with him. In finding Harry, she had found part of herself that had been missing.

She remembered Zac, what had happened to him, and her imagination began to prey upon her. What would they do – no, *what were they doing* – to Harry? Half-formed fears began to crowd into her mind, chasing away the comfort she'd found. Then her attention was caught by a painting in a huge gilded frame that hung on a wall near at hand. It was of a young man, St Sebastian the Martyr. It made her think of Harry. His hair was the same colour, the eyes had a similar cast, and his lips were parted, calling out in despair, his body tied to a tree and pierced through with many arrows. The blood from his wounds trickled down below his knees. With a cry of torment that echoed throughout the church and startled the *babushkas*, Martha jumped to her feet and ran from the church.

'There are only two things I require from you, Mr Jones, and then we can get this entire unpleasant business over with.' Beg made it sound as if he was about to do Harry a favour.

'You mean you can kill me.'

'I think life is so often overrated, don't you? Particularly when it involves so much suffering. In any event, I have very little time. The President is, after all, the President, and he is an impatient man. He requires that his instructions are carried out promptly. So although your suffering will not be prolonged unnecessarily, it will, I'm afraid, be intense. Until you tell me what it is I need to know. But that shouldn't be so difficult. Only two things.' He counted on his crooked fingers. 'First, of course, I must know who helped you. You understand that, don't you?'

'And second?'

'I would like to know why, Mr Jones. Why you have done this. Given your life up for a friend.'

'The first I will never tell you,' Harry whispered. 'And the second, you will never understand.'

'A pity. A very great pity. I would have enjoyed the privilege of talking with you some more, but . . . to business.' He crossed to the cupboard, his storehouse of terrors. When he turned back once more, he was holding a tray of surgical instruments that he laid on the desk directly in front of Harry. Pliers, clamps, needles, scalpels, even a saw. As battered as his eyes were, Harry couldn't drag them away. Beg knew it. It was always the same. His fingers hovered over the tray in a grotesque pantomime, as though it was a box of chocolates and he was having difficulty in making up his mind which treat to select.

'Please, Mr Jones, try to understand. There is nothing personal in this. Truly.'

'You'll be suggesting we hold hands next.'

'I will gain no pleasure in watching you suffer.'

'Screw you, Beg. This isn't a spectator sport for you, you get your rocks off on making people suffer. Is it instead of sex? What is it with you, is there no woman in your life? Or is it something else that does it for you – young boys, perhaps? Dead sheep? A pound of raw liver?' He was lashing out, trying to hit a target, struggling to hide his fear. 'Or is it that you're not only inadequate but undersized, too? The shortest dick in the boys' showers, was that it?' Harry was sweating now, the tension cascading down his face.

Beg turned, and something sparkled in his hand. 'I

think, on that front, you have no cause to be making any claims,' he snorted as his eyes dropped to Harry's groin.

'I'm freezing.'

'And afraid.'

Of course he was. Beg was holding a scalpel.

For the first time Harry tried to test his bonds, but the leather straps were thick and securely fastened. He could do no more than wriggle, or was it that he was shivering?

'Who helped you? Give me their names. Otherwise . . .' Beg took a step forward. The state of his hands meant that he was forced to hold the scalpel crudely, in the palm of his hand rather than with his fingers, but whichever way he held it, it was moving straight for Harry's uninjured eye. Harry closed it, not in any hope of protection but in order to try to compose himself for what was to come. Should he laugh, sneer, scream, suffer in silence? This might be the last decision he ever made. He wanted desperately to get it right.

'The names, Mr Jones. You don't need to go through this. Just give me their names.'

Yet when Harry opened his eye once again, Beg realized he wasn't going to cooperate. There was a strength, a resilience, a glimmer of hatred in this man that Beg knew he would have to overcome before he got anything from him. He lunged forward.

CHAPTER TWELVE

Harry felt the lance of the blade, the warm blood falling onto his shoulder, the deadening numbness that the body insists on in those moments when it struggles to deal with profound offence. His mind went blank, preparing itself for the tidal wave of outrage that would soon engulf it.

On cue, through the numbness, came galloping the messengers of intense pain. When Harry dared to open his eye, he found he could still see, and only inches in front of him, bending down to inspect his handiwork, was Amir Beg. Suddenly Harry's ear began to scream as though it had been thrust into a brazier of hot coals. A substantial chunk of it had been sliced off.

'You did that deliberately?' he gasped.

'What?'

'Missed my eye.'

'But of course. Without your eye it's impossible to see what is coming. That's half of it, and often the most important half. You must be able to see in order to be aware of what is to come, and for your fear to undermine your courage. You know how this works, Mr Jones. Fear can achieve what simple pain cannot.'

There was nothing simple about the pain that was sinking its teeth into the side of Harry's head. Beg took some medical gauze and began wiping Harry's shoulder, as though in concern. 'You don't think I enjoy this savagery, do you?'

'Every minute, you sick bastard!' Harry cried out as Beg dabbed at his ear. He couldn't defeat the pain, he could only try to fight it as long as possible, in the mind as much as in the body, which was why Beg was insistent on attending to both.

'Come, come,' Beg muttered in reproach, his breath upon Harry's burning cheek, 'you said you took an interest in Afghanistan, just across our border. You must have seen what the Americans and British have done there, been part of it, even. Oh, what do you call it? *Exceptional measures. Extraordinary rendition.* Strange language, but what can we expect when Vice President Cheney spent so many years compiling the dictionary? Neat bureaucratic phrases, designed to set Western consciences at ease. And how easy that has proved to be. The abuses were massive, they were carried on for years, yet in your parliaments and amongst your peoples there was barely a whimper raised in protest. And you, Mr Jones, I understand you were not only a politician but also a soldier. You bear twice the measure of guilt. Even if you weren't part of it, you most certainly were aware of it.'

'Only the photographs,' Harry muttered weakly. Splashed all over the media. He couldn't deny Beg's point. What had gone on in places like Abu Ghraib and Guantánamo Bay had come to sicken him. Acts that had been carried out in the name of extracting truth and approved, even insisted upon, by politicians who then repeatedly lied about such things. In the national interest. Whenever they were forced to argue their case and justify what had happened, they fell back on claiming that a few casualties were inevitable in defending that interest, weren't they? No need to look too closely. Although the strangest thing was that when the lies were exposed and the account presented, it was mostly only sergeants and lower ranks who were forced to pay, and not a single politician. It was the one time in his life when Harry had felt shame. The irredeemable tarnish on the brass. And Beg had been clever enough to open that old wound, and pull it apart.

This was no longer merely a matter of violence, a one-sided contest of brute force between gaoler and captive, it had become a battle of wills between two men, testing each other. There could be only one result, for it was never going to be a fair fight and at any moment he chose Beg could bring the game to an end by crushing the other man with a flick of a wrist, yet while it continued, it was real, and its outcome mattered, if only to the two of them.

'We are much the same, you and me,' Beg said.

'You're more flexible than me,' Harry responded,

panting in pain. 'I'd never bend as low as Karabayev's arse.'

'In a few minutes you will bend lower than you ever believed possible.'

'You serve him. Yet you loathe him, don't you?'

'Let me put it this way. I'd much rather have him sitting in this chair than you. And perhaps I shall. Soon.'

'Doesn't it worry you, sharing opinions that could get you on the wrong end of your noose?'

'But I do it only with those I know will never be in a position to repeat them.'

'Fuck you.' It was the best Harry could do. He was supposed to be playing mind games, but the pain of his ear was growing so intense that it felt as though Beg were slicing off another chunk. The battle with the injury was already exhausting him. Beg knew it, and would take advantage.

'You see, Mr Jones, pain is life. Without life there can be no pain, and so pain is the ultimate proof of a man's existence. And it is cumulative, layer upon layer of it, like oil on a painting, getting ever thicker. That's what we do, that's what this process is about. It's a form of art. Piling pain upon pain, to the point where you will give me what I want. We will paint a picture together. From the names.'

'Art? You couldn't even hold a fucking brush. And I've seen what you call your artwork, plastered over the wall beside the scaffold.'

'You *will* talk.'

'Name, rank and address.'

'We shall see.'

'Tell me, Beg, why do you hate your country so much?'

'Me? Hate Ta'argistan?' For the first time, Beg seemed taken aback, knocked off course by a thrust he hadn't expected.

'Your country has betrayed you. You were born for better things than this, playing the lapdog to a man like Karabayev.'

Beg's mouth twitched. How did this man see these things? Were his feelings so obvious? Then he realized this was nothing but a game. 'No, I don't hate my country.'

'You think when Karabayev goes they'll let you take his place? Look in the mirror, Beg. You're not the sort they let out into the daylight, not a half-man who makes women flinch and children run screaming from the room. You're a creature of the shadows. And that's where they'll keep you.'

With a snort of rage Beg lurched forward, and another chunk of Harry's ear was gone. Harry moaned. There would come a point where the pain would overwhelm him, drive him into unconsciousness and he would no longer be able to talk, but that point was still some way off. Meanwhile, Beg recovered his composure, shook himself, not just physically but mentally, grabbing control back from Harry.

'The pain in my hands is nothing compared with

what you will endure, Mr Jones. But I somehow sense that more blood is not the answer. I look at your body, with those marks, its scars, reminders of the battles it has fought, and they suggest to me that you are a man so accustomed to blood that I am unlikely to persuade you by shedding a little more, perhaps not even a lot more. In any event, I don't have the time to waste in playing with you. We must become more serious.'

The blood of which Beg was talking had now completely filled Harry's right ear, yet he didn't need to catch all the words to sense the threat that was being made. What came next? The fingernails? Sawing off an entire finger? Beg was right, the damage was done in the mind, and Harry was growing very afraid.

Beg was bending over something in the far recess of the room, on the other side of the cupboard, Harry couldn't see. He returned pushing a trolley. On it was a box with a prominent dial, and leading from it were thick cables, like car jump leads, with dull metal paddles of what looked like bronze or copper at their end. A red flex trailed behind the trolley to a power point.

'I suspect you have seen something like this before. It can deliver high voltage with low current – that means it causes very serious pain without killing you. You can see its advantages.' Beg flicked a power switch, fiddled with the rheostat dial and picked up the paddles by their insulated handles. 'We use these on the extremities. Start with your toes, then move up to your testicles. And after that, if you are still stubborn, your tongue. Layer upon layer, you see. I tend to linger over the testicles, avoid the tongue, if possible; it makes it more difficult to talk afterwards. Although very few push me as far as the tongue.'

'As you say, nothing personal.'

'You will talk, Mr Jones. They all do. Your friend, Mr Kravitz, did. It's only a matter of when.'

Beg was kneeling in front of Harry, the terminals in his hand. He touched them together, a harsh yellow spark shot between them that added the smell of ozone to that of the antiseptic. Sitting in the chair, naked, with his legs apart, unable to move, Harry felt desperately vulnerable. He was still damp, from the shower, and with sweat. He knew Beg was right. It was a matter of time. And pain. He would talk, so why not do it now?

Suddenly pain seared through his body, jerking it taut, forcing it against the bonds. Harry screamed. It lasted for only a couple of seconds. Beg was toying with him, letting him know what was to come. Beg withdrew the paddles and the pain began slowly to subside, but Harry still moaned. He spat out a filling that had cracked, he could taste blood in his mouth.

'That's good, a very good start,' Beg said.

Harry tried to mumble something. Beg drew closer, put his ear to Harry's mouth.

'I want to tell you something,' Harry whispered.

'Excellent!' Beg cried in triumph.

'You . . . you still smell as though someone's just poured a bucket of shit over you.'

Their eyes met, in hatred. And the pain began again. For longer, and far more intense. Harry lost control over his body, which fought to escape, fighting the leather bonds, his arms twisting until blood started seeping from his wrists. Harry was screaming, which satisfied Beg; it meant he was still conscious.

'Have you anything else to tell me,' Beg enquired, 'or shall we move further up the body?'

Harry was moaning, panting, sweating. Beg was right. Pain had a quality of thickness and it was pressing down on him, trying to suffocate him. His lungs were burning. God knew what would happen next. He didn't think he could take much more.

Yet, slowly, Harry became aware that something had distracted Beg's attention. It was his hand. While the electrical current had jolted his body back and forth, Harry's wrists had twisted within their restraining straps and the palms of his hands were now facing upwards, the fingers outstretched in their agony. And embedded in his right palm, surrounded by bruised and suppurating flesh, was Zac's chess piece.

Beg cried in both surprise and delight at his discovery. 'You see, Mr Jones, you can have no secrets from me!' His eyes mocked as he bent forward for a closer inspection and his broken, crooked fingers reached out to claim his prize. Harry felt the other man's fingers scrabbling at his palm. And something on Beg's exposed wrist glinted in the light. A Rolex – Zac's. Julia's.

Harry wanted it back. To reclaim what was hers. This bastard had no right to it. So, with every tattered shred of strength he could muster, Harry's own fingers closed around those of the other man.

Harry wasn't fully conscious, only half aware of what was happening. Everything was confusion, and pain, and through it all he heard more screaming. Yet this time it wasn't his own. It was Beg's.

Beg was trying to pull away. He grabbed a paddle, slapped it against Harry, but it required both paddles to make the circuit, not just one. He stretched out with his free hand, trying to reach for something from the desk, one of the cutting instruments, but as he scrabbled at it the scalpel dropped to the ground and bounced out of reach. 'Help! Help!' he screamed. It was pointless. The guards never responded to screams from this room.

Harry squeezed still harder, using all his scrambled physical and mental resources to crush the other man's crippled joints. It was as if his entire life had been reduced to this one moment.

Beg's body twisted, curled, like an autumn leaf. The resistance flooded from it, and he collapsed at Harry's feet.

'*Ya vas umolyau,*' he whimpered. 'I beg you . . .'

Harry tightened his grip. His slashed ear, his cracked ribs, he felt nothing any longer, apart from the all-consuming ache in his right arm.

'Please. Please!'

'Undo – my – straps,' Harry gasped.

Beg shuddered.

'Undo the fucking straps!'

Slowly, jerkily, like a robot with dying batteries, Beg stretched out and began scrabbling pathetically at the strap on Harry's left wrist. 'I need both hands,' he pleaded, sobbing.

'Try this for a work of art,' Harry muttered, and poured his last remaining resources of energy into his fist, knowing that very soon his own strength would be gone.

And, somehow, Beg undid the strap. Harry's hand was free.

Quickly Harry set about releasing the strap around his chest, then his legs. Only at the last did he free his right hand, and not for a moment did he loosen his grip upon the whimpering Beg.

When at last he was able to stand, he twisted Beg's arm and threw him into the chair. Within seconds it was over. For a second time, Harry had changed places.

'What . . . are you going to do?' Beg asked, trying to swallow but discovering his mouth was parched and everything was sticking in his throat – words, wild thoughts, but mostly his fear.

Harry was examining the Rolex he had liberated from Beg's wrist, brushing the face with his thumb. 'As much as I've enjoyed our little chat, I think it's time to leave.'

Beg's eyes were following Harry's every move, swivelling in their sockets, like a spooked horse.

'I wish I had more time to spend with you. You've been an excellent teacher.' Harry bent down and retrieved the scalpel Beg had dropped, examining its blade.

'You will kill me.'

'Perhaps.'

'Is there anything I can do to strengthen my case?'

'You could tell me how to get out of here. Then you might live.'

Beg managed to produce a rueful smile. 'But you can't. This is a prison.'

'Yes. The same thought had crossed my mind.'

'You speak no Russian.'

'Only a few words.'

'And you are naked.'

'There is that, too.'

'If it would help me I would tell you the location of every locked door and checkpoint in the place, give you the name of every guard, what football team he supports, who or what he is sleeping with.'

'And still I wouldn't escape.'

'Precisely. We both know that. And I don't think I'm in much of a position to lie.'

Harry had hoped that now the tables had been turned Beg would shrivel, fall to pieces, start to cringe and mewl, but now the pain in his hands had subsided, he was showing considerable mettle.

'This isn't your day, is it, Mr Jones?'

Harry was desperately assessing his situation. He needed clothes, and an escape route. He examined Beg, but the Ta'argi was a good eight inches shorter than him; his shirt and trousers would be useless. He considered taking Beg hostage but that would only serve to slow him down, and in any standoff there could be only one conclusion. They would both end up on the business end of a bullet; Karabayev would insist on it. Harry began rifling the drawers in the desk, searching for something, he didn't know what.

'I don't suppose there's any point in suggesting we come to an arrangement which would ensure both of us were still alive by this time tomorrow?' Beg asked tentatively.

Harry didn't bother replying.

'No, I thought not. But to show my good faith,' Beg said, as Harry continued to ransack the desk drawers, 'I have to tell you that a guard will be bringing me some fresh tea. Right about now.'

He wasn't showing good faith, of course, merely playing the game, trying to keep Harry unbalanced and indecisive. Harry threw the final, useless drawer aside and grabbed a handful of medical gauze, dabbing at his ear, cleaning up the mess as he struggled to figure out a plan of action. That was when, as Beg had promised, there was a sharp knock on the door. Harry jumped. He picked up the scalpel once more, and held it in front of Beg's nose.

'Get him in here. Any nonsense and I will slit his throat.'

'I'm sure you will.'

'Yours will be next.'

Harry scurried across the room to hide behind the door. There was another knock. Beg cried out, *'Vkhodite!'* Come!

The door opened slowly and into the room, head down, all his concentration focused on the tray of tea and scones, came a young guard. In one movement Harry had kicked the door shut, placed one arm around the guard's neck and pressed the scalpel against his cheek. The tray fell to the floor with the sound of a car crash.

Harry should have killed him, straight away. It was the only safe thing to do, particularly with his cracked ribs. It would take no more than an elbow from the guard and Harry would be down. Yet death had followed him all his adult life and Harry wanted to end it, shake it off. He wanted this boy to live. He'd once – only once – asked himself how many people he had killed, in the war in Iraq, the glorious wilderness of Afghanistan, in the jungles of Colombia and West Africa, in the cold mud of Armagh and all the other places he had fought besides, but he had stopped counting when he'd remembered Julia. He'd killed her, too, as good as. His list was already too long and he had no desire to add to it. This boy looked as though he'd left his mother's side only a few hours before and he was doing nothing more than his duty by delivering a tray of tea. Only an Englishman would die for a tray of tea. Anyway, the young Ta'argi was tall, his uniform might just fit Harry, so it wouldn't do to get blood over it. The guard's neck was in the crook of Harry's arm; he kept up the pressure, cutting off the supply of oxygen to the brain. It took only a few seconds for the young man's body to go limp. Collapsed.

Harry gasped as his ribs exploded in agony once more. He doubled up, choking, every breath as hard to take as if he had swallowed a mouthful of petrol. When, at last, he recovered, he stripped the guard of his tunic top and trousers, his belt and his boots. As he struggled into them, he vowed once again to lose a few pounds. He couldn't use the socks because the boots were at least a size too tight and pinched horribly. They would have to do.

All this time, Beg had been listening to what was going on behind his back, straining to interpret every rustle and gasp. He knew his moment would come next, when he would be brought back into the play, a game that would decide whether he would die or somehow escape with his life. 'You're very resourceful, Mr Jones. Truly, I admire you.'

'It's not mutual,' Harry snapped, banging his foot into the final boot.

Beg began talking once more, trying to fill the silence with words, to calm his own fears, to distract Harry from whatever he intended, but as he did so he picked up the chilling sound of the guard's gun being checked.

His flow of words stalled as he heard the cold, metallic clicks of the magazine being ejected, inspected, rammed back home, a round being forced into the chamber. Then came the softer sound of the gun being slipped back into its holster. Beg thought he might die with relief. For the first time, he thought he might live a little longer.

It was a surprising weakness in Harry Jones, to let Beg live, an act of folly, yet the world overflowed with surprises. It was what had always given Beg his advantage, spotting weakness in others, exploiting it, and them. Now he sat, his breathing growing more regular, waiting. At last, from the corner of his eye, he saw Harry. He was dressed in the guard's ill-fitting uniform, inspecting himself, making one final check. No socks, Beg noted, and trousers that were too short. Details that were certain to betray him.

Then he heard Harry's footsteps retreating, crossing to the door – he was almost gone! – but as Beg strained to catch every movement, the door didn't open. The other man seemed to have forgotten something, for the footsteps came back, the heavy boots scraping the floor. Beg could sense Harry standing behind him, could hear his breathing, as though he had just run a race, and he felt the prickle of fear rising on his neck.

He saw Harry move round the chair until the two were facing each other. Their eyes locked. Drained of emotion. Businesslike, somehow. As Beg watched, Harry bent down, drew closer. Whispered in Beg's ear.

'Nothing personal,' Beg heard him say.

Beg sensed the rush of horror through his bowels. He knew the other man was lying. Then he felt the pressure of the blade, sawing, slicing, as his ear was cut off. That's when he began screaming again.

Harry had no idea where he was, but as he crept into the corridor he saw the soft glow of daylight at its far end. He hurried towards it, only to find the window solidly barred, but through it he could see he was on the ground floor, with a view across the exercise yard. It left him struggling to work out his location from what he remembered of his previous visit. He knew that all the exits were guarded and there would be no chance of simply walking out unobserved, not with only one ear. It had stopped erupting blood but was still grotesque. Neither was the sewer an option, not in daylight, and he couldn't climb out of any barred window. That meant the third floor, right at the top, or trying to hang on until darkness, but this last option presented too much of a risk. Once they found Beg, Harry knew he would insist on starting the mother of all manhunts. He should have killed the bastard after all.

Harry was juggling with the idea of returning to the room and finishing the job when he was dragged back to the moment by the sounds of guards approaching. His first instinct was to run, but that would only give the game away, and he had the disguise of his uniform. It would do, at a distance. As the guards approached, he began to walk in the opposite direction.

He knew he had to stay out of close contact, but this was a prison crawling with guards, and he ran into another as soon as he had turned the corner. Incredulity spread across the guard's face as he caught sight of Harry's bruised and bloodied features. He muttered something, a question, in Russian, but Harry didn't understand a word, so he hit him. The guard cried out, fell to the floor, the files he had been carrying clattering around him. The commotion, in turn, aroused the curiosity of the other guards, who began calling. That's when Harry started running.

There was no plan to Harry's flight. He simply needed to gain some distance on the sounds of pursuit that were growing stronger behind him. An alarm bell began jangling. Within a few minutes every exit from the prison would be locked down, the guard doubled. For one dark moment he thought he might have to try to shoot his way out . . . No, better the third floor.

One of the abiding images of Harry's childhood – he'd been about ten – was one of the episodes that marked the end of the Vietnam War, the scenes on television of Americans scrambling onto the rooftop of their embassy in Saigon, waiting for evacuation helicopters, as hordes of Vietnamese swarmed over the walls and into the embassy compound. It had been extraordinary how many had made it out, despite the impossible circumstances. Not as impossible as his, of course. He needed a miracle, but first he needed a staircase.

He found it by accident, blundering through a door and finding himself on the stone steps that led from the courtyard to the governor's office. For a moment he contemplated changing course and crashing the court-yard, perhaps trying to steal one of the cars, battering his way through the gates, but he knew it was already too late. He had lost that vital, life-extending element of surprise. So he ran up the stairs, two at a time, using the banister to haul himself up still faster. Below him, he could hear his pursuers doing the same.

Then a shot rang out. It didn't miss by much. As he reached the second floor landing, a door opened; a guard appeared and shouted in alarm. Harry kicked him, watched him topple, sprang up the next flight. They were only feet behind him now.

The door to the governor's office was locked. He put his shoulder to it and it gave way immediately. When he burst through, for a moment it seemed as though he had jumped into a different world, one of almost comical calm. The empire around him might be in uproar, but Governor Akmatov had other things on his mind. He was standing by the double win-dows, a glass of vodka in his hand, naked from the waist down, except for his socks, staring triumphantly at the world outside. Bent over by the corner of his desk was his secretary. As Harry burst in, Akmatov turned and stared in disbelief, while she screamed and clutched at her loose blouse. Little wonder they'd turned the key.

Harry couldn't stop. In another couple of steps there would be guns trained on his back. To stand still would be to die, so he kept running, grabbed a letter opener from the desk, thrust it at the eye of the still-startled governor just as the guards arrived. The governor's grotesquely exposed body was now between Harry and his pursuers, and Harry was careful to keep it that way. The guards were sizing up the situation, waving their weapons, bristling with intent. He cast around for a means of escape, but there was none, nothing but the windows.

Akmatov's office windows were in the outside wall of the Castle. The previous day, when he'd been sitting and drinking the governor's tea, Harry had noticed a gang of workmen clearing the street below, with shovels, even planks of wood. The snowfall had been heavy, the drifts thick, and the heap of snow was deep. It gave him an idea, a lousy idea, he would be the first to admit, but better than the one being offered by the collection of muzzles pointing at him.

'Open the windows,' he instructed Akmatov. The governor, still in shock, was incapable of obeying, his hands desperately scrabbling to cover his dignity. Harry forced the point of the letter opener into the skin just below the eyeball; Akmatov screamed, the guards shook their weapons, but could not fire.

Clumsily, the governor reached behind him and loosened the catch. The windows swung open on a blast of chill air.

It was a ludicrous gamble for Harry, of course, but

the alternative was to be shot, or even worse, returned to the care of Amir Beg. And he still had one very substantial card to play. The governor. Harry's arm stretched around Akmatov's chest, and heaved with all the strength he could summon. Suddenly they were falling backwards, tumbling, twisting, three floors.

It wasn't, perhaps, total madness. Akmatov was beneath him as they fell. He was fat, and the snow might still be soft.

They hit with a crack. Harry's mind went blank from the renewed pain in his ribs. When once more he regained his focus, he saw the crack had been Akmatov's neck. The governor's eyes stared emptily, his mouth wide open, smelling of borscht. There was blood on the snow; Harry's ear again. And there were shouts from above, but no shots, for his pursuers wouldn't take the risk of hitting the governor; they didn't yet know that he was dead. Another body on Harry's list.

He grabbed a handful of snow and packed it to his ear, then picked himself up and began to stumble away. That's when the shooting started again, bullets spraying in the snow around him. He had to scrabble for every foothold; it was like trying to race through water. He pushed himself on, not daring to stop. As he tumbled into the road and began to run, he told himself he needed to find another pair of boots. This pair was killing him.

CHAPTER THIRTEEN

After Martha had fled from the church she had scurried back to the Fat Chance, but her nightmares had pursued her and now they seemed to have her surrounded. She was feeling wiped out. She'd had no proper sleep since she'd arrived in the country, and none at all the previous night. She wasn't well equipped for this job, waiting, staring at an empty coffee cup. The wooden chair on which she sat was unforgiving, but still her head dropped, the resistance slowly draining from her body.

It was Bektour, ever the young shepherd, who noticed. 'Come on,' he whispered, shaking her shoulder. He showed her to another of the alcoves, hidden behind a curtain. It was almost entirely filled by two well-worn, cushion-strewn sofas that faced each other a couple of feet apart. 'Rest here,' he said, 'it will be more comfortable.' And, usefully, out of his mother's way, although he didn't say so.

Martha sank into the cushions, which closed around her like protective arms, and she sighed in gratitude.

'This is where we take turns to sleep, when we're working at the screens.'

'You kids,' she muttered, yawning. 'All the same. Romantic night owls.'

'No, I'm afraid that's not it. It's simply that the rate we get charged for our Internet connection drops by two-thirds after midnight.'

'Revolution on a shoestring.'

'We do what we have to.'

'I won't forget my promise. I'll find some way to help, when I get back home.'

He closed the curtain, and within seconds she had fallen asleep, but she found little rest. Her dreams were turbulent; she heard the sounds of sirens. She was running, they were hunting her, in a world full of men, but no matter how hard she ran she couldn't escape, her high heels twisting under her, constantly catching in the broken pavement. What had happened to the practical shoes she had bought earlier that day? They were nowhere to be found when she needed them. And there was Harry, her father, and many of the other men from her life, all shouting after her as she tried to get away. She ran through a field, filled with ripe, waving corn, like Jamilia, but just as she thought she was free she found her way barred by a river, with no bridge anywhere to be seen. And still they came after her.

It was some time before she realized the sirens were for real. Even down inside the cellar they were unmistakable, police cars announcing their presence, racing through the streets of Ashkek. She shuddered, opened her eyes. There would be no more sleep.

Suddenly, from beyond the curtain, came the sounds of commotion. There was a sharp banging on the door, a distant cry. Pounding feet on the steps leading down from the street. A chair was knocked over. She peered through the curtain and gasped in alarm. She was confronted by the sight of a man in a uniform.

Then he turned.

'Harry!'

She brushed the curtain aside and threw herself across the bar. She was about to wrap her arms around him when she caught sight of his face. The bruises. Cuts. The swollen eye. The mutilated ear. He was swaying with fatigue.

He'd made it, but only just. He'd started running the moment he rolled away from the governor's lifeless body, but it made him a target of suspicion, and he'd soon had to stop, slow to nothing more than a brisk walk, even as sirens sprang up on all sides and vehicles crammed with policemen had hurtled past. He'd relied on nothing more than prayer to ensure they didn't stop to question why he was headed in the opposite direction. He'd tried to keep to side streets and the slushy back alleys, breaking into a trot when he could, finding it harder to walk than run, his heart thumping within his broken chest and his breath coming in snatches. By the time he clattered down the steps of the Fat Chance he was sweating profusely, both from the effort and the pain.

'You waited,' he gasped. The solitary open eye overflowed with a fusion of exhaustion and awe.

'Of course I did, stupid. And a good thing, too, by the look of you.' She was putting on a brave front, trying not to burst into tears.

'Thank you,' he whispered.

She put a finger softly to his lips, swollen where he had bitten them in pain. 'Be quiet. Do as you're told, for once.' She turned to Bektour. 'Please, help us.'

Before he could answer, there was another presence in the cellar, and a cry of anguish. They turned. It was Benazir. She was holding a gun, a Makarov, an old Soviet-era pistol. And it was pointing directly at Harry.

Less than two miles away from the Fat Chance, and much in the manner of Martha, the young prison guard was also emerging from the darkness. A violent noise was shaking the peace that had descended upon his tranquil world of unconsciousness. It was the sound of Amir Beg screaming.

As soon as he heard the guard stirring, Beg's cries began to take concrete form. They were no longer incoherent outpourings of his physical and emotional pain, but became specific demands. For a doctor. For the immediate presence of Sydykov. For the entire fucking army to be put on alert. And for the guard to be shot. There was a long list of reasons for the guard's condemnation – spilling the tea, falling unconscious on duty, most of all simply for witnessing the humiliation of his master; Beg didn't specify, it wasn't necessary. It was enough to be within reach when a man like him worked up an appetite for vengeance.

But Beg still had his back to him, hadn't seen him.

'I'll fetch help, sir,' the guard groaned, and stumbled from the room, hoping desperately that he would be able to spread the responsibility for this chaos, and find a new pair of trousers.

'Mother!' Bektour cried in concern.

'Get that man out of here. He brings us nothing but trouble!' Her words were fired with passion, and the pistol was shaking in her hand, but never away from Harry.

Deliberately, very slowly, Bektour moved in front of Harry, placing his own body between Harry and the gun. 'No, Mother,' he said defiantly, 'we owe him support, as Ta'argis. Or has Karabayev taken even that from us?'

'We owe him nothing! They are not here for us, these foreigners, only for themselves!'

'I'll go,' Harry said, still panting heavily and holding his ribs.

Bektour would not be moved. 'Please call the doctor, Mother.'

'Someone might have seen him come in here!' she snapped.

'So the longer we wait for the doctor, the more risk we run.' His tone was remarkably self-possessed for such a young man. He stared at his mother through his tinted glasses. 'Please. Call him.'

It was a moment when the balance in their lives shifted. This was more than mere youthful defiance, it was a claim to his own independence, and authority. His life, no longer hers. She seemed to grow older before she moved to a distant table and began pushing buttons on a phone. The gun remained pointed at Harry.

The doctor was the same one who had attended Zac the night before. He must have been local, for he arrived within ten minutes. He made a rapid inspection of Harry's injuries. 'Like your friend, you require a hospital,' he concluded.

'I know a fine one,' Harry replied through gritted teeth as the doctor felt across his ribs. 'St Thomas's. Just across the river from Westminster. I'll visit as soon as I can.'

The doctor shook his head in resignation, wondering what he might find in his bag that would be of any use in the treatment of multiple contusions, lacerations, abrasions, a missing ear and broken ribs.

'Nothing too strong, Doctor. I need my wits about me,' Harry said.

'You are sure?'

Harry nodded. Even doing that hurt.

The doctor picked up a packet of Ibuprofen. 'Only two at a time. I also prescribe plenty of rest.'

'I think Amir Beg might have other ideas.'

Harry's supposition was correct. While a prison surgeon bobbed nervously from foot to foot, cleaning and bandaging the injured ear with a huge wad of cotton, Beg began to hurl a welter of instructions at Sydykov. The major had returned less than an hour earlier from the trip to the Celestial Mountains; he listened impassively, his face carved from granite, as Beg began closing down the city.

His first order was that the airport should be closed and all flights cancelled. There would be complaints from airlines and demands for compensation, but Beg's anger was beyond price. The railway station could remain open but guards with weapons prominently on display would man every crack and crevice in both platforms, and an armed patrol would be placed on all departing trains. Roadblocks would be thrown across highways out of Ashkek – not a major challenge in a mountain city which had only a handful of routes leading out along the valleys, but it meant the capital would grind quickly to a halt. That was the point, Beg insisted. Anyone running would become an obvious target. Then he instructed that the guard outside Western embassies was to be increased, all visitors scrutinized and searched and to hell with the inevitable protests. It was a blessing in such circumstances that there were only three – American, German and Japanese. The British had long promised to open some diplomatic facility, but it had been yet another promise swept away in the recession, and another slight taken by the Ta'argis. The foreigners could go fuck themselves, Beg declared, his voice rising almost to incoherence while he waited for the painkillers to kick in. Then he turned on Ashkek. Every location that had ever been suspected of harbouring critical voices was to be raided and, if necessary, wrecked. No, Beg added, banging his fist on the table, better wrecked! Teach all such maggots a lesson. And as Beg roared at those around him in order to cover his shame, Sydykov took notes, pages of them, making sure he missed nothing, his impassive face never faltering, even when Beg instructed that every hotel room was to be searched. Every hospital, too, come to that, every sick bed examined, every blanket pulled back, every bandage lifted, every patient identified, every doctor's office inspected, every nurse interrogated. Then the entire process was to be repeated.

Beg demanded immediate results. No stone unturned, no arm untwisted, no corner left uninspected. He warned that Sydykov's own neck would be on the line if the man wasn't recaptured by daybreak. The major recognized the bluster, but knew he would need to be careful. This situation put many at risk, and none more than Beg himself. That's what made him so dangerous. Yet if he fell, the resulting tidal wave might swamp smaller boats like Sydykov's.

It was only when the name of the President came up that Sydykov raised an eyebrow. The troops stationed around the Presidential Palace were to be doubled, Beg instructed, which confused the major. It implied that Beg had an extraordinarily high opinion of this man

Jones to think him capable of such grand folly as breaking into the palace. Unless, of course, Amir Beg had finally succumbed to the temptation of ambition and the troops were being sent to prevent Karabayev getting out . . .

Beg roared, his hands flying out as he tried to orchestrate events, his head held rock still, his lips twisting in pain as the doctor dabbed nervously about his ear. Meanwhile Sydykov scribbled away in his notebook, and minute by minute an entire capital city was laid waste as they stepped up the hunt for one man.

The sirens were a constant presence on the streets, but none had stopped outside the Fat Chance, yet. The doctor had finished strapping up Harry's ribs.

'What next?' Martha asked quietly.

'The border with Afghanistan is only thirty miles away,' Harry said, testing his breathing now his ribs were constricted. 'My plan was to make for that.'

'Was?'

'It's through the mountains. On foot.'

'So what's the alternative?'

All she got was a silence.

'I'm working on it,' Harry said eventually.

'If the plan was good enough this morning, what's changed?' she persisted.

'He needs a hospital, not a trek through the mountains,' the doctor insisted.

'You have me now, Harry,' Martha said.

'I know.'

It was the tone that betrayed his meaning, as though she had presented him with a flat soufflé. She was the problem, not his ribs. He knew she would react badly.

'Martha, it's the middle of winter,' he protested, getting his argument in first. 'There are no roads, no motels, no sushi bars, no Starbucks. Everything's buried under God knows how many feet of snow, and the lowest pass out is at something like twelve thousand feet. That's getting on for halfway up ruddy Everest.'

'But you can't get out any other way.'

He chewed a knuckle.

'I'm coming with you.'

'You can't.'

'And why not?' she snapped, hotly, facing up to him.

'I'm trained for that sort of thing. You are not.'

'Your training was twenty years ago, Harry. And by the look of you, you've forgotten most of it.'

'I won't let you.'

'Since when did you start telling me what to do?'

'You should have been on the plane, like I told you. Why on earth weren't you?'

'Because she's in love with you.'

It was a new voice in the argument. They both turned. It was the mother.

'She's in love with you, Mr Jones. That's why she stayed. And that's why you can't stop her coming with you.'

'But . . .' Harry was lost for words. His eyes settled on Martha. The flush that had spread into her cheeks told him it was true.

'You mentioned dinner when we got home,' she said, awkwardly. 'I thought maybe I'd take you up on it, that's all.'

'Martha—'

'Don't say a word!'

'It will be dangerous.'

'I always suspected falling for you would be.'

'No, the mountains.'

'I know that, you fool!' she bit back. Then the fire subsided. 'What a girl will do for dinner with Harry Jones, eh?'

'I don't know what to say.'

'I'd prefer it if you said absolutely nothing. Not until we get to the other side of the mountains. Anyway, I've been shopping for you. A whole load of winter gear. Pipe, slippers, the lot. Everything an Englishman could need in the mountains.'

'You've got a lot to learn about me,' he said, smiling. 'I'm Welsh.'

'Now, where did I leave them?' she said, turning, searching the cellar for the bags.

'I burned them,' Benazir said defiantly.

'You what?'

'I burned them!' she shouted, defiant.

'But . . . in God's name, why?'

'We want nothing to do with you, nothing of yours

here that could betray us. And I *will* shoot if you don't leave. Both of you.' The gun began waving once more. 'Enough. The doctor is done with you. Now go!'

Another siren passed by outside. The woman's eyes grew wide with alarm, the gun shook all the more. Harry knew that even if she didn't shoot, she would have no hesitation in handing them over to the authorities. She would do anything if she thought it might save her son.

A new siren started screaming, very near at hand. It took them a second to realize that this one wasn't passing. It had stopped right outside. Already they could hear the thumping of car doors, the clump of impatient boots on pavement, shouts. The doctor's face turned grey with fear. They were being raided. Then came the sound of battering at the upstairs door.

'Quickly, come with me. There's a back way out,' Bektour instructed them.

'No, Bektour!' his mother cried, flinging her arms wide, imploring him to stop. 'They don't stand a chance . . .'

But the son was hustling them towards the rear of the cellar, and the doctor was hurriedly repacking his case, hiding the blood-stained swabs of gauze inside. As Bektour led them on, Harry glanced over his shoulder to see if they had left any sign of their presence. He could find nothing but a dirty coffee cup.

And, at her table, a mother wailing in grief.

*

Beg's world was filled with many twists and torments. His ear was now heavily anaesthetized, yet still gave forth frequent shrill cries of distress, but that alone wasn't sufficient to account for his pain. It was more than the ear; mostly it was the agony of humiliation. As much as he screamed at others and demanded that they leap back in time in order to carry out his instructions more quickly, he knew there could be no hiding place from the responsibility for this fiasco. The humiliation would follow him for all eternity, or at least as long as men were meant to have two ears. There was only one way to prevent others from sniggering behind his back, and that was to terrify them, to leave no one in any doubt as to the terrible consequences that lay in wait for any man unwise enough to be caught sneering at Amir Beg. They might remember, but they would never dare mock.

So he threw everything into the hunt for Harry. The Briton would become the first victim of a new purge, an example for others to fear, and of how no one could flout Amir Beg for long. The rules of this new game were simple; no hold barred, no arm untwisted, no room unransacked, no life left alone. The search for Harry allowed neither respite nor reservation.

They didn't catch him at the Fat Chance, didn't even sniff his presence or catch the faint, lingering hint of a Western woman's perfume. That didn't prevent Beg's men from turning the place over, breaking chairs, ripping down curtains, smashing bottles – at least, those they didn't steal. They kicked and cudgelled into pieces every single computer monitor they found, then they beat up the doctor, and slapped around Bektour's mother. But they didn't hang around too long. They had many more lives to ruin before Amir Beg would be satisfied.

Bektour led them through back streets, constantly glancing over his shoulder, pausing at every corner, until they came to a car park behind a block of crumbling dwellings. He stopped beside an ancient and dust-smeared Lada – Harry reckoned it must have been at least fifteen years old – and bent down beside the front wing, reaching beneath it. When he stood up, he had keys in his hand. 'Belongs to a friend of mine,' he explained, 'part of our group. He won't mind, not if I return it with a tank full of petrol.'

'And windscreen wipers,' Harry added. There were none.

'He takes them off, to protect them from the frost. And to stop them being stolen, of course.' Bektour unlocked the vehicle. Martha and Harry climbed in the back, and Bektour reversed it out.

'Could do with new shocks, too,' Harry muttered, but only to himself. He was scarcely in a position to be fastidious. The back seat was filled with clutter, the marginal paraphernalia of a young man's world – CDs, a woollen hat, road maps, a cheap plastic anorak, an ice scraper, a rucksack filled with overused gym gear.

Without asking, Harry grabbed the hat and placed it tenderly on his head so that the dressing couldn't be seen. He also clambered into the anorak, stretching it across his uniform. So long as no one looked too closely, it provided a reasonable disguise. Then he opened the map, stared at it, trying to make sense of the ribbons of road that led from the city.

'So what's the plan?' Martha asked as they passed a police car screaming its way in the opposite direction.

Harry looked up. There was a hard glint in his eye. It was the only answer she would get. Harry went back to poring over the map.

Bektour drove through the streets, not quickly, cursing at each clumsy gear change, trying not to attract attention. Every street seemed to have some security presence, men with weapons at the ready, peering suspiciously through car windows. Harry raised a prayer of thanks for the filthy windows, but as they joined a line of vehicles waiting to cross an intersection a militiaman, an AK-47 in the crook of his arm, began prowling between the lines of traffic, bending low, peering inside the cars. Every step was bringing him closer, and not even the dirt would prevent him seeing them. Bektour moaned, froze, Harry felt sick, as though his stomach had been hollowed out. Martha smiled. The militiaman smiled back, moved on.

'Seems I have my uses, after all,' she whispered as the line of vehicles began to move again.

After only a few hundred yards, the traffic once more

began to slow. Ahead it had stopped completely, gleaming brake lights suddenly spreading along the road. 'It's the underpass by the university,' Bektour muttered, 'they must be checking every car.' Quickly, before they were held tight in the jam, he swung the wheel and turned aside.

'We've got to get out of the city,' Harry said.

Bektour nodded.

'And then?' Martha asked.

'The mountains,' Harry whispered, his voice almost lost beneath the grumble of the old exhaust. 'There's no other way.'

Soon they were driving through an industrial estate full of workshops and warehouses. It had seen better times. Many of the facilities were closed, even those that bore foreign names. Gates were padlocked, windows broken, metalwork rusting, pallets overturned, yards covered in old snow. The only facility they passed that appeared to be thriving was a German-owned cigarette factory. But the roads through the estate were mercifully empty, not a police car in sight.

On the far side, Bektour turned a corner and the met-alled road surface came to a sudden end. The car began to roll along a pot-holed track.

'Lock your doors,' he instructed solemnly, as he fastened his own. 'This is what we call the Kremlin. We don't really want to be here.'

The state of the buildings on all sides was pitiful.

'It's an illegal settlement,' Bektour continued, weaving

his way along the track. 'It's so violent here that even Karabayev hasn't dared try to bulldoze it. There'd be blood running in the gutters – if there were any gutters. Anyway, it provides cheap labour to the factories. Easier to turn a blind eye. That's what you can do when you're setting up the eternal empire. Leave everything for tomorrow.'

The track meandered through an extraordinary confection of huts, hovels, shacks and assorted ill-defined constructions that someone called home. All were of only one storey. Some were ancient, built with walls of thick mud with cracks as large as a man's wrist running from their window openings; others were built more stoutly, from industrial brick, often set like forts behind walls or barriers that had been thrown together from corrugated iron or plywood.

'Reminds me of Fort Apache,' Martha whispered, 'after the Indians arrived.'

The most prolific building material seemed to be tattered sheets of plastic, in hues of black, blue and garish yellow. Many windows had no glass and were filled with cardboard, and there was no indication of any communal facilities, no running water, no drainage, not even a shop. The only sign of a power supply appeared to be an illicit electricity cable that had escaped from an abandoned warehouse and snaked away through the community in a tangle of wires. The tracks and alleyways that branched off in many directions were built of nothing more than frozen mud, on which seemed to live little but rubbish and yapping dogs. Absurdly, most of the better, brick-built houses sprouted satellite dishes on their roofs and had securely locked metal gates on their outside walls. There was a hierarchy, even here.

There were a few people about, who cast suspicious scowls at this unknown vehicle. Strangers clearly weren't welcome here, or safe. They passed two young women, arm in arm, who despite the conditions were dressed in bright clothes and high heels, heading off for what Harry assumed must be the nearest bus stop or taxi rank and a night shift in the city centre. A pack of young children scampered across the track in front of them, some barefooted even on the frozen mud. They stopped as they saw the car bouncing over the pot-holes. Suddenly stones rained down upon the Lada's roof and windscreen, before the children disappeared, taunting, up an alleyway. Every inch of this place seemed to hold a sense of menace.

'Why are we here?' Martha asked, a little frightened.

'You don't find any policemen in the Kremlin,' Bektour replied. 'Anyone in a uniform here disappears faster than free cigarettes.'

Harry tugged the anorak more tightly around him. It was bright red; he was mortified to discover it bore the logo of Manchester United. He'd always been an Arsenal man.

'And this way we can avoid the roadblocks,' Bektour continued. 'I can take you on. To the mountains.'

'We need supplies,' Harry said. 'Anything that will keep us warm. Food. Better clothing.'

'That won't be easy,' Bektour replied. 'We'll find nothing here.'

'Do what you can, whatever you can,' responded Harry.

They continued weaving their way slowly along the lanes of the Kremlin. Harry hadn't seen anything as dismal and threatening as this since West Africa, yet, eventually, with a thump of gratitude from the front axle, they left the heart of this other world and climbed back onto a ribbon of concrete, a road that led them out through the outskirts of the community. Here there were signs of more productive lives – a vehicle-repair shop, with mechanics in oiled clothes crawling beneath broken cars, a small mosque set back behind a high brick wall, a scrap metal yard, its rusting waste spilling out onto the road, and, a hundred yards ahead, its small window protected by a metal grille, a shop.

'Let's stop here,' Bektour suggested. 'Get what we can.'

'Whatever we can,' Harry said, unnecessarily, his voice betraying an edge of concern.

Bektour pulled off the concrete roadway and parked beneath the branches of a bare oak tree. Martha thrust all her remaining currency into his hand. 'Food, clothes, anything to keep us dry and warm,' Harry repeated, his words a hollow echo. The shop appeared pitifully small.

The afternoon light was beginning to fade as Bektour disappeared inside. Harry and Martha sat back, in silence, nursing their anxieties, which was why they failed to notice the group of young men approaching the car from the rear until the moment they were deafened by a fierce pummelling on the roof, and by that time it was too late. The driver's door was wrenched open – Bektour had forgotten to lock it – and a jeering face forced its way inside. Harry couldn't understand what was said but knew it screamed of trouble. The face belonged to a scruffy youth whose front tooth was broken, whose cheek bore a vivid recent scar and whose eyes were fixed hungrily on Martha, molesting her. Other faces were pressed to the windows, threatening worse. Five of them. Too many for Harry.

'Harry?' Martha cried in alarm, but all he could do was squeeze her hand.

Suddenly there was a shout from outside. The thug was already clambering over the front seat, but as he heard the cry he stiffened, stopped, then ducked back in alarm, his head banging fiercely against the door pillar. Then he was outside once more, his hand clamped over his forehead trying to staunch a flow of fresh blood, not looking back, running in the footsteps of the others as they fled towards the heart of the Kremlin. For, a short distance down the road, their boots pounding on the roadway as they drew closer, were two heavily armed policemen.

When she saw them, Martha clutched at Harry's

hand ever tighter. 'No, it's not possible. Is God asleep?' she whimpered in despair.

The two policemen had slowed, clearly having no intention of pursuing the men into the depths of the Kremlin, but they would inspect the car, ask questions, ones that could barely be understood, let alone answered. Harry's disguise would be discovered, they would be undone. They had been saved, only to be hurled down from a still greater height. If this was any example of a divine sense of humour, Harry decided it was uncommonly dark.

That was the point when Bektour emerged from the shop. He was carrying a small bag of purchases, and he was shouting. Harry could make out only fragments of what was being said. Bektour was hurling abuse after the retreating thugs, then conversing in a quieter voice with the policemen. Harry thought he heard mention of a sister and her boyfriend. Bektour was trying to head them off.

'I think you'd better kiss me,' Harry said to Martha.

As the two officers approached, they found Martha and Harry in each other's arms. Bektour made some comment, the policemen began laughing, exchanging ribaldry as Bektour threw his purchases into the front seat.

'*Spasibo! Spasibo!* Thank you. I think we've overstayed our welcome here,' Bektour called out to the officers, waving his gratitude. And, trying not to appear in too great a hurry, he started the car and pulled away. The policemen waved back. Only then did Martha and Harry tear themselves apart.

'Show a little more enthusiasm next time, dammit,' she said. She sat back and sighed, smoothing down her coat as the policemen disappeared from sight.

They drove on in silence. Then Harry stretched forward to the front seat and took the bag of provisions.

'That's all they had,' Bektour said in pre-emptive apology. 'It was such a small place. Little more than a cigarette kiosk.'

Inside the flimsy plastic bag were several bars of chocolate, three cigarette lighters, and a large bag of hazelnuts. But no clothing. Harry struggled not to betray his distress. All they had to face the task of escaping across some of the highest mountains in the world was the contents of this plastic bag, the clothes they wore and the gym kit from a teenager's rucksack. It wasn't enough. He looked up to the mountains that lay ahead. The skies had cleared and the sinking sun had begun to set the tops of the peaks ablaze, yet the brilliance of the passing colour only served to emphasize how enduringly grey and forbidding the rest of the countryside remained. The night would be ferociously cold.

They drove for a few more miles, leaving the lights of the city behind them, climbing gently, the windows misting, but the road grew steadily poorer, more narrow, the way increasingly choked by snow. Eventually the car began sliding, its wheels scrabbling for grip, not finding enough. It became apparent they could go no further.

'I'm sorry,' Bektour said.

Harry laid his hand on the young man's shoulder. 'Bektour, such words are pointless. You've been as fine a friend as a man could ever hope to have. And all for a stranger.'

'It was always the way in old Ta'argistan. Perhaps we shall be able to remember such things once again. Before it gets too late.'

'Some revolutions take a lifetime. Others arrive in a weekend. There is always hope.'

'I'm the impatient type.'

'Good.'

As they sat in the back seat of the car, they began a tally of their clothing. Martha had her cheap boots that were little more than trainers, a pair of trousers and the thin bright green coat in which she would have flown back home, plus the cheap anorak she had bought that morning.

'And this,' Harry said, pulling from the gym bag a sweat shirt that brought with it a strong smell of stale male sweat.

'Is that really necessary?' she asked, examining the stains and trying to ignore the smell.

'Yes. These, too,' Harry instructed, producing a pair of desperately underwashed gym socks. 'As gloves. The cold is our greatest enemy out there. Next to Amir Beg, of course.'

'But he's behind us.'

'He'll be ahead of us by morning.'

She struggled into the clothes, looking like a clumsily stuffed rag doll, while Harry brought out the rest of the contents of the bag. 'I need to put on these shorts,' he announced. 'You may wish to cover your eyes,' he said as he began to unbutton his uniform trousers.

'Do I have to?' she whispered. But there was no coquettish smile, she was beginning to understand what lay ahead of them.

Harry slipped off the guard's boots with a sigh of relief; already his toes were raw, but when he tried to replace them with the trainers he found in the bag, he discovered the new footwear was impossibly small. Ta'argis were so much smaller. So the boots would stay. After he had finished rearranging himself, he forced them back on his feet. Even the effort of putting them on made him wince.

Their other supplies were now packed into the empty rucksack and it was zipped closed. Then Bektour stripped off the sweater he was wearing, leaving him clad only in a T-shirt. 'Here, take this,' he said, handing it across.

'No,' exclaimed Martha, 'you've already done too much—'

But Harry's hand was reaching out to accept this last gift. He knew, as did Bektour, how priceless it might be. 'Another debt we owe you. Thank you.' He thrust it at Martha. 'Wrap it around your head. You'll need it.'

As soon as she had opened the door she understood what he meant. She'd never been a wimp, but this was different from anything she had ever experienced. She shuddered as freezing air began attacking every inch of exposed skin. She tied the sweater tightly around her head, then pushed her hands deep inside the old socks. They helped Bektour turn the car round, man-handling it across the ice. They said their farewells. Moments later the car began slipping downhill. Harry and Martha watched it until it had vanished from sight.

'Come on, girl,' Harry said, 'a nice warm bed is wait-ing for us on the other side of those mountains.'

It was a remark that should have called for a riposte of some sort, but as she looked up she found she had to bend her neck to an impossible angle before she could see the tops of the mountains. For the first time she began to comprehend the reality of what lay ahead. She said nothing as they began walking into the rapidly fading light.

It had been Harry's intention to walk through the night, it was safer that way, hidden from prying eyes, and although they had no torch the moonlight reflect-ing back from the snow would be strong enough for them to see. Yet as soon as they set off they found their progress slow; where there was ice their footwear slipped, and where there was soft snow they sank into it up to their calves. The day had already wrung the last drops of strength from them, and although Martha uttered not a word of complaint, she was clearly exhausted. Harry felt no better. They had to stop.

The blanket of snow that covered the landscape around them hid most of its features, but about an hour after darkness they stumbled across a small shelter, a shepherd's retreat used in summer, when the pasture was rich and green and the sun so hot that the stones on the tracks would burn their feet. It was a pathetic construction of old scraps of wood panel, with a single sheet of plywood leaning up against the opening where a door should be. Sheets of plastic were tied over branches to form a roof. Inside, Harry pulled out a cigarette lighter: the interior was bare, apart from a couple of armfuls of old straw that had been thrown or blown into one corner.

'Welcome to the best room in the house,' Harry muttered.

'It's . . .' She was about to declare it freezing, using plenty of colourful adjectives for elaboration, but it would have been pointless. Even inside the shelter, the simple act of breathing left wisps of frost hanging in the air. 'It's charming, Harry,' she declared. 'How romantic of you. I have to admit I'd fancied the idea of a dirty weekend with you but not quite . . . this dirty.'

'A couple of hours. Then we carry on.'

'Chance of a fire?'

He shook his head. 'One spark and the entire structure will burn. Tell the whole country where we are.'

They scraped the straw together to form a crude

mattress, but only after Martha had inspected it closely for any trace of life. They sat side by side, munching chocolate and nuts.

'We must try to get some sleep,' Harry said.

Martha looked at the straw. Some of the strands were moving in the draught. She shook her head. 'Not possible.'

'Martha, you'd be surprised what's possible. Comfort's a little like pain. It's a state of mind. Stay positive.'

'I don't even have a blanket.'

'You have me.'

'Then you'll have to do, I suppose.'

'I could always start making a speech. Sleep is all but guaranteed.'

'I'll try the more conventional route, if you don't mind,' she said, nestling into his arms. 'By the way, you smell like an old sweatshirt.'

He held her tight, trying to cover as much of her body with his as he could.

'We'll make it all right, won't we?' she whispered.

'Course we will.'

'Men lie when they get a girl in their arms.'

'Trust me.'

'You know, one day I'd like to.'

She forced herself closer to him in the straw, sharing the heat of their bodies. It wasn't as she had imagined it might be.

CHAPTER FOURTEEN

A couple of hours, Harry had said, yet daylight was seeping through the cracks and holes in their shelter when he woke. His abused body had demanded rest, even on the earth floor of an open igloo. When his eyes cleared themselves of sleep, he discovered Martha looking at him from close quarters.

'Been awake long?' he asked, stirring.

'Forever.' Her eyes were tired, her teeth trembling, chattering. She hadn't been able to sleep, to shut herself off from the cold. Not the best way to start their day.

He groaned as he moved. Every muscle was stiff and truculent, every movement sent out a blast of complaint from his ribs. At least the cold would have closed the wound on his ear, he reflected, preventing it from bleeding further, so why did it still hurt like hell?

As he watched his breath form vapour trails just beyond the tip of his nose, Harry's mind wandered to what lay ahead of them. The border with Afghanistan was approximately thirty miles away as the crow flew. That sounded encouraging. Thirty miles was nothing compared with what they had made him do at

Hereford, little more than a day's gentle yomp, even in full gear. Except that neither of them bore the slightest resemblance to crows. Picking their way along snow-covered trails, through ravines and valleys, up the sides of mountains, would require much more of them than thirty miles. Anyway, the border was nothing more than a line on a map that had been dreamed up in some imperial outpost and bore no resemblance to the realities on the ground. Even when they had reached it they would still be a long way from safety, with many more miles to make through the mountain wilderness of Afghanistan before they found anything that resembled help.

Long before that they would somehow have to find a pass through the mountains, which would take them up to twelve thousand feet. At that height even the trees had trouble surviving. During the night, whatever warmth the air had drawn from the day would be sucked back out and they would be attacked by temperatures of minus twenty. That was before the wind got up, forcing the cold into them, like a hammer driving nails. They couldn't withstand those sorts of temperatures for long, not in their ludicrously inadequate clothing.

Yet there was one consideration more powerful than all the others. Amir Beg.

Harry should have killed him, he was clear about that now. It had been an unforgiveable lapse to let him live, a moment of pathetic weakness, for now Beg would do everything within his considerable powers to capture them. If the mountains didn't get them, he would. He'd stop at nothing to get at Harry, and his appetite for revenge would consume Martha, too. That was why they had to take this route, because it was the shortest. With every hour that passed, the obstacles would grow more difficult, their strength less reliable, and the pursuit more desperate. They had to get out very soon, or they wouldn't get out at all.

That was Harry's plan. It inevitably had many weaknesses, but also one potentially catastrophic flaw. Beg would have worked all that out, too.

Harry stretched, groaned some more, it was time to get on with it. They – *he* – had already wasted precious hours asleep. He tried to wriggle his toes inside his boots but he couldn't feel them. A bad sign. They were too cold, and the boots too tight. A perfect recipe for frostbite. So instead he wriggled his fingers. He had no gloves, and during the night, as Martha had used one of his shoulders as a pillow, he had kept his hand warm by lodging it in her armpit. The other, he now discovered to his surprise, had somehow infiltrated its way inside her anorak and was clasped both firmly and warmly to her breast.

'I'm sorry,' he stuttered, a little startled, 'I didn't mean . . .'

Her wide eyes stilled his feeble protest. 'You animal,' she whispered, then smiled.

'Martha, I'm so sorry you got mixed up in all this.'

'I'm not.' And, reluctantly, she rolled out of his arms.

Harry clambered awkwardly to his feet and started a series of exercises, stretching his limbs and swinging his arms. 'Gets the system going,' he said, looking at Martha, who was looking unimpressed and had retreated to a corner.

'I'd prefer a filter coffee. Maybe some low-fat yoghurt with fresh raspberries on the side,' she replied.

'We need to generate some heat, but not so much that we start sweating. That'll soak our clothes, which will freeze. We have to pace ourselves.'

'Preferably in a warm bed. With a great dollop of crème fraiche.'

'What?'

'On the raspberries, you fool.'

She began flapping her arms, yet found these get-up-and-go calisthenics genuinely difficult. She was wearing so many layers of clothing that even bending an arm was a challenge. 'I feel like some medieval knight,' she protested.

'Be grateful.' Harry was sitting back down trying to ease off his boots. They were very stubborn, and it was a struggle. When at last the feet appeared, they were unnaturally pale, except at the points where they had been rubbed raw. Martha gasped when she saw them.

'It's fine,' he said, trying to reassure her. 'White is fine. Not fun, but fine. It's when they go black that life becomes a bitch.' He spent several minutes massaging them, taking considerable care, encouraging the blood to circulate, but along with renewed life came the pain, and it was all he could do to force them back into the boots.

'That must hurt like hell,' she whispered.

'Reminds me of something Amir Beg said. That pain is life.'

'Did he?' Martha's eyes were drawn to the bulge beneath Harry's woollen hat. 'The bastard.'

'But he was right. Up here in the mountains there isn't any comfortable alternative. If it stops hurting and you feel nothing, that's the time you should start to panic.'

'Are you going to be all right, Harry? Here am I all dressed up like Santa Claus but you . . .' She cast a critical eye over his assorted items of clothing that were so inadequate they barely covered the skin in places. 'You're not exactly dressed for the job, are you?'

'One night sleeping together and already you're criticizing my wardrobe.'

'A girl's got to have standards.'

'Just consider this as my underwear,' he said, and began pulling the shelter apart, gathering together the various lengths of rope and pieces of plastic sheeting. He squatted on the floor and started tearing at the plastic, then reached for the cigarette lighter and began burning through the rope until he had several shorter pieces, unravelling the strands until they were reduced to string. This string he used to tie the plastic around his arms, securely, so they wouldn't slip too much, but not so tightly that his circulation would be cut. Then he began stuffing straw inside the plastic. She stared at him in bewilderment.

'Not pretty, I grant, but better than freezing,' he declared. He tore a hole in a larger piece of plastic and placed it over his head to form a poncho, tying it at his waist and once again stuffing the space inside with straw. 'It helps insulate. Traps the air,' he said, 'like a string vest.'

'You look like Worzel Gummidge's grandfather,' she declared, shaking her head at the results. 'It's difficult to take things seriously with you dressed like that.'

'It's because I take things seriously that I've got to do this.' He folded up the larger remaining sheets of plastic and bound them with more rope, slinging the bundle over his shoulder. 'Just in case.'

'Of what?'

'Wish I knew.'

The old hut around them was now in a state of far greater decay than even they had found it. It got worse as Harry began dragging out branches and large sticks that had been used to prop up the walls. He selected two that were stout and reasonably straight. 'Walking sticks,' he announced, handing her the smaller one.

They stepped outside, the plywood board that had passed for a door falling flat in front of them, causing an explosion of snow. Despite the decrepit nature of the shelter, they knew it had served its purpose, for as much as they had suffered inside, out here the air was cold enough to chew.

It was then she remembered her present. She dug deep inside her clothing until she found the appropriate pocket. 'Oh, I got you this.'

'What is it?'

She handed across the Red Army medal commemorating the Battle of Berlin.

'A medal? Just for sleeping with you? You give every man a medal? Points out of ten I've heard of, but – a medal?' They were still testing each other, sorting out the pecking order, neither willing to give ground.

'You're a pig, Harry Jones.'

'And you, Martha Riley . . .' His look said it all, everything she wanted to know. He took her in his arms, brushed his warming finger across her cheek. They held each other, sharing everything they had, not only their body heat but also their feelings, which included their unspoken fears.

'Oh, and something for you,' he announced, his fingers digging beneath the plastic coverings and into his pocket. They came out clutching the chess piece. 'For you. For luck.'

She looked at it, and shook her head. 'You keep it for me, Harry. Save it, for when we get home.'

'It's not the only thing I'm saving for when we get home.'

'Come on,' Martha said, sighing as she pushed him away, 'last one to Afghanistan buys the drinks.'

They set off, walking away from the morning sun that was beginning to set fire to the mountain peaks ahead of them, which appeared like the jagged teeth of some snow beast, waiting for them.

Their progress was slow. The snow was covered with a crust of ice, but they couldn't tell how thick it was. Every step they took was a gamble, a stride into the unknown as their feet crunched through the crust. They had no way of telling if the snow beneath them was secure, or whether they were stepping onto a roof of fragile ice that was about to collapse and hurl them into a chasm beneath. The snow tugged at their heels, held them back, sometimes sucking them in up to their knees. And when the sun hit the ice, it began to melt, and they slipped.

Despite the difficulties, there was an intense, austere beauty to this place. The morning air had the quality of finest crystal, enabling them to see for miles. Snow eagles hovered above their heads, the wind picked up snow from the mountaintops and sent it spinning off in wisps of ice that sparkled in the sun like a firestorm. Cascades of blue ice several hundred feet high marked where waterfalls had been caught even as they fell to earth and turned to stunning, twisting sculptures.

They walked for two hours, stopped to rest, and for Harry to readjust his straw jacket, then walked another two. It was their pattern for the day. Harry showed Martha how to squeeze snow into a hard ball which would then slowly melt in the hand, providing a trickle of water to slake their thirst. The air was dry up here as well as cold, stinging their noses and mouths as they breathed, and nothing made them breathe more heavily than their struggle with the treacherous snow. They both began sweating; they would pay for that later.

Bektour had said the road he had put them on led through a valley that would take them all the way to the border. The road petered out into a stony track, but if they could follow it, it would lead them to where they wanted to be. It sounded simple, but the track and everything surrounding it were buried beneath many feet of snow, so during the afternoon they climbed the valley's north side to make the most of the sun and to gain a vantage point for their way ahead. Yet when Harry looked back he groaned. Laid out behind them along the floor of the valley was a trail of footsteps. It looked as though a dying fish had been thrashing its way through water. It could be seen for miles.

'A problem?' Martha enquired.

'We have to assume they'll be looking for us soon. Once Amir Beg has ransacked the city and found no trace of your cute nose or my bloodied ear, he'll turn his attentions further afield. He's not a fool, he knows this is the shortest route to safety. He won't be far behind.'

'So it's a race,' Martha said, panting, still recovering her breath from the last stretch of their climb. 'How long did these hikes take when you were in the Scouts? Or was it the SAS?'

'Oh, that depended,' he answered evasively. He'd probably have managed four miles an hour, for many hours, and be done by nightfall, but then he would have had proper equipment, a clear idea of where he was headed, and an instructor screaming in his ear. He wouldn't have had a woman in tow. They'd been walking six hours, and had probably covered only as many miles. Martha was undoubtedly slowing them down, but he would never say so.

Yet perhaps she picked up on his thoughts. 'It'll get easier, the higher we go,' she said, sitting on a rock, nibbling at a few of the remaining nuts.

'You reckon?'

'I know. When I first got myself elected, I was on another parliamentary delegation, to Dharamsala in India. It's pretty much a community of refugees, those who have fled across the border from Tibet so they can be near the Dalai Lama. It's his headquarters. We had tea with him.'

'Noble of you. Most of our parliamentary colleagues would have preferred a rum and Coke, preferably in the Seychelles.'

'Yes, I began to wonder about that myself. I don't seem to have learned this game very well, do I? That trip was in the middle of winter, too, but I was thinking – India. That's T-shirt and jeans territory, right? I totally overlooked the fact that Dharamsala is in the foothills of the Himalayas. We arrived late one evening in a blizzard. Froze everything I had until the shops opened the following morning. Gave the brass monkeys a run for their money.'

'I'm sure you did,' he muttered, blowing on his fingers to restore their feeling.

'While I was there I met two nuns. They'd just arrived from Tibet. Walked out of the Himalayas, just to be near the Dalai Lama, in a pair of trainers and cheap Chinese clothing. Seemed incredible to me. It had taken them three weeks, yet somehow they survived, so I asked them why they'd done it in the middle of winter, and not waited until summer. And they said it was because of the snow. When it froze solid it was firmer, they could trust it, made it easier to walk, while in summer they'd disappear up to their waists. And that's what we'll find as we go higher, Harry. We're lucky, really we are.'

She was playing the game, too. Attitude was everything, in the mountains, and Martha Riley had plenty of it. What she failed to mention to Harry was that the two nuns had been part of a group of ten, that three hadn't survived, and the rest had been taken straight to hospital suffering from frostbite and malnutrition. Neither did Harry think this was the moment to remind her that she was talking about Tibetans, who lived on a plateau at fourteen thousand feet and who had spent a hundred generations acclimatizing to the cold. They both knew they had to remain positive, for the mountains took raw pessimism and beat it into despair. Yes, attitude was everything.

Harry glanced back once more to the trail of broken snow that had followed them all the way from the hut. 'You're right, it'll be better when the snow gets firmer,' he said. And to hell with the cold. It was beautiful up here, on their own.

It was as he was glancing back in the crystal air that he saw two specks in the sky, at a great distance. Hawks, perhaps, hovering, catching the updraughts that came with the sun. It was several seconds before he realized that it couldn't be, for hawks didn't hover at a hundred and fifty miles an hour.

The Mil Mi-24, known in the West as a Hind, was a helicopter gunship that had been in operation for more than thirty years. It was a Soviet-era creation and became the backbone of Moscow's military effort during the war in Afghanistan, but like so much of the hardware of that era, it continued to be employed long after the original idea had begun to creak and rust. The Ta'argi air force had only four of these machines, two of which were grounded, waiting for spares. The remaining pair was heading straight up the valley towards Harry and Martha.

As they drew closer, Martha cried out in alarm. The Hinds were odd, even ugly, with two cockpit pods in tandem. It gave them a curious bug-eyed appearance, like monstrous flying insects. Killing machines. In Afghanistan those on the receiving end knew them as Satan's Chariots. The sound of their whirling rotors went before them, creating a wall of harsh noise that pounded up the valley, bouncing off the walls like a barrage of artillery. Instinctively Harry and Martha tried to scramble away, but it was pointless, there was nowhere to go. They were on the side of a mountain, it was difficult enough to walk, impossible to run. Martha slipped, fell flat on her face, lay half-buried in the snow. The Hinds came on, thud-thud-thud-thud, following their track. Every sound was magnified in the valley, noise echoing from the walls until it pounded inside Harry's skull and rattled his senses. His wounded ear was agony.

It was impossible to think, there was only instinct left, and his instinct was to save Martha. He struggled to reach her in the snow, stumbling, the air around him shaking, trying to push him over, and he was on his knees, struggling to lift her, hugging her to him. Her eyes stared into his, filled with fright. They grew wider still when they looked over his shoulder. Less than forty yards away, hovering, hammering at them, was the first of the Hinds.

The nose dipped, an almost graceful movement, in the manner of a duellist acknowledging his foe. The two pilots in their separate pods were looking directly at Harry, and close enough for him to see that one had a moustache beneath the Ray-Bans. Then the craft rotated, slowly in the thin air, and the rear cabin door slid open. Inside were six men, in winter gear. Harry recognized one of them. Sydykov. The Ta'argi raised a gloved hand, then pointed a finger, claiming his victory.

It was only as he waited for the first shot, that Harry remembered the prison guard's pistol strapped to his waist. It was an old version of the ubiquitous Makarov, short-range, not accurate beyond twenty feet, and with only three rounds in the magazine. A pea-shooter, when he needed a cannon. The 9mm bullets would bounce off the Hind's windscreen, wouldn't touch the rotors, and he needed a miracle to wipe the cold smile off Sydykov's face, but he had to try. Anything but kneeling in the snow, waiting. He sprang to his feet, scrabbled desperately beneath his plastic poncho, but his hands were frozen, he had no feeling in his fingers. He sensed he had the weapon in his grasp, but even as he dragged it from its holster his numbed, clumsy fingers betrayed him. The pistol tumbled into the snow. Harry threw himself forward, desperate to retrieve it, only to see it slip beyond his reach, down into the valley below. As it disappeared, it took with it Harry's last flickering hope.

The Hind was held stationary beneath its thudding rotors, blasting out noise. Harry looked up, his eyes filled with ice, saw Sydykov's imperturbable face split by a thin smile of triumph. Beside him in the cargo compartment, a soldier crouched with an assault rifle, taking aim.

Martha saw that too. 'Harry?' She called out, very afraid.

He stretched out his hand, took hers, tried to hold on. A final touch.

'Don't you go giving me this goodbye crap, Harry Jones,' she cried above the hammering air. 'Damn it, we only just got together!'

Her eyes spoke of love, of fear, of a desire to stay alive that burrowed deep to her core. It reminded him of another time, on the side of a mountain, when he'd been able to say goodbye with nothing more than a glance.

Julia.

In his mind everything had been white, even though inside the torrent of snow and rock that had swept them both away there must have been almost complete darkness. His senses had been overwhelmed, they couldn't be trusted, and perhaps that was why he remembered it as an entirely silent experience, despite the noise of the mountainside crashing around him. There had been just one word – Julia. Then nothing, until he had woken in a hospital bed, and she was gone.

There had been another recollection that he carried with him afterwards, no more than an impression, and perhaps false. Of how it had started. The first sensation, of the earth moving, the snow slipping, the merest fraction. That first sign had been so insignificant, no more than the beat of a butterfly's wing, yet it had destroyed his world, had swept it away.

Now Harry's memory was playing tricks with him

again. He could feel that butterfly once more, its wings trembling against the ground, and his world slipping away. He couldn't hear the helicopters any longer, or see Martha. There was nothing, except whiteness, which became darkness, until Harry was entirely alone.

The snow on which Harry and Martha were lying was fresh, and thick, and had neither melted nor had the time to freeze tight. It lay on top of a thick slab of old snow that had been compacted and formed a solid base, yet old and new snows were not fully attached. The bond between them was weak – too weak to resist the explosive pounding of the helicopters. Even as Sydykov stared, his victory vanished in front of him. The earth moved, just a fraction, but then more, much more, and the avalanche swept down the side of the mountain until it smashed to pieces on the valley floor, finishing up amongst the conifers that hugged the far side.

Clouds of snow and confused air were thrown up, grabbing at the Hinds. They were old, not the most agile craft, their maintenance and their pilots lacking in mountain flying hours. Not an ideal combination. They began to rock, bucking in the sudden updraught, the pilots struggling to regain control while those in the cargo compartment held on to anything they could find, several growing air sick. Yet better than being buried beneath a mountain.

When at last the tumult had subsided and the Hinds

could recover their station, Sydykov found himself besieged by relief as well as nausea. The mountain had done his work for him. He was glad his task had been completed without the need for enforced brutality; unlike Beg, he hadn't lost contact with his humanity. He was a traveller in a rotten world, and wished only to get through it as quickly and as cleanly as possible. Yet Beg, that supercilious bastard, was a man for trophies and would demand proof that his orders had been carried out, and since his ear had been sliced off he wasn't in a mood to listen to reason or much else. He was a head-on-the-plate man, the type who would believe in nothing until he had his crooked fingers around it. Sydykov sighed. He knew they would have to go down and search, find something to satisfy Beg – a shoe, a glove, a hat, preferably with the skull still inside.

As he surveyed the wreckage of snow, boulders and shattered trees two things tore at his composure simultaneously. The pilot began yammering in his earphone, some pitiful crap about the weather closing in and them having to pull out. He said a storm was on its way, almost upon them. High in the mountains everything was pushed to extremes, and weather conditions could change as quickly as a man broke wind. As Sydykov looked up the valley he could see a wall of angry grey air heading towards them at remarkable speed, as solid as flint, blocking out the sun. The mountains had been disturbed, pulled fresh out of shape, were angry, and blamed these intruders. Sydykov knew better than to take the mountains for granted. He swore. The helicopters would have to back off.

And in the same breath as he cursed, down below, on the valley floor, he saw something move. Some *one* move. A figure, crawling through the mangled snow towards the trees. He ordered the aircraft down, and valuable moments were wasted as the pilot argued, but Sydykov insisted, invoked Beg's authority, and so they dropped. The Hind was already bucking like a startled horse as the storm found them.

It was the woman, they were close enough to tell that now. Sydykov knew they couldn't land, not in this weather, and they couldn't linger, either. He ordered them to start firing. Yet the rear compartment of the Hind was tight on space, only two men could fit in the doorway at once, and the craft was juddering, badly. Typical of the Ta'argi air force on minimum maintenance, the nose-mounted machine gun was inoperative, while the rear compartment's mounted machine gun had been removed. Screw it, the most they got to do in a normal year was a couple of presidential fly-pasts, not bear-hunting all the way up here. They were down to AK-47s. The assault rifle could fire hundreds of rounds a minute, but a single magazine held only thirty, and they had less than twenty seconds before the woman disappeared into the trees. The mathematics were finely balanced. She crawled, they fired. Even as she made the thick stand of firs and pines they kept firing, blasting away wildly, shredding branches, shaking the forest, until a giant foot kicked the Hind sideways, and even Sydykov had to agree it was time to go. In any event, the pilot had already made up his mind. He had no radar, no instruments he trusted and a ton of airborne ice bearing down on him. By the time he heard Sydykov's instruction he'd already thrown the main stick to one side and was putting the chaos behind them. They could come bear-hunting some other day.

Sydykov watched, his eyes streaming in the draught from the rotor blades, until the scene of destruction was swallowed by the storm's foggy maw. 'I'll be back,' he whispered, slamming shut the compartment door.

To live through one avalanche was immense good fortune, to live through two was a miracle. In the case of Harry's second avalanche, God arrived in the unmistakable form of Martha Riley. Once again, as he fell, somersaulted, was pushed, dragged, battered, kicked, his mind filled with white brilliance – this time he decided it wasn't the snow, the brilliance was simply the colour of his fear. It carried him along, scrambling his senses until it dumped him in a pit of unconsciousness that seemed bottomless. Yet he must have stopped falling at some point because gradually he became aware of sounds around him. For some extraordinary reason nothing hurt, not his severed ear nor his ribs, but he could feel a tugging at his legs, which seemed to be attached to the wrong part of his body and were now somehow way above his head. It was some while before he realized he was stuck head first beneath the snow. His arms were in front of his face and had created a chamber of air that had certainly saved his life, now someone was pulling on his foot. He hoped it was Martha. He wanted to cry out but his mouth was packed with dirt and snow, and he needed to save the air, he wasn't sure how much longer it would last. Don't panic, slow the heart, control the breathing, try to ignore the fear. Hurry, Martha, for heaven's sake hurry. He wanted to push, to help her, but he was stuck fast and could only waggle his left foot, but as soon as he did the sounds of scraping gathered pace, grew almost frenetic.

It seemed to take forever, and at times longer than he thought he had. He could no longer feel his feet, feel anything, his mind couldn't focus, closing down, wondering where the brilliance had gone, why everything was growing dark. Was this what it was like for you, Julia, those last moments? Drifting? Sinking? I'm glad it didn't hurt, no pain, my love . . .

He was only vaguely aware of his hand being pulled from the snow, then his shoulders coming loose. Suddenly there was light, the nightmare was coming to an end. He was almost free. Or dead.

'Julia!' he gasped, as he lay spread on the snow, spluttering, filling his lungs.

'Take a second guess,' Martha muttered, leaning over him.

His eyes blinked, only half aware. Then they met

hers. Even with ice still clinging to his lashes, he could see what he had done.

She swallowed, as if it were a stone in her throat. 'I'm sorry it wasn't Julia,' she whispered.

'No, Martha, don't!'

'She was your first thought.'

'It wasn't like that.'

'You must have loved her so much.'

Tears began to wash the ice from his eyes. 'She's dead, Martha. She's dead.' Now Harry knew why he was able to withstand physical pain, because it was nothing compared to his loss – or the hurt he had inflicted on Martha. He took her face in his frozen hands. 'Let's make an agreement, you and me. No more ghosts. For either of us.'

'Yes, please, Harry.'

Yet even as he kissed her, he realized something was wrong. She was perspiring prodigiously, her face a mask of sweat from her effort in dragging him out. She had been digging frantically for almost half an hour with nothing but her bare hands, which were raw, the nails torn. And to his alarm he saw that the sun had disappeared, swallowed in a fog of freezing mist that would suck the body heat from them both, but mostly from Martha in her sweat-soaked clothes. He knew he'd had the easiest part of the deal, lying buried, waiting to be rescued, lost in memories.

He tried to scramble to his feet, but only made it to his knees, still unsteady. 'How did you find me?'

'The roll of plastic you had on your back. One end was sticking from the snow. I just kept pulling on it, like reeling in a fish.'

'You're something special, Martha.'

'And there was you thinking I was slowing you down.'

'Was I?' he lied. He stared at the ground, in shame. 'I'm looking forward to you slowing me down a little more, when we get back home.'

'Then it's a deal.'

But her voice was weak, she was gasping for air. He had to get her out of her sweated clothes. Yet as he raised his eyes, he saw something else. Alongside the damp, there was a dark stain on her clothing, both front and back.

Blood.

It was her turn to lie. 'It's nothing,' she said. 'Doesn't hurt. They got a little touchy after we slipped away.'

He had heard nothing of it, buried beneath the snow, but as he looked around at the devastated forest he recognized the marks of the aerial attack that had left branches shattered and tree trunks scarred.

'Can you walk?' he asked.

'I think so.' But now the adrenaline that had sustained her throughout her frantic efforts to release him had drained, she had turned from tigress to trembling kitten and was finding everything more difficult. Clumsily, and only with his help, she made it to the shelter of a nearby tree, where he sat her down, trying to make her comfortable, leaning her back against the trunk. He began peeling away the layers of clothing, sweatshirt, jacket, and by the time he reached her cotton shirt he found it drenched in blood and sweat. He used handfuls of snow to wipe her skin clean.

He discovered two wounds. The first was on her back, left side, just below the ribcage, where the bullet had gone in; he guessed a medium-sized cartridge, probably one of the assault rifles. It seemed almost innocuous, clean, small, no bigger than the tip of his little finger, but entry wounds usually were. It was the exit wound that most concerned him. This he found on the lower part of her stomach, just above her hip. When a bullet hits something that offers resistance – bone, muscle, a major organ – it releases a huge amount of energy and begins to oscillate, ripping at everything in its path. This can cause the most terrible exit wounds, but this wasn't; it was only a little larger than the wound on her back. It seemed the bullet might not have hit anything of great consequence. Yet it was a wound, straight through her, and still she said it was nothing.

'Get your hands off my body, you animal,' she gasped as the compacted snow slid across her stomach. Good, she could still fight, and would need to. The flesh was unnaturally pale and her teeth were beginning to chatter. Hypothermia. As if having a bullet through her wasn't enough. Already the sweat on her clothing was turning to ice, yet the cold was helping to constrict the veins, stem the flow of blood.

'Take me to a hotel, Harry. Have your wicked way with me, if you insist. Just get me out of this bloody place, I'm freezing . . .'

She needed warmth desperately, but as he cast around him he found nothing. Their bag of supplies, as pitiful as they were, had gone, lost in the avalanche. They had been left with nothing but their clothes and the contents of their pockets. He patted himself down – yes, he still had one of the cigarette lighters. Enough for a fire, perhaps. He began scrabbling around on all fours on the forest floor like a foraging bear – a few stones, a couple of handfuls of old bark, dead twigs that had collected amongst the roots of the trees and in the hollows of branches. With the stones he formed a small hearth on the snow, then built a rough tepee of twigs with other kindling laid to the side. He scratched around inside his plastic clothing to claim what was left of the straw. Finally he ripped the pocket linings from his trousers, soaked them in the remaining lighter fuel, and carefully placed them in the heart of the fire. His hands were shaking as he brought the lighter to the face of the tinder. A spark, which died, then a second and a third until finally the lighter offered up a weak flame, its fuel almost spent, but it was enough. The cotton caught and started feeding on the tinder, which began to smoke. Soon they had a flame, then a fire.

Yet it wouldn't be enough. A small fire, on its own, would never win a straight battle with the damp forest and the excruciating cold of the night that was to come.

They needed more. With one of the broken branches that lay scattered about, Harry began to scrape out a shallow trench in the snow beside the trunk of a fallen tree, just long enough and wide enough to take two bodies. Then he draped the plastic sheeting over the trunk, weighing it down with rocks and stretching it so that it formed the roof and ends of a tent. He collected armfuls of broken fir branches, laying them thickly over the plastic to provide a layer of insulation. Smaller, softer fronds from the trees he scattered over the snow floor of the trench, and on top of those he laid the sheet of plastic he had been using as a poncho. They had their shelter. There was just enough room for two tightly pressed people.

For all the pain he was feeling, Harry could see from the set of her lips and the greyness around her eyes that she was feeling more. As soon as he had dragged her inside he began removing her clothing.

'Hey, you incorrigible romantic,' she muttered, still mocking as he fumbled with the zip on her trousers. Even as he watched, the colour was leeching from her face; he prayed it was mostly the fading light. Her jacket, once bright green, was smeared on one side with a crust of coagulated blood and sweat, and the cotton shirt beneath was worse. He took them off, as tenderly as he could. In the pocket of her jacket he found her panty liners; these he used as makeshift dressings on her wounds, spreading them gently over the angry skin, binding them in place with the bandages from around his own head. Her wounds were still oozing blood.

'Bet you can recommend a good surgeon,' she said.

'Shut up.'

'I can't, I'm a politician.'

He looked into her eyes. He could see the fear lurking just beneath the mockery she used as a shield. He dressed her once more, in all the dry clothing he could find – Bektour's sweater she had been wearing around her head, the sweatshirt, the anorak, his own woollen hat, then he laid her down on the floor of the tent, trying to make her comfortable.

'How do you feel?' he asked.

'Better than I otherwise would, thanks to you.'

'No, really, how do you feel?'

'I feel nothing.' She ran her tongue across lips that were strangely dry. 'Isn't that when you said we should start panicking?'

'I'm not finished with you yet, woman.'

He went to the fire, stripped off his uniform jacket, leaving him bare to the waist, then used it as a glove to pick up the now super-heated stones he had placed around the edge of the hearth. He took them back to the tent, and laid them carefully out on the floor, so that they began to warm the inside. He buttoned up his jacket once more, as securely as he could, remade the fire, then crawled back inside the tent and lay down beside her. He held her tight.

*

As the body grows cold, and unnaturally so, its functions change. Blood vessels to the hands and feet constrict and the blood supply slows as the body concentrates on major organs. The extremities begin to lose sensation, stop functioning, might even freeze, get frostbitten. As the cold grows more intense, the decline deepens, passing from fingers and toes to hands and feet, then arms and legs. What is discomfort becomes pain, what is at first clumsiness grows to incapacity. After that, the body's in real trouble.

Normal body temperature, or normothermia, is around 37 degrees. As its temperature drops the body begins to shiver, sometimes uncontrollably, while it struggles to generate more heat. Below 35 degrees major changes take place, it's not just the hands and feet that close down but more important bits, too. Another degree down, below 34 degrees, and the blood supply to the brain begins to suffer, and confusion sets in. The pulse begins to slow, breathing grows shallower, the uncontrollable trembling eventually ceases, the body doesn't have sufficient energy left even to shiver. It falls asleep as it prepares for an enduring siege in an attempt to protect the final stronghold of life, the heart. Everything else is expendable.

Harry knew of the dangers of hypothermia, he'd been trained by some of the best people in some of the worst places. And his improvised heating system was working remarkably well. The plastic sheeting and insulation from the branches had trapped the heat given off by the stones and his own body, and although it was minus 25 degrees outside he'd been in far worse situations. Yet still it wasn't enough. It wasn't just the hypothermia; Martha's system had to cope with a bullet through her guts. Unknown to Harry, the bullet had nicked the spleen, and it was slowly leaking. While the cold caused the entrance and exit wounds to constrict and all but close, the wounds inside proved more stubborn. Even as Martha lay silent and asleep, she was bleeding.

Harry had fallen asleep, too, despite his determination to watch over her. His own body had been put through the wringer, and while Martha felt nothing, every muscle and joint in his own body was screaming in protest. Sleep was the only protection. When he woke in the middle of the night, his arms were still folded gently around her, his body sharing its warmth, but he found that she was colder than ever.

He knew she wouldn't be able to walk. He would have to carry her. He'd done that before, carried a man much heavier than Martha, two days and two nights. But that had been through the deserts of Iraq in the lead up to the first war, not through ice-covered mountains. It had also been more than twenty years ago, and the man had died anyhow. Yet if the sun was strong in the morning, and he could get Martha up to a spot where she might draw from its strength, then anything was possible. Hell, what did it matter if he had to carry her all the way to Afghanistan? Anyway, what choice did he have?

As the light of the new day began to penetrate the forest and trickle inside their makeshift shelter, Harry examined the still-sleeping Martha. He hated what he saw. The skin was not only unnaturally cold but luridly pale, like wax. The flesh around her eyes had shrunk, turned grey, the lips blue. The defences of the body were turned inwards, locked in what was clearly a monumental fight. She desperately needed that sun. He rubbed his thumbs across her forehead, trying to wake her, but there was no response. He pinched her cheeks – still nothing – tried again, began shouting in her face, growing more anxious with every breath, until eventually her eyelids flickered and opened. She was awake but very confused. The eyes took many seconds before they were able to focus on him and she remembered where she was.

'Life's a bitch, eh, Harry Jones?'

Her voice was weak, little more than a gasp. Harry noticed that her breath didn't condense into a warm fog the way his did.

'Morning, Martha.'

'Is it?'

'Of course. This is the day we get out of here.'

'That's great, Harry . . .'

'Get you fixed up. Then take you off on a long holiday. Somewhere warm, I'm thinking. Mauritius. Seychelles. Wherever you want. Plenty of sand and sea. Get you in a bikini.'

'Compare scars.'

Her eyelids were closing once again, her strength almost gone, but he couldn't let her sleep. He was terrified she might never wake up. He shook her gently. The eyes flickered open once more.

'So much to find out about each other,' she whispered, 'so little time to find it.' She knew she'd never make it.

'Martha . . .?' He didn't know what to say.

'Thanks for trying, Harry.'

'Don't give up on me, don't you dare!'

'Silly man, you still think you're in charge, don't you?' She tried to smile, but it didn't work. A puzzled look crept slowly across her face. 'Do you mind . . .?'

'What?'

'If I made friends with Julia? Would that . . . be all right with you?'

He wanted to scream, to rage, to tear the world apart.

Her voice was almost inaudible. 'Don't let the weeds grow on my grave, Harry,' she whispered. 'No weeds.'

'I don't . . .?'

He didn't understand. What did she mean? But her eyes had closed and she wouldn't respond.

All through the night he had tried to keep the fire going and the stones reheated, but now he ignored them. They weren't working. He knew there was something else going on, something inside her, guessed there was bleeding. And he didn't want to leave her, not for a second, even to tend the fire. He lay down, his body across her, his arms around her, protecting her.

Her breathing grew more shallow, until it was all but impossible to detect. Almost an hour later she stirred. Her eyes opened, but did not see. The lips parted, but at first he could not hear what she was trying to say.

'Martha? Stay with me, Martha!'

Then the words came, in a wretched sigh.

'For a moment, I thought we were going to make the earth shake, you and me.'

And her hand reached out for him, but there was no strength, flailing, like a ribbon in a draught, barely touching him, yet causing more pain than he thought he could endure. Then her arm fell gently to her side. When next he looked, her eyes had closed.

For another hour he lay there, holding her. Only then, when the fire outside was long spent and he found his own body growing cold inside, did he give up hope, and finally let her go.

CHAPTER FIFTEEN

Harry was no stranger to death. They'd been travelling companions for much of his adult life and he had grown familiar with its many forms, yet such uncomfortably close acquaintance hadn't made him lose his reverence for life. There was, to Harry's mind, no such thing as a good death, only the ending of a good life, and Martha's had been one of those. Death was a cheat, a charlatan who offered eternal peace but so often left behind nothing but perpetual torment. In Harry's view, death never deserved the final word, yet he knew that death, in the form of its surrogate, Sydykov, would be back. That bastard didn't deserve the final word, either. He owed that much to Martha.

The heavy, cloying mists left by the storm were beginning to break as the morning took a firm hold on the skies. He hadn't much time. With a sense of desolation he took apart their shelter and laid Martha on a bier of young branches, her skin as pale as the snow that surrounded her. He set about emptying her pockets of everything they contained – her purse, a pen, a few scraps of paper, which would make excellent kindling if only he could find something to light it with, the reading glasses she so hated to wear, and a nail file she had probably forgotten was ever there.

She lay stretched on her bed of green. He didn't know if Martha had been religious but offered up a short, silent prayer in any case, and not just for her. If there were a God, Harry was going to need him, too. As he stared down upon her the sun, freshly hauled above the mountaintops, filtered through the trees and brushed gently across her face. She was at peace, yet he had never been further from it, and he let forth a pitiful cry of fury, like a wounded animal. Then he picked up Martha's body and began walking.

The avalanche had kicked all sense out of the countryside and everything it had touched was left in ugly, ragged confusion. Several times Harry almost stumbled as he made his way through the mounds of boulders and broken snow. Further up the valley, beyond the footprint of the landslide, the mountains drew together to create a ravine, deep and filled with massive boulders fallen from above, and barely wide enough for a road to pass through. Between the rubble of the avalanche and the ravine ahead lay a stretch of the valley floor that offered the only section of flat, undamaged snow in sight. This, Harry reckoned, was where Sydykov would come, the only spot where a helicopter could land safely.

Harry took Martha's body to a point near the middle of the area torn apart by the avalanche. He found an exposed spot – in the sunlight, she deserved that – and laid her down in the snow. In the rapidly clearing air she could be seen for miles. He knelt down, brushed his fingers through her hair, pushed a stray wisp tenderly into place, kissed her lips. There were tears on her cheeks, but they were his own.

Then he left her. He scrambled into the shadows and waited.

They came out of the early morning sun, even while the mists still clung to the hollows of the valley floor. He heard them before he saw them, the thump-thump-thump of the rotor blades, then, as they drew closer, the whine of the turbines. Two of them again, the Hinds, powering their way up the valley but slowing as they came close to the broken mountainside. They began circling, high up; it wasn't long before they spotted Martha's body.

Harry knew this was where he had to take his stand. He had few enough options, and there was no point in trying to outrun them all the way to Afghanistan. They would pursue him like a rat in a barn, so better that it be here, where Martha had died.

The Hinds were cautious after yesterday's confusion. They spent several minutes circling, before one dropped slowly from the sky and, as Harry had suspected, came to rest on the section of the valley floor before the ravine. The other stayed aloft and at some distance; they didn't want to risk another avalanche. The lead

Hind settled slowly, testing the snow before trusting its full weight, and even when it was on the ground the pilots kept the rotors turning. For a while the scene was enveloped in a blanket of snow thrown up by the downdraught, but as the rotor blades slowed, so the squall subsided and the rear door was hauled back. A grim smile of satisfaction tugged at Harry's lips. Framed in the opening was the unmistakable figure of Sydykov.

He jumped onto the snow, testing it, kicking at it with his heel, then his toe, sending small splinters of ice flying. His men followed, crouching beneath the circling rotor blades until they had gathered at a safe distance beyond. Harry watched them from his position, hidden behind boulders less than a hundred and fifty yards away. He could see Sydykov gesticulating, his breath forming vapour trails as he gave his men their instructions. Then they spread out and advanced upon the rubble left by the avalanche, beginning their search for Martha. Harry knew their progress would be slow. They would be forced to clamber over the chaos of destruction, as he had done. In any event, they were in no hurry. Martha wasn't going anywhere.

He tried to calculate how much time he had. Perhaps five minutes? Once they had found Martha they would search around for any trace of him – he hoped he had obliterated any sign of his presence. They would seek, not find, then they would be back. Yes, five minutes max.

He approached the Hind from the rear, hidden out of sight of the pilots in their pods, using what little cover he could. It would take no more than one backward glance and it would be over. He left a trail of footprints behind him, no chance of hiding those, but as he drew close to the helicopter his tracks disappeared, mixed in amongst those left by Sydykov and his men. He crept up behind the rear rotor, kept as close as he dared, the whine of the blades thrashing in his ears, scything at him, trying to suck him in. Neither of the pilots climbed out, none of the troops looked back; he hauled himself into the rear compartment.

The space was small, little more than five feet in height, not sufficient for a man to stand upright and able to hold no more than eight men, tightly squashed. Harry was familiar with Hinds. Way back, during the Soviet invasion of Afghanistan, he'd trained the muja-hedin to use Stinger missiles, those grey hawks of the battlefield, preying upon the Hinds, smashing them out of the sky, but that familiarity had been at a con-siderable distance. He'd never been this close, never inside. He moved to the rear, next to the rotor shaft. The walls were covered with thick soundproofing material to dampen the brutal battering from the engines and rotors; he pulled at it, there was a ripping sound as it came away from its Velcro fixings to expose a metal panel about two feet square, hinged at the bottom. He flipped the latches at the top and the panel fell away. He caught his breath in anticipation. Behind it was a cat's cradle of wires, hoses and pipes running up towards the rotor head.

If the turbines were the heart of a Hind and the electronics its brain, the hydraulics were its backbone. Without the hydraulics, nothing worked; it became little more than a load of tin. And there, in front of him, were the system's guts. The layout was similar to a NATO Apache – not surprising, given the plagiarism and outright theft indulged in by Soviet designers. A dual system, two sets of everything, so that if the main system failed or was damaged, the secondary system would take over. That's how vital the hydraulics were. In-built redundancy, nothing left to chance, an essential precaution when you're being shot at by a bunch of hairy-arsed Afghan mountain men.

But Harry had no gun, hadn't even a knife. He came armed with nothing more than Martha's nail file. Somehow he would have to make it enough. He had no difficulty picking out the hydraulic pipes from amongst the scramble of electrical cabling and oil and fuel pipes. They were high-pressure hoses braided with stainless steel, capable of dealing with intense internal forces, even if they did look at least fifteen years old. These pipes gave him his chance, his only chance; if he could knock out the hydraulics, he would cripple the entire craft.

He examined the nail file then tore his eyes away; he didn't want to dwell on how pathetic it seemed. He held it like a bayonet, placed the point in the centre of the hose, and pushed. It made not the slightest mark. He pushed harder, with exactly the same result. He twisted it like a screwdriver, round and round; it didn't leave a scratch. He stabbed as though with a dagger, but it was futile. No matter how old the hose was, it was a match for Martha's nail file. With a final desperate lunge he thrust at the hydraulics once more. The nail file struck, then bent in abject surrender.

His head was pounding, his ear screaming, his time running out. He began to rifle through his pockets for anything he might use. 'Martha, don't let me down, not now,' he pleaded. He found her credit cards, reading glasses, the pen, everything she had left, and all of it totally bloody useless. He cast around the cabin in despair, what else was there? He searched his pockets once more. Julia's Rolex. A small key for a locker, the only item he'd found in the prison officer's uniform. Nothing else. It was pointless. He slumped back against the wall of the compartment, his eyes closed. 'I'm so sorry, Martha,' he whispered. He felt drained, his knees refused to support him any more, he slid slowly to the floor, defeated. Sydykov would be back in moments. It was over. Everything.

It might have been different. He had been a brilliant soldier, an inspiring politician, a man who could have made a real difference, and perhaps he already had, in many ways, but there could have been so much more – *would* have been more, if Julia had survived, or Martha. It shouldn't have finished like this. He'd already won so many honours, more than any man of his age, yet they meant nothing now, for it was all going to come to an end, here, in this frozen waste of Central Asia. And no one would even know about it. No more medals for Harry Jones, not even posthumously. They didn't hand out medals for failure.

Random images collided inside his exhausted mind. And he remembered Martha's medal, tucked away in his top pocket. Her gift, from the Battle of Berlin. He pulled it out. It was made of dull brass that glistened as he turned it. *Za Bzyteey Berleena. For Defeating Berlin.* It had on it a red star and oak leaves, dangling from a begrimed ribbon of red, black and gold stripes.

And the ribbon had a pin. A sixty-something-year-old pin, manufactured in some Siberian gulag and rusted to match, yet nonetheless a pin. A pin . . . He was armed once more! He hauled himself to his feet, reached yet again for the tangle of cables and pipes, his fingers closing on one of the hydraulic hoses. He forced the point of the pin into it, and pushed. And pushed, and pushed still more.

He felt it move. Only a fraction, a little like those butterfly wings on the mountainside, but it was enough. He pulled the pin out of the casing, and escaping behind it came the faintest mist. The second pipe took longer, offered more resistance, perhaps the pin had been blunted, but he got through that, too. Slowly, the access tunnel with its cabling and pipes was filling with a fine mist, tiny droplets, of hydraulic fluid.

He knew he hadn't much time, Sydykov would be back very soon; it might already be too late. He snapped the cover into place, reattached the sound-proofing that hid it, swiftly checked that he had left no sign of his presence. Then he returned the medal to his pocket. 'Thank you, Martha. Now just a little bit more of your magic, please?'

He stuck his head out of the compartment. He could see signs of movement, a head bobbing through the jungle of moraine left by the avalanche. He jumped down to the snow, and within seconds was gone.

He only just made it back to the cover of the boulders before Sydykov and his men reappeared, like bathers emerging from a sea. Four of them were carrying Martha. They had made a perfunctory search around the body for Harry, but found no sign. The situation was clear, he had been buried beneath the mountain-side, and no one would find his body until they came to clear the road after the spring melt, and even then they would find only what the wolves had left. Beg would have to make do with just one trophy. Martha. They threw her into the back of the helicopter with as little grace as a sack of coal.

Harry watched, transfixed. The sound of the engines grew louder, the rotor blades turned faster, drifting snow blew into a storm as cautiously, hesitantly, the Hind lifted into the air. A hundred. Two hundred. Three hundred feet into the air.

The puncture holes were minute, but the hydraulic

system in the Hind operated at extreme pressure. It was slowly losing that pressure, not so much yet that the alarm was activated, but enough to make the craft a little more cumbersome to handle, as if things weren't bad enough in these conditions, at such high altitudes, towards the limits of the Hind's service ceiling, which made the controls sluggish and unresponsive, difficult to read. That's why the pilots didn't notice, at first – that, and the fact they had so few flying hours up here that they couldn't tell the difference between altitude sickness and a bad curry. There were so many things to take care of – updraughts, downdraughts, ice on the blades, the viz shot to crap. Didn't help that they were packed behind with all these bodies. It was normal for the craft to wallow like a mother pig. Things would be better when they got up a little airspeed.

It is when a helicopter is travelling at its slowest that it is most vulnerable. The controls don't respond so well, it is more difficult to fly, more unstable. So the pilots noticed nothing out of the ordinary until the hydraulic alarm started to scream at them. The senior pilot's first instinct was to drop the nose, put on power and throw his craft away from the mountainside. Yet, inevitably, as he grabbed anxiously at his sticks, he over-controlled and over-torqued massively. This would, perhaps, have been no more than a momentary discomfort, had it not been for the hydraulics. As the pilot demanded more of his systems, the hydraulic fluid was pushed around at still greater pressure, which meant that more of it escaped – and that made the craft still more difficult to handle, which meant the pilot demanded ever more of his systems . . .

It was like an inexperienced driver trying to control his first skid on ice, except this was several hundred feet above the ground. As Harry watched, the Hind began to pirouette and stumble through the sky, lurching forward, up, aft, as the pilot yanked at his controls in ever-growing panic. He might still have been able to stick the Hind on the ground, but he never got the chance. The fine mist of hydraulic fluid was floating around the engine and gearbox. It was highly inflammable, and they were exceedingly hot. The Hind blew up with terrifying explosive anger. Harry threw himself behind the boulders as a firestorm of hot gases and debris shot across the valley. He was burying his head in the snow when there was a second explosion as the Hind hit the ground. By the time he looked up again, he could see nothing but flames.

High above the scene the second Hind circled, inspected, hovered in indecision then flew away.

It seemed forever before Harry could approach the scene. The fire burned with an extraordinary ferocity and there were several more minor explosions, yet contrary to his first impressions, not everything was in flames. The explosion had scattered chunks of wreckage across a wide area, and as soon as it became safe, he began a methodical search. What he found in many places sickened him; pieces of charred and torn wreckage, not just of the machine, but of those on board. The explosions had shown no mercy. He had to try to find Martha, but there was nothing, except for a single sleeve of her bright green jacket that seemed almost spotless and unsoiled, as if it had just come from her wardrobe. It was all that was left of Martha Riley, except the memories. He took the sleeve and dropped it into her funeral pyre.

A little further away he found one of the soldiers. He had been blown clear of the fire, was relatively undamaged. Harry stripped him down to his shorts, and dressed himself in the winter kit the soldier had been wearing.

The last thing he tried on was the boots. The boots! Even in the stolen socks they slipped on remarkably easily. His feet were still screaming, but this time in relief. He sat in the snow, tied up the laces, stood, stamped, jumped, tested them.

Then, in those boots, Harry walked all the way to Afghanistan.

PART THREE

The Avenger

CHAPTER SIXTEEN

It took Harry almost three weeks to find his way home. The journey wasn't without incident, much of Afghanistan was still a place of hazard for any Westerner, but nothing compared to what had gone before. The world around him seemed to have changed as he travelled in from Heathrow Airport; people with their heads down, eyes fixed on the ground, making sure their feet were still there, their jobs and homes, too. The middle of an economic meltdown wasn't the best time to fuss with other people's problems. But he'd changed, too. He was a different man from the one who had left with Roddy Bowles, and Sid Proffit, Malik, and Martha. He felt as though he was viewing everything at a distance; nothing was quite in focus. Harry hadn't known what he'd find when at last he arrived back in London; he'd hardly expected marching bands, but on all sides he was met with a damp blanket of indifference and incredulity.

There were his friends, of course, but like everyone else they were distracted, many assuming he had been away on a protracted holiday. Some even expressed envy, until they saw him and caught sight of his face. A Harley Street plastic surgeon had tidied it up and was even talking about growing him a new ear on the back of some genetically modified mouse, but in the meantime he changed his hair style to hide the worst effects. He had also lost weight, too much and too quickly, and there were shadows around his eyes that spoke of turmoil and made people feel uncomfortable. In any event they had other, more pressing distractions than events that had taken place in a country they had never heard of; the month of January had been the wettest on record, many rivers were flooding once again, despite last year's assurances, and Big Ben had suddenly stopped. No more chimes. It was taken as an omen. Harry spent two days on his return, hitting his phone, digging up apathy, getting nowhere. Yet it was the Establishment, rather than any individuals, that upset him most. It seemed as if no one in a position of authority wanted to know, as though they had better things to do. When he tried to report Martha's death to the office of the Westminster coroner, it was made clear that they weren't about to become involved in a problem on the darker side of the planet when there wasn't even a body. They suggested the police. So Harry phoned Scotland Yard, spent a considerable time on the phone explaining the situation, and they sent an inspector, but he was clearly sceptical and kept insisting that the Yard couldn't sort out political problems. He also repeatedly failed to spell Ta'argistan correctly as he sat taking notes.

'Strange, sir, but the authorities in –' he searched for the name yet again – '*that country* say they know nothing about the matter,' he declared, closing his notebook in a decisive gesture. 'But rest assured, we'll look into it.'

Harry did not rest assured. The Chief Whip wasn't around, away burying his mother amidst claims that the local hospital was riddled with a super-bug, so Harry tried to phone the Foreign Secretary, but his call was returned by one of the junior ministers. 'Of course I'll put a few ferrets down the rabbit hole, Harry,' the minister said, 'as soon as I get back from my next junket. A week of sweating my way up the Zambezi, can you believe it? Those buggers Stanley and Livingstone have got a lot to answer for.'

Harry grew increasingly exasperated. He was working on too short a fuse, he would be the first to admit it; he was a long way off recovering from his ordeal, even physically, let alone with what was tearing at him inside. Yet the Establishment seemed concerned with little more than ticking boxes on lists, not taking him seriously. So his spirits lifted when, one afternoon, there was a knock on the door of his parliamentary office in Portcullis House and a man introduced himself as Superintendent Ron Richards. He was not in uniform but it seemed, at last, that the Yard was giving the matter more weight.

'I hope you don't mind me saying, Mr Jones, but I've been an admirer of yours since you were a minister in the Home Office. I was only a sergeant then.'

'Then you have grown, Superintendent, while I . . .'

Harry spread his hands and indicated his room with an expression of mock despair. His ministerial office had been ten times the size.

'Why bother with an office, when you have the entire world.'

'Thank you. Will you have tea, coffee?'

'Something stronger, perhaps? This is an informal visit, Mr Jones, off the record, if you don't mind.'

'Then you'd better sit down, Ron, and call me Harry,' he said, reaching for the Scotch.

They sank the first mouthful, then the policeman chewed his lip. 'It's like this. The Ta'argis aren't being very helpful. So far as they are concerned, nothing happened, and if it did, it must be down to you.'

Harry sighed, sensing where this was going. His ear began to throb once more.

'It's a delicate one. You can understand that, can't you, Mr Jones?'

'Harry,' he insisted, but the superintendent was clearly feeling ill at ease.

'It seems some journalists are trying to stand up a story that there might have been . . .' Richards cleared his throat. 'A lovers' quarrel. Forgive me, but you and Mrs Riley, were you . . . close?'

'She died in my fucking arms!' He found it difficult to contain his anger at the implication.

'OK, but do you have any proof of your allegations?'

'Apart from a couple of broken ribs, multiple lacerations and no bloody ear, you mean?'

'Yes, apart from that,' Richards responded, holding his ground.

'I can't believe this. You're doubting my word? Accusing *me*?'

The superintendent leaned forward in his chair, making the distance between them less formal. 'I'm trying to show you what you're up against, Harry.'

Harry closed his eyes, fighting to suppress the surge of outrage that was swamping him. 'She was murdered, for pity's sake. You trying to tell me that doesn't matter?'

'What I'm trying to tell you is that it's a swine of a job investigating an alleged offence in a country on another continent when there's not a shred of physical evidence. Not even a body.' The superintendent sipped his whisky. 'The Ta'argis have sent me a copy of her visa. It's fully stamped. Date and time in, same on the way out. They say she left the country, voluntarily and in fine shape.'

'Then ask Sid Proffit, for God's sake.'

'Oh, I intend to.'

But, of course, Sid would be able to prove nothing, either, merely that he saw Martha leaving the plane. 'Look, I've got her credit cards and IDs,' Harry said, diving into the drawer of his desk. 'How am I supposed to have got hold of those?'

'How, indeed. They prove only that *you* were with her, Harry, not the Ta'argis. Just digs you in deeper.'

'Damn it, Ron, what the hell am I supposed to do?' Harry demanded, thumping the desk in exasperation.

'Wait till something else turns up. There's not enough here to go on.'

'Martha Riley won't be turning up!' His head was pounding, his heart, too.

'Harry, take it from me, nothing's going to happen here in a hurry.'

'So what the hell happened to justice?'

The superintendent stared, warning him. He fought back.

'I won't let it rest, Ron. This isn't just some parking ticket I can write off and forget!'

'That's what I thought. And that's why I'm here, man to man. To make sure you don't raise your expectations of what we can do. And to advise you not to get yourself in too deep, not to take things into your own hands. It can only cause you trouble.' He stood up and finished off his drink. 'I'm sorry.' He sounded as if he meant it. The policeman placed the empty glass down on the desk and walked from the room without another word. Harry was left, staring at a closed door. He picked up the phone and furiously began punching buttons, thinking of calling a couple of editors, but the time wasn't right for the whimsies of the press and probably never would be. He jammed the phone into its cradle, then picked up the entire piece of equipment and hurled it into the wall. It ended on the floor, imitating a disemboweled octopus.

Everywhere Harry looked, it was the same. It was more than indifference, it was as though he had become an embarrassment. No one wanted to know, they preferred to pass by on the other side, to look away, waiting for the grass to grow and cover everything up.

Even Zac didn't help. He couldn't be found. Harry found a message from him on his answering machine, but it was vague, saying he would call back, but he hadn't. Seemed to have disappeared yet again. Then, late one night, while Harry was at home, very much on his own, the phone rang.

'Harry?'

'Zac!'

'Harry, you marvellous goddamned idiot. They let you out.'

'You know my persuasive talents.'

'How . . . the hell are you?' The voice was breathless and the words came a little slurred, but Harry sensed it wasn't the drink.

'I'm in great shape, for one of Amir Beg's guests. And you?'

'Oh, some medical stuff they're seeing to. That's where I am now, surrounded by some good-looking nurses. They're pouring all sorts of shit into me, just to keep themselves out of harm's way.'

So that's why he was having trouble talking. Harry didn't much care for what it implied. Zac's treatment in Ashkek must have been even worse than he'd thought.

'Harry?'

'Yes, Zac.'

'I don't really know what happened . . .'

'I'll fill you in one day.'

'I want to come and see you. Soon as I can.'

'You up to the travelling?'

'They're letting me out of here on parole in a couple of days. Then a plane to London. So we can talk. If you've got time.'

Harry assumed Zac wanted to offer his thanks. 'There's no need for that, Zac.'

Yet there was more in the matter than Harry had realized. There was an edge to Zac's voice that was insistent and even suggested desperation. 'Sure there is. There's nothing but broken bits in my mind, Harry, and I've got to know. I need your help putting all them screwy little pieces back together again.'

'Trouble is, Zac, whenever you and I get together, some bastard out there always seems to want to kill us.'

'I'll see you. Couple of days tops, Harry, I swear. Even if it does kill me.'

He was as good as his word. Two days later Harry got a message; Zac was in town. They arranged to meet that evening at the Special Forces Club in Knightsbridge, tucked away in a backstreet behind Harrods. It was in a discreet Edwardian red-brick terrace, no nameplate outside its modest black door, its membership traditionally reserved for those who had served in intelligence and special operations communities. It was a place of secrets, whose walls were lined with memorabilia of those who had gone before, some of whom were household names, others whose real names had never been known, somewhere for Harry and Zac to talk without fear of eavesdroppers, and particularly reporters.

Yet although the club might ban journalists, that didn't stop their newspapers. It was while Harry was waiting for Zac in the bar that he picked up a copy of the *Evening Standard*, its late edition. Buried some way inside he found a small item, that Mrs Martha Riley, the MP, was believed to have disappeared walking in the mountains while on a recent visit to Ta'argistan. It was thought she might have had an accident, presumably a fatal one. A Ta'argi consular spokesman was reported as saying that it would inevitably be many weeks before any attempt could be made to locate the body. 'Spring comes very slowly in Ta'argistan,' he was quoted as saying. The *Standard* concluded that a confirmed death would involve a by-election, but that given the economic circumstances and the government's crumbling popularity, no one was in any hurry. In the meantime, until the situation became clearer, matters in Martha's Midlands constituency would be taken care of by a neighbouring MP.

Harry crushed the paper into a small ball and threw it in a bin. The Establishment had spoken, or rather whispered. He ordered a drink, a stiff one, not bothering to wait for Zac.

He was standing at the front door of the club, waiting, when Zac's taxi arrived, but it took Harry some time before he realized that it was his friend. The man who prised himself out of the back seat was not the man Harry had known; he looked little better than the tattered figure who had been hauled from the cell. Zac's once broad, straight back was bent, and he held on to the taxi door for support, then the railings as he hauled himself up the club steps.

'I know, I know, I look like shit,' he said as Harry took his hand. He stared at Harry's ear. 'Don't look too good yourself.'

'Just come from the consultant, as it happens. They're going to grow me a new one.'

'Give me his name. I could use him.'

Harry looked into Zac's face. It had a tautness that spoke of intense strain, a sheet of chalk where there should have been a tan, and eyes that were distant, halfway to another world.

'Fuck,' Harry breathed.

'Yeah, I know.'

'What did that bastard do to you?'

'We talk. Over a drink.'

'You allowed to drink?'

'Harry, those dumb-shit doctors tell me not to drink, not to fly, not to look at nurses' butts. What's the point in stopping me? Ain't gonna make no friggin' differ-ence.' He was still holding Harry's hand; there was a faint trembling, more butterfly wings. 'Those quacks tell me that I might have a few more months if I behave myself, but I don't know how, Harry, and I guess I'm too old to learn.'

Harry stood on the doorstep of the club, his eyes brimming with sorrow. Zac braced his shoulders and threw him a look of scorn. 'I think this is the point where you're supposed to ask me what my goddamned poison is. It's a vodka martini.' He handed Harry his coat as though he was a cloakroom attendant and walked stiffly to the bar.

Soon they were seated in a quiet wood-panelled corner, beneath a portrait of a long-tressed French girl who had been a wartime resistance fighter, deceased, Dachau. Two vodka martinis stood in front of them, mixed to Zac's meticulous instruction.

'To the enemy. Up its arse,' Zac suggested in toast, raising his glass with great care.

'Which particular enemy?'

'Big C. Eating me away, Harry.'

'And I don't suppose your stay at the Ashkek Hilton helped you any.'

'That's partly why I'm here. I don't remember much, but it seems like you pulled me out of one hell of a hole. I need to say thank you.'

'My pleasure. I was doing no more than returning the favour.'

'That was a long time ago.'

'Makes no difference.'

'So can we stop saving each other and just sit down and drink, like two regular bastards?'

'Well, I guess we can always try.'

They drank, and ordered more.

'One thing you can tell me, you all-American hero,'

Harry said as the second martini began to take hold, 'how the hell did you end up in bed with the President's wife? I know you've always displayed a remarkable lack of judgement when it comes to women, but even by your standards that was awesome.'

'That's the bitch of it all, Harry, I never did. I was set up.'

'What?'

'Oh, I met her, sure I did, at some business reception. Cute. With a track record, apparently. And I flirted with her, of course I did, but no more. I'm not a complete dickhead. You go screwing with a President's wife in a place like Ashkek and you ain't gonna come out with any balls. Then a week or so later Papa Karabayev was off on some foreign trip, I was out on the town, pretty loaded, and I get a message that she wants to see me, and a car's waiting. So I get in and I'm taken to the Presidential Palace outside of town. A back entrance. Taken up some stairs, into a room, hang around admiring the wallpaper, then I get a message that she's changed her plans, is sick, that's what I was told. Never saw her. But others saw me, of course. Next day I'm playing a poor game of chess in the park and suddenly I've got the muzzles of half the palace guard sticking in places I really don't want them. By lunchtime I'm making buddies with Amir Beg, and he's showing me photographs of the presidential missus getting a real going over from some guy who Beg claims is me.'

'But? There has to be something.'

'No, Harry, not guilty. I never had the pleasure, but I sure as hell paid the price.' He was breathing heavily with the effort of talking, and the memory. 'I was framed.'

'Why?'

'You know, old Amir never got round to telling me. Too busy beating the crap out of me.'

'Could it have been to do with your work?'

Zac shook his head. 'Can't think so. I was clean, truly. Oh, there was some funny shit going down at the uranium mines, all sorts of strange whispers, but I never went near any of that. It was like I was picked out in a lottery. They needed a fall guy, and I won first prize.'

'Why you, I wonder.'

'I was available. And American. I got the impression they don't like Americans.'

'Or Brits.'

'Yeah.'

'There was another American, too, Zac, although she'd lived here a long time, long enough to become an MP. Friend of mine. Name of Martha.'

'Do I remember her? I seem to think there was a woman, a cute redhead . . .'

'She didn't make it, Zac.'

'Jesus.' He sighed. 'I'm sorry. I feel terrible about that.' He gazed into his drink, shaking his head mournfully. 'What a senseless waste. As you can see, I really wasn't worth it.'

'She didn't do it for you, Zac, what she did she did for me. And for herself.'

'Can tell she meant a lot to you.'

'You'd have liked her, too, although whether she'd have taken to you is another matter.'

They exchanged forlorn smiles, built on an old friendship where insults were used as endearments.

'She said something, it still bugs me – in fact she said a lot of things that bugged me,' Harry said, trying to make light of it. 'Right at the end, she told me not to let the weeds grow on her grave. She made a point of it, but I'm damned if I know what she meant.'

'I can't claim to be much of an authority on what women mean.'

'It was important to her.'

'Which makes it important to you. So to me, too. Harry, if you'll allow me, I'd like to raise my glass. To Martha. And to you. To you both.'

'Yeah. That would have been good,' Harry said softly. 'Perhaps even great.'

They sat, and they talked, and they drank, until they got too drunk. It was when they started singing, Harry's maudlin song about the barman, and all those good resolutions they drank to forget, that the doorman called them a taxi.

'Where are you staying?' Harry enquired as he helped his friend into the back of a black cab. Zac seemed to be having trouble lifting his left leg high enough to get it into the cab, and ended up stamping at it like a horse.

'At the 41, next to the Royal Mews,' he said, when at

last he was done. He slumped rather than settled into his seat, his energies almost consumed. 'It has eleven different types of pillow and a rather fine bust of Napoleon. And did I mention the exceptionally pretty Polish maids?'

'Not much point in suggesting that you start acting your age.'

'And if you keep the window open, I'm told you can also hear the bands at Buck House. It's what I most admire about the British army. Your bands.'

'You keep your windows open in January?'

'Had them open all the time in the Ashkek Hilton.'

'I remember.'

'Although they never left any chocolates on my pillow.'

'Maybe I'll point that out to Amir Beg, next time I'm through.'

Mention of the name seemed to knock the last of the strength from Zac. He let forth a sigh of deep inner weariness; the time for banter was done. 'Harry, if you don't mind, let's go by the river. I do so love it at night.'

'Me, too,' Harry agreed, even though it would mean a wild detour. He gave instructions to the cabbie. 'So how long are you staying, Zac? When do you plan to go home?'

'Home?' The word was uttered with an unmistakable degree of confusion, as if he were reading the instructions for assembling a new toy. 'I'm not sure, Harry, been away so damned long. Anyway, I've got a bit of thinking to do. Don't want distractions. So I guess I'll be staying a few days, until I've sorted things through.'

'Things?'

'You know. Dying things.'

His face looked ashen in the street lights. They didn't talk any more until they were on the Embankment and approaching the Albert Bridge. It stood out brilliantly against the night sky, lit with thousands of bulbs. 'Slow down, will you,' Zac instructed the cabbie, 'there's no hurry.' He turned to Harry. 'You know, someone once told me they named this bridge after Queen Victoria's husband. Beautiful, isn't it? Doubt P.J.'s likely to name anything after me, except maybe the trash can. I've made a mess of things. Too many loose ends.'

'Haven't we all? But your life has been pretty exceptional, if you ask me.'

'It's had its moments, but it's what comes next that I'm thinking about right now. You know, Harry, this cancer, it's not a great thing to be with. I don't want to spend enough time with it for us to become friends or anything. Know what I mean?'

'I think so. I'm sorry.'

'Don't be. I'm not here to complain, just to sort things out. I always knew I'd never die with my slippers on, but I don't want to die in a medical smock and pissing through a straw, either.'

Harry said nothing. He understood, would feel the same. They drove on in silence.

'The 41,' Harry said eventually as they passed by the

ruined hulk of the Battersea power station silhouetted on the other side of the river. 'It's pretty up-market.'

'Sure ought to be, the prices they charge. Hell, it's not like I'm saving for my old age or anything.'

'Come and stay with me, Zac. At home. Until you're sorted.'

'Why?'

'Many reasons. So you can teach me how to fix martinis, for one. And because if I were in your position, that's what I would want. I won't get in your way, Zac, whatever you decide.'

'Appreciate that.'

'There's something else. What you said, about being set up. If that's so, I've got a personal interest in finding out why.'

'Martha, you mean.'

'I think that's perhaps what she meant. About not letting the weeds grow. Cleaning things up.'

'She was American. That's what she would have wanted. Screw the bastards.'

'Who are we talking about here, that's what I want to know? Who in hell's name are they?'

But Zac didn't reply. He had fallen asleep.

'Hello, Roddy.'

'Ah, Harry, is that you?' Bowles spluttered, his features stretched taut in alarm, like an Edvard Munch canvas. 'Been meaning to catch up with you,' he lied.

'And now's your chance.'

They were standing in a stairwell where Harry had been lying in wait. Ever since Harry had returned Roddy Bowles had been avoiding him, turning on his heels in corridors, suddenly disappearing from crowded bars, avoiding eye contact. Harry suspected he had even been sending his secretary ahead to scout out the ground and make chance encounter impossible. So Harry had decided to ambush him.

Unlike many of his colleagues, Bowles had chosen not to move his office to the glass and steel extension of Portcullis House across the road from the main Parliament building. Instead he had stayed within the honeycomb cake of the old Palace of Westminster. The centre of power and gossip had tended to gravitate to the new facilities, but it meant that MPs' rooms in the old Victorian building were quieter, less brash than the hi-tech boxes of Portcullis House, and they were far more lavishly decorated. Bowles was a man who preferred Pugin to Peter Jones, and had little interest in the machinations and rumour that swirled beneath the atrium at Portcullis. He preferred Gothic nooks and crannies, and dusty shadows, so he had stayed. It was also a much better place to avoid the likes of Harry Jones, yet now he could avoid him no longer. Harry was on the back stairs, facing him, blocking his path.

'You'll have to forgive me, Harry, I'm in such a desperate hurry, late for dinner. But could we get together very soon? So much to catch up on. Give my office a call.'

'I already have. Twice.'

'Truly? I didn't know,' he blustered. 'My secretary, been unwell, distracted. I'll have a word with her, get her to put something in the diary. Now, if you'll excuse me . . .'

He tried to pass, but found he couldn't. Harry was clutching his arm, the fingers digging deep into the flesh. There was also a look in his eye that frightened Bowles.

'Well, perhaps I could spare a couple of minutes, Harry, as it's you.'

'The Terrace, I think.'

'But . . .'

He was about to say it would be dark and deserted, but presumably that was the point. If there was to be a scene, better it shouldn't become common gossip. They walked silently through the labyrinth of corridors, meeting few people at this dining hour and ignoring those they did, until they came to the carved oak door and steps that took them onto the Terrace. It was a large paved area nestling between the wings of the old Palace and overlooking the Thames. And it was, as Bowles had predicted, deserted and decidedly uninviting.

'You sure, Harry? Brass-monkey time out here. How about a drink inside?'

But Harry led him on, to one of the darker corners, where the coverage of the CCTV cameras would be at their poorest, until they were leaning on the balustrade and peering into the dark, turbulent waters of the Thames. A stiff breeze was slicing along the river, whipping up disgruntled waves and tugging at Bowles' hair.

He got out a packet of cigarettes and offered one to Harry. It was declined with a cold stare. The cigarette took several attempts to light. Bowles suddenly felt very isolated. In the distance, to their left, they could see the lights of the traffic pouring across Westminster Bridge, and he very much wanted to be with other people, not just with this strange man who was still gripping his arm. It was hurting.

'Can't tell you how sorry I've been about—'

'Shut up, Roddy.'

'You know, as leader of the delegation I should have—'

'Yes, you should have. But you didn't. Instead, you've been spreading rumours about Martha and me, that we were having an affair, got involved in some lovers' quarrel.'

'No!'

'It doesn't matter, Roddy. As it happens, I did love her, although we weren't having an affair. How's your curator friend, by the way? Still working her way through your collection?'

Bowles wriggled in discomfort. 'She's fine, thank you. Look, Harry, man to man, I'm sorry if anything I've said has been misinterpreted, but—'

'But bollocks, Roddy. We both know what's been going on. The difference is that you don't know what I know. And I'm just about to tell you. You see, when you didn't return my calls, I telephoned your wife.'

'You what?'

'No, not about you and your art collection. Even in this place there are still some basic codes of conduct. At least, I like to think so.'

'She's not well,' Bowles blurted pre-emptively, 'gets very confused.'

'Like your secretary, you mean? You really must get a bigger box of excuses, Roddy.'

Bowles threw the remains of his cigarette into the river. It was turbulent, looked angry, slapping impatiently against the Embankment, a high tide doing battle with the water flooding down river from the recent rains.

'You do your wife an injustice,' Harry continued. 'She sounded pretty up-to-date to me. I reminded her we'd talked earlier, about Ta'argistan, that I'd been there with you, talked to the people in government. She was very friendly, asked if I was involved in the airport project.'

'That stupid—' But Bowles bit back his outburst. It was time to listen.

'Didn't come as much of a surprise, Roddy. You were so far up the President's backside that at times I suspected you had parking rights. You monopolized the Minister of Transport, then someone told me that you stayed on for a couple of days after the official visit was over. And it wasn't to look for Martha and me, either.'

'Look, Harry, where the hell is all this going? So I'm interested in helping the Ta'argis. Nothing wrong with that.'

'And helping yourself, of course. I spoke with a friend in the City, she put out a few feelers – you know what that place is like. Seems you're involved with a consortium that's been raising a whole shed-load of investment money for Ta'argistan.'

'And why not? They need a new airport, new hotels, new roads. Fuck you, Harry!'

He was growing angry, which suggested he was a little scared. On the bridge an ambulance, with sirens blaring and emergency lights flashing, was forcing its way across the river in the direction of St Thomas's. They followed its progress. Perhaps it was a colleague, a fellow MP. That's how some of them died, in the ambulance.

'Let's hope that doesn't mean another bloody by-election,' Bowles said, trying to steer the conversation onto firmer ground. 'We're in enough trouble as it is. Have you heard the latest? There's a whisper doing the rounds that the PM might be forced into calling an early election. You know what that would mean. This place will become an abattoir. I don't take things for granted. It could all come to an end for us soon, Harry.' It sounded like a plea of mitigation.

'So stuff a little money away while we can, is that it?'

'Harry, for Christ's sake, the Ta'argis need to move forward, I want to help them. What's wrong with that?' Bowles began fumbling with his pack of cigarettes once more.

'I think this is the point in the conversation where you're supposed to lead me astray a little, suggest that a man with my experience would be most welcome on board, that there'd be room in your enterprise for me, too.'

'What? After the stunts you pulled in Ashkek?'

Ah, so Bowles knew more about what had gone on than he was admitting. 'You're letting your knickers show, Roddy.'

'I'm helping the Ta'argis build a new airport. That's it, and that's all of it.'

He lit his cigarette and took the nicotine down deep. As his hand came up, it was trembling slightly, and Harry couldn't help but notice the set of expensive cuff-links that glittered in the half-light.

'Your efforts to improve their infrastructure are to be applauded, Roddy. And, I presume, well rewarded. Except they don't seem to have shown up in the Register.'

Bowles' entire body jerked, as though he'd been stroked with a red hot poker. The Register. It was to modern Westminster what the tumbrels had been to Paris during the revolution, the means by which a politician's financial entanglements were supposed to be faithfully and fully recorded, a proposition that was pursued by many with almost as much sincerity as their wedding vows.

'Damn you, Harry,' Bowles spat, 'don't you dare patronize me, not you with all your inherited wealth, a man who's never had to do a day's work in his well-heeled life.'

On another occasion Harry might have argued the point. The army, the House of Commons, they'd been real jobs in his eyes, but he had grown used to the petty jealousies that others found so difficult to hide.

'I think I can guess how it goes, Roddy. Not only do the parliamentary authorities not know of your little scheme, but I suspect the tax man doesn't, either. There'll be nothing in your name, of course, you're not stupid enough for that, but I suspect your wife's been signing a lot of the documentation. Yes, your poor, confused wife.'

'Leave her out of it!'

'But it's you who got her involved, Roddy, not me.'

Bowles once more discarded his cigarette and immediately lit a new one.

'The government says that will kill you,' Harry said.

'Fuck the government! And fuck you, too.'

'Talking of which, it began to get me thinking about your curator. And your magnificent art collection.'

Bowles began coughing as though he was ripping out the lining of his lungs.

'Is that how they pay you, Roddy? In a few minor Pissarros and Picassos? Pay the girlfriend, too? I have to admit, your taste is excellent, you'll be able to sell that collection any time, anywhere in the world, without the Inland Revenue ever getting to know about it. Those paintings are your pension plan, as good as gold and far more reliable than dollars.'

Bowles looked down into the dark, turbulent waters, then glanced along the Terrace, making sure they were alone and not overheard. 'What is it you want?' he said, his voice still hoarse from the coughing.

'What I want,' Harry replied softly, 'is to know what's really going on in Ta'argistan. I want to know why they need a new airport, new hotels, new roads. What's going on that is about to turn a country that's the arsehole of Central Asia into something that's fragrant and attractive to some of the meanest, most sour-nosed money men in the world. And I want to know it now.'

Suddenly Bowles was flying through the air, across the balustrade, and was dangling upside down, held by his legs, staring at the oily river. The contents of his pockets began falling around him – lighter, pen, mobile phone, keys, wallet, dropping into the dark water and disappearing, except for his cigarettes, which were dragged away in a giddying dance by the fierce current. The cold spray whipped up from the river was hitting him in his face. He began to scream.

'You're crazy!'

'I agree,' Harry replied, calmly, letting his grip on Bowles slip a little.

'You wouldn't!'

The grip slipped a little more.

'I can't swim!' Bowles cried, but it was turning to a whimper.

'Not the answer I need, Roddy.'

Bowles tried to twist and stare around him, surely someone was watching and would come to his rescue, but the Terrace was deserted, the winter's night dark, they were in the shadows. And his belt was about to burst over his hips.

'All right! All right . . .' he cried out in submission.

Harry pretended not to hear, kept him dangling, made him repeat his cringing surrender, this time with considerably more passion, before hauling him up. Bowles slumped onto the paved floor, sobbing.

Harry stood over Bowles, not letting him up, while the other man grew ever more wretched, answering questions, filling in gaps, protesting, pleading, wiping away tears of humiliation, until at last Harry was satisfied. Only then did he allow the other man to scramble to his feet.

'You must be mad! If you'd let me slip, I'd have died,' Bowles said, still gasping for air.

'I know.'

'Harry, listen to me, please,' Bowles pleaded, mounting one last defence. 'It wasn't my fault. I told you not to go to Ta'argistan in the first place.'

'That's right.'

'Nothing that happened to you there had anything to do with me.'

'I accept that.'

'But you're going to ruin me anyway, aren't you?'

'Yes.'

'For pity's sake, why?'

'Many reasons. But mostly because of Martha.'

'I don't really know what happened to Martha.'

'No, of course you don't. But you should have asked,' Harry replied, disappearing into the night.

CHAPTER SEVENTEEN

When he returned home later that evening, Harry shared what he had discovered with Zac. For a while, they both sat silently, staring at the fire in Harry's hearth, chasing the consequences. They both knew where it would lead.

'I thought your policeman friend warned you not to take things into your own hands,' Zac said eventually.

'And not to park on yellow lines,' muttered Harry. 'Anyway, we're talking Roddy Bowles. The creep doesn't count.'

'Even so.'

'Even so *what*, Zac? I hate it when you go all enigmatic on me. You're an American, for God's sake.'

'You're going to see this through, aren't you?'

'Of course. To the end.'

'Me, too.'

Harry turned to look at his friend. 'Look, Zac, I think I know—'

'Shuddup, Harry.'

'What?'

When Zac turned from the fire his eyes had regained

some inner spark. The body was weak, but the will was still overpowering. 'For this one time in your life, Harry, shut the fuck up and listen. Listen hard. We do this together. And we do it my way.'

'What way is that, Zac?' Harry asked softly, although he already knew.

'The way you would do it, if you were in my shoes.'

Harry poured them both another drink. And then he listened.

Dictatorships never depend upon just one man. They rely on a System, which is built of many parts. Take one part away, destroy it, and the entire System may become unstable and begin to fall apart. Karabayev knew that, he was a master at playing the Ta'argi system, which was why he had risen so high and survived so long. Power abhors a vacuum, and he had learned it was better not to create one.

Yet when he was shown the evidence, he felt he had no choice. He looked out from his office with its sweeping views of Ashkek, and his instincts slowly hardened. Ashkek was his city – oh, there were some cities in Ta'argistan less loyal, and one or two he hadn't dared enter for several years, but this was his place and he refused to be made a fool of in his own home. Yet on his desk, in the folder in front of him, was the evidence that Amir Beg was trying to do precisely that.

Karabayev had been told that the American who had been caught screwing his wife had been dealt with, as he had ordered. Amir Beg had given his word on that, just as he had recounted how the Englishman who had caused so much trouble over the matter was also dead, buried somewhere up in the mountains. So how was it, asked the President, that he was holding a photograph of the two of them, posing for the camera, shaking hands, smiling, almost jeering as it seemed to Karabayev, and standing in front of the British House of Commons with a time code on the photograph bearing last week's date?

Not that Karabayev believed in the implicit integrity of photographs, they could so easily be faked, he'd seen to that himself for one or two of the show trials he'd needed to arrange while on his way up. A thought even flitted through his mind that the photographs of the American with his wife might not have been what they purported to be, but such thoughts were quickly pushed aside by the other item in the folder. A computer printout of a bank statement, one of Amir Beg's, from a foreign account. The existence of the account didn't trouble Karabayev, they all had such arrangements, a pension plan for those who lived long enough to enjoy such things, although he was shocked to see that Amir Beg was receiving a higher kickback from one of the Ashkek casinos than was he. Even that could be taken in his stride and easily corrected, but what couldn't be so lightly dealt with was the evidence in the bank details of Amir Beg's deliberate treachery.

Karabayev had long known of Beg's envy and had sensed the lack of loyalty, but evidence had been hard to find. Yet here it was, staring at him. The seducer and his friend were still alive, and it was Amir Beg's doing.

He couldn't drag himself away from the photograph. His eyes kept coming back to the jeering face of the American, imagining it sweating above his wife's own, and his anger grew to a point where it overpowered his caution. He wouldn't be mocked, and neither would he be betrayed. He wasn't only the President, he was also a man, and he was as mad as hell.

He summoned Amir Beg, and when he arrived at the Presidential Palace a little later he was met by the Presidential Guard, but instead of receiving the usual salute he was bundled into the back of a car and driven straight to the prison. At first he struggled, then he threatened, but as he was dragged towards the Extreme Punishment Wing he began instead to plead. He was pleading ever more fervently as they dragged him up his own scaffold and placed the rope around his neck. He kept demanding to know why, what was the reason, but no one bothered to reply. Had this sort of thing ever needed a reason?

Karabayev had long wondered about Beg's private life, and particularly his sexuality. Beg had never married. He had never been found with his trousers round his ankles, yet none of the inevitable rumours this conduct inspired had gained any lasting life. He was a loner, not as other men, and Karabayev had come to the conclusion that Beg's time in the gulag had crippled more than simply his hands. Yet when, later in the day, he saw the new photographs that landed on his desk, the President laughed. They showed Beg with an unmistakable bulge beneath his trousers. At last Karabayev had discovered what turned the poisonous little runt on.

A damned good hanging.

It was afternoon, around the time the English have tea, Harry said, but Zac was having none of that. No tea, no cake, he insisted, in language that was characteristically colourful. In any event Zac's appetite had all but disappeared and it was beginning to become apparent on his shrinking frame. So they made do with one drink. A martini. Zac chewed the olive very slowly, as though it was rarest caviar.

They reminisced, about good times and the good people they had known. Zac even talked about P.J., and it was as if she were still there, beside him. Eventually, laughing gently after yet another story, he ran his finger around the bottom of his glass, checking that the final drop had gone. 'Guess it's time for a bit of weeding, old friend.'

'I'm going to ask you just this once, Zac. Are you sure?'

'You know, P.J. put that exact damned question to me just before we got married. I went ahead and did it, anyway,' he replied, putting down his glass and rising stiffly from his chair.

Hervé d'Arbois was punctilious for a Frenchman and arrived only seven minutes late. Harry was there to greet him at the door. D'Arbois was in town only briefly, but had been tempted to delay his departure a couple of hours by Harry's offer of dinner at the Special Forces Club, a venue he knew only by reputation, and by the enticing suggestion that Harry was at last in a position to close the chapter on Zac Kravitz. They sat at a quiet corner in the dining room studying the menu.

'If you're tempted by the Dover sole I'd recommend having it grilled with nothing but a little butter and lemon. The béarnaise sauce is . . .' Harry shrugged apologetically. 'I think there's been an outbreak of Turks in the kitchen. But we could wash it down with a bottle of Chablis. A grand cru. Protected by a stout glass bottle and a thousand years of tradition. They can't screw that up.'

'My dear Harry, it seems I am in your hands.' The Frenchman bowed gracefully, sitting beneath a portrait of Charles de Gaulle.

'Did you ever meet him, Hervé?' Harry asked as the waiter delivered their first course.

'Naturally. Many times. The first after my unit returned from Algeria. I was barely eighteen.'

'You didn't resent what he did, giving Algeria its

independence? After so much blood had been shed for it?'

'Unlike you, I suspect, my friend, I have always regarded myself as more of an administrator than a politician. There are some things that must be. You accept them and move on.' He dipped his fork into a shell of crab meat. 'In any event, and without being too indelicate, most of the blood that was shed was theirs.'

'You've come to an age where you can be philosophical about such things.'

'I don't think it's so much a matter of age as of attitude and experience. We have both been soldiers, Harry. We know that sometimes there are no easy answers. That's one of the reasons why, if you will forgive me saying so, I have never been tempted by a career in politics.'

'I take your point. How's the crab, by the way?'

'Very English.'

'You should have joined me with the potted shrimp,' Harry said, digging his fork into the tub of brown crustaceans submerged in solidified melted butter.

The Frenchman laughed. 'Even your persuasive powers backed by an entire case of the finest burgundy couldn't bring me to that, my friend.' He raised his glass, while Harry inspected something unpleasant that was dangling from the end of his fork.

'I think you're right,' Harry said, abandoning his starter and reaching for his own glass. 'Poor bloody shrimps. Why do we have to drown them in congealed butter?'

'We all suffer for our traditions.'

'Yet when you French call them *crevettes* they become a thing of beauty. Except . . .' He paused. 'Isn't that what you called them in Algeria? Those you threw out of the helicopters a thousand feet above the Mediterranean?'

'You know what it's like in war, Harry. Sometimes you have to take a short cut. And there was never a shortage of Arabs, no matter how many we tried to teach to fly.'

Harry seemed to recall that many of them had been weighed down with concrete. He was tempted to suggest it was a strange type of flying lesson, but the waiter was back, removing dishes. Harry moved on.

'Hervé, I promised you an update on Zac.'

'Ah, the exceptional Mr Kravitz.'

'He and I want to thank you.'

'For what?'

'If you hadn't mentioned him to me, I don't think Zac would have got out of Ta'argistan alive.'

'I am happy to have been of help.'

'I don't know whether you keep up to date with what's going on in Ta'argistan?'

'I must admit, I am a little out of touch . . .'

'Chaos. Confusion. There's talk of an attempted coup. Apparently Karabayev's strung up his right-hand man, Amir Beg. Did you know that?'

'As I said, I am a little out of touch,' d'Arbois repeated. As a holding position, it left a lot to be desired.

Harry sipped at his wine, his eyes fixed on the other

man. 'I wonder if it had anything to do with the quarter of a million dollars I sent Amir Beg.'

'You what?'

'I sent him a quarter of a million dollars.'

'From your own account?'

'Yes.'

'Then it appears you have wasted your money, my dear Harry.'

'I don't think so. There are ways to get rid of bastards you hate without throwing them out of helicopters, you know.'

'You set him up?' D'Arbois gasped.

'Precisely. That amount of money paid into his account was bound to look like a bribe to anyone who discovered it. And it's so damned difficult to keep your account details secret when you're taking kickbacks from as many people as Amir Beg.'

The Frenchman began spluttering, incredulous. 'You send that sort of money to all the people you hate?'

'Can't afford to. This endless bloody recession's kicked the hell out of me, too. But if I'd sent any less, I don't think Karabayev would have jumped to conclusions. A quarter of a million's about the going rate, don't you think? For jumping to conclusions?'

'I have no idea,' d'Arbois protested, laughing, spreading his hands in bemusement and reaching for his glass.

'All that confusion at the top. It's bound to play merry hell with the uranium-mines project.'

The glass stopped halfway to the Frenchman's mouth. 'What project is that?'

'Don't you know? I think I've pieced it together. Zac heard rumours about it, then Roddy Bowles filled in a few more bits of the picture. It's a fascinating one. I'm sure you'll be interested.'

'I'm sure I shall.'

'You see, Hervé, the Soviets turned out to be very poor house guests in Ta'argistan. When at last they drove away, they left all their radioactive rubbish behind. Mineshafts full of the stuff, and none of it properly stored. So there's been an international project to help the Ta'argis clean it up, funded by Western governments under their foreign-aid programmes. And while their engineers were knocking around the old uranium mines, they stumbled across something else. A mountain range full of a mineral called heleonite. Very rare up to this point, but apparently it's going to transform our lives. It's the new silicon, reckoned to be the next really big thing in computer chips. It'll transform Ta'argistan, too. Better than oil. That stuff's going to make the country, or whoever's in charge, richer than Croesus.' He paused. 'Hervé, you're spilling your wine.'

The glass was suspended halfway between the table and his mouth. The Frenchman had been sitting as if carved from stone. 'Your tale, it's too distracting, Harry,' he said, slowly lowering his glass.

'So, naturally, everyone wants a piece of the action,

the inside track,' Harry continued. 'Who can make Karabayev smile, and who can get him to sign, that's the name of the game. Whoever gets their hands on his most sensitive parts first will have found the key to everlasting prosperity. Except, of course, the man's an animal. Instinct, rather than intellect. Distrusts everyone, even Ta'argis, but particularly foreigners. Hide of a rhinoceros but deep down exceedingly temperamental.'

An expression of amusement brushed around the Frenchman's lips. 'I find it's a common quality amongst politicians.'

Harry lowered his head, accepting the point. 'And this whole enterprise is like a long-distance race, everybody bunching on the bend before they get to the home straight, putting their best foot forward. And trying to trip up the competition. Which brings me to Zac.'

'Ah, yes, Mr Kravitz. I was wondering.'

'He was set up, you see.'

'Rather like you set up Amir Beg?'

'Very much so. Except Zac was accused of sleeping with the President's wife, and by doing so humiliating the President. Doesn't get more basic than that, does it? No way back from there. But it wasn't the wife getting screwed, you see, Hervé, it was the Americans. With a background like Zac's, Karabayev's never going to believe he's not working for the CIA or some other bunch of cowboys in Washington, no matter how hard they've tried to wash their hands of him. Coming into the home straight, the Americans have fallen flat on their face, giving everyone else a huge advantage.'

'It's an exciting theory, Harry,' d'Arbois said, 'but who would do such a thing?'

'Almost anyone. The stakes are too high to be squeamish.'

'But who, specifically?'

'Zac doesn't know.'

'A pity – for your theory,' the Frenchman suggested, flattening a wrinkle in the starched tablecloth with the palm of his hand.

'Yes, I guess that's right. But let me pursue it. You see, there's one huge flaw in this get-stinking-rich scheme. It all depends on Karabayev staying in place. Otherwise . . .'

'Of course. There is nothing. And you think he's in danger?'

'You won't have heard this, Hervé, not being close to the scene, but I reckon getting rid of Beg was a huge risk. Opens up all sorts of intrigue. And there is an opposition movement, I met some of them while I was there. In fact, I've been helping them, sorting out a little funding.'

'Democracy?' D'Arbois couldn't hide the disdain that strayed into his voice.

'I know, a bloody terrible idea, but so is Karabayev and Beg. He cut off my ear, you know. Even put a noose around my neck. That gives me attitude.'

'I saw your wound, I was trying discreetly to ignore—'

'They also killed a friend of mine. A rather extraordinary woman called Martha Riley.'

'Then I am very sorry for your loss. But it confirms the dangers of playing with places like Ta'argistan. Leave it alone, Harry. Don't try to play God.'

'There's another way of looking at it, Hervé, that what happened to Amir Beg suggests the dangers of playing with me,' Harry said, very quietly. 'Or with Zac. He's an unforgiving bastard, that man.'

'He's fortunate to have you as a friend. As, I hope, am I. But you will forgive me.' He glanced at his watch. 'My train, you understand?'

'You haven't had your fish.'

'My *soul* may wait for eternity, sadly my train will not,' he said with an engaging smile, playing on words.

'Come on then. My car will take you, it's waiting outside.' They rose, Harry hurriedly signed his club account as d'Arbois collected his coat. A black Mercedes was parked in the road, the engine running. The two men walked down the steps of the club together, knotting their scarves.

'You know, Hervé, I have dreams about my time in Ta'argistan. I still have that bloody rope around my neck, and Martha dying in my arms. I can't break free of it.'

'But you saved an old friend.'

'You're right. And it was you who brought us together. I'll never forget that.'

They climbed into the back of the car, and the Mercedes set off through the back streets and rat runs.

'Yes, it was you who brought us together, wasn't it, Hervé?' Harry said, picking up their conversation. 'And that's what got me thinking. Because if Zac was set up, then so was I.'

'I beg your pardon?'

'Was that it, Hervé? You and your business pals, wanting a little extra leverage? Screw the Americans through Zac, then go one better and screw the British through me? Leaving the field clear for – well, whoever's bought you for the moment.'

'That injury to your head must have done more harm than you realized, Harry,' the Frenchman said stiffly.

'You've always worked on the shady side of the system, ever since you started dragging Arabs from the Kasbah and trying to teach them to fly.'

'Your conclusions are preposterous, my friend.'

'I don't think so. And I'm not your friend, Hervé.'

'Then I think I should get out.'

'No, I'll get out. I need a walk. Some fresh air. He'll take you on.' Harry tapped the driver on the shoulder and the Mercedes began to pull over to the side of the road, its indicator flashing.

'Where are we?' d'Arbois demanded. It was a dimly lit street, he didn't recognize the location.

'Near the Embankment,' Harry said as the driver opened his door to let him out. 'Waterloo in ten minutes.' He took the driver by the hand and gripped it firmly. 'Thank you,' he said. His voice was soft, almost forlorn.

'You're welcome. Wish I could say any time . . .'

'Oh, there's something I nearly forgot. Should have given it to you earlier.' Harry unhooked the Rolex from his wrist and handed it across.

The driver examined it, rubbed its face, like a long-lost friend, then attached to his own wrist. 'See you in hell, Harry.'

'Be sure to keep a corner warm for me, Zac.'

Without another word the doors were slammed and the car was underway again. It wasn't until they hit the Embankment that it slowly dawned upon d'Arbois. 'Zac? You are Zac?'

The car speeded up. It was a thirty-mile-an-hour limit, but Zac didn't appear to care.

'Stop the car!' the Frenchman demanded. 'For God's sake, let me out!'

He tugged at the door handle, but it wouldn't move. The child locks had been activated. He tried the window, but the same story there, too. He began banging on the window, but there was no one to see. The street lights were flashing past, they were doing sixty, still gaining speed, pushing him back into his seat.

Construction work was taking place on the Embankment. The previous week a heavy lorry had swerved off the road in the ice and hit the river wall. The damage had required that a small section of the wall be taken down and repaired, and the job was half complete, a temporary barrier in place, separating the pavement from the dark, swirling flood waters on the other side. When the Mercedes hit the kerb it was doing eighty, and swept through the temporary railings as if they were bales of straw. For a moment the Mercedes lifted its head and its headlights arced high in the sky. Then it fell back, and hit the water. It floated downstream in the heavy swell for a few seconds, before it disappeared from sight.

Many people saw the accident, but no one jumped in. It was too dark, too deep, too cold, a deathtrap for anyone who tried. Instead they called the river police, and by the time their launch arrived, Zac Kravitz and his passenger were nowhere to be found.

Karabayev's cautious instincts had been correct. He should have listened to them. Beg was gone, and so was Sydykov; it left a huge hole in the security apparatus around the President. Far from strengthening his authority, it made the system around him look tattered and vulnerable. Matters began to drift quickly out of control. Large crowds began to appear on the streets, apparently prompted by messages passed around the Internet and through Facebook and Twitter. Bektour's timing was excellent, and his resources greatly enhanced. His network had received a huge boost through support that came from an entirely unexpected source. Much to the astonishment of his friends, Roddy Bowles declared that he was selling his entire collection of paintings and donating the proceeds to the cause of democracy in Ta'argistan. Even more to their astonishment, he went on to announce that he was retiring from

Parliament with immediate effect in order to devote his energies to other, unspecified charitable works.

The demonstrations in Ashkek were too large to be dispersed by troops without resorting to arms, and by the time Karabayev ordered them to do so, it was too late. His authority was gone, they would not fire on their own, not with their wives, and brothers, and sons amongst them. And soon Karabayev was gone, too.

They called it the Snowdrop Revolution.

Superintendent Richards entered Harry's room. He had a raincoat draped over his arm and an expression to match the weather.

'This is getting to be a habit,' Harry said.

'A dangerous one, Mr Jones.'

Harry noted the formality and didn't bother to reach for the whisky.

'Too many friends of yours dying,' the policeman continued.

'I'm a natural optimist. I'd like to think it won't be happening again, Superintendent,' Harry said, offering him a seat, while he stood at the window, gazing out across the rooftops of the rain-streaked city.

'The two who died in your car, the American and Frenchman. We've completed our investigation. Almost all the evidence points to a tragic accident. And that's what we'll be telling the coroner.'

'I see.'

'The driver was very ill, on medication, and the

passenger had been drinking. That might explain the accident, of course, and why neither of them was able to get out. But I have to tell you there are aspects I don't fully understand.'

Harry turned from the window to face the policeman.

'For one thing,' Richards continued, 'the passenger was in the back seat. That seems strange, if they were friends. It almost suggests that someone else had been in the car with them.'

'I see your point, Superintendent.'

'And the child locks were on. You don't have children, do you, Mr Jones?'

'No.'

Richards let the reply hang heavily between them for a moment before continuing. 'A good friend of yours, was he, the Frenchman?'

'I'd known him a number of years.'

'You see, sir, his seatbelt was undone – as if he had been trying to get away. You'd expect that. But there was a mark, a bruise on his jaw, almost as though he'd been hit.'

'Always a risk in an accident, I suppose.'

'There was also a mark on your other friend's knuckles.'

They were staring at each other, their eyes tangling, trying to catch the other's true meaning.

'But, as I said, the best we can do is conclude it was nothing but a tragic accident.'

'Is there anything else, Superintendent?'

'No, sir.' The policeman rose from his seat. Then his shoulders relaxed, his duty done. 'Ah, yes, there was just one thing.' His hand went to his pocket, his voice grew softer. 'I'm not supposed to do this, Harry, there should be paperwork a foot high, but . . .' He produced the Rolex. 'It was on Mr Kravitz's wrist. Perhaps he borrowed it while he was staying with you.'

He handed the watch across. It was still ticking through the soil of the river. Harry turned it over, used a thumb to rub the smear of silt from the back.

Thank you. J.

He choked, unable to hide the tears, as he read the inscription. Then his eyes found the policeman. 'I can't find the words to say how much I appreciate this.'

'No need. It's back where it belongs, that's all that really matters,' Richards said. 'Stay safe, Harry,' he added, over his shoulder, as he walked to the door.

Harry didn't reply. He was in another place.

The chimes of the newly restored Big Ben pulled him back. He crossed to his desk and slumped dejectedly into its leather chair. He opened the top drawer. It had a broken lock, where he'd once lost his key and forced it in temper. Now, more carefully, he reached for a small box, trimmed in red silk, one of the few possessions that remained from his mother. He opened it, and placed the watch inside, laying it next to his medal, and a battered chess piece.

ACKNOWLEDGEMENTS

The book is set in the mythical Central Asian republic of Ta'argistan, but those who know the region well might recognize more than a passing glimpse of Kyrgyzstan and its capital of Bishkek in my descriptions. It's eerie that the revolution I write about in the final pages actually took place a few weeks after the book was first published. Kyrgyzstan has received a good deal of bad publicity as a result, but I spent a fascinating time there soaking up the atmosphere and mountain air, and was treated with supreme hospitality by new friends I made, particularly Isken Sydykov and his son, Bektour Iskender. I can only wish all my friends in Kyrgyzstan a safe and successful future in the difficult days that inevitably lie ahead.

And while I have invented the Fat Chance Saloon, if you are passing through Bishkek in leisurely times I can thoroughly recommend Fatboy's Cafe, where Isken and I spent many comfortable and informative hours.

Several people helped me with the parliamentary aspects of the novel, illuminating some of the more perilous aspects of politicians' visits abroad. My old friend Nigel Evans, MP for the Ribble Valley, offered enthusiastic advice, as did Andrea Skyring from the International Parliamentary Union, and as is typical of him, John Whittingdale MP has always been there to answer questions of irritating detail. The book is dedicated to his beautiful daughter, Alice, my god-daughter.

There have been many technical and medical issues for me to tackle in this book, and I've received unstinting help from Major General (retd.) David Jolliffe, the husband of my cousin, Hilary, Lieutenant Colonel Pete Davis, and Major John Taylor, who by happy coincidence turned out to be the son of a former irrepressible political colleague, Sir Teddy Taylor MP. Dr Philippa Swayne has once again also helped me with many medical matters, as has David Perry with all my nagging questions about airports and airlines. I can only hope that I've understood and correctly reported the information they have all so freely given me.

Martin Fenner, head of section on Central Asian matters at the Foreign and Commonwealth Office, and various people at Human Rights Watch, have also been very kind. I would also like to thank Mike Atsoparthis, the British Honorary Consul in Bishkek, for his support and advice.

My rock in all matters concerning Harry Jones remains Ian Patterson. Ian helped create the character and has played a vital role in leading him through the many minefields I've cast in front of him. Our mutual friend, David Foster, has also come to Harry's assistance over thoroughly enjoyable lunches in the Chalke valley. Work should always be that hard.

And every writer should have a wife as wonderfully patient as Rachel, and kids as supportive as Will, Mikey, Alex and Harry.

Michael Dobbs
Wylye, 2009/10

Read on for an exclusive extract
from the next electrifying Harry Jones thriller

OLD ENEMIES

By Michael Dobbs

Coming from Simon & Schuster in 2011

PROLOGUE

Villars sur Ollon, Switzerland

She was a girl with hazel eyes and a face that with every smile reflected her happiness at being part of the world. Still a month short of her seventeenth birthday, she lacked a cynical side, which was perhaps something of a surprise for a teenager from New York. That's why she trusted the two men sitting in front of her.

Casey didn't know them, but that seemed not to matter. Had her mother known what she was doing she would have shouted at her, and perhaps even her father, too, if he'd been around, but she was far from home and the old rules didn't count. So much of what she'd found since she'd arrived at the international college in Villars was carved from a different world and she was determined to embrace every bit of it. Anyway, Switzerland was safe, everybody said so, particularly up here in the mountains, and she'd been here less than three months, barely enough time to get homesick. Soon Casey would be packing her pink suitcases and returning to Manhattan for the Christmas break, so before her Mom took over her life once more and smothered it in single-parent angst she wanted to stretch her wings and seek out a little excitement.

The two men nodded, encouraging, as she buried her nose in the sweet mist that rose from her mug of hot chocolate. A snowflake settled on Casey's eyelash, another high on her cheek. There had been a heap of snow this past month, so tomorrow she planned to go heli-skiing, unseasonably early, Ruari's treat. After that, she had decided, she would sleep with him. Their first time. For the heli-skiing, too. There was so much that was new to her here and she couldn't resist sharing it, even with these two strangers as they sat on the balcony of the coffee shop, while the snowflakes melted and slid down her face like fading innocence.

The chocolate chilled rapidly in the thin air and she finished it quickly, leaving a thin line of froth on her upper lip. She was a little nervous, burbling, hadn't even got close to mentioning what she wanted, and her cheeks rose in a guilty blush.

'Not to worry, we understand,' one of the men said, his English sharpened by an accent she couldn't place, but everyone here seemed to have some sort of accent, even Ruari. 'We know what you want.'

He slid a small sachet across the table. He wore a wedding ring, it reassured her. She glanced nervously around her, but they were alone on the balcony, looking out over snow-topped roofs that stretched like pieces of a jigsaw into the valley below. Inside the transparent plastic sleeve were six small tablets. E's. For her and Ruari. Another first.

'How ... much?' she mumbled, staring at them, her habitual smile replaced by a frown.

The man shook his head. 'We're not dealers.'

'Then ...?' She was confused. They were too old to be part of the club circuit.

'Buy us another coffee. That will be enough.'

Her fingers stretched out for the sachet, covering it with her palm; it felt cold, almost clinical, and she hesitated one last time before tucking it inside one of the pockets of the colourful Russian felt coat her mother had bought her as a going-away present. The man waved at the elderly waitress, and soon fresh drinks were steaming in front of them. As she sipped more chocolate, freed from her embarrassment, Casey relaxed under their gentle questions before glancing at her watch and gasping in surprise. 'Wow, this girl's got to be out of here. I'll be late for class!' Suddenly she was on her feet, leaving in a fluster of thanks and apology, her hand still firmly thrust inside her pocket.

As she hurried away, her boots crunching through the crust of fresh snow, the smiles of the two men faded into rock.

'She didn't pay for the fucking coffee,' one said drily.

'She will,' the other whispered.

Casey kept her most intimate possessions tucked inside a small silk purse. It was the colour of kingfisher blue, and beneath its gold clasp she had squirrelled away a photograph of her parents when they had still been together, and a more recent one of herself astride Trixie, her horse, along with the ring her grandmother had given her before she'd left for Switzerland. The ring was old-fashioned, too large for any of Casey's fingers, but her grandmother was one of those special people in her life who understood her better than almost anyone. Those secrets she wasn't told she still somehow guessed, in return offering Casey a gentle word of encouragement or occasional caution. But she never judged. 'I was there in the Sixties, sweetheart,' she would say. 'Sure hope you have as much fun as I did.' And now her grandmother's ring was nestling next to the note from Ruari. He was eight months older than Casey, almost seventeen, and when they had first grown close at the start of the term he'd given her a piece of paper with her name written on it. He'd proved to be a talented artist, because he'd turned the capital C into a face that bore a remarkable resemblance to Casey, with her snub nose and hair swept back behind her head, while the tail of the Y seemed looped in the form of a heart, although when she'd pressed him on that he'd grown embarrassed and pretended it was only her backside. Boys could be such idiots.

Their ski instructor, Mattias, picked them up from the school; you got door-to-door service when your parents were laying out more than seventy thousand dollars a year in school fees. Their equipment was piled high in the back – helmets and sticks and the fat skis used on powder – and Mattias had driven them to a football pitch on the outskirts of Villars that was now covered in a blanket of thick, fresh snow. In the centre of the pitch stood a small canary yellow helicopter. Their adventure was almost underway. As they clambered from the school van their boots sank in deep; it would be wonderful up on top, so long as the weather held. Casey glanced across the valley towards France, praying that the clouds piling up in the direction of Mont Blanc would steer clear of them, at least for the next few hours. It was glorious on this side, no wind, nothing but sun, a glorious day that would lead to an even more perfect night.

She turned her eyes on Ruari, who had streaks of red in his brown hair and a razor nick below his left ear. She grabbed his arm, urging him on. She'd not told him what she was planning, for later, when their friends and the teaching staff would be wrapped up in an end-of-term party, but she thought he'd guessed. She couldn't contain her excitement, squeezed him tighter, then slipped in her heavy boots, falling onto her back on a duvet of pure white, dragging him on top of her. Any excuse. The instructor turned away, smiling to himself, pretending not to see as they scrambled to their feet, laughing.

Mattias greeted the pilot warmly, they were old friends who had made this trip dozens of times, and the pilot began helping stow the skis in a wire basket that ran along one of the skids. Mattias had already spent half an hour briefing his students, and now he instructed them yet again on what to expect, how to behave in the helicopter and on the snow, what to do in the event of an avalanche. One final equipment check to make sure they hadn't mislaid their hand-sized avalanche transceivers or the folded aluminium probes, then all was ready. 'Today is a special day,' he declared, laying his hands on their shoulders. 'I promise you, it will be one of the sweetest adventures of your lives.' They giggled; he didn't know, of course.

As Casey climbed into the open-sided cabin, she was too wrapped up in her own world to take any notice of the other passengers already on board, two men, one of whom sat inside the passenger compartment while the other had begged a favour and taken a seat alongside the pilot up front. They were entirely anonymous and unremarkable. Both wore reflective sunglasses with scarves around their chins and sun cream plastered across their noses. Their heads were covered by thick woollen hats so that very little of their faces could be seen, and what was visible was covered in stubble. They offered no sign of acknowledgement. So Casey couldn't be blamed for what was about to happen. She was young, had eyes for Ruari, no one else. There was no way she could recognize these men as the pair she had met at the coffee bar a couple of days before.

And there were other distractions. The turboshaft engine began to whine, the giant rotor blades above their heads turned, her world began to tremble and scream. Even when Ruari shouted into her ear she had trouble making out what he was saying, so she used it as an excuse to lean on his shoulder and look into his laughing eyes, unaware. No, you couldn't blame Casey for that. She was in love and on the verge of the sweetest adventure of her life. Or so she had been promised.

Casey sat next to Ruari, facing the rear of the helicopter, with Mattias and the stranger opposite. Their knees almost touched, there was so little room. Outside, through the open door hatch, the scenery grew more rugged and spectacular as they climbed past the tree line and up towards the peaks. She pulled out a camera and began taking photographs, wanting to share the experience with her grandmother. The view of Villars was extraordinary, with wood smoke rising from the chimneys of its huddled chalets, while beyond she could see the valley of the river Rhone as it thrust its way towards Lake Geneva, with its power station chimney standing tall and steaming. In the great distance were the French Alps, where ribbons of ice crystals were being blown from the mountain tops like the fluttering of Tibetan prayer scarves, while behind her, she knew, in the direction they were flying, lay the peaks of Les Diablerets and the town of Gstaad where her mother had taken her shopping only a few weeks earlier, before the snows came and blocked the pass. It was where she bought the silk purse. Her fingers searched for it once more, beneath the folds of her ski suit, and she nestled closer to Ruari.

Casey had lost herself in the beauty, the noise, her rising sense of expectation, when she felt Ruari stiffen. His body tensed. He reached for her hand and squeezed it, too hard, so that she almost yelped in discomfort. It was only when she followed the direction of his gaze that she saw why. The faceless stranger who sat opposite him had turned in his seat. He was holding a pistol. It was aimed at Mattias's chest, barely two feet away. Casey didn't understand; there had been no argument, no raised voices. Even Mattias was looking on with an expression that suggested more confusion than concern.

'Stand up,' the stranger mouthed at Mattias. The

words were flung away in the downdraught yet their meaning was unmistakable.

The guide shrugged his shoulders, indicated his seat harness, still assuming this was some sort of pathetic joke. Then he saw the finger tighten on the trigger, only fractionally, but it was enough to persuade him that it would be unwise to test the stranger's sense of humour too far. Cautiously, not taking his eyes from the snub nose of the gun, he unclipped his safety belt and edged along the bench, trying to put a few more inches between him and danger.

The helicopter flew on, ever higher.

The gunman jerked the barrel, once, twice; with desperate slowness Mattias rose to his feet. His head was bowed, he couldn't stand full height in the cramped cabin. His eyes turned towards the pilot's compartment, hoping his friend had witnessed everything and would intervene. What he saw there made him suddenly sick. That's when he knew he was a dead man.

He was beginning to rage inside with the injustice of it all when, even above the racket of engine and rushing air, he heard Casey scream. At the same moment he felt a horse kick him in the chest, smashing through his sternum. His breastbone was no match for a 9 mm slug fired from a semi-automatic Beretta. It didn't hurt, there was no pain, only numbness, which was flushing all the way down through his bowels. He knees were buckling. That made him angry, he was a mountain man, his legs were his life. He was still filling up with anger when, at more than six thousand feet, his knees gave way and he tumbled backwards into oblivion.

The pilot hadn't been in any position to help his friend Mattias. He was already dead. He'd been flying on a path that had his craft rising straight and steady through the mountain air when the passenger in the left-hand seat reached over and twisted the lever that engaged the auto-pilot controls. The pilot had barely enough time to blurt out a protest when he, too, was shot. Two bullets. No one in the rear passenger compartment had heard the sharp retorts, no one saw what was happening on the other side of the bulkhead until Mattias stood up and noticed the pilot slumped over his controls, but by then it was already too late. Afterwards there was nothing more than a slight kick of the aircraft, like hitting a small air pocket, to betray the fact that the auto-pilot had been disengaged. The passenger up front now had control.

In the compartment behind him, the three remaining passengers were lost in their own individual worlds. Casey was old enough to love but far too young for death, even to comprehend its meaning, yet suddenly her world was filled with it. She couldn't stop screaming. The helicopter had become a coffin.

Beside her, Ruari was bent forward, straining against his harness, his senses focused on the gunman so close at hand. They both knew that if Ruari found the chance he would hurl himself at the attacker, even though the man was fifty pounds heavier and nearly half a foot taller, but Ruari wouldn't get that chance, not stuck in his harness. The attacker stared from behind his sunglasses, expressionless, alert.

All the while the noise from the engine and the rotors beat down upon Casey, numbing her thoughts, driving her fear still deeper inside her. She fumbled with the lock of her safety belts, releasing the catch, sinking to her knees as she struggled to breathe. Suddenly Ruari reached for her, trying to help, to hold her, but it was too late, she was slumped on the floor, trying to crawl away, her ski boots slipping as she struggled.

But there was nowhere to go. She sprawled nearer the access hatch but daren't move any closer. She whimpered, raised her head, looked at the gunman.

'Please,' she whispered.

He made no move. The gun remained pointed at

Ruari. It seemed as if Casey was of no importance to him.

Beyond the hatch she could see the mountaintops that had so excited her and the vast blue void that filled the spaces between. The helicopter twitched, she sank still lower to the floor, reached out to grab one of the metal supports beneath the seats, clinging to it in fear, afraid to move in any direction.

'Please!' she begged once more. She began to scream, piercing stuff that not even the pounding of the rotors could suppress. Ruari's hand stretched out, shaking as he strained for her, but still he couldn't reach. The pitiful screaming continued. She was a young girl, in a state of terror, pleading for her innocent life.

The helicopter banked sharply, like a fairground ride, until it was almost on its side. For a moment the screaming stopped as Casey needed all her strength to cling to the seat support, fighting the gravity that wanted to break her grasp and rip her free. She was losing the struggle. She slipped, a few inches, then a little more. Her boots were no longer scrabbling on the floor, they were dangling over the edge of the compartment, outside, in the void. No matter how Ruari strained, time and again, he couldn't get to her, couldn't touch her, couldn't save her. Her lips twisted into shapes they were never meant to make while her fresh, hazel eyes drowned in fear.

At last, although it was only seconds, her fingers gave way. She was tossed from the helicopter, like a sweet wrapper in the wind. That was when she started screaming again, but this time there was no one with her to hear.

The Eastern Highlands, Zimbabwe

The events that led up to what took place in the Swiss mountains had begun in another time zone and on a different continent less than five weeks earlier. The timing would eventually prove to be important. The matters that began to be put in motion typically required months to plan, but time was to prove a particularly inflexible factor. Corners were bound to be cut, knuckles scraped.

Moses Willard Chombo stood at the window of his bungalow perched in the hills of his country's Eastern Highlands and snorted in frustration. It was eighty degrees, the humidity that was so unexpected in these elevated parts made him short of breath and the rain that had been threatening all morning was now tearing itself from the sky and trying to batter its way through the roof. He couldn't even see as far as the military gatehouse that had been installed at the entrance to his

drive; the only immediate sign of life was a column of
ants clinging with growing desperation to the outside
of the window frame. Even the weather made him feel
impotent.

Chombo was the man who had emerged from the
dung heap left behind by the deeply psychotic Robert
Mugabe to squeeze into the dead man's shoes, but
Zimbabwe was still a deeply troubled country,
exhausted by the years of Mugabe's madness, and the
new president's mood was as overcast as the skies.
He was watching a waterspout erupt from the gutter
and cascade onto the lawn, where it was tearing at
the roots of an hibiscus bush, when he heard a door
open behind him. The wood was swollen and warped,
the hinges complained, like everything in this country,
and through it came Takere, the head of the president's personal guard. Behind him were two white
men, in their thirties, neatly dressed and well-
muscled.

'You are late,' Chombo remarked in Shona, the language he shared with Takere. It was more observation
than rebuke. The president was a big man with an ox's
chest who didn't rush to judgment, the sort of man
who preferred to seek salvation and revenge in his
own time. It was a caution that had held him back

while others had rushed into the hands of the death squads.

'My apologies. There are more potholes than tarmac on the roads out of Harare,' Takere responded, cautious, with a tightness in his lips that made him lisp. He was nervous, sweating, despite the fan that churned the air above his head. 'Your Excellency, this is—'

But a wave of Chombo's hand cut Takere's introductions short. 'We need no names, not for a meeting that has never happened. Have you searched them?'

'Of course.'

'Then search them again.'

'But—'

Yet even as Takere protested the shorter of the men had raised his hands to the back of his head and patiently spread his feet. He understood their language, felt no need to keep the fact secret. Takere patted him down, then the other. Again he found nothing.

'You will understand the need for caution,' Chombo said, this time in English.

'That's why I fly El Al,' the shorter man said. 'It never gets blown out of the sky. And why? Because it gives a damn, like you.' His accent was clipped, rolling from the tip of his tongue, South African.

'You address him as His Excellency Mr President,'

Takere said sharply, taking exception to the man's relaxed tone. 'You show him respect.'

Blue eyes stared at Chombo, holding his gaze. 'Respect? That is a rare commodity in this part of the world,' he said slowly. 'But I assure you, my respect for the President is at least as great as any he has for me.'

Takere's nostrils flared but Chombo burst into laughter. Flies would seek a second opinion before settling on this man. His mind ran back to Micklethwaite, the visiting British Minister, a man of phenomenally damp palms and absolutely no trace of respect.

'Yes, the West will give you aid, enough of it to transform your benighted country,' Micklethwaite had explained over tea in the glass-fronted embassy that looked out along Harare's Norfolk Road. 'Zimbabwe can become the flower of Africa once more.'

'Then we shall be grateful.'

'There are conditions.'

'Of course.' There were always conditions.

'These upcoming elections of yours, they must be fair and free, and seen to be so. You understand that. None of us want to go back to the old days.'

'Mr Micklethwaite, you sanctimonious white bastard,' Chombo had thought, but did not say. 'Mr Micklethwaite, I can lay my hand on my heart' – he had done so with an exaggerated gesture – 'and assure you that there is nothing I want more than for my country to make a fresh start with you and our other Western friends. But …' There were always buts, too. 'I must ask for a little patience. We have our customs.'

'You know our position on corruption,' the Minister had insisted casually, reaching for a biscuit.

'Ah, yes, you mean the corruption that permits rich businessmen to buy votes in the British Parliament and the US Congress?' Chombo had replied softly. For a big man he could speak very softly, which somehow made the words shout all the louder.

'I'm not interested in an empty debate, Mr Chombo. You know what I mean. Your country has a dark past in such matters.' He had hesitated. Even Micklethwaite had to admit it was a clumsy turn of phrase. Biscuit crumbs fell carelessly down his shirtfront.

'And a dark future, I assure you,' Chombo had replied, smiling, deflecting the tension as he had rubbed the skin on the back of his hand. 'But you must understand the way we do things in this country. Zimbabwe is desperately poor. Many still live on the edge of starvation. Sometimes the only thing of any value they possess is their vote. And if they give it, they expect something in return.'

'And we expect something in return, too,' Micklethwaite had replied.

The white man still played the imperialist, using what he called humanitarian aid as a hammer to beat former colonies into submission all over again. Mugabe had been right about that, at least, even if he had made a total fuck-up of the potholes.

Since that conversation Micklethwaite had been sacked and replaced by yet another damp palm, but it would make no difference, the British still danced to the tune of the American organ grinder, who knew nothing of Africa. And yet Americans believed in self-help, so what better way of confronting his current problem, Chombo thought, than to use other white men. Like these two. Security consultants. The expensive name for mercenaries.

The ceiling fan turned idly above their heads, and from nearby a pair of hornbills, spooked by a guard, screeched in alarm. The two consultants stood patiently. Chombo didn't offer them refreshment or invite them to sit down.

'You have discussed matters with Takere,' he said.

'Yes. And what he suggested is pointless,' the shorter man replied.

Takere's eyes, tired and bloodshot, flared in agitation,

but he said nothing. He sensed he was out of his depth, that it might be wise to tread water for a while.

'Look, you want to ... *change the mind* of an important newspaper owner in London, and in something of a hurry,' the mercenary continued. 'Well, there's no point in offering him money, he has plenty. If his office burns down, it will still make no difference, he will move into a new one. And if, as Mr Takere has suggested, he were to meet with a tragic accident ...' The mercenary spread his hands wide and shrugged. 'He would simply be replaced by others. You do not change a man's mind by smashing in his skull.'

Chombo considered the point, breathing deeply to massage his thoughts. 'Then what is it that you suggest?'

'We distract him. Give him something else to think about. It's difficult for a man to know where his mind is when you are *ripping* out his heart.' The man rolled the sound of the word in a manner that gave it added menace.

Takere began cracking his knuckles in confusion, but Chombo thought he was keeping pace. 'His wife, you mean?'

The mercenary shook his head. 'No, not that. They live in London, it's sewn up as tight as an antelope's arse with all the anti-terrorist precautions. And if he has any sense he'll have a security company taking care of his home, fitted it with panic alarms, CCTV, that sort of thing. There will be regular patrols, maybe bodyguards. They might even have constructed a secure room inside. To break an operation like that would be very difficult, take time. And time, so your Mr Takere tells me, is one thing you don't have.'

Chombo didn't bother to dispute the point.

'Anyhow,' the white man continued, 'he may not even like his wife.'

A smile spread slowly across the President's face. It took considerably longer to reach his eyes, which remained fixed on the other man, who wasn't like the last pair of 'consultants' Takere had brought him – Englishmen, who'd been halfway up his backside trying to establish parking rights before the draught from the door had time to settle, which was why they had been thrown out just as quickly. But Chombo's instincts told him that this one was different.

'Yes, as you say, there are many problems, so many problems,' the President said. 'But I expect you have brought with you a solution. An expensive one.'

'It will be double the fee that was originally indicated. Half up front, the rest when it is underway.'

Suddenly Takere came back to life, beginning to understand that these two men had played him like a fish. 'We said only a third up front, with the final installment afterwards, when the job is completed.'

'We are all of us in this for high stakes, putting our necks on the line. "Afterwards"? What is "afterwards"? I may not be around to collect, while you, Mr Takere, might not be around to pay.'

Takere looked in uncertainty towards his President, waiting for his cue to throw these cheating bastards out into the mud.

'So how is it that you propose to distract him?' Chombo asked.

'Not through his wife.'

'Then how?'

'His eldest child. At school in Switzerland.'

'Ah! The snow. It hides many things,' Chombo replied softly. 'We should have more snow in Africa.'

And so it was that Casey's fate had been sealed. She wasn't the eldest child of the newspaper owner Chombo was so desperate to get at – that was Ruari. It was simply Casey's misfortune to be his friend, and to be in the way.

Michael
DOBBS

WAR WITHOUT WEAPONS. ONLY VICTIMS.

The Edge of
MADNESS

POCKET
BOOKS

Michael Dobbs

EDGE OF MADNESS

*The build-up of steam in the reactor core blew the
pressure-release valves. The noise sent out a scream
that made all who heard it freeze with terror ...*

Cyber-war. When a few strokes of the keyboard
can bring the world to its knees.

It begins with small things. Power failures. Blackouts.
Transport breakdowns. A plane that falls out of the sky. A US
warship steers off course and into Iranian waters. A rogue
calculation almost bankrupts the London Stock Exchange.

These are just warnings. A test for what is to come.
The real war hasn't started yet. When it does, there will be
madness, and millions will die as governments fall
and systems collapse into chaos.

Two Presidents and one Prime Minister have two days
in which to prevent it. And they have Harry Jones ...

ISBN: 978-1-84739-843-7
PRICE: £7.99